ALMOST PERSUADED

Dick Curran was born and brought up in Newcastle. After studying English at Manchester, he lived and worked in London, Brighton and Hull, before coming back to Newcastle in 1997.

He has written several full-length plays and dozens of shorter pieces which have been performed at venues all over the country including Live Theatre with the RSC, and The Customs House at South Shields, as well as pubs and Medieval castles (well, one).

Recent plays have been chosen for Manchester's 24:7 Festival and Liverpool's Write Now Festival. 'Islanders' was chosen as Best Fringe Production 2010 in the MEN Theatre Awards, and after being selected for the Re:Play Festival, toured in Spring 2011. He has also set up a production company – Farnes Productions.

Dick has won a number of other awards including The Drama Association of Wales Short Play; and the Yeovil Octagon and Arundel Festival Joy Goun Prizes. He had a short film script produced for a TAPS showcase at ITV studios, and the radio version of 'Therapy' was as runner-up for the BBC Alfred Bradley Bursary Award.

ALMOST PERSUADED

DICK CURRAN

RED SQUIRREL

First published (this version) in the UK in 2011 by
Red Squirrel Press
PO Box 219
Morpeth
Northumberland
NE61 9AU
United Kingdom
www.redsquirrelpress.com

Printed in the UK by
Martins the Printers
Sea View Works
Spittal
Berwick upon Tweed
TD15 1RS

ISBN: 978-1-906700-32-4

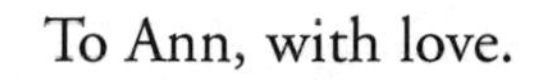

To Ann, with love.

Contents

PART ONE
PROJECT MANAGEMENT

CHAPTER 1

I made my way along the platform through families and couples saying goodbye. There was no one to see me off and I was glad. I was free to take any train I wanted, my journey was paid for by those who needed my services, and there would be a room full of beautiful women waiting for me at the other end. I swung my bag into the luggage rack, dropped my newspaper on the table and sank into my generously wide First Class seat. I was in my prime, at my peak. If only Louise could see me now.

Admittedly, I hadn't yet met any of these women; I was travelling nowhere more exotic than Berkshire; and my freedom of choice was restricted to those trains which would take there in time for a course on Project Management, but still I felt elated and optimistic.

Travelling First Class and on expenses helped. Just before Christmas, Finance had discovered a huge underspend on the 1995/96 budget for what Senior Management insisted on calling the Y2K Project. It had to be corrected by 1st April and training was a good way to use up money, so dozens of us suddenly found ourselves being despatched, First Class, around the country in the name of education. This was my turn and I intended to enjoy it. It made a pleasant change from half-heartedly trawling through software changing "31/12/99" to "31/12/1999" in the battle to stave off what the media were in their turn insisting on calling The Millennium Bug.

The last time (in fact the only time) I had been away on a course like this, I had still been involved with Louise, so I had been on no more than polite terms with the other delegates and I had counted the hours until I would be back home. This time, with Louise behind me, I would take full advantage of my opportunities and enjoy my good fortune. Even the spectacular dullness of the subject matter could not spoil the prospect of a week away from work, everything magically covered by expenses.

I was even being paid for this time: travelling through England in the late winter sunshine, reading my Independent on Sunday and consuming Vegetable Tikka Massala with Leaf Tea Large. I took out my Walkman with the tape I had prepared for just this moment, and settled back, gazing out at the pale green Midlands countryside to the sound of 'I Heard that Lonesome Whistle' and 'I Miss A Lot of Trains'.

I woke with a jolt and a full bladder as we pulled into

Peterborough. My mouth tasted of stale spices and I took a drink of cold tea which did little to freshen it. There was nothing worth looking at outside. I had once had sex on a station platform, so I assumed other people must have done as well, but perhaps Louise and I really had done things that no-one else had since Adam and Eve.

I waited until the train was well out of the station before heading for the toilet. When people were all settled down it would be more difficult for a thief to roam the First Class compartments inconspicuously, looking for unguarded bags.

The toilet at the end of the carriage was occupied, so I headed on past the buffet to the first of the toilets in standard class accommodation. It was free. Scratched on the wall at eye level was 'Vinny shags convicts wives'. I wondered if he really did (it seemed like a very dangerous thing to do), and if so how often, and how soon after sentencing.

My bag was still there when I got back, but the magic of the journey was gone. One of the foam earpiece things was missing from the Walkman, and it irritated my ear when I put it back on. I had read everything I could face reading in the paper; the novelty of sitting in a bigger seat than everybody else had worn off; and I had that crumpled, depressed feeling you get from unsatisfactory sleep. And the train was running slow and late.

The train out of London was slower, and colder and

smelt of stale wet cloth. Worst of all I was no longer getting preferential treatment. I tried to avoid catching anyone's eye. For all I knew, that skinny boy in the too-small jacket might be Vinny himself and the woman across from him, a convict's wife.

When we finally arrived, the first thing I saw was a large colourful advert for the Grand Hotel - with swimming pool, sauna, exotic food, and attractive smiling staff. I began to regret my choice of accommodation. The Halfway House B&B was cheap, and traditionally the place to stay for those trying to make a profit on the fifty-five pounds a day allowance. I was. At that precise moment, though, I would have loved a big, expensive, comfortably corrupt hotel with Cajun Chicken baguettes available from room service.

Worst of all, two of my colleagues were waiting for me there: Andrew Punchley, a jovial red-faced bully who worked in Credit Control, and Andrew Mulholland, a dull family man whose idea of a wild night was half a bottle of wine and a Top Gear special.

There was a bitter wind across the station forecourt, there weren't any taxis, and the payphone wasn't working. Not for the first time I wondered if it was worth holding out against carrying a mobile phone. Still, it was important to believe in something. I crossed the road to a telephone box, rang The Halfway House and waited, gazing at the brightly lit orange curtains of the nearest house while Mrs Mullen made her way from her television (The Darling Buds of May - repeat) to the phone. I pretended to listen to her directions, promised I was not intending to pay by credit card and then found my way by asking directions of anyone I met who looked local, sober and non-violent.

The Halfway House was a pleasant surprise. While it wasn't the Grand, my room smelt as a hotel room should - clean and impersonal - with complimentary tea, coffee, biscuits, and little plastic pots of Tippex-style whitener.

I still remember my first hotel room. I was nine and it was a thrill like first love: walking into a clean, bright bedroom with a colour television, freshly laundered sheets on the bed, and my own sink. And a lock on the door. It was all the more intense because so short-lived; next day we were taken away to a self-catering place in Cromer.

Back in the Residents' Lounge I asked Mrs Mullins if there were any messages.

"Palmer. Tony Palmer. No. Right. Thanks. Good." I pretended to be pleased, but I would have liked someone to talk to – even Punchley and Mulholland - and it was very frustrating to be stood up by people I despised.

Mrs Mullins was staring at me, so I decided to make the best of it by getting four cans of Holsten Pils (it was a very limited bar) and retreating to the sanctuary of my room.

I turned on the TV and lay on top of the bed with my hands behind my head. I was halfway through my second can when I heard voices on the staircase. I muttered vague prayers that if it was those two, they would leave me in peace. I lay still and silent; my prayers were answered and the voices faded.

I put out the main light, turned the volume down low and flicked through a bizarre range of unfamiliar satellite channels. There were toothpasty Americans talking manically about God; truck racing from Iceland; and a discussion programme which moved effortlessly from considering the capacity of fish to feel pain, to Satanic child abuse. I opened another can.

I was dreaming about being a squirrel in the safety and warmth of a carpeted hollow tree when John Major woke me up, being reassuring about the future of his government on the Today programme with John Humphrys. He seemed to be trying to reassure himself more than anyone else, but it was a gentle way to wake up. I rose from the warmth of my bed to the warmth of the bedroom, and into the ensuite bathroom for a shower.

When I came back, wrapped in a large cream towel provided by the establishment, the radio had moved on to 'Thought for the Day'.

"I was, as perhaps you were, listening to those reports earlier about genetically engineered crops. The word 'miraculous' was used. And, you know, I was put in mind of a really miraculous event many years ago when a carpenter's son took a few loaves and a few fishes and with them fed five thousand people. And that says so much. For all we try to do through the wonders of technology to enrich our lives, the love of Jesus can, and already has done, so much more - through the wonders of His Truth..."

It was following the rules. It was odds on that someone or something would soon 'bear witness to' someone or something. Then the bastard claimed that this difference between the divine way and the human way put him 'in mind of a story'.

A sinner had gone to a monk (this was in the olden days when there were such things) to ask forgiveness. The monk told him that all he had to do was fill a small jug with water.

I knew this one. Basically the sinner had lots of unsuccessful ordeals ahead of him as he tried to fill the jug. All failed until he broke down and shed a tear of remorse, which splashed into the jug and filled it. Or some such shite.

Being born in the late Sixties, I was just old enough to have had teachers and priests who felt duty-bound to tell small children about the fires of Hell, and my eldest brother had actually gone so far as to become a priest. I had eventually emerged with only minor psychological damage, but their medieval horror stories had steeled me against this pallid, ecumenical wittering.

As he concluded, the speaker claimed insanely that this still 'resonated in today's world' and passed us back to the studio.

"You out of your pit yet?" Andrew Punchley banged on the door, and dragged me back into the Twentieth Century

"Wanker," I muttered. I turned the volume down in case he thought there was something weird about listening to Radio Four. "Yeah, mate. Down in a minute."

On the way downstairs, the breakfast smelt good, so I managed to smile at them as I approached their table.

"OK here isn't it?" said Punchley grinning at his plate of glistening bacon, sausage and egg.

"Yes. Better than I'd expected for the money, down here."

I asked for scrambled egg and no sausage which drew a slight frown from Mrs Mullen.

"It's OK – give him the works and I'll take the sausages," Punchley interfered. "I like a good breakfast when I can get one. Especially if someone else cooks it."

I didn't like the idea of his fork in my breakfast

"Heavy night?" I said to John.

"Fairly."

"No," Punchley corrected him. "Don't think you get out enough, mate," and he made an 'Under the Thumb' sign.

"Didn't have your mobile number, Tony," said John, "Otherwise. . . "

"No worries," I said.

"He doesn't have one," Punchley said, shaking his head. "Didn't miss much last night though. Quiet here. Mind you those Croatian-I-think-they-were birds were all right"

"Probably just being polite," said John Mulholland, unnecessarily dampening down any suspicion that he had been considering being unfaithful.

"Imagine what else they might do to be polite - eh?"

I asked Punchley how long he was down for. I knew he was going back on Wednesday, but hearing him say it would make me feel better.

"All week. Same as you, mate."

"You sure?"

"Yeah. I got myself switched to the Project Management gubbins you two are doing. Whole week. They don't seem to care what courses we do as long as we're using up the budget. So we'll be like the Three Musketeers."

That was very bad.

"Nice one."

"Week's a long time to be away from home," said John.

"When you've been married as long as I have you

won't think that," Punchley told him through a mouthful of bacon before turning back to me, "John here's offered to drive us into school in his nice new Orion."

How was it that these people with all these terrifying responsibilities (John had a new Persimmon home and at least two children), thought it was a good idea to buy new cars that must have cost half their salaries?

"All we need now," continued Punchley, "Is some nice tottie on the course and I'm in clover."

I didn't like the fact that I felt the same. Two young women came in for breakfast, and Punchley gave me a very peculiar expression which I realised was meant to be a knowing look.

"Morning, girls," he called out. The better looking one smiled back.

"Don't think much of yours," he chuckled.

I prayed they hadn't heard, but I still felt obliged to smirk back at him,at the same time trying to turn my head at an angle which meant they couldn't see me do it.

CHAPTER 2

The traffic jam began on the outskirts of town and stretched to the junction with the main road from London. I was in the back and the radio was on, which made it difficult to join in the conversation. This was not a problem and I gazed out vacantly through the rain at the smart, large houses, and damp fields as we edged past them.

On the radio was Local Drivetime, hosted by a gulping DJ called David Simonside who subjected us to some soft rock before passing over to Newscene. This was a selection of recent crimes in the area served up with global atrocities, disasters, and scandal. Then there were adverts for a Rover garage, crap lager, and a clinic which specialised in cosmetic surgery.

"Specialises," I attempted, leaning forward to make myself heard. "Does that mean they normally just do eyebrows and stuff, but if you want a heart operation they'll give it a shot?"

John made a polite, token 'Huh' in response. Punchley said nothing. I shrank back again.

The radio went back to The Hollies, Simply Red and The Pet Shop Boys with the promise of a special feature to follow on the alarming rise in gangland crime in the area. Andrew Punchley was scornful about that.

“Gangland - round here?” He waved at the fields we were passing. “Gangbanging sheep more likely.”

He turned around to me, and I felt obliged to laugh but then Traffic Action kicked in with news that there had been accident on the road ahead. They weren't able to name the victims yet, but they gave us details of the unfortunate vehicles - a Peugeot and a Transit.

"Well, we could be worse off," John commented philosophically, as we were handed back to David Simonside, who was now practically begging us to have a good morning.

"Yes," Punchley concurred, "Could be at work." Then he was off. "Been on eleven courses now, counting this. Learned precious little, but I've made a few quid. Bournemouth, Windsor, Stratford, the lot. Shame I couldn't bring the wife and girls really - save on going to Tenerife. Or the girls from Credit Control.

"You win every way. Makes the old CV look a lot better. And the more money they've spent sending you on courses, the harder it is for them to justify getting rid of you.” He was right so rather than agree with him, I closed my eyes and pretended to sleep. John Denver came on the radio.

"One for you - eh, Tone?" said Punchley.

"No," I said quickly.

"His dark secret," Punchley continued. "Country and Western. Line Dancing. All that."

"I don't," I said, flushing with embarrassment, anger and a sense of injustice. "It's different. The stuff I like."

"Wife's sister does line dancing to try to get her weight down," said John. I gave up and went back to pretend-sleep. "And it's not working."

I pretend-woke when we were reversing into a parking space at Hanlon Hall, the home of AJA Training.

"Nice old building," said John.

It was. The place could have been a college or a large nursing home except that it exuded health and middle-ranking corporate hospitality. The core of the building was an Eighteenth Century manor house, with 1960's concrete improvements, and a newer accommodation annex at the back.

No doubt elderly lords had once been smothered with pillows here by impatient and greedy relatives; and serving girls had been deflowered by the same lords in their youth, but now the landed gentry's presence was reduced to a few portraits on the walls, and the odd piece of antique furniture herded behind thick blue cord in Reception. The building had been taken over by business suits, contact lenses, flip charts, quiche salad and juice drinkers. A snack kiosk in the corner was called "The Butlers Pantry".

There were a few traditional male red-faced lechers and a smattering of public sector/charity types with jeans and beards but overall the place was the preserve of the smart, the healthy and the not unsuccessful. Conversation was dominated by house prices, physical fitness and the bloody traffic. Reception felt like the lobby of a good hotel and the smiling, efficient faces behind the desks reassured me I was welcome here. This could be heaven if I managed to make physical contact with at least one of those clean attractive women, and avoided the man from Redditch with bad breath and a worse drinking problem than my own.

A beautiful woman at the enrolment desk gave me a smile and a slip of blue card in return for filling out a form.

“This is your AJA Delegate Card. It gives you full access to delegates' rooms and facilities and food.” I thanked her with full eye contact. "Your course room is A4, to the right at the end of this corridor. But if you'd like to go to Hospitality for coffee or juice, you'll be called through when it's time. This leaflet," (I liked her hands),"Gives information about our facilities - dining rooms, games rooms, sauna, bars and so on. I hope you enjoy your time here." Smile.

She reminded me a little of a teacher at my Primary School, Miss Glade, whom I had a crush at the age of eight. Nothing had come of it.

"More paperwork," I said jauntily, and laughed, pushing a blast of air through my nose while jerking the bottom half of my face upwards. It was meant to indicate sophisticated, world-weary amusement but it came out as a sort of dry, false sneeze.

John was next, and he got less of a smile than I had. Good. It was useful to have him with me; someone to talk to and move away from as required. There were a lot of prosperous-looking interesting women around, and I had a week in their company miles from home. All I needed was a can of Woodpecker Cider and Heaven 17 playing and I'd be a teenager again. Things got better when Miss Glade queried Punchley's registration details and sent him to another desk.

"See you in there, mate," I said, as I led John quickly away to Hospitality like a tug-of-love child.

I strode happily down the corridor, playing at half-catching people's eyes as I went. I smiled and usually they smiled back. For a moment I was sure that I saw Louise. She had short, spiky black hair and features which my brother Richard had described as 'Elfin'. I hadn't liked it, but I knew what he meant. There was no reason for her to be here, but I was in a magical expenses-paid world where anything was possible, and I imagined the pleasure of seeing the regret in her eyes as I sailed past. Perhaps I would give her another chance; it would be good to look into those dark mad eyes, tamed at last.

She turned around. Of course it wasn't Louise, but I smiled and sailed past anyway in the hope of leaving some regret in whoever she was. Hospitality was really part of the main dining-room, separated by a sort of garden trellis made of cream-coloured plastic and devoid of plants, real or fake. Through it, I could see three plumpish young men in dark suits poring over large sheets of paper. Each had an empty plate and coffee cup by his side. Perhaps they were taking a course in doing breakfast. I turned to suggest as much to John, but he had moved away. He was talking to a large-jawed rugby-looking type in early middle-age.

"John Mulholland! You old bugger. The devil are you?"

"Great. Yeah. Great."

They were both grinning stupidly.

"Seeing you in the suit and everything. God, what would you have been wearing last time I saw you? Rebel without a cause - but not without a drink, eh?" They laughed together.

"Must be ten years." Pause. "God." Long pause. "What brings you here?"

"The M25. Ha, ha. No. RDBMS DBA course. Three days."

"Oh, this is Tony. I work with him, Bernard."

"Good to meet you." Bernard shook my hand.

"Bernard's an old friend from college."

"Fantastic."

It was a shock to realise that Bernard was the same age as John and only a couple of years older than me. But then I was getting bad at guessing ages now that an increasing number of oldish-looking people were actually younger than I was. I stood next to them like an irritated dummy as they talked.

"Drink? Tonight? Yeah, great. Fujitsu - Old Street. Harrow. Bought about six years ago so the mortgage is a harrowing experience. Ha, ha. No - engaged though. Frances. Kids? Good for you. Next May. Like to come? Great. Project Management course cancelled due to unforeseen circumstances. Ha, ha, ha. Anyway get some more coffee. Have you tried the," quote marks in the air with both hands, "Cappuccino? Tonight then mm? Main bar. Six.

"Good to meet you as well, Tommy," said Bernard, as he strode past me to the drinks dispenser.

"Knew him at college," John informed me again.

"Fantastic," I repeated. It was wasted.

"You fancy the drink with us tonight?"

“Yeah – great.” As an absolute last desperate fallback.

At that point a female voice called us through.

"Project Management - this way please." She gave us Delegate Welcome Packs and a smile as we filed past her.

John and I took up a good position, sharing a PC in the back corner of the room, but as I watched the others filing in, it did not look promising. Men, suits, spectacles and personal organisers. The only woman in the room, between two dullards on the front row, was very earnest looking, even sickly. Then another woman came in accompanied by a tall man with a stupid moustache. I couldn't see her clearly at first because he was in the way.

My feelings about the week, and my whole life, changed completely as she sat down, took off her jacket and shook back her long dark hair. I watched jealously as she smiled at the moustache man, and chatted to him in a soft Scottish accent. She was sitting diagonally in front of me, so I could see the right side of her face, her neck and a part of the top of her shoulder. I had never been in love with anyone with a soft Scottish accent before that I could remember. The seat to her left was still free. Andrew Punchley walked into the room and parked himself in it, giving her his most lecherous smile and "Hi."

My anger at this intrusion into her personal space was interrupted by the arrival of our Course Leader, an upright slightly leathery man in his early fifties.

"Good morning." There was a slight roll on the 'r' and the 'oo' was short. The polite conversations in the room abated.

"Welcome to Room A4 - the only room I have ever taught in to be honoured by having a paper size named after it."

Polite smiles. The man with the moustache looked puzzled, but that might just have been my malicious imagination. The Scottish woman's smile was unforced and comfortable. I caught a glimpse of her tongue as she finished smiling. The Course Leader's Scottish accent was harder and more clipped than hers, like a church minister or a school teacher; a little disciplinarian perhaps. That word immediately shot my thoughts back to the woman in front, whom I loved and would marry.

"At least the humour cannot deteriorate from that point," he went on. "My name is Campbell, Andrew Campbell. For the next five days I will be, to use current jargon, your Course Leader, as we consider 'Project Management and The System Life Cycle'.

"I hope you will not grow too tired of the sound of my voice over this time, not least because I hope to hear as much as possible from you yourselves. This course has cost you, or those who choose to invest in you, a good deal of money, and my job is to enable you to gain maximum benefit from your time here. And I hope some of you will even want to come back." He stopped and seemed to be staring inquiringly at me. I was glad when he resumed.

"One of the folders in your Delegate Welcome Pack contains Feedback and Reflections Forms. Obviously you will be making your own notes, but if you could also give me your thoughts on each day of the course it will help us in the never-ending process of revising and improving our Product.

“Before beginning the course proper, I would like to

try to stir you out of Monday morning torpor with something which I like to call The Creeping Death. This is not some exotic Oriental disease." He paused for laughter and was disappointed.

"I would like each of you in turn to introduce him or herself to the rest of us. As well as the obvious - your name, organisation et cetera - I would like you to tell us about your background and experience, and what you hope to gain from this course. And any other details of your life you think that we might benefit from hearing."

Two more people came in now. A thirtyish woman in glasses and a business suit, and what I at first thought was a flustered looking little boy. They apologised and took the seats to my left. I smiled politely and went back to concentrating on what I could see of the exposed flesh of the woman in front.

"Well we are still one short, but I'm sure they will forgive us if we begin in their absence." He smiled. "All right, would anyone like to lead us off?" There was silence. "Strange," he said, slowly, "No-one ever does."

It would be a good idea to start. It would ease my own nerves and earn the admiration and gratitude of everyone else, including the woman in front with the Scottish neck. I was about to speak when suddenly, on my right, I heard John.

"OK, I'll go first. I've cracked." Everyone laughed.

"Excellent. And after you, we'll go around the group

from the chap to your left."

That was me: the chap to the left of John Mulholland. 'Tommy' as Bernard had called him.

"My name is John Mulholland. I work at Bridge Systems - a software supplier and consultancy. I have about eight years computing experience mainly with Oracle Financials although I have recently been drafted into a Y2K Project." There were murmurs of recognition.

"I would like to formalise my Project Management experience with a view to using it in larger projects - if anyone lets me." There were a few soft, nasal laughs around the class, "And discovering how to avoid the mistakes I've made in the past." People liked that. "My hobbies include squash and golf but I'm not sure of my vital statistics." More laughs.

To John, "Thank you. Excellent. Very good." To me. "You have the idea?"

"My name is Tony Palmer. Like John I work at Bridge Systems. I've been involved, analyst-programmer, with Ingres databases for a few years but I've been on Year 2K as well now."

What was I saying? No-one called it Year 2K. It was Y2K or Year 2000. I realised I had also stopped talking.

"And done some theoretical Project Management theory, but that was a while ago, like, not really practised, more 'I learn it from a book' needs consolidating. And I don't play golf."

I tailed off to baffled silence.

"Right - and techniques you are familiar with?"

"Do you mean the names?"

"Yes." What else could he mean? "Gantt charts?" He was trying to help. "Critical Path Analysis?" he added. He was pitying me now.

"Yes. Both. A bit."

He gave me the most insincere reassuring smile I had seen for quite some time, and we passed on to the new woman on my left.

"My name is Joanne Carr. My background is in Mathematics and Statistics rather than computing, but through a slightly unorthodox career path..."

This was boring but I wished I had achieved that. I had sounded like a fraud with something to hide; barely articulate with inverted snobbery about golf – perhaps due to some anti-Scottish sentiment. People must be wondering why John Mulholland tolerated me.

Joanne Carr finished off her spiel and the little boy next to her started up. He was Warren from Belfast and he had been working in IT for five years since graduating. He "wanted to get involved in Project Management and managing projects". He was nervous, which people probably found endearing. Endearing. I wished I had been endearing.

I wouldn't have been much worse if I had told the truth

My name is Tony Palmer. I have been sexually inactive for about a year now - ever since I was dumped, without explanation, by a beautiful bitch called Louise Jackson with whom I had planned to spend the rest of my life. I enjoy listening to Country music and I drink too much, which might be to compensate for the lack of love in my life, but it's probably just because I like it too much.

I have recently come to realise that I am closer to my mid-life crisis than to my childhood; I might even be having it now. I don't remember much of my early life. My parents died when I was twelve and I was brought up by my aunt and uncle and elder brother, Richard who is the only one of my family I have any time for, even though he became a priest. My younger brother, Robert, went bald at the age of twenty-one in what could have been an attempt to precipitate middle-age. He has three children and a wife; we see each other rarely and that's just fine. My sister, Susan, is also dull, despite having artistic pretensions. She works in art administration, whatever that is, and she seems to spend a lot of time attending openings and networking. She enjoys exotic holidays, and I suspect she hopes to marry for money.

I am also, and I hope she will excuse my boldness, deeply in love with the Scottish woman on the row in front of me. I earn £24,000 a year for my involvement in the futile attempt to prevent computer systems all over the world crashing on 1st January 2000 (note to self:Survival Hampers) as programs fail to cope with year 99 being followed by year 00; and I am bored out of my mind.

This distracted me from Andrew Punchley's speech, and then it was her turn. She was a little nervous. She took a few deep breaths and pulled her hands up against her thighs and the tops of her legs. Her nails, her ribcage, her lungs were exciting me at the moment. I longed to hear her voice.

"My name is Helen Palmer," she said softly, "No relation."

She glanced back in my direction with a playful smile and everyone tittered. She was looking straight into my eyes, and the blood which had been gathering lower down my body shot up to my face, which surged from pink to red and then purple. I could do nothing to stop it, and was left feeling hot, sickened and exhausted.

"I live and work in Swindon," she resumed at last, but I missed the next part as I was preoccupied with the battle with my skin colour and heart rate, and looking around to see who had noticed. As I began to recover, I learnt that she was interested in finding out to what extent formalised techniques could be used, across a wide range of situations, to introduce control and accuracy in planning, "To improve productivity and stop the appalling way I waste so much of my time."

I was more impressed with the way she moved in her

chair as she spoke than with what she actually said. 'Creativity in Project Management', was not a phrase I would excuse many people using, but my love for her was banishing my sad old cynical ways. I knew these feelings. Louise had made me feel like that.

It turned out that the man with the moustache next to her was also called Palmer. People found this hilarious.

"In my case, Terry Palmer," he said. "Again, no relation to either of these young people." I didn't blush this time, although I tried to, as cover for my earlier attack.

"I am a VME COBOL contractor, have been for fifteen years now and I am ready..."

A genuinely interesting fact had finally emerged. He was paying for this course himself. Cash. Money that would otherwise have gone on food or drink or furniture. Something like £1100, plus expenses and loss of earnings. Unlike the rest of us, this was costing him a lot of money; he must have believed that this course was actually worth attending. Madness.

"OK," said Campbell briskly when we had all finished. "By my calculations that means our missing delegate is Mr Clegg." No-one disagreed and he made a note.

"Right. Project Management. What is it? How does it work? Why does it matter? Does it matter?

"To answer the last of these questions will take only

one word. Yes. To answer the remainder will take the rest of this week and the rest of your working lives.

“In fact more than just your working life. The world is becoming more complex, potentially more chaotic all the time. Without direction, without control to hold it all together there is nothing.

"I am a Scot. There are nearly as many Scots here as there are Palmers," he smiled, "And to paraphrase the words of another Scot: Project Management is not a matter of life and death - it's much more important than that."

I stifled my first yawn of the course. A course for which the twelve of us (including the absent Mr Clegg) were each paying, directly or indirectly twenty-seven pounds and fifty pence per hour including lunch. It would have bought each of us fourteen hundred large sliced granary loaves or a return plane ticket to the other side of the world and a fortnight’s holiday with half board at a hotel in Sydney. Between us, we could have put down a 20% deposit on a decent three-bed terraced house in Leicester.

"To take a simple example. If you are having a dinner party it is important to tell your guests both when and where it will be held. If you do not do so, then your meal, however well prepared, will be a failure. You may feel you do not need me to tell you this, but it happens all the time in business.

"People build bridges which fall down over rivers which don't exist. Tunnels fail to meet in the middle. Banks collapse, countries disintegrate, wars are lost," he paused for effect, or perhaps for breath, "People die - because of poor project planning.

"Any questions? No? Now if you could turn to page 9, chapter 1 of the course notes..."

We were off. I set my brain to the appropriate state of semi-consciousness, polling for phrases like "turn to page" and "switch on your PC" and "Fire!". Looking around, I suspected that I was not the only one doing it.

Helen remained beautiful. She had become more desirable through the morning while I had become less. She had shown herself to be intelligent, self-confident and happy whereas I was ludicrously self-conscious and consumed with lust. It hadn't started well and I was afraid she was out of my league. But I had to try. It was the only thing worth doing in life.

I turned my attention to Terry, the moustachioed half-wit sitting next to her. He was too old and bedraggled to be a serious rival. Experience told me, though, that once I thought this, the same man would next appear with a hand caressing the shoulders of the woman in question and his head up her skirt, but I needed something to build up my confidence, and belittling others was the most reliable way.

My attention was distracted by the sound of the

Joanne woman to my left scribbling frantically. Any minute now she would be putting her hand up and asking if she was to write on both sides of the paper. She saw me looking.

"You make a lot of notes don't you?" I whispered.

"It helps me stay awake."

When Mr Campbell released us for our first break, I avoided making too obvious a beeline for Helen, who was being talked at by Terry, and I ended up walking down the corridor with Punchley, just behind her. Although I didn't really want a conversation with Punchley, I reckoned that if I talking to him it would be easier to chat with whoever he was sharing a PC with. Oh, it was that woman, Helen.

"What do you make of this so far?" I asked pleasantly. We were following quite close behind the most beautiful woman in the world, which made this inane conversation quite bearable.

"No complaints," he smirked, "Especially where I'm sitting. Nice isn't she?"

He was not speaking in an undertone, or anything like it. I was horrified and I wanted to shush him. He saw the change in my expression.

"You fancy it as well, do you?"

There was a character in the Bash Street Kids called Wilf, who was always pictured with the lower half of his head hidden inside a green pullover. At this point I instinctively tried to imitate him, while at the same time slowing down and trying to slow my companion down with me.

I also made no reply to the question, so that anyone who could hear but not see us (the couple in front for example), might be in some doubt as to whom it had been directed. If this failed, then I hoped that my silence would at least show that while I did not disagree with the literal truth of what was being said, I felt that its tone was wholly inappropriate and demeaning for all involved.

"Wearing a wedding ring. But then so am I," Punchley sniggered. I stayed silent and prayed for him to shut up, especially as Helen and Terry in front were slowing down.

"Palmer - same name - could be in there, you reckon?" he persisted.

We were only five yards behind her and I was doing a lot more blushing than I would have expected on the first day of a course on 'Project Management and the Development Life Cycle'. It would be difficult to slow down any more without a reason, but I couldn't stand much more of this. I twisted slightly, bent forward and stumbled. It might explain my red face as well, I thought.

"What's up?" cried Punchley.

Of course, Terry turned around at this, and then Helen. As I fell to the ground I realised that, whether or not she had heard Punchley's conversation, this tumble would do little to impress her; but it was done, so I sat up on the ground holding my left ankle and wincing as a small crowd gathered around me.

"Feel so stupid. Just twisted it a bit. It's fine. Just go on without me, I'll be OK," I said in best War Film hero style.

"Are you sure you're all right?" said Helen, with apparently genuine concern.

"Oh yeah, I'll be fine, " I smiled back bravely.

"Do you want to go to the sick bay?"

"No - it's OK. I'll go to the toilet." It seemed a natural refuge to me, but it produced looks of surprise from the huddle around me. "To bathe it," I explained quickly.

Luckily this seemed to satisfy them and no-one asked for details. There were a couple of half-hearted 'Do you want a hand's' which I managed to turn down gratefully. It was not so difficult. Once the novelty of seeing someone else's injury has passed and there is no likelihood of its worsening dramatically, people rarely turn down an opportunity to leave the victim. The chances of seeing me twist the other ankle and make for the toilets on my hands were very slim, so they left me. Despite the fact that this was what I wanted, I still felt a little hurt.

As they walked away, John and Helen were chatting. There seemed no end to his popularity: wasted on a man as married as he was. Punchley was bobbing around them trying to break in.

"We were just talking and then whoomf..." I heard him say as I hobbled away through the swing doors.

Now I was faced with new complications. How long would it be appropriate to hobble like this for? Would I remember that it was my left ankle that was injured? Should I get it dressed or strapped up? If there were other people there when I reached the toilet, did I have to go through the whole fiasco of bathing my ankle in front of them, balancing on my one good foot like a ballerina, with the other leg at right angles in the hand-basin? Perhaps I could just put the injured foot down a toilet and flush water over it at regular intervals while a queue formed outside.

Again I prayed, and again my prayers were answered. The toilet was empty apart from Warren, the little boy from Belfast. We nodded to each other, and I limped past him to a cubicle. Perfect witness. I locked the cubicle door, pulled down the lid and sat on it, relieved to be away from them all.

This did not last long. I was not doing well. I had become a curiosity: the blushing, golf-hater who falls over for no good reason, and can't say "Y2K" properly. Instead of developing my devil-may-care Lothario persona, I was hiding, sitting on a toilet seat, with my trousers on and a fictitious sprained ankle.

I had to do some planning and prioritising - Mr Campbell would have been proud of me. My short-term objective had to be for this whole sorry episode to be forgotten, so I could merge back into the world of the normal as quickly as possible and work on my long-term objective of seducing Helen.

Although this seemed a remote possibility now, I remembered how unlikely it had once seemed that I would ever persuade Louise to get in to bed with me; let alone sustain a relationship of almost two years during which she gave at the very least a convincing pretence of love.

The first part of my plan was quite simple. I had to be brave about the pain, and make my recovery as fast as would be credible given that the water here was not piped in from Lourdes. If asked, I would say I had bathed my foot, but I would not go into detail.

I flushed the toilet - it seemed the most natural thing to do - and then limped back to A4. The idea of returning like an infirm elderly relative, being offered chairs and mumbled sympathy, was not an appealing one, but I had no choice. I would just have to work harder at developing that Lothario persona.

"Ah ha," said Campbell as I entered, "I thought we'd lost another."

"You OK?" asked John, as if I was his feeble little brother.

"Yes, fine." A few of the class turned to look at me.

"Dunno what happened," I mumbled.

Punchley, who had turned round for a good look, spoke up, "You could sue them."

I laughed politely, hating him more than ever.

"Is there a problem?" Mr Campbell asked tetchily.

"He sprained his ankle coming down the corridor," explained Punchley helpfully. If he died, I really would feel nothing but pleasure. "I was with him." The people who hadn't been looking at me, now looked at me.

"Is it serious? Do you need to go to First Aid?"

"No, no thanks. It's not so bad. Healing up fine, just twisted it a bit really, you know," I pleaded.

"We were wondering - could he sue?"

"Ha, ha," said Campbell, unamused. The class probably had me down as a chancer now as well.

I concentrated on blending in to the back wall, and willed Campbell to start teaching again. Joanne half-smiled at me. Could she have guessed? She had been behind me when it happened and I doubted my fall was convincing. I gave an approximation of a brave face and looked hard at the manual.

“We can resume now at Section One proper. Page twenty-two - Understanding Importance."

I sighed with relief. We were back on the course again, and soon I was safely anonymous again and bored.

CHAPTER 3

Lunch was the predictable, pleasant cross between airline food and good school dinners. And it was all free with our little blue laminated cards.

"Get as much as you can now, and just get a burger tonight. Don't want to waste money on food," Punchley told me. "Soup," he added, ladling out as much as possible into his bowl.

I ignored him, and moved away. The morning had dragged once the relief of anonymity had subsided, and it was good to be able to move around and make choices. I had done two hours of limping, and it would soon be plausible for my recovery to start. Rounding the dessert island, I was faced with Helen on her own for the first time. I had to make this count.

"Not many vegetarian options, are there?" she said.

"No," I answered brilliantly.

"Can you manage all right?" she asked.

"Oh ho yes," I bellowed, over-stressing the nothing-to-worry-about jollity of the 'ho'. I was embarrassed and I started blushing again, just in case she hadn't realised. I wanted to get away, but I remembered that embarrassment is more attractive than rudeness so I tried to smile, "More embarrassing than anything else."

"Right. I'll stop mentioning it then." I agreed, and we

exchanged a smile. At last.

Punchley, of course, had noticed the exchange, and he sidled up to me.

"Using the sympathy angle there, were we?"

At least he had waited until she was out of hearing this time, or I might have had to stage another accident, flinging my trayful of food into the air for added effect.

"Something about women on a course," he told me, "The wife being three hours down the motorway helps, as well, I suppose. Doesn't apply to you that though, does it?"

It occurred to me that he might be thinking I was gay.

I limped over to my classmates. Helen was already hemmed in by Terry and Ian, a dour Mancunian, so I sat next to Joanne who was in deep conversation with a woman I didn't recognise. Helen was having Leek Soup and the Lentil Roast; I had chosen haddock, which I hoped she would see as a step closer to vegetarianism than the other options.

"Joanne told me you were here," a woman said.

I looked up. It was the woman next to Joanne. She was looking straight past me at John. Him again.

"Yeah. How are you doing, Rachel?" John replied.

“Fine,” she smiled. “Still here. Still in marketing.”

Was I missing something here? Was there anybody he didn't know? I was ready to fight now, and while these women were not as debilitatingly gorgeous as Helen, it was time I made my mark. And become known for something other than my ankle.

"Is it sore?" Joanne asked me suddenly.

"Pardon?"

"Your ankle."

"Oh. Not too bad. I feel a bit of a fraud, everybody asking all the time as if I've only got a few months to live or something."

"What's the problem?" asked Rachel.

"Twisted my ankle."

"Sports injury or something?"

"No. Walking down the corridor really."

I couldn't help but think that this course was not going to be remembered by everyone as the time they met that wonderful man, Tony Palmer.

****

Most of the able-bodied went for a walk around the grounds after lunch. The only exception apart from myself was Ian, who made no pretence at being glad of my company, as we sat facing each other in silence in the lounge. I turned self-consciously and looked out across the grounds at the strolling executives for as long as it was credible that I could want to. A car alarm went off for a few seconds then died abruptly. Ian remained silent. It was no good, it was rude not to talk to him. He might think I thought he was socially inept.

"Quite a nice day, isn't it?" I said. "Funny how only a few miles can make a difference."

"Global warming," he explained.

"Are you staying here?" I asked and he nodded. "I'm at a B&B myself."

He said nothing. Admittedly it wasn’t a very interesting thing to say, but there was no need for him to look at me like that - as if I was a television which had been left on, and that was where the noise was coming from.

"Good to get away from work for a few days though."

"Young baby. Wife's not very happy with me coming away. And it's not as if it's Centre Parks is it?" He was right, it had a lot of advantages over Centre Parks, including the absence of his family, but I let him think I was agreeing with him.

"Cheaper, though," I suggested.

"Spent half last night on the phone," he countered.

I had to admire a master at work and I fell silent. He offered me an Extra Strong Mint. Concern about my breath overrode concern for my teeth, so I took one. He stood up.

“Get some more,” he muttered, “Butler's Pantry. Twenty per cent mark-up.”

I relaxed as he left and looked up at the sheet of silver-blue sky. At one side of the grounds was what I suppose was a summerhouse. I would have enjoyed walking towards it across the crunching gravel and the yielding grass, with my hands behind my back like a dashing young squire taking the air, but for the time being I had to be the sickly younger brother, destined for the church.

I turned around, hearing John's voice. He was with Helen, Warren and another couple from the course.

"...This afternoon's lecture on Project Planning has been cancelled due to unforeseen circumstances." They all laughed. John was now Oscar Wilde.

"Lovely, out there now - like Spring," Helen said to me, the last traces of her laugh still lighting up her face.

I smiled and nodded, "Mm, looks like it."

"It's hard to imagine people used to actually live here - in the Middle Ages or whenever." This was Warren.

"It is a beautiful house." That was Helen again.

"Wouldn't fancy cleaning the windows, mind," I chipped in, and Hallelujah, a few smiles. Including a big one from Helen.

"Are you from Newcastle?" she asked, and I nodded modestly. I loved her voice and I could feel a stupid smile forming on my lips. There was nothing I could do about it, so I let it grow.

"Lovely accent it is," she said. "Lovely place as well. Very friendly. Ex-boyfriend from there, that's how I know it."

That was either very good or very bad. I carried on

giving her the benefit of my lolloping grin.

"Great night life - what I can remember of it." She laughed again. I laughed again. "My cousin lives there now as well. Went to college and never left. Loves it."

I could feel that my grin had widened still more, and I had added an imbecilic, wide-eyed stare and automatic nodding.

I straightened up. It was very pleasant to be pummelled into jelly by my adoring lust, but the spectacle was unlikely to excite her much, and she must have seen it plenty of times before. I straightened up a bit more, then worried that I looked unnaturally stiff so I flopped back again. I must remember to become a vegetarian. It was morally right anyway.

"Do you go home much yourself? I suppose it's a long way from Swindon up to Scotland."

"You're not wrong there - what a trek."

"Must be hard that, like," I said, sensitively, and cranking up the old accent. It seemed to work. She looked touched. I also felt that I was no longer the ankle man.

"How's the ankle?" asked Warren.

"Not too bad, thanks."

"A few beers tonight should numb the pain," said Punchley, joining in as usual. "Do you fancy it, Helen?"

"Sounds cool," said Helen. Right. Time for action. "But I think Carl's coming over." Oh.

"Are you married?" Warren asked me, out of nowhere.

"No."

"Courting?" Courting? Where had he picked that word up from? John and Bernard were coming over to move in on Helen, and Warren was waiting for me to say something.

"What about you?" Anybody so unlucky?

"There is someone," he confided with an air of mystery that meant he'd be married to the lucky woman and in a semi within a year. "And, as I said to my brother last weekend, she might just be the one - if you know what I mean."

Warren talked to me about her all the way back to A4.

The free food, an enthusiastically heated room and the natural aridity of Gantt charts did for the afternoon, especially as Mr Campbell was now sticking to the manual with the rigidity of an Orthodox Talmudic scholar. Relief came when the network went down after a couple of hours, and Campbell told us we could leave.

“Hope the forced early finish won’t adversely colour your Delegate Reflections on the day too much,” said Campbell as we were gratefully packing up.

“No chance of that, mate,” I muttered.

The only problem, as Ian pointed out grimly, was that the more delays there were now, the less chance there was of an early escape on Friday.

CHAPTER 4

This had been an amazing sequence of events, I thought, looking at her.

"I never guessed," I said, then I stopped.

Helen smiled at me, amused but not mocking. She understood. There was no need to speak, so I stayed stopped, and lay there watching her, mesmerised. She poured lime juice over vodka and ice, sipped it without swallowing, and leant over me. She was wearing a loose white blouse and a short kilt, and her hair was down, spread over her shoulders. Our hands touched as I reached to take the glass from her. Her skin was soft and warm. She didn't release the glass. I looked at her, puzzled. She shook her head and pouted very slightly. Suddenly I understood. My drink was still in her mouth.

I lifted my head from the pillow towards her gorgeous female face, desperate for the touch of her moist lips. My mouth was in a state beyond dryness, and my eyes stung as I opened them. I sighed, and lay perfectly still, as consciousness and disappointment washed over me.

When I was sure I was awake I began my standard checklist.

It began simply enough. Tony. Tony Palmer.

In my bed. In a Bed and Breakfast place - in Berkshire. I looked away from the ceiling to check the next bit.

Focusing took a while; but happened eventually. Yes, it was my room.

I continued. Underpants and socks - no, sock. Next thing?

Oh my God. Turned the volume down yesterday. I sat up straight and checked the time. Five to eight. Late but not too late. I lay back down and continued.

Not sure. Taxi? I concentrated. Nothing. Walked perhaps?

I had played pool. We had somehow managed to find the only rough pub in town. The Eagle and Child. Bloke selling watches, phones and lighters from a black bin bag. Won three games in a row.

My body had woken up properly now - it was calling out for fluid, but I hadn't yet got the energy to move, so I lay still and continued my catechism.

Beer? Well, yes. Whisky? Yes, towards the end and, yes, kebab. Still taste it.

By myself, probably at closing time.

No, not sick. Moderately close - slight nausea on getting in to bed. As usual, hadn't bothered to drink the water that would have made all the difference now. Thoughtless bastard.

Not sure how I had got separated from the others. I had definitely come back by myself because I remembered worrying about waking Mrs Mullen as I fell through the door. I must have unlocked it without realising, and then fallen through while trying to unlock it again. But she hadn't woken up; I felt sure she would have let me know if she had. This was all good. Best of all, I didn't have that vague sickening feeling of remorse which meant there was something awful lurking to be remembered. I dared to allow myself the beginnings of a sense of well-being, which I had learnt to be wary of.

I was ready for refreshment now and I hauled myself out of bed. 'Refreshment'. The water would taste sweetish, and as it left the tap it would flow down and splash up from my hand pure and clean, as if trying to preach to me. And it did.

It had no lasting effect on the dryness of my mouth. I was expecting this as well. I was made mindful of the Parable of the Sinner and his Jug. But I knew that the liquid had to be rushed off to those parts of my body most urgently in need. In time, though, some fraction of the moisture would be passed back to my mouth as saliva. The healing process had begun. I gulped down three more big mouthfuls, and felt suddenly dizzy, so I leaned on the sink for support until it passed.

When I was back on the bed I trawled my memory for embarrassing moments - humour in bad taste, grotesquely unsuccessful seductions, fights, police.

None of the above - despite the whisky. Helen? No. The only women I remembered apart from barmaids were Joanne and her friend Rachel. They'd appeared unexpectedly but not stayed long, which was probably down to Punchley.

Still nothing bad. I had managed not to tell people about my ankle or my love for Helen. I had been a little full of myself after winning that third game of pool, and I remembered refusing to go on with the others. I had stayed in the pool pub, talking to the barmaid and anybody else who'd listen including the man with the black bin-bag full of merchandise of uncertain provenance. I had definitely gone on about Newcastle at some length, with particular reference to its lowlife, which I pretended to be familiar with. Well, I wouldn't have to see them again, so it didn't matter.

Otherwise nothing. So, why so rough? Early start. Very. Five o'clock, straight from school. I had drunk to excess, but not to ridiculous excess. Perhaps those days were gone. Perhaps I would never again set fire to my hair.

It would have been sweet just to turn over on my bed and sleep through the morning, but I had things to do. It was a shame I had no tomato juice. It would have been so welcome now, with a dash of Worcester Sauce, but, as Mr Campbell would have said, I was paying the price of not planning ahead.

I knew the other ingredients I needed for resurrection: orange juice (fluid, vitamin C and sugar), grilled or fried food (bulk and salt), tea and coffee (fluid and caffeine) and three or four visits to the toilet. These together would purge me and cleanse me, working together with the magical natural restorative powers of the body over time, to end my pain.

First, I needed some breakfast to swamp my headache. I dressed as quickly as I could, brushing my teeth at the same time, and made my way downstairs. There was no-one else there.

"You wouldn't have any. . . er tomato juice would you?" I said when Mrs Mullen appeared with a glass of orange juice.

"Instead of this orange juice?"

"As well?" My headache was making me bold.

She looked at me strangely, perhaps to make it clear that this was not a regular occurrence.

"I'll see," she said eventually and left the room while I gulped down the orange juice. She came back with a very small glass of tomato juice.

"You'll be wanting the same breakfast as yesterday," she told me, still holding the glass.

"Yes please." She released it. "Thank you. Oh, and please could I have it with no egg please?"

Asking for less seemed to be as unwelcome as asking for more, but she didn't actually refuse. I sipped the tomato juice, tasting its richness and thickness immediately. There was no Worcester Sauce in it, but there were limits to my courage. She turned away.

"Just going to give the others a knock," I explained to her uninterested back.

I went upstairs quickly, not bothering to limp, and knocked gently on John's door. Nothing. I knocked harder.

"Yeah?"

"It's me. Tony."

"Oh."

"It's gone quarter past eight."

"Oh."

"Are you going in?"

"No."

"What do you mean?"

"Last night. Sprained ankle. Bloody agony."

"That's me not you, man. Are you still pissed?"

"No. I have. Tell Campbell. Tell Mullens. Stop in bed."

I went back downstairs.

“Looks lovely that,” I said as she put my breakfast down. "Mr Mulholland won't be down. He's still in bed. He's sprained his ankle as well."

"I don't do breakfasts in bed."

"Right."

"He was in very late last night - noisy," she said.

"Perhaps because of his ankle," I attempted. She looked scornful. "Though I wasn't with him." Her scorn deepened and I buckled under it, and concentrated on my breakfast. It was nice, which cheered me up a little; and then Punchley appeared at the door looking like death. This cheered me more. He walked carefully to my table

"John's out of action," I said, "I'll ask Mullens to get us a taxi."

He looked as if he needed a good breakfast, so I put a piece of bacon in my mouth as I spoke to him.

"We're running a bit late, though," I told him. "No time for breakfast, mate."

****

Punchley was pale and almost mute in the taxi, and he followed me like a lamb into A4.

"I'm sorry we're late. And John - Mr Mulholland - can't make it in this morning. He sends his apologies."

Mr Campbell did not like to be interrupted, but I was a paying adult so he had to endure it.

"He's sprained his ankle." People looked surprised.

"I was not aware that the condition was infectious."

"It is a bit of a coincidence, isn't it?" I was blushing again and I felt exposed. "But his sounds really bad."

I braced myself for more sarcastic comments, but there were none. I was grateful for this. Given that teacher had been interrupted by a late-arriving and possibly mendacious boy bringing bad news to an already diminished class, his manner was more kindly than I would have expected. It was also surprising how quickly the interest of the others had faded. They weren't all hungover, surely?

Mr Campbell looked weary as well and soon set us to work on an exercise. John's absence reduced the class to ten and we were put into pairs. Joanne and I, on the stricken back bench, shared her PC. She seemed happy to do the work, which left me free to daydream about Helen.

My hangover only served to increase my lustfulness. Helen had caught my eye twice, which she could only have done by deliberately turning around. To think, she was making all that effort for me. I wished I could show her the fullness of my gratitude. I loved the way the tops of her ears were rounded. She rubbed her right thigh again. That was the fourth time since I had come in. I don't think I had missed any.

Still, working with Joanne made a change from John. Was I the only person in the world who found him boring? I wondered how many more ankles would have to go before I would be working with Helen.

"Well that's one done," Joanne said suddenly, showing me the Gantt chart.

"Honestly? Great. I promise I won't be as useless as this every morning - I hope."

"Good night was it?"

"Is it that obvious?"

"Oh no. Don't worry. You seemed to be going for it when we saw you though."

"I was led astray. I don't normally..."

"Poor you." She let me get away with the little boy lost. "How's your ankle?"

"Oh lot better. My head's not so great though."

"And your friend?"

"John? Sounded quite bad, this morning. Weak ankles run in our company." She smiled.

Terry and Warren hijacked me on the way out. "Good night last night. How's John?"

"Still in bed. Where did he do his ankle in?" Terry was puzzled for a moment.

"Oh, course you'd gone. Coming out of Berlins - wine bar. Just a little step but he went over on it. "Weak ankles seem to run in your company." He laughed, I didn't. "We had to half carry him back to your hotel didn't we, Andy?"

I knew Punchley hated being called Andy, so that was something. We collected our coffee and moved away from the machine. Terry was still talking.

"Quite surprised to see you this morning, Tony, the rate you were going through it - impressed."

"Well I am feeling a bit fragile," I said, "But I thought I ought to come in. Try and help keep the numbers up. Otherwise we'll be down to nine - what with John and old Compo missing."

I grinned. They looked shocked. God help me, I thought, confronted with such witlessness. Two people haven't turned up, so I am pretending that this makes me feel that I ought to come in myself. It's a joke. Admittedly a bad one. As is the reference to characters in a Sunday night sitcom. Compo and Clegg? Yes? No? Sorry about the odd two syllable word.

"Oh, course, you were late. You won't have heard... The other, Mr Clegg, the one who didn't turn up - he's dead. That big crash and all the hold-ups yesterday - that was him. Went into the side of a van."

Terry chipped in, "Talking to someone who saw it - glass all over the road and blood. There was a picture in the paper as well. Green 405 - total write-off. Used to have one myself, nice car. Heavier on fuel than you might expect, though."

"Driving up from London to the course, crashed only a couple of miles away."

It was hard to imagine a more pointless death. Terry had something more to contribute.

"There but for the hand of God..."

When Helen appeared with Bernard, I just walked over to them without a word of explanation. Helen smiled gently. I began to blush but I didn't care. That was hangover-induced recklessness, probably.

"It's the hustler," Bernard said, laughing. This was

better.

"Painting the town red, by the sound of it," Helen said, pretending to disapprove. I liked her doing that.

"How's John then?"

"Still in bed I would think."

"Weak ankles seem to run in your company," said Helen and we laughed and laughed.

"It was good to see old John again," said Bernard. "Even if it half killed him. Married life I suppose."

"Did you have a good night?" I asked Helen hypocritically.

"Yes, lovely. We went to The Jade Palace on the way out of town. Chinese. Near the racecourse. Really good. I'd recommend it - although that's usually a mistake." We smiled at the wisdom of this observation. "Did you hear about the accident?"

"Mm, yes. Makes you think."

I couldn't help wondering if his course fees would be refunded.

I was beginning to feel hot now, and my half-digested breakfast was bringing on mild nausea. Then the coffee kicked in and a sudden pain cut across my bowels. I made an inaudible excuse, not wishing Helen to associate me primarily with toilets, then performed an awkward, slightly painful swivel-turn, and limped out of the room.

Joanne and Rachel smiled politely at me as I passed them. They seemed to be getting on very well. Perhaps their closeness was a defence against the threat of lecherous inanity presented by Terry and Warren, who were standing next to them, trying to join them, like atomic nuclei trying to fuse.

It was good that so many men were so stupid. It helped compensate for the fact that so many women were trapped in pointless marriages. So why did I spend so much less time copulating than I would have liked?

How could anyone want to take their clothes off with Terry, for example, and suck on bits of his flaccid, hairy naked white flesh? Or want him to reciprocate with clumsy prodding, and panting and slurping? Never mind pledging allegiance for life and exchanging bodily fluids.

On the way back, I passed a fat man of about forty-five with the bluish complexion of an electric shaver user. He was barking fierce laughter into a mobile phone, while caressing a buttock (his own) with his spare hand. The other one had a wedding ring on. It was worrying.

****

I got through a morning of Critical Path Analysis by the simple device of letting Joanne continue doing all the work. I hadn't got the energy to concentrate, but she seemed satisfied with me making appreciative and supportive noises.

Perhaps inertia was the way forward, because at

lunchtime I found myself sitting next to Helen without even trying.

"Nice these, aren't they?" She was holding a piece of Vegetable Bake on her fork. I was having the same, and she was right. They were nice - crunchy on the outside with a sloppy mixture of carrot, leek, mushroom and tomato inside.

"Yes, crunchy on the outside and... not in the middle."

"Are you vegetarian?" she asked.

"Moving towards it." And with a bit of encouragement. . . from you. . . in bed. . . I think I'd get there.

This was a lot less stressful than trying to manipulate everything. Even being joined by Punchley didn't get to me.

"If I'd thought I could have brought John's card in," he said. "Could have had two lunches."

"I've got a Platinum Privilege card," said Warren. "Five grand and it covers as many training courses as you like for a year. Only reason I'm here I think. Trying to get their money's worth."

"You could book yourself on to every course going and just come in for the freebies," I suggested. Helen smiled so I continued. "If you lived round here you could treat it as a free restaurant. Though I suppose you might get noticed after a while."

"They might just think you were a very keen student." That was quite witty for Joanne.

"You could sell courses on your card to other people, couldn't you? Cut price. Savings all round. Not really doing AJA Training any harm either. Keeps the classes full."

"Food," objected Ian, "AJA'd lose out having to provide all the food for nothing."

Ian, the voice of doom, did what he did best, "Actually a few free meals might push them over the edge. I've heard things aren't too good for them at the moment."

Helen leaned past me with a look of real concern.

"Yes, it's true," added Terry, "Take-over bid supposed to be coming. Hardware division's losing money hand over fist."

"But if they were taken over they'd probably stay very much as they are now?" Helen persisted, inexplicably. The vegetable bakes on our forks were forgotten.

"I wouldn't have thought so," said Ian.

"It's just that Carl's firm does a lot of work for them," she said pitifully. "He's just started up on his own, you see, and they are his biggest client." End of mystery.

"There'd be bound to be cut-backs," Ian continued. "Chop it up and hive it off. That's what they do."

"They're breaking everything up at the minute," said Warren.

"Yes, you go into a Post Office now and it's about

twenty different companies you're dealing with."

"World's gone mad."

"Schools have advertising now. At Robert's school they've got billboards up, advertising."

"And sponsors for everything."

"It's all marketing, isn't it?"

"It's all part of Theme Park England," said Terry from last Sunday's newspaper.

"When I go back to Newcastle..." which I had last done about two years earlier and might never do again, with what was left of my family scattered like myself in outposts of dullness throughout England.

"...It's amazing all the countries you go through. You know - Bronte Country, James Herriot Country, Last of the Summer Wine Country, Captain Cook Country. . ."

It would have been a very circuitous route, but why let the facts stand in the way of a good theory?

"They'll probably start selling passports next. We'll have a borderless federal Europe, but you'll have to cross half a dozen time zones to get to Tescos."

Helen wasn't paying any attention. She was sitting silently in her own worried world; perhaps upset that we could chatter like this while her life imploded, so I changed tack.

"You OK?" I asked her. Nice guy. Concerned.

"Sorry? Yes. Not sure what to do. Carl's business."

"Right."

“Perhaps best not to worry him.”

“You’re probably right. It’s all speculation, isn’t it?”

She agreed, and touched my arm. This was fantastic. The most beautiful woman I had ever met was beginning to realise that she was married to a loser and appreciated that I was opening her eyes to the fact. The only problem now was that I was full of wind - the final instalment of the price I had to pay for last night. I left to spend a few moments alone, after first checking that Helen was going for a walk outside with the others after lunch.

"I'll meet you out there, if that's OK. Sure I’ll manage it."

I did a very slight brave wince as I limped away and she smiled back. It wasn’t exactly lustful, but it was a start.

When I felt ready, I left the house by the west porch, and joined the others at the summer-house, like the young squire I had imagined being the day before. Although it was but early February, the weather was not inclement and the sunlight tolerable strong. The party was resting, and I fancied, with the walk following so close upon luncheon, that some of the ladies especially might be quite knocked up. They were conversing little, which confirmed me somewhat in my thinking, but they were by no means out of spirits, rather they were enjoying the tranquillity and the repose.

After exchanging pleasantries with the company, I endeavoured to make myself agreeable to Mrs Palmer.

This most pleasant activity was too soon curtailed by the clock (which read some five and twenty minutes after one), so there was little time to savour the moment, much less for suggesting to the same lady that she and I could slip around the back, and expose each other's eager flesh before rolling around on the cold grass, legs akimbo, making manifest the Holy Spirit to one another. So we didn't.

Within a few minutes of re-entering A4, torpor overwhelmed me. The vegetable bakes didn't help, and after nearly two days, Campbell's attempts to interest us in his subject were getting desperate.

"For those of you who think that Project Planning is a matter of deciding on the most efficient and cost-effective way of balancing a hundred thousand angels on the head of a pin..."

That wasn't fair on Medieval philosophers. At least they didn't ask their students to split into groups and analyse irritatingly whimsical data about widget production.

By the end of the afternoon I felt sick, sweaty and in desperate need of sleep. The only thing that would get me out tonight was the possibility of helping Helen betray her husband, and when I looked around I found that she had already left. I trudged out of the classroom to ring for a taxi.

There was a queue at the payphone. Some bastard was

phoning his wife for a crisis discussion about their child going to the dentist. Helen and Ian came towards me, deep in conversation.

"Sure you're OK if I try again?" Helen asked him. They seemed to be getting on well, the marrieds. Ian even managed an approximation of a smile as he handed her his mobile.

“Course. Just hope you get him this time.”

"Thanks, Ian. Just need to catch him before he leaves. Can't believe I forgot my phone the one time I really need it."

"Coming over again tonight is he?" I asked innocently.

"Mm yes."

"How long have you been married?" asked Ian.

"Six months."

"Oh I see," and they laughed.

"You're not married are you, Tony?" said Ian.

Helen finished dialling and seemed to be staring at me.

"Oh no," I said in a hearty kind of voice.

"Like your freedom, eh?" Help.

"Has its advantages. And its disadvantages." I said, uncontroversially.

"Any plans?" he pressed on, taking advantage of the universally acknowledged fact that a single person's private life is public property.

"Hi, love," said Helen on the phone, turning away.

"No. And do you find that the number of times you have sex has tailed off dramatically since you got married? And which of you is more bored with the other's body?"

This actually came out as, "No, nothing at present," followed by a silly gasping laugh which Rachel and Joanne got the benefit of as they appeared.

"What have you got planned for tonight then - another wild night, ankles and all?"

"No," I replied. "Sleep, sleep and more sleep. Getting a taxi back to bed."

"We're going into London."

"The ballet."

"Really?" I tried to sound interested.

"Swan Lake. Still tickets. Could squeeze one more in - if you're not too tired."

"Thanks. Thanks but..."

"Don't know what you're missing," said Joanne with a bright smile.

The man with the child in peril at the dentist's waved me forward as if he was doing me a personal favour. Helen was still on Ian's mobile as the four of them drifted away together, leaving me to order a taxi, young, free and singlishly.

****

John had pushed a note under my door saying where

I could meet him and Bernard. His sprain must have recovered as well. I turned on the TV and opened one of the cans of Guinness I had bought on the way back. It was too warm and spurted out on to the carpet. I rubbed at it half-heartedly with my handkerchief and John's note, then looked for more paper. All I had to hand was Campbell's Delegate Feedback and Reflections folder. I had finally found a use for it. I tore a couple of sheets out and lay them on top of the damp patch. The TV was showing a programme about arranged marriages. That would be the only way I would ever get with someone like Helen, and I had no family to arrange it. Self pity? Yes. Justified? I thought so.

I switched channels, and caught the end of a prize quiz on a religious channel, followed by a speech that was a cross between advertising blurb and a sermon, delivered by the host of the quiz show. It was worse than Thought for The Day. I could do better than this.

"Can you, Tony? Can you do anything, Tony?"

"Yes," I told myself. "And I'll prove it." I dug out a pen and started writing, for the first time, in my Delegate Reflections folder.

"All the devils in Hell have been numbered and named. We have their measure, attack us though they may. We can resist them with the treasures of our age – Project Planning and electronic technology. We do not fight our enemies any longer with clubs and spears, but with heat-seeking missiles, and sound business practices. We must harness our new tools to the good fight. This is the will of the Almighty. It must be, for He has given us these tools, as once He gave us fire and the sword."

It was the first creative writing I had done since Primary School and it felt good. Heavy exposure to vintage country music had probably helped. I went to the toilet, intending to come back and complete it, but then I allowed myself to become distracted by an old episode of 'A Fine Romance'. It was better than I remembered it as being, so I decided to get into bed with my cans to watch it properly.

CHAPTER 5

I woke very early on Wednesday. I tried to get to sleep again, but my body remained stubbornly awake, so I slid out of bed and peered through the curtains.

It was still quite dark. I was up before the rest of the world, which was a novelty, and I wasn't sure what to do. Apart from hammering on Mrs Mullen's door and demanding breakfast, I could not come by any food, so I decided to make full use of the amenities by running a bath, and making myself a cup of coffee with the Tippex-style whitener. I drank it in the bath, and ate two packs of complimentary biscuits. When I tired of playing Cleopatra, I shaved and dressed, then sat by the window watching the sunrise slowly lighting up the sky.

Now what? A conscientious student would have filled in some Delegate Feedback and Reflections forms and gone through their notes. I decided to go for a walk.

It was nearly seven and though it wasn't cold (Ian's global warming), there was no-one else about. Apart from a passing worry that I might be mistaken for a prowling felon, this felt good. I walked briskly, listening to the pavement echoing my steps and the sound of my breathing. Other sounds carried as well. When I reached a T-junction at the end of the road, I heard running water and I headed towards it.

I owned the deserted streets and I wanted to breathe in the pleasure of possession before all these curtains opened and the strangers spilled out to spoil things. It would have been nice to have a dog with me at this point, to run along by my side through the dew and piss on crocuses, but a dog is for life, not just for taking on spontaneous walks during residential Project Management courses. I was a responsible kind of person afraid of responsibility, so I walked alone.

I came to a park with heavy cast iron gates and I walked through. The sound was coming from a small, stepped artificial waterfall cut in light grey rock. It fed the narrow leg of a pond which I followed around.

A young woman in tight jeans and a quilted grey jacket was throwing scraps of bread to breakfasting ducks. She looked good in those jeans. I could see her face clearly now in the early morning light. She had a friendly expression, challenging yet open, and lively eyes. Her white shirt was open at the neck, to the top of her breasts.

"Hello," I called out.

She looked up, squinting slightly. I walked towards her.

"Hello," I repeated, "How was the ballet?"

"Oh, it's you," said Joanne. "God, my eyesight. I didn't take you for an early riser."

"Not usually. Had an early night last night though, so by six o'clock this morning I was sitting bolt upright in bed and wide awake. What about you?"

"Only when the ducks need me. No, not usually. I'm a bit erratic in my hours." Her eyes were full of life, and her skin looked fresh and healthy in the crisp air.

"Can I have a go?"

"What a cheapskate - not even bringing your own stale bread."

"It's very hard to get hold of; stale bread shop's not open for hours yet."

She placed two slices in my hands.

"You can manage to tear it up yourself?"

"Is that how you do it? I was just going to give it to them whole. Anyway, how was the ballet?"

"Really good."

"Swan Lake wasn't it?"

"Yes. Perhaps that's why I felt the urge to come down here. Duck Pond doesn't have the same ring to it though, does it?"

"Might do in Russian." I paused, "Says he, hoping it is Russian."

"You're OK - it is. Bloke called Tchaikovsky."

"That's a relief. Nothing worse than doing a knowledgeable joke and not having the knowledge. I went to the ballet once. Years ago." With Louise. "Nutcracker Suite." That was appropriate. "Really enjoyed it." The things she had done to me still made me shudder. "It was all the activity on the stage, that's what got me, so much movement and so graceful. And no-one fell over." Louise had taken my hand and put it inside her jacket, then inside her blouse. "Although I was probably too young to appreciate it properly."

Then she had reciprocated, lower down my body with her soft warm hand, at which point I had lost all interest in the world outside my trousers.

"You should have come with us."

"I know. Stupid. I wasn't really thinking when you asked; and you'd gone by the time I'd changed my mind."

"Sure you had more important things to do - like drinking with your mates."

"They aren't really mates."

"Not even John?"

"No." A duck quacked. We both looked at it and smiled. "I mean he's better than Andrew, but that's not saying a lot."

She nodded. "So how are you getting in today?"

"Taxi again. If John's still out of action."

"I could give you a lift. I'm staying at the Grosvenor." She yanked her head back to indicate where it was, slightly pursing her lips as she did.

"Thanks. That'd be great, if I can give Punchley the slip."

"Yes – do that. I'll be there until quarter to. It's this way," she said at the gates. I was going the other way. "So if you want a lift... Can you remember the name of my B&B?"

"Actually, I can. I save my ineptitude for the course."

"Bye then. See you later."

"OK. Thanks. Hope so. Bye."

Considerate and grown up; intelligent and thoughtful; and possibly flirting. Life had a meaning again, which was nice. Things were looking up. I even managed to buy some tomato juice and Worcester Sauce from a shop which I was sure hadn't existed the day before. I'd get the number of the Grosvenor as soon as I got back and book my lift before John had the chance to get up. Just in case.

****

But the selfish bastard was up and about in the breakfast room with Andrew Punchley, laughing.

"Thought you'd be out of action today."

"Went to the A&E," said John. "Got it strapped up. Your's OK, now?"

"Yes, more or less. You can't drive though can you?"

"I doubt it." Good.

"But you can. Or Andrew. My insurance covers any other driver."

"Anyway where've you been?" Punchley asked me. "I gave you a knock." What was it to him?

"Just went out for a walk. Woke up early. Couldn't get

back to sleep."

"God, imagine that. Getting out of bed when you don't have to. You want to try having kids." The family men laughed again. The drive in was not going to be fun

****

John's return not only screwed up my lift with Joanne, it also meant that I was working with him again, and Joanne was back with Warren.

"It's not as much fun working with John," I told her in the break.

"Really?" she said coldly.

"Yes."

"I need to talk to Rachel."

Rachel was standing by the door with a stupid, sulky expression on her face. What was her problem? She was holding a Paddington Bear folder. That was stupid as well; she wasn't a child.

"Did you have another wild night, last night?" asked Helen. I hadn't even noticed her coming over.

"No. Took it easy. Keep a clear head for school."

"Yes, strange in a way, being in a classroom again."

"Well it's a lot better than school as I remember it," I said, as my slow-moving brain digested the fact that she had made a clear decision to move away from the others and talk to me.

"Yes," she agreed, and then she laughed. "Mind you it was getting a little bit boring there yesterday afternoon."

Yes. How wise she was. She had a beautiful laugh. It was unforced and natural and somehow suggested awesome, life-changing possibilities for anyone who managed to become intimate with her. If Joanne was trying to be the ice-maiden, she was way over-playing her hand with competition like this around.

"You were saying you don't get home as much as you'd like," I said, reminding her of our common Northness. "Where exactly are you from?"

"Fife." Thank God for that. I had only been seven years old, but it counted.

"It's beautiful up there," I sighed. "The fishing villages - Crail, Pittenween."

"You know it?"

"Visited – years ago. Bit different to Swindon." She nodded a little sadly, and I showed how deeply I understood with a furrowed brow. We even walked back to class together. If she had had a bag I would have carried it.

At half past eleven a woman from Reception came into the room. I was surprised to hear her saying my name. There was an important message for me. I had a sudden feeling of dread. Helen looked at me with concern as I limped to the door so I smiled back bravely. Perhaps it would be something she could help me with.

In bed.

The receptionist had gone by the time I reached the door, so I lost the limp as I hurried to Reception. I hated not knowing. Even Money: bereavement; 3-1 burglary or fire; 25-1 something good. It was work. Never thought of that. I had forgotten all about it. I had to ring Luke, a Project Manager three years younger than me.

"I don't have a mobile for you," he complained. I said nothing. Luke was responsible for Payroll systems. A routine for calculating sales reps' commission had failed and I had made the mistake of leaving my name on comments in the code.

"It's a while since I was involved with this."

"It's serious," he said, and listed the managers who were putting pressure on him. I yawned. "So if we can't get it sorted you'll have to come back." Suddenly he had my full attention. I could have cried. They were threatening to bring me back early from camp just when things had started getting interesting with no less than two women.

“Give me some time to think. I'll ring you back at half-twelve,” I said in desperation.

So instead of having lunch with the rest of them, I had to go back to the payphone. I became increasing stressed as one by one my suggestions were tried and failed. I could hear Luke sighing, as he kept reminding me that this had to be working by Friday. Fear is supposed to concentrate the mind, but I was just flailing about, saying anything that came into my mind to delay the summons back to work.

"How many reps did you say were on the list?"

I could hear some fumbling on the keyboard.

"One hundred and twenty nine."

"One hundred and twenty nine?" I repeated, "As in one hundred and twenty eight plus one?" Please God, I thought.

"Can you go into the code and read the variable declarations at the top?"

Yes. Hallelujah. Sitting there on line thirty six was a small integer variable (which could hold positive values up to one hundred and twenty-eight) storing the total number of reps. I remembered thinking at the time I should increase it. But I never had. Perhaps something more pressing had come up - like a Fantasy Football transfer deadline or a call of nature. Whatever the reason, I had not got round to doing it before being moved on to make other mistakes on other systems.

"Yes," I said. Helen's interest was giving me the strength to defy Fate. "That'll be it."

I talked him through amending the code, recompiling, and rerunning the application. It ran sweetly. Luke sounded so grateful and relieved. Career strategy note: always leave bugs in your code that you can heroically clear up later on.

"Tony," said Luke. "Tony, thanks a lot. Great what you've done there. Great."

"No probs, mate." I was delighted with myself. Boffin cum brain surgeon cum streetwise Lothario. Best of all, I could stay here. I made sure I told Helen the good news first.

“Got it sorted – eventually”.

"Did you?"

"Big crisis in Payroll. Thought I might have to go back for a minute." No reaction. I had come back from victorious battle to find out she didn't even know there had been a war on.

"Thought you were on Y2K," said Warren.

"Seconded. You know the way it is. Hard work over the phone. I felt a bit like air-traffic control in a disaster movie, talking the plane down blind after the pilot's had a heart attack."

"Things can be difficult over the phone," said Helen, dreamily. I suspected we weren't having the same conversation. "Misunderstandings happen. Not just with practical things either."

'Practical' obviously covered all the mundane trivia outside the ethereal universe inhabited by herself and her husband. I murmured dishonest sympathy, but she just took out her phone and walked away. When I turned back the others had gone, leaving me with Terry, who decided this was the time to tell me of the misery of his life as a contractor.

"Money's good, though, isn't it?" I suggested.

"Not worth it. Cost me my family. All that working away." It probably would have happened anyway, mate - face like yours. "You know what happened? She went off with my accountant. They must laugh at me, together, in bed." He stopped.

"Sorry. Sorry." He blinked a couple of times. I was afraid he was going to start crying. "I don't know what's come over me. Thanks, son, you're a good listener. You're lucky. You're all so young."

I could have set his mind at rest with regard to that one, but it would have been difficult to do it tactfully. He took a drink from his empty glass of water.

"Sorry, just feeling sorry for myself. Embarrassing."

"No, no - it's better out."

I was on the brink of asking him if he wanted to go out for a drink that night, despite my other plans, but I managed to stop myself. We were living in an age of refreshing honesty, and it would have been deeply dishonest to invite him out if I didn't really want to.

He began to brighten up a little, anyway, thinking he had found a sympathetic ear. By the time we reached the lounge, he was chatting almost happily about places he had worked in - South Africa, Saudi Arabia, Indonesia; and the wildish times he had had there, with all the short-cuts and comforts which money provides.

"And I suppose everybody's got their own problems. There's that Helen, seems to have everything going for her, and then she comes back off the phone... but it's none of our business, I suppose," he tailed off as Helen appeared.

She smiled at me, or perhaps at us. It was a very friendly smile, and my hopes rose again. Perhaps she saw I was being nice to Terry, and she found displays of kindness erotic.

"Got through to Carl," she explained.

"Oh good," said Terry.

“Fantastic.”

That was that. I should have known not to waste time on her when the more realistic possibility of Joanne had been within range. The same way I should have gone to London with them, instead of wasting the night skulking by myself in my hotel room. Plenty of time for that after my funeral.

Back in A4, Campbell was shuffling papers and transparencies around; and John and Joanne were deep in muttered conversation. I said 'Hi' and hovered next to them. I was ignored. I began counting, and I had reached twenty before John acknowledged me.

"What about you for tonight?"

That depends on what more interesting people are doing.

"That depends..." It was time to be open. I looked at

Joanne. "You any plans?"

"They're going to London for the night," said John.

"Again?" I was suspicious.

"Old friends," Joanne explained. "Rachel's really. She'd arranged it weeks ago and I don't want to let her down."

"OK. Shame, though." Only now did I realise why she had been distant with me. "And look, sorry about this morning. I should have rung, to tell you." They both looked surprised.

"She'd offered me a lift in," I explained to John. "Problem is I don't have a mobile."

"I know," said John, laughing.

"Oh," said Joanne. "Right."

But it was too late. I felt sorry for myself and angry with myself. We were halfway through the week and I knew how it would all work out. I had not been not as open as I could have been about my willingness to carpe diem with other delegates, and there was only one solitary night left after this. Then it would be over, and I would be left with the bitter taste of untasted fruits in my mouth on the lonely train home.

CHAPTER 6

The next day there was a bomb scare, so we went to the races. Mr Campbell had been discussing the evolution of Critical Path Analysis theory, and Joanne was sitting the other side of Warren, so when the alarm went off I felt like cheering.

"Don't know why they're bothering," Andrew Punchley explained to Warren from Belfast, as we traipsed out to the Assembly Point. "It's all over now, you know. Cease-fire."

I mentioned the races as a rebellious joke, but the idea quickly picked up momentum. First Punchley, John and Bernard. And then Warren, and even Terry. After a short, agonising hesitation Joanne agreed too.

Not Helen though. She smiled and shook her head sadly. Probably afraid of a drain on the joint bank account as her bone-headed husband headed for well-deserved bankruptcy.

There was just time to make the first race, and I manoeuvred a place in the back of Terry's car next to Joanne. With barely a glance over our shoulders we headed for the gates. Terry swung the car left, accelerated hard away and we were free.

The sun was warm through the car windows and it shone on the first signs of Spring. We tore through villages with corner shops, sub-post offices, nice old pubs and medieval churches. The houses were large and solid with neat gardens, and second cars in the drive. Warren passed round some Opal Fruits and I offered Joanne the strawberry one.

"So, the age of chivalry is not dead. Thank you, sir." Our hands brushed together as she took it and popped it in her mouth. I tried not to stare.

"This is great, isn't it?" said Warren.

It was. We laughed, gay and carefree. Joanne had a bottle of fizzy water, and I didn't wipe the top after she handed it to me. She was a girl but she was good fun all the same. I was ever so glad I was here – not with Bernard and Andrew in the boring car. Even Terry had cheered up.

We sang 'Summer Holiday' and 'School's Out' and laughed ever so much. Terry parked the motor car in a muddy field, and we rushed over to the turnstiles with ten minutes to spare before the first race. I knew more about betting than the others and I tried to explain my favourite - a Heinz.

"A Heinz?"

"Yes. Six horses - fifty-seven bets. Like Heinz varieties? Fifty-seven varieties. On the tin." Blank expressions. I felt a little sympathy for Mr Campbell.

"Six races is fifty seven bets, because you have fifteen doubles, twenty trebles, fifteen four-folds. . . " I tailed off and decided to explain a Placepot instead.

"If your horse finishes first, second or third in each race you get a share of the pot."

"But the same horses aren't running in each race."

This took a while as well, but I didn't mind, especially when the horse I would have backed in the first race came nowhere.

"Cheapest way to gamble," I explained to Joanne. "Pick a horse, don't back it and celebrate when it doesn't win."

She was happy as well because her Placepot horse came second, and we slipped away from the others to the bar. We sat together by the window looking out across the course, swigging cans of lager and chewing on surprisingly pleasant sandwiches.

"Do you go to the races much?" she asked. "You seem to know a lot about it, with your Heinzes and your Placepots."

"Not that much. Too expensive."

"This is my first time."

"What do you think?"

"It certainly beats Project Management."

"By more than a short head." We smiled.

We were picking our horses for the next - a four runner Novice Hurdle over two miles – when Warren and Terry tracked us down.

"I fancy that Belpton Boy," said Warren, "It's the

favourite," he explained. This was on the strength of a third in a nothing race at Plumpton.

"I like Sunset Mirage," said Joanne.

I settled for Mowthorpe, the outsider, leaving Terry with Caesar's Pet. Joanne and I left them to keep the table while we strode out through the bookies in the pale sunlight.

"Yours is eight to one over there," she said. "Six to one everywhere else."

"You learn fast."

"Yes," she said, "I do."

We watched the race together. It was clear from the off that Sunset Mirage was out to make it a true test of stamina, and as they passed the judge with a circuit to go, Caesar's Pet was already under pressure and getting tailed off. Going into the back straight the other two were reeling in Sunset Mirage. He already looked done for toe when he made a total Horlicks of second last and his jockey pulled him up, leaving Belpton Boy and Mowthorpe going to the last together, both handy enough if good enough.

"Do you know much of the jargon?" said Joanne.

"Not really. God, did you see how Belpton Boy pecked on landing there?"

I yelled hopefully as Belpton Boy's jockey wobbled and Mowthorpe pulled away, but the bastard clung on and then started closing the gap again.

"Oh, for Christ's sake," I muttered. Mowthorpe began to toil and the nearer he got to the finishing line, the smaller his lead became. It was like some excruciating mathematical puzzle, as his lead went from five lengths to three lengths, then two, then one, and then, as Belpton Boy's nose was level with the his rump, they rushed by and past the finishing post. Mowthorpe first.

"Enjoy that did you?" asked Joanne.

"Yes. Never worried."

"I had that in my Placepot thingy," she said.

That was nice as well. I was forty pounds up. I could bet ten pounds in each of the last four races, lose them all and still come out even. I grinned at Joanne. This was great. Then the others appeared. All of them.

"Sorry. Got a bit lost," explained Andrew.

No need to apologise, we haven't missed you.

We all went down to the paddock to see the horses for the next. In the middle, the connections had already started gathering. There was a fine display of hats, tweed, and small-checked heavy cotton shirts with woollen ties. These, I explained, were the owners. I also explained that as this was a small country jumps track on a Thursday afternoon, and the next race a nine-runner selling hurdle, we were unlikely to see any sheikhs or members of the Royal Family.

New money was represented by a couple of prosperous looking suburban families who were trying to avoid a bunch of drunks in their thirties. None looked blue-blooded, and if they had ancestors who had fought the French alongside brave Harry, it would have been on a ferry going to a UEFA Cup match.

Some of the onlookers commented on how beautiful the horses were and how gracefully they moved. Others concentrated on trying to see which had not been gelded, and which were defecating. There was some concern about the earnings of the stable lads and lasses, but true harmony was only achieved when the jockeys began to mount.

"God, they are small aren't they?"

"Yes. Specially compared with the horses."

"Must be very strong to control them. Powerful."

"Horsepower."

"Not allowed to bet are they - jockeys? Trainers are though, and they must know as much."

"Is that Lester Piggott over there?"

Warren was responsible for the last of these comments. I hadn't the time to list everything that was wrong with it, and I tried to edge as far away from him as possible without actually leaving the racecourse. Unfortunately this took me away from Joanne, but she had been swamped by the others now, so I went off on my own to look at the first prices being chalked up.

Venture Capitalist was seven to four. It wasn't an attractive price, nor short enough to convince me that there was confidence in it, so I had a fiver on an outsider owned by one of the prosperous-looking suburban families. It came nowhere, but so did Venture Capitalist, so I still counted the race a success on the strength of the money I had saved.

I had ten pounds on Louise's Lolly in the next, figuring I had to get something from that relationship. It was one of half a dozen horses in with a chance as they came into view.

"Come on, Louise." I shouted, "Lazy mare."

I heard a woman laugh and realised Joanne had appeared next to me. I grinned back.

“You’re on Louise’s Lolly?”

“Yes.”

My horse was one of three who cleared the second last together. And then a thing of great beauty happened. A close exciting finish at the end of a testing race, the essence of the sport, with horses and riders flying together across the turf in desperate competition, was replaced by a foregone conclusion.

As the commentator put it, in his plummy English, "Louise's Lolly is now pulling away from two tired horses coming up to the last. She's over, and the others have nothing left to offer."

And they didn't, bless 'em. Louise's Lolly strolled up to the post on her own, handing me fifty pounds plus my stake money as she did so.

“How did you pick that one?”

“Long story. An ex, actually."

"Louise or Lolly?"

"It was Louise. Very 'was'.” I felt sophisticated all of a sudden.

"Tell me more - hold on, what number was it?" We checked the racecard. "Right. Thought so - I had it in that Placepot thing you insisted we all put on."

"Have all yours been placed?" They had. “That's great. Just two more to go."

“What are you on in the next?” she asked me. I went for it.

“Dennis the Duck, for sentimental reasons. You?"

"The same, of course.” That was nice. “First thing I chose."

I put twenty pounds each way on Dennis the Duck at sixteen to one. It was a beautiful, dappled horse with a dignified stride. Gerard Manley Hopkins would have had a few quid on it if he had been there. The favourite was called Atkins Loft Insulation, which would have been less likely to get his money.

We went back down to watch the race together. The sun was still shining, and I was on my third can and still winning.

"Lovely this, isn't it? The time between races always drags on TV."

"Spend a lot of time watching racing on TV, do you?"

"Whey aye, pet. Unless there's a decent leek show on, or I have to take one of my whippets down the vet."

We were right by the rails and Joanne smiled with pleasure as all eighteen horses galloped past, tightly grouped; then we stared after their shining rears racing away from us.

They had the best part of a circuit still to run, and Dennis the Duck had taken the lead by a couple of lengths. They went out of sight behind the trees.

"Too early, too early," I muttered, "Jockey's an idiot."

Emerging from the trees, Dennis the Duck's lead had stretched to six or seven lengths. Perhaps the jockey knew what he was doing

But as they entered the back straight, my earlier fears were confirmed. Dennis the Duck began to tire, his lead melted away, and he was swallowed up by the chasing pack.

"Told you he was an idiot," I said. "The Duck's exhausted."

Meanwhile the plummy commentary continued from on high.

"Atkins Loft Insulation has it from Delilah's Friend, Jutting and Dennis the Duck. These four are now pulling clear of the remainder, who are headed by All At Sea."

"Anyway," said Joanne, "Who is - sorry was - Louise?"

"Lovely name isn't it – Atkins Loft Insulation?"

Atkins Loft Insulation quickened again after the

second last, pulling five or six lengths clear of Delilah's Friend and Dennis the Duck, who were alongside each other, well ahead of the rest. The race was over and done with. There was no catching the leader, but as long as Dennis the Duck kept plugging away for a place, I would be happy - and well up on the day.

Then, completely unexpectedly, Atkins Loft Insulation made a complete mess of the final fence. Perhaps too full of running, he took off early, hit the top and landed flat-footed and winded. The other two jockeys saw their chance and urged their horses over the final flight and past him. Then the clown riding Dennis the Duck pushed too hard, so the horse veered sharply across the course and almost into the rails, allowing Delilah' Friend to get ahead. I was still cursing when he straightened up and, using the rails as a guide, accelerated towards the line, closing the gap on the leader.

"Come on, come on, come on, come on - no," I said as they passed the line together.

"I think he got there," said Joanne.

"No. Another hundred yards and he would have."

"I thought he did," she said. I shook my head. I knew how Fate worked, and I had sound superstitious reasons for being pessimistic.

"It'll be a photo."

It was. I was going to hug her if I won. Another reason to be disappointed when my bad luck was confirmed.

The announcement did not take long.

"... The result. First number seven Dennis the Duck..."

"Yes," I roared and hugged her. Should I kiss her? "Genius jockey," I said instead, "Always thought that." She smiled after I let go, and watched me do a little dance. "Sorry - got carried away."

"Don't be. How much have you won?"

"Three hundred and twenty - plus either eighty or sixty-four. Three hundred and eighty or so." Plus my stake back.

She looked pleased for me. The day was shaping up perfectly, unless I messed it up. On my way to the bookie, I began to worry that I had been a bit heavy-handed with the hug. There must be pleasanter things than being squeezed by an over-friendly, slightly intoxicated male, flushed with greed and vague lecherous intention.

The bookie read out my number to the man with the money bag, as he tore my ticket in half.

"Four hundred and twenty four pounds." He counted out the fifties, twenties, tens and coins, put them in my hand, and then took them out again.

I heard the end of the announcement, "... called for a steward's enquiry."

"Don't worry we'll not forget you," the bookie assured me as he handed back half of the ticket.

"Would you believe it? I was actually touching the

money."

Joanne was laughing, so I tried to make the best of it. "Steward's enquiry - story of my life. Can just see it. Day of Judgement. St Peter gives me the nod by a short head and I'm halfway through the Pearly Gates when he calls me back because there's been an objection."

"It's just money," said Joanne, teasing me.

"And your Placepot?" I reminded her - although I'd forgotten it myself until now.

"Oh God, yes. Outrageous this Stewards' Enquiry, isn't it? Disgusting. Tell me, how much will I win?"

"Dunno. Depends on how many favourites have been in the frame really. Could be quite a lot if your horse gets placed in the last."

"Yes? Take them to the European Court." We passed Punchley on our way back to the Grandstand.

"How are you doing?" he asked.

"Not bad - if this stands after the Stewards'. You?"

"I should have stayed on the Project Management course"

"As bad as that?" I asked him happily. Joanne interrupted.

"Did you hear that? Result stands."

“You sure?”

“Yes. Shall we get your money?"

“If he's still there.”

And he was, the lovely man, silhouetted against the

beautiful late afternoon sky above a throng of lively humanity bound by a common love of things equine. He nodded acknowledgement and handed over the money.

"Can I keep it this time?" I quipped.

"Well - we'd like it back on the next race - if you don't mind." It was humanity at its warmest and its finest.

"What have you got in the last for your Placepot?"

"You're My Flame," said Joanne.

"Right." I quickly consulted my Racing Post to cover my embarrassment. "Second favourite - eight horses - you should have a good chance."

"What are you backing, anyway?"

"I quite like the look of You're My Flame, actually," I said, meeting embarrassment head-on, "But I don't want to jinx it for you - and it's not much of a price."

"Very considerate."

I finally put a hundred on Dream On at Six to One. This was more than I had ever bet before, and it wasn't even a horse I really fancied, but winning had changed my sense of proportion. And although we talked a lot about her Placepot, I gradually became convinced about the claims of Dream On. Perhaps I could pick them after all. And though her winning the Placepot might increase the chances of us ending up in bed together, taking seven hundred pounds from a bookie would be pure pleasure as well - and uncomplicated.

There was another thing. Every now and then I felt

unsure about whether or not I was really attracted to her. From certain angles, there was something I didn't quite like about her face. A little too sensible, something priggish about her mouth. But I had experienced this before, and I had learnt to ignore it. Love has a nasty habit of reappearing overnight.

"Hey, what's the matter? You look miles away."

"Sorry, deep in thought."

"Really? I'm impressed."

"It happens."

"They're off. That's what you say, isn't it?"

Dream On fell at the fourth fence, but I was still £400 up, and it was something of a relief to have my feet reminded how the ground felt. Another horse fell with it, but not one wearing the red and gold of You're My Flame.

"Well that's down to six," I said encouragingly.

"I just hope it gets around; some of those fences look very high to me," she said, as they headed out into the country. "It's awful when you can't see them, as well."

As they reappeared, Fate Fantastique was ten lengths ahead; You're My Flame was leading the chasing group of three, but tiring.

"I hope I haven't jinxed your horse by saying I wasn't going to jinx it," I said.

Joanne was holding the rails and staring intently down the track.

"I need to be in the first three?"

"I think so," I replied, agonisingly uncertain.

"Come on, come on, come on," Joanne muttered as they came up to us. You're My Flame was holding on to third place, a neck ahead of Zoot Suit; and it seemed to be staying at a neck, and then perhaps a little more, and still holding, and then the jockeys' hands fell as they reached the line; still third. Joanne flung her arms around me and gave me a big kiss on the cheek. I analysed its significance. Friendly? Flirtatious? Both? Or the obvious - she was happy because her horse had come in. I only hoped I was right about them paying third place.

"There's nothing like winning, is there?"

"It's something I could get used to."

"How much?"

"Have to wait, I'm afraid. Tote has to calculate it. So it might not be as much as all that," I said like a true friend, prepared to warn her selflessly of bad news.

"If we go over by the Tote it'll come up on the screen when it's calculated." I was actually more anxious than her by this point. The third horse did count in an eight horse race. It must do. Mustn't it?

"Sorry about yours in that one," she said generously. "And thank you. I've really enjoyed this. And I wouldn't have known about this Placepot bet thing if you hadn't shown me. Is that how much I've won?" She pointed to the screen.

No, she didn't understand. That was just the Tote returns on the last race, but luckily, before I said so, I saw the Placepot payout alongside.

"Yes, you're right. One hundred and sixty-four pounds and twenty-five pence."

She grinned at me with pure, unfeigned delight. "Good this, isn't it?"

“Nothing like it. Well not much.”

At this point I need to add a note of caution. You very rarely win. Usually you lose. Even more rarely does it happen that two people together both win, let alone experience a run of good luck like ours that day. Given that the bookies have to make a living, pay staff and cover expenses, it is inevitable that they will only infrequently hand you more money than they take from you. Most millionaires don't gamble. Gambling can seriously damage your wealth.

But this time it hadn't. Look, Ma, top of the world. And then the others appeared again.

“Let's go and help these two spend their winnings.” Laughter. Not from me. This could be tricky. I should have prepared an escape route rather than just forget about them in the hope they'd go away or die or something

"I'd love to" said John, “But I need to get away. I've got to go to Slough. The wife's cousin," he added glumly. That was rid of one of the bastards.

"Ah. Shame, mate," I said. And then we had some more luck. The queues heading for the exit slowed down, then stopped moving entirely. After a few minutes, policemen appeared, ushering us out in various directions. As we allowed ourselves to get separated from Andrew and Bernard, the last thing we heard was that they were heading for The Bluebell.

I knew where it was and how to avoid it. It was all in our hands now. Then I heard myself asking Joanne if she wanted to go to The Bluebell. She was as surprised as I was.

"I'm not sure I fancy a whole night with that crowd," she said. Thank God one of us had sense.

"Me neither."

"So why suggest it?"

It was a good question. To give her a chance to escape? To play it cool? Or just to screw things up, because things were normally screwed up and that was what I felt comfortable with. I'm not sure how Lothario operated, but I'm pretty sure it wasn't like this. Concentrate, Tony.

We went into the first pub we passed, to give the others the time to get well away.

"What I'd really like to do," I said, "Is go for a victory meal, celebrate our success. The two of us."

It sounded spontaneous. Not knowing how twisted I was, she probably thought it was.

"Great. Any idea where?"

"Don't mind. Something nearby," and ending in bed.

"Italian? Chinese?"

"There's a place called The Jade Garden. Looked nice. We passed it on the way here."

Joanne interrupted me, pointing at the television in the corner. It was local news, with footage from the race meeting.

"It's Terry." The camera caught his face for a second as it panned across the crowd to the police.

"Hope teacher doesn't see this."

Someone, a bookmaker from what we could make out, had been attacked after the last race. Stabbed.

"Of course - all those police."

"It's like being an absent-minded driver. Have you ever been in an accident? No, but I've seen a lot happen around me."

"Are you saying nothing ever happens to you?" she said, putting her hand on my shoulder. "Poor you."

"So what about a Chinese banquet for two?"

In the restaurant we ordered a bottle of cheap champagne. She asked me when my birthday was.

"Thought so," she said. "Leos and banquets go together. How do you feel about it - being a Leo?"

"I'm proud of it - we are generous, warm-hearted, noble."

"Arrogant, vain, unspontaneous..."

"Oh so you believe in it, then?"

"I think there might be something in it. Like the way a Leo isn't interested enough in other people to ask them when they were born."

"I was just about to," I protested.

"No you weren't." She liked it when I was in the wrong. She kicked me gently under the table.

"Have we moved on to footsie?"

"What do you think?"

"I'm not an expert."

"I am. Represented my county at schoolgirl level. Do you not believe in anything like that, though?"

"Footsie?"

"You know what I mean. There's no need to pretend you're stupider than you actually are. Astrology, religion, spiritualism."

I hadn't got a Christian with me had I? Or some New-Age bollocks?

"I went to school with someone called Horace Copes."

"Now you're getting juvenile."

The tone of that irritated me. But it was the nearest we came to discord, and it didn't last long. She asked about Louise again. I told her an edited version, giving the impression I had outgrown her, rather than that I had been utterly besotted, and devastated when she dumped me. I moved on to the safer territory of lapsed Catholichood and family tragedy. I was concerned that she might think I was using it to make myself more interesting, but she didn't seem to, and as far as I could tell I was sincere.

"It would have been good to talk to them as an adult," I heard myself saying. "Understand them better. I was just a sulky twelve year old."

"I'm sure you weren't."

"I was."

"Or if you were, I'm sure they saw through it."

My love of Country music she found harder to understand, but she was prepared to let it go. Her liking for Billy Joel I pretended to let go in return.

We drunkenly stumbled into each other, and kissed outside the restaurant. I looked down into her face and we kissed again, with an embrace, slight sigh and then a light neck kiss. We smiled, asked each other how we were and then kissed again. Whether it was the rich food, the drink or the deteriorating conversation; or because it had now become a real possibility, I started to have my doubts about the idea of sleeping with her.

And when she said, "Shall we go for a drink somewhere then? Decide what to do," I realised she felt the same.

The magic had gone; just like that. I started to feel embarrassed. We both did. Instead of laughing she was now smiling politely. I decided to drink my way out of trouble.

Once we were in the pub she quickly became, or pretended to become, very drunk, and I just found her irritating. And I expect that was mutual as well. The uncertainty had gone. We would not be sleeping together after all, against all the odds given the way the day had gone. Sad in a way, but at least, with that decided, I could relax again.

CHAPTER 7

Next morning's standard checklist started and ended abruptly with:

Tony. Tony Palmer. In Joanne's Bed and Breakfast. In her bed.

This was confirmed by the fact that she was walking towards me in her underwear. She looked very attractive now. This could have been the usual aphrodisiac effect of my hangover. It could also have been because she had woken up first, showered, and was now standing over my weak, degraded self. This gave her the universally attractive qualities of self-sufficiency, and control. I loved the shape of her mouth.

"Are you OK?" she said, in a friendly half-whisper.

"Think so," I smiled.

Her smile back was just as lovely as everything else about her almost naked body. She moved closer. I thanked God for that. Hazy memories of the night before were nudging into my mind.

"You look great," I said, and she smiled. Was there pity in her smile? "Sorry I was so drunk last night." I just wanted to touch her and hoped I didn't sound too whining.

"It was fine."

Fine. Not the sort of notice Lothario would have got.

"Thanks."

"Hey, I had a great time, Tony," she said kindly. "And I was hardly sober either."

"Perhaps just too much good luck to last," I began, sadly, "Last day as well."

She looked sad as well, I thought.

"Want to sit down? Here?" I just wanted to get closer and closer to her body. I wanted to make things better - in every way.

She winced. "It's just... time," she said.

"Yes, suppose you're right."

I saw that she had seen me see her wince.

"Not that I wouldn't like to," she said, trying to cover it. I pretended it had worked.

"I'll even take my other sock off." I moved that foot under the quilt, pushing the sock off with the other as unobtrusively as possible. She sat down and we kissed and then rolled around a little on the bed - her one side of the quilt, me the other. "You going in today?" I asked.

"Better really," she said.

I checked the clock. Ten past eight. She saw me doing it.

"Just it would be good," I said, "To try to make up for last night."

"For who?"

"Obviously I was only thinking of you."

"Yeah, right." At least we were sparring again.

"I could stop over tonight, you know," I continued. "Not that I'm besotted with you or anything. I might just decide to live here." She laughed in a way that suggested she really would like to stop tonight.

"I would really like to," she said. "Only trouble is," gee whizz, I'm dreaming my life away, "I ought to go back home." She didn't say she was going to, though. That was promising.

"My partner's mother's coming for the weekend."

"Oh," I said. The word I believe is crestfallen. I also realised how little I knew about her home life.

"No," she said, quickly, "It's not an excuse or anything - far from it." There were some real highs and lows here, but I had no idea which way it would end. "Wish you'd had the wit to suggest something earlier in the week. Sorry - attempted joke. My fault as well anyway, I know."

I stroked her left collar bone to make her feel worse.

"When's she coming over?" I asked casually, putting the 'partner' on the back burner for the time being and concentrating on the bastard's mother.

"Tonight. Not till late though," she added, hesitantly.

"So..." I counted to five. No response. "Have you seen the Grand Hotel? Do you know what I'd love to do? Go there and spend some of the money we've won. Be a lovely way to finish the course, beautiful expensive hotel room; lots of time. I think we deserve it after the work we've put in this week."

She bit her lip.

"I'd li-," she broke off in a short exasperated sigh.

"Is she with you for the whole weekend?"

"His Mum?" The partner was a man then. "She's with us a week." A whole week? I had a chance.

"Could you not get delayed? Give a man and his mother some time together?" That didn't get a smile; so I tried to apply a little pressure. "If you've all week to make up for it." There was an implied 'we've just got tonight'.

"Hey," she warned me.

I raised my hands to show that the last thing I wanted to do was to put pressure on her.

"It's just it'd be something I'd really regret, not having that time with you."

"Oh, yeah," she said cynically, but believing me. And she was right to. "Tony, I'm not playing games when I say this. I'll see if I can do it. I'd like to. Really like to." That was good. "Anyway we can always phone each other later."

It took me a second to understand what she was talking about. The future. All of us back at home. That was no use to me. It was a long way off, and there would be plenty of time for minds to change and practicalities to get in the way. No use at all.

"It's just feels like it should be part of this week. Might be too late some other time - and I would like a proper night with you."

She smiled. We had a couple of very pleasant kisses after I had cleaned my teeth with her toothbrush.

"If I can't work something out for tonight, we could at least sneak out for an hour together at lunch?"

I pretended this would be better than nothing, while making clear that it wasn't what I really wanted.

"I do think these courses should be longer, don't you?" I said as we started dressing. "I mean, you barely scratch the surface of Project Management in a week."

"I know. Such a rich and enthralling subject."

"And the people you meet. Now I suppose I'd better pull my trousers on over my black and white spotted baggy underpants and shin down a drainpipe in front of the vicar."

"No, you're OK. I'll come down with you."

"Will we not be seen?"

"If we are - and if we're asked, I'll tell them you've just called around to..."

"Help with your bags?"

"The age of chivalry not being dead..."

"Actually I reckon it's just the sort of thing the age of chivalry was actually all about, really - illicit romantic encounters and... stuff."

We finished dressing and kissed like a happy couple before boldly walking downstairs together. I smiled at the woman in Reception, who smiled back approvingly at my bag-carrying behaviour. I knew without asking that we were keeping this secret, so I declined her offer of a lift.

"John'll be expecting me to come in with him."

"What are you going to say to him?"

"I've been giving that some thought, you'll be surprised to hear. And I've decided that I've just been for another one of my early morning walks."

"In last night's clothes?"

"Why not? It's not as if I'm going to meet anyone interesting out at that time in the morning is it?" She glowered at me playfully, which was nice. I passed her bag back and we clasped hands tightly, like a slightly edgy happy couple.

“Thanks, Tony, see you in a bit,” she said, and smiled.

Then she turned away to go and pay her bill, and I headed back to my hotel as fast as I could manage. My limp had gone completely now. Once in, I sneaked up the stairs. Over the banister I could see the back of John's head, chewing his breakfast. I washed and changed quickly, and then threw my clothes into my bag. I was downstairs again within five minutes.

"I gave you a knock," said John in a half-reproachful, half-defensive tone."

"Oh, I went out early again."

"Andrew's having a shower." I remembered Joanne had had one of them this morning. I'd missed it, unfortunately.

"I just want bacon, tomato and toast, please," I told

Mrs Mullen, without thinking. She nodded and even gave a hint of a smile. It was easy as that. Just don't cringe.

"Good time, yesterday?" John asked

"Yes. Fine. All got separated on the way out."

"I heard. Sure Andrew would have liked to help you spend you winnings. Said he tried to wake you when he got back, but he was too scared of the landlady to knock really hard.

“Looking forward to getting home,” he continued. “A week here's about as much as I can manage,” and then he went back to his breakfast and Breakfast TV.

I felt very differently.

CHAPTER 8

Only slightly late, I dumped my bag in the corner of A4 with the rest. I passed Joanne on my way to my seat.

"Good morning," I said casually.

"Good morning to you too, sir. Did you sleep well?" Then she added, considerately, "How's the head?"

"It's still on my shoulders. Yours?"

"Been better - but OK."

The class began with what was as close to a telling-off as Campbell was able to give us, directed at those "who had not felt the need yesterday to come back for the rest of the day."

I exchanged glances with a few of my fellow conspirators, and received an indulgent smile from someone called Helen in the row in front. She was attractive in a text-book kind of way, but not really my type. I smiled back; she was a useful decoy.

"And it was," said Mr Campbell, "A false alarm, as the more observant among you will have worked out for yourselves." There was some light laughter, which cheered him up.

I needed to know what Joanne was doing, even though I knew that she wouldn't know herself until she had phoned home. The uncertainty left me in a such a state that the whole of the first session's thirty-seven loaves worth of day-trips to Scarborough or whatever, washed over me without anything permeating. It had nearly finished when there was a knock on the door. Reception, again. This time Miss Glade. That first morning when I had lusted after her so childishly seemed a long time away.

I realised she was saying that it was me again that they wanted. I was less worried this time. If it was work, I was ready to fight. I had something to fight for and there was no way I would come home early now.

“Your hotel doesn’t have your mobile number," explained Miss Glade leading me to Reception. Apparently you've left some clothes behind in your wardrobe."

I could have kissed her. I went into a brief 'Silly Old Me' routine, which I stayed with on the telephone. It seemed to irritate Mrs Mullen, so I persisted with it while I arranged to pick my clothes up at the end of the day. I wanted lunchtime free, in case I was getting the consolation prize.

I was telling my not very interesting story to John when Joanne passed.

"Just going to make that phone call," she said. I was shot through with nervousness. Then I realised John was talking to me.

"So you see I was hoping to get away early today," he finished, apologetically. I stared at him neither understanding nor caring. All that mattered was the conversation Joanne was having on her mobile a few yards away. "So if you could get them earlier." He seemed to be pleading now.

"Oh," I realised, "You mean my clothes?" You're afraid I'll delay you getting back to your poxy family by making you take me back to the B&B. "No bother. I can always get the train back," I said helpfully. "Might stay on a bit, anyway." He looked bewildered. "It's nice here."

I said this against my better judgement. In my experience there is a law of Fate, which states that if there are two possible outcomes - one good (finally managing to have successful sex with Joanne), and one bad (not) - then preparing for the good increases the probability of the bad occurring and vice versa. Presumably the Fates don't like being taken for granted.

So I added, "Although I'm not sure yet." This was a very slight concession, and unlikely to appease the Fates.

Being released from his lift-giving obligations cheered John up, and as it was what he wanted to hear, he didn't ask any more questions, but went off to ring his lucky wife.

I waited around with the few stragglers who had managed to restrain themselves from telephoning spouses, hoping to get a chance to interrogate Joanne. I couldn't help worry that she had no intention of staying, and was trying to spare my feelings while extricating herself from a drunken mess. The Mother in Law probably didn't exist and she had planned a weekend of conjugal sexual athletics with her partner. When she reappeared, she was deep in conversation with married Ian and married Helen, which I was afraid was the wrong kind of company. She smiled, a little too kindly for my liking, as they went past.

I caught up with them just outside the class, and I told them the tale of my wardrobe and my missing clothes.

“I could take you if you like," said Joanne. "I've not got to get back urgently tonight or anything."

"You don't?"

"No."

“Great,” I said, choking with gratitude. Ian and Helen looked surprised. “John’ll be pleased," I explained as John joined us. "Won't you, John? Isn't it great? I don't need a lift to get my stuff so you can get away without having to wait for me. Thanks, Joanne."

"No problem. I’m having lunch in town with Rachel today."

"Lunch?" Who cares? As long as you don’t screw anybody during it.

"At lunchtime. We’ll grab a sandwich somewhere."

"Of course. Yes. Great. Enjoy it."

That was our last exchange until the evening, apart from my attempts to indicate, through a code known only to myself, that I had booked the Grand Hotel for the night. I stopped in case it gave her second thoughts about staying with me.

Despite his comments about the day we had missed, Campbell still managed to finish early on the Friday. He didn't even ask for our Feedback and Reflections Forms.

"Told you," I said cheerfully to Ian, "Never been on a course that hasn't finished early."

"Still hit the traffic, though."

"Missing you already."

We gathered up all the course materials, exchanged contact details and said our farewells. Joanne and Rachel were having a last conversation so I waited in the corridor, taking the opportunity to bin course materials and contact details.

****

When we turned into the pretentious sweep of the Grand Hotel's driveway, I started to doubt my extravagance – even at the weekend saver rate - but my doubts faded as we booked in at the elegant reception area; and by the time we were in the room itself, with the bed, bathroom and the view from the window, I felt fully justified.

"Love hotels," I whispered as she looked out of the window, and I dared to give her a first hug from behind. She turned her head back and gave a hiccoughy, contented kind of laugh. We were getting on fine, I thought.

I will not bore you with the details of our night together. I will spare you tedious accounts of how we undressed each other, and the sheer carnal pleasure we experienced between those crisp white sheets. And how often.

We laughed as well, but not too much; and as the moon slipped across a deep blue sky, we lay against each another, saying how glad we were that we had stayed.

"I'm glad we stayed."

"Me too."

"Very glad."

"Good."

"Is it going to be difficult for you?" I asked.

"Mm?"

"At home."

"You're very considerate all of a sudden aren't you?" I responded by registering deep hurt at her cynicism. It seemed amusing at the time.

"I'll sort it out later," she said. "I don't like lying to him particularly, but there wasn't a lot of point in trying to explain the full truth over the phone."

"Is it," I was going to say 'an open relationship' but that sounded too outmoded and trite, like something from a 1970's documentary on 'The Permissive Society' and I knew she would laugh at me. "I mean is it... Is it

OK... Understood between you - doing this?"

"Do you mean is it an open relationship?"

"Yes, that's it. If you don't mind me asking." We were lying naked, high up in the bed, our shoulders on the pillows and my arm around her in manly fashion.

"Yes it is. Well, more or less. I said that's what I wanted, more or less, when we started - or not long after - and he didn't say no - in so many words. It's amazing how you can manage not to have the most basic conversations with someone you spend so much time with." She was talking sense.

"It doesn't happen much - but it's good because I know I'm not doing it to prove a point or anything."

This was a bit too much sense for my liking.

"I'm here with you because I want to be." That was more like it. She had a startling way of switching her tone, which I liked, "Really want to be," she said, and lightly rubbed the side of her left leg over my right. I liked that as well.

She woke up at 7:36, spent fifty-six more minutes in bed, then she got up because she really had to be back by midday. She spent twenty-two minutes in the shower (the first nine by herself, the rest accompanied by me). Then we dressed, with a not entirely linear progression, in a little under forty minutes. We were down for breakfast just after 9:30.

We passed Helen and "Oh hello, this is my husband

Carl. Carl, this is Tony and Joanne from the course," coming out of the dining room.

"Hi. This beats the conference centre, doesn't it?" I said, boldly.

"Yes. Surprise, though, seeing you both here."

"Lovely rooms aren't they?"

"Oh yes - yours is too?"

"And the food?"

"They do a really good breakfast."

"Good. Ha, ha."

“The expression on Helen's face,” said Joanne, as she sat down, laughing and shaking her head, "First time I've seen any sign of life there."

"Not much going on between the ears is there not?"

"Not a lot, no."

"Never really talked to her."

"Her Carl was right about the breakfast, though, I'll give him that.” Joanne was still smiling as she finished her scrambled eggs and toast.

"Shame you can't stay longer," I said. She nodded. "Would you want my number?" I asked. “It’s my landline, but I might get a mobile.” In case you call and I miss it.

“You – a mobile? I’ve heard it all now,” She said writing her own on the back of the breakfast menu. “Menu should help you remember who I am.”

"I’ll remember. Is it OK to ring you sometime?"

"Yes - that's why I'm giving you my numbers."

"Is any time particularly good or bad?"

"No. But give me some time first, though, in case... What about you?"

"Any time. Sounds like it might be easier for you to ring me."

"Yes, perhaps."

"Have you got kids?" I asked, trying to get a clearer picture of what would be at the other end of the phone.

"No. You?"

"Eh?" What an unnecessary question that seemed. "No." It brought home how little we really knew each other. I took another mouthful of almost black tea. Lukewarm. A wave of sadness swept over me. I was about to be left alone, and I had felt so strong and happy and loved only minutes ago.

"You OK?"

"Just feeling a bit... Do you ever get it - you know like when you fall asleep on a train and wake up not knowing where you are? Disorientated. Panic." She nodded to show that she thought she did. "Suppose I'm just sorry you're going."

She reached for my hand under the table and squeezed it. "Do you want a lift anywhere?"

"No, you're OK. Thanks. 'S been great - really enjoyed last night and," trying to lighten the maudlin tone, "Most of the night before," realising that, being a

Software Engineer and not a puppy dog I was not going to be cute for long.

"And the day as well. I think we could be lucky for each other." I smiled back at that. "Not that you believe in that kind of thing of course." She released my hand. "If I said that bomb scare was me would you believe me?"

"What?" I tried to read her face. I liked that face a lot now. "No," I didn't know. "Well...possibly."

"OK then."

"Was it?"

"Might tell you next time. Give you an incentive."

"If I needed one." Sometimes people who appeared most sensible turned out to be the most dangerous. I wondered if I would ever be able to tell her the truth about my ankle. Best not try now, Tony.

"Sure you won't have a lift anywhere?" she asked, when she finished packing.

"Trying to feel a bit less guilty about leaving me here? Alone."

"Not really, no. Just thought you might like a lift."

"No, you're fine. Thanks." I didn't want to tell her that I had booked the Weekend Winter Saver Special for two. It had seemed a good idea at the time, perhaps it hadn't been. It might well have served to harden the Fates against letting her stay the full weekend. It also made things a lot more complicated when she asked how much her share of the bill was.

“It’s OK - I’ll get it.”

"No. You're not paying for me stopping here," she said.

"It's not that."

"Well what?" This was too complicated.

"Seventy quid?"

"If I'd known it was that much I'd have taken up your offer."

"I'm glad about that bomb scare," I said, as I walked with her to her car

“Me too. Lucky, wasn’t it?” she smiled.

"Just a shame we've had so little time. Be nice to. . ."

“Yes. Just give me a week or two, though."

Keep it light, Tony, keep it light.

She turned and unlocked the door, then we embraced and kissed. She picked her bag up, opened the door and put in on the passenger seat, then came back to me again. Then she got in, a little awkwardly, and wound down the window. I stuck my head in for another goodbye kiss. It seemed the thing to do.

"Best of luck on avoiding Helen and her Carl," she said, after she had turned on the ignition.

"Thanks very much pet." I handed her a Delegate Feedback and Reflections Sheet on which I had written nice things about her, and all my contact details.

That got a surprised and pleased laugh and a final half embrace and kiss through the window before she drove off with a wave and a beautiful smile.

I trudged back across the gravel of the car park, through the hotel foyer and back to my achingly empty room. I tucked the breakfast menu with her number on it into my Delegate's Reflections Folder. It was pointless to stay and pointless to go. I sat on the bed in silence. I had been abandoned and I felt sick.

I tried to develop a few viciously possessive fantasies about being her husband and waking up next to her each morning, but I couldn't hold them. I needed to get out of the room, into fresh air.

"Hi, again," said Helen on the stairs.

"Lo."

"Where's Joanne?"

"She's gone," I said in a fairly unfriendly way.

"Oh, we thought you must be taking up the Weekend Winter Special - really good value, isn't it, Carl?" He appeared behind her. "I hope you don't think I'm prying, but..."

"What?"

"It's just that I didn't realise you knew each other..."

"Oh no," I laughed condescendingly, "Known each other for years. We nearly got married actually, but we decided we'd be better apart. It's always great when we see each other - in every way - and without all the staleness and routine of marriage... Well, you'll know what I mean."

She looked angry, but she couldn't reply. Carl knew his role without instruction, and he was already preparing his manly shoulders for whatever was required.

"Well goodbye - so nice to see you again," I said and stalked past them.

"Goodbye," said Carl solidly.

I had never really lied before. It felt good. I carried on stalking, not looking back, leaving them to do whatever losers do. I took a door, any door, and hit the cold fresh air like a diver hitting the water.

It was time to change my life. I had potential and I should realise it instead of just thinking about it. You have to keep moving to stay alive, like a breathing shark. You have to be working towards something, selfishly and single-mindedly, if you wanted to be really loveable.

And I could do it. I was in my prime, reasonably healthy, reasonably attractive, reasonably well-off, employable, and insurable, with a pension on the go. And Joanne had liked me. I wasn't sure how much, but she was not someone who would do anything she didn't want to.

I passed a pub. I knew what would happen if I went for a drink, even one pint on my own, and I was tired of wasting time. I'm not sure if I'd read The Great Gatsby then, but I instinctively knew the procedure. Make a list of what you want from life, and how you can go about getting it. This was my only chance, I had to take it.

Unlike so many people, I was free. My crimes were minor and far enough away to escape punishment; at least until my turn came in the two-seater settee next to the big, bearded bloke in the white smock, settling down to watch 'Tony Palmer - The Video', with his hand on the remote and a strong smell of burning flesh downstairs.

I had to buy a pen and notepaper to write that list. It was as if I had been on a Project Management course and taken it to heart. I needed to find a newsagent. That was it exactly - goal and method in quick succession.

It was a bright clear Saturday morning and I felt bright and clear and part of it. Sloth was truly one of the Deadly Sins. And the Deadly Sins were the route to self-destruction, as they had always been, even in 1996, in our classless, quality of life, society-less society.

I saw a newsagent across the road, next to the park I had met Joanne that morning. I could sit in my warm coat and do my planning. Yes, I had finally grown up, there and then, wallop, on the way from the Grand Hotel to the newsagent.

****

I staggered out of a taxi seven hours later, blinking at what was left of the daylight and apologising to lampposts. It was Gary's fault.

I had walked into him as I came out of the

newsagent's; and he had recognised me as I began apologising.

"Tony." He seemed pleased to see me. When I realised who it was I felt very flattered and pleased he was pleased.

Gary had been the tallest in his class at the age of nine, and the course of his entire life afterwards had been shaped by that one dominant fact. He had won all his fights in the playground, including those against the boys who had been tallest in the class at the age of eight. He had stolen from shops at the head of a gang of pre-pubescents without serious mishap, moved into petty crime and random violence with the onset of his teenage years, and eventually been caught and punished. He had temporarily reformed then relapsed, after which he had become suddenly and mysteriously well-off and moved away from Newcastle when he was about twenty.

I had known him when we lived near each other as seven year olds, and on the strength of this sentimental attachment he always treated me with more respect than I deserved. He was an impressive, if sometimes socially inappropriate acquaintance. I wished that Joanne had been here with me in the newsagents so that she could be impressed, and at the same time I was relieved that she was not, in case she had not been. It would have been stressful.

I had bumped into Gary from time to time, usually in pubs, during adolescence, but we had not met since I had moved away. This seemed like a strange place for him to end up.

"I'd heard you'd moved down south," I said as we left the shop, "Didn't know it was here though."

"Surprised?"

"No."

"You are."

"OK, then. Yes."

"And you?"

"Oh, I was just down here on a course - AJA up the road - computers. Just stopped over a night at the end of it." I wanted to tell him why I had stopped over, but I felt shy. "You're living here permanently?"

"Yes."

"Are you doing anything at the minute? Fancy a drink?"

I wasn't sure that we'd have much to talk about, and I was afraid that it might become awkward, but I didn't want to seem unfriendly, and with Joanne gone, I felt like some company.

"I don't really drink now," he smiled, thinking of when he did. "Trying to stay fit. I've got a snooker club nearby we can go to if you like."

"Great."

"You're not a journalist now are you?" he said suddenly, looking at the notepad I had in my hand.

"No, no," I laughed. "Computers, like I said."

Most of the people scattered about the snooker hall had a vaguely criminal appearance. I hadn't realised that places like this existed in picturesque small towns. It was quiet, the only real noise coming from a dangerous-looking group of four near the corner. They included a blonde woman in jeans, white shoes and T-shirt and a broad, burly man in a tight fitting blue denim shirt and a number two crew-cut. I knew I shouldn't catch their eye but I couldn't help looking at them. Gary saw me and laughed.

"Yes. Schoolkids, eh? God knows where they get the money from. Still, less said about that the better," he grinned. "So you're in computers? Everywhere now, aren't they? Perhaps you could have a look at some of the stuff I've been offered."

I was afraid of getting involved with stolen goods, but I didn't know how to refuse.

"Not hardware," he said quickly, as if he had read my mind. "Software, you know, for helping run this place. I don't really understand it all myself, and I don't trust salesmen."

I had no idea how serious he was, but I knew there was little chance I could tell him anything useful.

"Aye, no problem," I said, "Cheers," and slid my pint towards his glass.

"Slimline tonic," he explained. "Not a lot of point in running and working out if I'm getting pilatic all the time as well." 'Pilatic' was nice. It was like being sixteen again.

"You seem to be doing well on it." I took a drink and looked around. It was a bit of a dump. "It's a nice place, this."

Gary seemed pleased and he led the way over to a table near the fire exit. A short, slim sallow man in a yellow v-neck jumper nodded through the cigarette smoke at us as we reached it.

"Tony, Scouse Johnny. Tony's an old friend from home - just bumped into him." Johnny said nothing, but nodded upwards to acknowledge receipt of the information.

"You like it here?" I asked Gary, a little awkwardly, and took a couple of self-conscious mouthfuls of beer.

"It's all right isn't it, Johnny?"

"Coppers are still bastards – like everywhere."

"Right."

"Fiona likes it here – the wife. Nice countryside close by," said Gary. "And we've got the eldest at a good Primary School."

"Are you off the drink completely then?"

"No, just cut back a bit. Well, a lot." It had been my intention to keep away from the subject of drink, as I anticipated confusion over whether or not I would pay for them at his club. Now I had accidentally drawn attention to the fact that my glass was nearly empty.

Luckily I still had a pocketful of cash. "I see you haven't - another pint?"

"It's OK - I'll get them."

"I'll get it - they're my profits." Please let me spend money. "You can get your own after that."

He didn't want me to feel uncomfortable. That was very considerate, but it meant that it would be impossible to leave, and I was not looking forward to making small talk with Scouse Johnny. Luckily we were soon joined by a more civilised man called Brendan, and then others came over when Gary came back. They were all friendly enough towards 'Gary's mate from Noo-Carstle', and they all seemed keen to buy me drinks. This was all very nice, but unwarranted kindness from sensitive and possibly violent strangers made me nervous.

"Are you doing anything this afternoon?" I said even though I had told myself not to say anything which might make it harder to leave.

"Some of the boys are off to the races," said Brendan, "You interested?"

I turned to Gary. My instinct was to let him speak for both of us, but as we were not in any conventional sense of the term, a couple, I had to answer for myself.

"Sounds good, aye. Went on Thursday actually. Did you hear about the stabbing?"

"Day off was it?"

"Sort of." They looked unconvinced. "There was a

bomb scare so we had time to kill." I felt good about mentioning bombs in such a matter of fact way. If the opportunity arose, I would mention the Basque bloke I knew at University, the bits of shrapnel possibly removed from my Grandad at Ypres, and that night drinking after hours off the Old Kent Road.

"Well, matey," said Gary, leaning back and putting the palms of his big hands solidly on his thighs, "I'm going to have to leave you in the company of these gentlemen for a while. Going to get my dinner - lunch as they call it here - and see my family. Never thought I'd be a new man, eh? Should be OK for the races though. When are you heading back to Newcastle?"

"I - no hurry."

"Right, should see you later then. Bye Brendan, Scouse."

And he was away again, to token 'Changed man since he got married' comments. Despite his new domesticity, Gary was still not the greatest conversationalist I had ever encountered, but the group (myself in particular) missed his presence.

There are occasions when embarrassment and a sense of not belonging can render you physically incapable of hearing properly. I say 'you', it certainly happens to me. The condition makes it impossible to get involved in a conversation. It's not that hearing itself is actually impaired. The words are still heard, but they seem disconnected from meaning and are gone before you can absorb them. It is like hearing a familiar foreign language that you aren't fluent in. The longer it goes on, the worse it gets, as you become more and more desperate to break into the conversation.

I was overcome with this aural dyslexia almost as soon as Gary left the table, and despite a couple of yesses and a trip to the bar to show I wasn't scrounging drinks, I soon faded into a fidgety silence. The rest of them weren't saying a lot either, but they belonged there. Their conversation seemed to consist mainly of rhetorical questions and curt exchanges, but it was no doubt full of relevant facts, and rich in bonding detail.

It got worse. They must be wondering why I had turned mute. Did they think I was trying to make a point? I became aware of the man on my left studying me. Someone said something about picking their children up from their ex-wife.

"Kids," I blurted out, with rather more scorn than I had intended.

"What?"

"Kids - take over your life. You got any?"

"Yes, two," he said. He must be wondering why I was so interested. There were no good reasons unless I had children too. "You?"

"No, not me." He didn't look as if I had won him over with this.

It might have been part of my creeping insanity in the situation, but I thought he looked familiar, although I had no idea how. Perhaps he had been on the news or a crime programme. I tried not to stare at him too closely. I had stumbled into the world of Vinnie and his convicts' wives and I didn't like it.

I was missing Joanne. I wished I was with her rather than sat here - an unknown outsider of dubious sexual proclivities in a crowd of violent homophobic strangers and nervous criminals, responding to their warmth and friendliness with sullen silence, and occasional prying personal questions.

When I did finally recognise him, it just created more indecision. Should I say I knew him or not? Would he think I was spying on him? Would he not want it known that he frequented the Eagle and Child? Or that he did business there out of a bin bag?

I wasn't sure about saying nothing either, and my indecision was making everything worse. I needed to do something. He was definitely looking at me strangely now. He wasn't big but he looked as if quite a lot was compacted into his short muscular body. I wished Gary would come back. My heart was pumping blood so fast it was almost hurting. My beer was going down alarmingly quickly. I regretted not smoking. I had nothing to pretend to be doing, nothing to look at, nothing to say and masturbation was out of the question.

"Do you get in The Eagle and Child much?" I finally managed.

A hundred cropped heads turned and looked at me.

"Sometimes, yes."

"Oh, I thought I'd seen you in there," I said eagerly, my voice sounding in my head like a Famous Five falsetto. He looked puzzled. He had thought Gary said I didn't live here. "I was in on Monday night - playing pool with some people from work. That course we were down for." He might think that having a job was weird, but at least I had explained myself.

"Oh right," he said and nodded. "One of the few decent boozers in town, that. Most of them are too stuck up or full of tourists."

"Aye," I agreed, fervently and Geordily. It was like learning to speak again. I was still clinging on to the conversation by my fingertips, though. Then Brendan spoke.

"Do you want a game?"

Of? They were all looking at me and waiting.

"Aye. No problem," I said, my mind racing though the possibilities from arm-wrestling upwards.

He picked up his cue. He meant snooker. Of course he did. It was a snooker hall. This was a relief but it had implications. I was going to have to play snooker in public with petty criminals. If anything would find me out, this would, but it was too late to back out.

He gestured for me to lead the way to the tables. I nodded back and tried to smile. My mind was choked with visions of ripping the baize and of huge bets - losing money I didn't have, or even worse, winning. I lurched forward, trying to guess which table he wanted me to go to.

Instinctively adopting a subordinate role, I went around the pockets, taking out the balls and rolling them down to him, making sure that they travelled far enough to be within his reach, while not so fast as to risk cracking his knuckles. No bets were mentioned, and at least I was away from Scouse Johnny and friends.

"Tony did you say the name was?" I nodded. He put out his hand and shook it without mishap. Things were going well. I wondered how I would spoil it.

I won the toss. I said a little prayer as I broke off. I hit the ball too hard, I thought, then too soft, but it reached the pack, three or four reds split fron the pack, and the cue ball came round the table to rest half a foot from the top cushion. Respectable. Never in my life had I been so pleased to be respectable. And it got better.

On my next visit, I clipped in a red close to a corner pocket, coming round the pack to leave me, much to my surprise with a simple straight blue into the middle pocket. I potted this, and by some miracle I was left with an easyish red into the other corner pocket. I managed to pot this as well, although an unfortunate kiss left me snookered for the black. He frowned sympathetically.

I was almost enjoying myself. After a near miss I tutted, hoping to give the impression that I might just be a useful little player on my day, although I was a bit rusty. I wasn't and there was nothing to rust. But soon, with Brendan's assistance, there were only five reds left on the table. I was going to lose, but I was acquitting myself without shame, which was an outcome for which I would have considered selling my soul earlier on.

Gary reappeared, smartly dressed.

"I hope you're not playing him for money," he said.

"Hey, he's not bad," said my friend Brendan, narrowly missing a red and leaving it so easy to pot that I was glad to have the chance. I was part of the gang, I could relax.

However, being part of the gang meant that I was off to the races again, and this time instead of sitting next to Joanne, I was sharing a back seat with Scouse Johnny and being driven by a man who had had as much to drink as I had. If we killed anyone I would be jointly responsible for accepting the lift. The good news was that there seemed no requirement to talk. I began to relax as we passed through the same villages I had gone through so happily with Joanne only two days earlier. She had gone back to her partner and I was getting on with my own life. I would have liked to see her cope with this as well as I was. They began talking as we crossed the same muddy car park.

"Do they know who carved that bookie up yet?"

"Think they got someone."

"Anyone you know?"

"Perhaps just some pissed up day-tripper." The other twisted his face in disagreement.

I decided to chip in.

"If everyone who lost at the races reacted like that, there'd be a shortage of bookies pretty soon."

Hoped for response: "Ha, ha, ha - and knives."

Actual response: silence.

There was a noisy crowd at the turnstiles, and I might have imagined it but I think the crowd opened a little to let us through. I was still sober enough to know that it would be a good idea to slip away from these people before I accidentally insulted someone, or became involved in some kind of criminal activity that I was spectacularly unsuited for.

It was not difficult. No-one paid any attention when I said I was going to the toilet, and when I emerged I went to the far end of the enclosure. The view wasn't good but I was unlikely to be disturbed. I put twenty pounds on the second favourite.

To reassure those of you bracing yourselves for another blow by blow account of another day at the races, this will not happen - for two reasons.

Firstly, this horse didn't win. It barely got a mention. And so it continued; and a horse race you don't win on is nothing more than a few animals running around, driven, sometimes cruelly, for the entertainment of the rich and the profit of large ethically unsound companies, and what could be less worthy of report than that?

Secondly, most of the afternoon is a blur. I remember losing narrowly on the next two races, and not even betting on the one after, which I sullenly watched from an awkward angle at the bottom of the grandstand.

I was feeling the cold, and just about to leave when I bumped into Gary again. He led me over to a small group which included a few women dressed in the approved ladies' race-going fashion. They had a table, and someone had produced champagne. I managed to manoeuvre myself into a position between the person currently being poured champagne, and the person on their left.

My plan worked. The champagne was ice cold, and it tasted sharp and clean after the beer. The ladies didn't say much. Their role seemed to be smiling and nodding while the suited men they were with talked. I tried one of them in conversation.

"Are you from round here?"

"Yes, nearby."

"How's your luck going?"

"I don't really gamble much. I leave that up to him," she said, indicating a hard-looking man in a suit.

I laughed.

“It's a good day out though, isn't it?” She said nothing.

Perhaps she was concerned that our intimacy was a little too much for all but the most liberal of observers. Perhaps she had a point because I was at that point imagining her naked, with her mouth slightly open, hair spread out on the pillow.

She asked Gary for a light. The man who was with her gave her a disapproving glare.

"He doesn't smoke now - hasn't for ages."

"Excuse me, but I think she is only asking him for a light to calm your ludicrous jealousy and show there's nothing between us, unfortunately."

Again, this was thought rather than said. Despite my growing confidence I still had some sense left.

This had brought her man and Gary into open conversation, and other people were suddenly interested. Despite standing so close they had not yet spoken.

"So, Gary, how's things?" It went quiet. There was tension. These two were big men in this world, even I could tell that.

"Just fine, enjoying it," he said and smiled. The interrupted conversations resumed, and people were laughing and talking again. I wondered if any on the women were currently unattached. It was what Vinny would have done.

This confidence was ridiculous. One respectable defeat at snooker, and an unbroken jaw after greeding a glass of champagne and saying hello to a friend of a friend from primary school was no solid foundation on which to take chances. I must be getting drunk. Be careful. Especially as I had started thinking of clever things to say. I ought to make my excuses and go, but it would be awkward, and besides I had a full glass of champagne again and it still tasted good.

By seven o'clock, I was staggering into the lamppost mentioned above after going back to my hotel to get the rest of my money and cards, on my way to meeting up with the rest of them again to go to a casino.

By ten, I was dancing confidently with a woman in a tight, dark blue dress. I had never met anyone who dressed as well before or looked as glamorous. Deep down, though, she was probably just as insecure as me. I complimented her on her earrings, and she laughed when I said how well they matched the carpet. She touched the top of my hand, and then covered her mouth hesitantly for a second. She was called Victoria, a name which had not done anything for me until that moment. Joanne was back enjoying domestic bliss with her 'partner', why shouldn't I enjoy a different kind of bliss with Victoria?

It transpired - I am not sure exactly when I became aware of it, or how (it was a gradual process like the childish understanding of sex or the onset of baldness), but there was a point at which I definitely did not know and a point at which I did know - that she would accompany me back to my hotel room and have sex with me for money.

After the dance, she had leant very close to me, and shown more interest in me than I could possibly have merited. It was hard to believe, but she was making it very clear that she, like the rather dowdy and homely Joanne Carr, wanted to sleep with me. The idea seemed a very good one. When the financial aspect dawned on me, I had tried to behave nonchalantly, although I was surprised. Then again, I liked Victoria a lot. It was her living; it was not necessarily a criticism of me. To use a helpful analogy - if you analyse systems for a living, there will be some systems that you enjoy analysing more than others, but you still expect to be paid for analysing them.

In the taxi back to the hotel, however, I began to panic. Suddenly we had nothing to say to each other, and there was only so much smiling I could manage. The only subjects I could think of were AIDS; hotel security staff; and the occurrence of robberies by prostitutes of their clients (often assisted by large and violent men), and the unsympathetic attitude towards their victims of the police, media, hospital staff - even friends, relations and work colleagues. I was also rather frightened of her. Two hundred and fifty pounds was a lot of money to pay for something I increasingly felt that I didn't want; but I had no idea of the etiquette of the situation.

Besides, I didn't like her so much now; she seemed rather mercenary and materialistic. How much would it cost to persuade her to go away? And how much to get her to go away without telling anyone? I had no idea how to raise the subject, and I didn't want to upset her. Could I just pretend to fall asleep and let her rob me peacefully? I was grinding my teeth while considering this. It was probably annoying her, so I stopped. I wondered if Joanne would have sympathised with me or just despised me. At least I would have had a chance of getting her to understand me. I loved her so much.

After an agonisingly long time we reached the hotel. I paid the taxi driver, who gave me a less than friendly look, despite a large tip. Then I tried to bundle Victoria into the hotel as quickly and unobtrusively as possible. She didn't like this. She was giving increasingly irritated responses to my muttered "It's just up here" and "Can you just em..." and "No need for a drink". It was becoming more and more difficult to imagine how I could make clear my intentions (if I knew what they were); nearly as difficult as imagining pushing my penis inside her body. I had had enough trouble with Joanne the first time, and she was nice.

We met Helen and Carl at the door. I was giving them plenty to talk about anyway. I wondered if Victoria looked to them like a prostitute. Probably less than I looked like a drunken lecher. I collected my key in the manner of an adolescent buying contraceptives while Victoria went up and down in the lift at my suggestion.

The relief, as I got the bedroom door closed behind me was colossal. When she came to the door a few seconds later, I was even able to speak clearly and coherently.

"Nice hotel this."

"Yes. I used to work here - as a waitress."

I have veils available, and I will exercise my right to pull one discreetly over what followed. After she left I consumed most of the contents of the minibar, but whether this was driven by guilt, triumph, relief or anything else I leave it to you, gentle reader, to surmise.

****

Next morning I rang for a newspaper. I hypocritically asked for an Independent or an Observer. I got the latter, featuring 'The Changing Relationship of the Sexes in Britain Today'. I made myself tea and then coffee and then sick.

I ate a large, tomato juice-included breakfast at about half-ten and paid for my Weekend Winter Saver Special. I had a quick drink in the pub by the station without meeting anyone I knew and then took my place in the corner of an almost empty carriage with my newspaper to hide behind. My train left on time and I was soon speeding through the outskirts of town and away. The countryside looked dignified but friendly, and the air fresh and clear. My fear and guilt and embarrassment were fading fast, now that I was heading away at seventy miles an hour, all expenses paid - or at least most of them.

PART TWO
PRIVATE ENTERPRISE

CHAPTER 9

Within a few weeks I was redundant, considering self-admission for alcoholism, and feeling lonely.

The redundancies were announced on April 1st. The date seemed appropriate with the Millennium bearing down, and organisations the world over desperate for computer staff, but it was not a joke. Accounts had discovered that their original blunder, which had paid for all those training courses, had not been a blunder at all. This meant that the underspend was now an overspend, and the department had to do some serious shedding of staff. This included me.

I was delighted. We were being paid a lump sum including four months' pay in lieu of notice (the last time I had managed to save any money was for Subutteo World Cup '82) and it was quite exciting to be escorted off the premises, black bin bag in hand, by Group 4 security.

The way I saw it, those remaining were the unlucky ones. They would have to work harder and longer hours until panic set in and management began to re-employ the staff it had made redundant as contractors on twice their previous salaries. Whatever happened, most of us were pretty employable. After all, we had received a good deal of training recently.

Not everyone was quite as sanguine, particularly the older and more settled. They went home while the rest of us went to the pub to celebrate the windfall and our new found freedom.

The pub, again, though. I had stayed there until midnight and then rung Joanne to tell her the news. Me and alcohol – so predictable – and now I was facing a miserable hungover Saturday afternoon trying to piece it together. I couldn't remember much, except that she kept saying she couldn't talk. It hadn't stopped me though. I also remembered that she kept calling me Mr Brown. This was presumably to throw any listeners off the scent. It had amused me a lot at the time. Less so now.

I shouldn't have rung her. Her only communication since the course had been a message to say she would be in touch again, which I suspected was designed to prevent me calling her. I had shown maturity and restraint by honouring that, and now I had messed up. I would end up like Terry, the lonely contractor. I had no sympathy for him, but I didn't envy him, and I didn't want to be someone people didn't envy.

Still, prosperous misery would be better than

miserable poverty, and activity would probably make me feel better. I could go contracting. There were thousands of companies paying handsomely for temporary staff to join in the battle against the Millennium Bug. If I had to, I would call it "Y2K". Perhaps I could buy a Cadillac and drive past Joanne's house smoking a fat cigar.

The first step was digging out my CV. If I wasn't going to get love letters, then job offers would have to do instead. It looked good, and it would be a shame to spoil it with a spell in a drying-out clinic. That was the self-admission for alcoholism sorted out. Apart from anything else, I was probably better off self-medicating from Threshers, than with whatever the authorities decided to pump into me instead.

Lonely, though. In an enterprising new world of families and individuals, the individuals, especially those without jobs, tend to be lonely. I wanted to speak to Joanne, but I didn't want to pester her again. I wished she would ring. Then she did.

"Look," I said, getting in there first, "I'm sorry about last night."

"Don't start again. You did enough apologising last night."

"Did I?"

"You can't remember?"

"Not really."

"So do I need to tell you I was calling you Mr Brown

because that's the name of the User Group Chairman."

"I know it was a stupid time to ring, and I'm sorry I was so..."

"Tony," she warned.

"Did you manage to explain it to your...?"

"Tom? I didn't really have to. He's pleased at any chance he can get to feel aggrieved at the minute. He just went into a bigger sulk than usual at being woken up and I left him to it." This was good news. Although I didn't like the idea of them sleeping together.

"Anyway," she continued, "Is it definitely true about your job going?"

"I managed to convey that much at least then. Yes."

"You should be OK for getting something else though, shouldn't you?"

"Would hope so. I was thinking about contracting. I'm mobile. No ties." Did that make me sound like a desperate and dangerous loner, rather than a young man with a cowboy soul?

"But you've got no definite plans?"

"No," I replied.

"I suppose you haven't really had time."

"And I was busy yesterday, as you know, getting pissed."

As the relief of being forgiven, or at least being told to stop apologising, wore off, I began to feel disappointed. This was not the highly romantic and erotically charged conversation which I would have liked.

"It's just I might have a proposition to make," she said. I resisted the temptation to make any of the crude and obvious comments bobbing around in my head, and made an interested noise instead.

"I'm not exactly certain of the details yet, and it's probably not, strictly speaking, legal - although I'm not sure." She paused. "Do you suppose they tap phones at random?"

"Hang on." I adopted an official-sounding voice. "Excuse me, but if you're listening in on this conversation could you make yourself known - clear your throat or something?" Silence. "No, we're OK - unless they're really cunning."

She laughed at that anyway. It was a nice laugh. Then I remembered that I was supposed to be preparing myself for this 'proposition'. I didn't like the hint of illegality much. I felt naughty enough with no job, no wife, no children, no religion, no parents, and no friends, without being led into crime by someone I had no reason to trust.

"I know I'm being vague," she admitted. I let that hang. "I'd really rather discuss it face to face, if that's possible."

"Yes. And I'd be good to see you again. Really good," I said unambiguously. The silence at the other end of the phone suggested that I had gone blundering in too far, so I tried to get back to business.

“I'm sure I'll be interested to see what you have to offer." Why did every comment have to be laced with red-nosed end of the pier, how's your father, tickle me coconuts with your turkey drumstick style double meanings? "But can I not have a clue now?"

"It's a bit tricky," she said, as if I was the one being unreasonable.

I continued trying to sound hard, self-reliant, and positive but matter of fact.

"I'd like to know more. And you can trust me not to talk about it, even if I say no. Is there a lot of money to be made out of it?"

"There could be, yes," she replied quickly, "Depends how far we take it."

"Good. What's happened here's made think. There's people terrified of losing their stupid jobs - and I mean stupid. I don't want to get like that. I want to get some control. Even if it means taking chances. Would this fit in with that?"

This was all untrue. Being asked to put my belongings in a bin-bag and leave the building with a fat redundancy cheque was about as near to the Wild Side as I was ever likely to get, but I wanted to hear what she had rung up about. And she must want to tell me, otherwise she wouldn't have started.

"It's a bit complicated to explain over the phone," she said.

If this was the game she wanted me to play then I would do it. Not a problem.

"I don't want to play games," she said.

"Me neither." And I added in my best dynamic manner, "So let's meet up then."

"Right. It's just, I don't know when. To be quite honest you've taken me aback a bit with your enthusiasm."

I was enthusiastic about seeing her, not about whatever stupid plan she had in mind.

"What about next week?"

"I can't," she said.

That wasn't good, but I had somehow got the upper hand. I was sounding uncharacteristically decisive and assertive. People liked that, so I continued with it.

"Why don't you put it in a letter? If you're worried about phone taps and emails being intercepted. Give you time to work out when we can meet as well."

"A letter? Don't know when I last wrote a letter."

"Just think of it as a fax you put in an envelope."

"I can trust you, can't I?"

"Yes. Your instincts haven't been wrong so far, have they? Send me a letter - I'd like that."

"You're dead set on this aren't you?"

"Mm."

"Bastard."

"Hey, that's no way to speak to a potential

accomplice."

"A letter eh?"

"You have got my address then?"

"Yes. You know I have. You put it on that Delegate Reflections Sheet – as you know."

"Lots of other things as well."

"Yes. I know."

"Have you still got it?"

"Yes."

"And I've still got the breakfast menu," I said, "In my course folder actually, for safe keeping." She said nothing in response, which I took to mean that she wanted me to change the subject. So I did. Nice guy. "And how are things with you? You lost your job as well?"

"No - worse luck. There's not a lot happened really since I saw you last. Work is dull. Personal life slowly deteriorating." Excellent. "I've seen quite a lot of Rachel - for reasons you'll understand later."

Less excellent. I felt sure Rachel disapproved of me. I wasn't sure why – perhaps she was just a good judge of character. This even took the sheen off the news about the deterioration of Joanne's private life.

"Did John ever say anything to you about her?" she asked suddenly.

"Who? Rachel?"

"He didn't, then."

"Are you saying something happened with them?"

“I’m not saying anything."

"He's not the type."

"How well do you know him?"

"Not very well - obviously. He's married."

"You're very right and proper all of a sudden." She had a point there. I said nothing. "Defending your friend."

She didn't have a point there. I had no wish to get into an argument defending someone I had no wish to defend.

"I keep telling you, he's not my friend. And I'm shocked, Ms Carr. I didn't realise things like that happened on Project Management courses. I hope you didn't become entangled physically with anyone?"

"Oh no - I was as celibate as yourself I'm sure." Then there was another lull.

"So - this letter," I said.

"Yes - OK. If not I'll give you a ring. Did you get that mobile?"

"Not yet. I. . . "

"Will you be in, most of the time?"

"Being unemployed you mean?"

"No plans to emigrate or get married or anything? Mind you, I shouldn’t be putting ideas in your head.” Jealousy – good. “I need you for my accomplice." Crime again – bad.

"I’ve no plans."

"And it would be nice to see you," she said, tentatively

beginning a nice end to the conversation.

"You too."

"Catch up."

"Yeah. OK. Bye. Thanks for ringing look forward to hearing from you take care of yourself, bye."

"Bye."

I went over to the window again, and leant against it. She would get in touch again. I liked people who said they'd get in touch again and did, and I was pretty sure she was that kind of person, so I felt a little ashamed that I would be photocopying her letter, especially with all this trust between us, but I knew I would.

She had too many cards in her hand, that dame. I just needed a little security, a little insurance, and in this business I was going to get nowhere with Eagle Star. And it would be a dumb guy who went into the lions' den, turning down an opportunity to have incriminating photographs of the chief lioness somewhere. Just in case.

Still lonely though. I wanted someone to talk to, and my brother Richard seemed the obvious, in fact the only, choice. With Louise gone, and Joanne an unknown quantity, he was probably the person I felt closest to in the world.

He had been sixteen and I was twelve when our parents died and he had become a sort of semi-parent in league with my Uncle Patrick and Aunt Eileen. Two or three years later when we were a little more like equals he had decided to become a priest. Despite this act of lunacy we stayed as close as we could given the fact he was living in a seminary with other deluded young men. We had never been a religious family. We would have been too embarrassed to pray together, and it had been fun trying to shock him by telling him about my attempts to lose the virginity he was sworn to.

Three or four years ago, he had got himself moved into a nearby parish and we got on better than ever. There was an interesting balance now. He was quite unworldly; and he had a childish view of the material world which he seemed to think I had mastered. He was older, wiser and more responsible than me; yet I had the sensible well paid middle-class job. I still found something ridiculous in the idea of him being a priest, and he could laugh at my sexual disasters. Despite his occupation, he was a lot less sanctimonious and moralistic than Robert or Susan. It was impossible to imagine either of them helping me through Louise or now talking about the pros and cons of Joanne.

Having said this, Richard had been a little strange over the past few months, often brooding or excitable for no obvious reason. This had worried me. He was about the right age for a mid-life crisis, which in the case of priests has to involve a Loss of Faith. It would be messy; I had scrupulously avoided responsibility until now and I didn't like the idea of my big brother becoming a dependent.

On the other hand, a mid-life crisis might do him good. The bleakness of Aetheism has to be a more solid basis for life than renouncing sex, property and freedom in exchange for the service of a non-existent omnipotent creature, whose communications are ambiguous at best and often contradictory.

I would enjoy telling him about Joanne. I could already imagine his careful questions and mild shock. I could drive the twenty miles to his house in less than half an hour, and I thought the drive would do me good.

I know cars are a malevolent force in the world, polluting the environment and devouring precious resources; placing globe-destabilising power in the wrong hands; and being responsible for more carnage than all the European medieval wars combined, while destroying what little sense of community we have left. But it was a nice sunny day; and you can wait ages for a bus; and have you any idea what the trains were like after seventeen years of Conservative government?

I had the music sorted as well, for daydreaming while I drove. I turned up the volume for 'Me And Billy The Kid', and again for the first chorus of 'Tonight I Think I'm Gonna Go Downtown', and yet again for 'Lord of the Highway'. I'm not sure it helped my driving, but I enjoyed it.

By the time I reached his presbytery I was full of things to say. I knocked vigorously at the door, but there was no reply. I felt let down. I wasn't good at dealing with disappointment, despite all my practice, and I was sulking as I walked away down the path, disgruntled and kicking at pebbles. Then I stopped. I thought I heard a noise. It could have been my name being called. I turned around but there was no-one at the door.

I realised I was standing next to his priestmobile; further evidence that he wasn't out on parish business. It was a warm day, perhaps he was in the garden. It would be maddening to come all this way, and then miss him because he was out in the back. There was an alley down the side of the house. I walked down it and tried the latched gate at the bottom. It pushed open. At first I thought he was there in a sun lounger thing facing away from the back door, but as I went up to it, I saw that it was empty.

Now I was sure he wasn't around, I wanted to leave the garden quickly. I didn't like being where I shouldn't at the best of times, and to an outsider I must have looked like a speculative burglar. It was hard to overstate my unsuitability for a life of crime. I ought to tell Joanne.

This thought was obliterated as I glanced through the living room window, and saw my brother spread out on his back on the floor. His shoulders were loosely propped against an armchair, his head was tilted back and his eyes were closed, presumably to intensify the pleasure he was getting from the attentions of a dark-haired woman in an unbuttoned white blouse. She was kissing his neck and chest, and her short black skirt was tight around her as she leant forward. I liked the look of her a lot, and I just stood there, gazing in awe. I don't know how long this went on but finally, after one last stare, I managed to haul myself away, across the lawn and down the side of the house with comically long strides, looking dead straight ahead, and grimacing with the effort of keeping quiet.

"Christ, everybody's at it," I said, when I had got back to the safety of the car. I drove four hundred yards, and around a couple of corners before parking and allowing myself two minutes of disbelieving head-shaking and bitter laughter.

"It's supposed to be the new age of Victorian Values, and we've got priests shagging in the middle of the afternoon - and not even in bed."

I wondered if, being a priest, he would use Durex. Given the evidence demonstrated here, of his flexible, not to say free-wheeling attitude to the church's teaching on such matters, there was no telling.

I was confused. I had been happily going off to discuss my problems and aspirations with regard to sin and sex with someone who would listen, and even enjoy listening. Instead of which I had discovered that he was quite involved enough with his own sin and sex to make my own preoccupations seem like nothing.

I had no idea what to do. I didn't know how to tell

him I knew without admitting that I had been sneaking around his garden and peering in through windows. He might bring it up first. I wasn't sure I'd be able to manage that either. It was unlikely he'd seen me; he had been very busy, but it wasn't impossible. If so, what would he make of my silence? It was difficult.

It was very difficult. If he had just been my brother it would have been simpler, but he was more than that. He always knew more than me; he was there to be relied on.

When my uncle arrived to tell us about our parents, I had been out in the garden playing football, badly, by myself, concentrating a lot more on my commentary than on the ball. There had been a car crash three hours earlier.

"They died instantly."

"Oh aye."

"They would have felt nothing."

"Oh right."

At the exact time it had happened, I had been sitting looking out of the window - and, instead of doing my homework, dreaming about being orphaned. Sometimes I tell myself that I have just imagined it, but I'm sure it's true. I had been imagining their car crash, and then Uncle Patrick came to tell us the news.

Richard had immediately taken on responsibility for me and Susan and Robert. He managed it very well. It must have forced him to grow up quickly, and deprived him of a lot of his adolescence, which, come to think of it is a little like being deprived of dandruff. Still, it must have changed him, going from being a sulky teenager to discussing your brothers and sister with social workers and concerned relatives.

For all I teased him about his sudden adulthood, then his sudden sanctity, it had always been reassuring to know that Richard was there, and able to save us from the worst the world could confront us with. The transformation from brother to parent to priest I could cope with. But this was different. I had never imagined him being anything so irresponsible as a philandering priest.

Apart from anything else, now for the first time I could remember, I knew something he didn't.

I drove home in silence trying to decide what to do. I tried to imagine what Richard would have done in this situation. I could get no further than 'the right thing probably' which wasn't very helpful. And I felt very uncomfortable about knowing what I knew; and, worse, having seen it. It is easier to pretend you don't know something than to pretend that you haven't seen it. I would have to work hard on erasing that picture from my mind.

CHAPTER 10

Monday morning's post was interesting. There was a postcard from my sister Susan in the Maldives. It was a complementary one from her hotel, but I assumed she had paid for the stamp herself. I had also won a quarter of a million pounds and a luxury holiday for two in Lanzarotte. This was not yet completely cut and dried, however. I had been entered in a draw for the former; and to collect the latter I would have to go to a country club in Derbyshire where I would be set upon by a team selling timeshares. I considered going. If I behaved in a sufficiently anti-social manner they might give it to me in order to get rid of me, but I had less belief in my will-power than theirs, so I decided against it.

The item which made the post interesting was a hand-written envelope. Even then these were so rare that I knew it had to be from Joanne. I delayed opening it by spending more time on the other items than they deserved. I hoped to be told that I was the greatest lover she had ever experienced and that she longed only to place herself in my powerful, loving arms again as soon as possible. In case that was not what I was about to read, I squeezed everything I could out of the pleasure of anticipation.

I quote the letter exactly and in full.

Dear Tony,

It was good to talk to you before. I'm glad you got in touch. I've just put the phone down, and I now wish I'd said all this when I had the chance. I tried to ring you back, but you had gone out. Have you thought about getting an answering machine? Basically, would you like to meet up to discuss my plan? The work would start as soon as you were ready. I'm not sure how much you'd make - it depends how you would like to operate. We need to talk about it properly, that's one of the reasons I'd like to see you. So let me know if you are interested and we can work out where and when. I've got a Privilege Card now - I remember you talking about how useful they could be. I'd like to talk some more.

Hope you're feeling OK,
Joanne.

I reread it. 'Hope you're feeling OK' was possibly quite warm. And the 'one of the reasons' comment was nicely ambiguous. Was the mention of the Privilege Card a hint that she'd like to go back to the Grand Hotel with me? If so, I would have preferred something clearer and, ideally, more lustful. I put her letter with the Breakfast Menu in the Course Reflections folder which was fast becoming a collection of souvenirs, and returned to the other great concern of the moment, my brother.

That lasted about twenty seconds. It was too difficult so I went back to the letter. Light flooded in, albeit gloomy light. The whole thing was a waste of time. Even if the scheme was a failsafe route to wealth, there were other safer ones. Like working. There were a number of salient facts to consider in deciding whether or not to contact her:

1. Although I quite liked this woman, I hardly knew her and had no reason to trust her or her judgement.

2. I had not the temperament for crime, nor the experience - apart from speeding and parking offences, drink driving, tax evasion, claiming benefit while working, under-age drinking, failure to possess a valid TV licence, use of cannabis and amphetamines, allowing a dog to foul in a public place, stealing from an employer, illegal copying of documents, breach of the data protection act, shoplifting (attempted) while a minor, blasphemy, slander, and smuggling contraceptives (unnecessarily) into the Irish Republic. Moreover, I had no real financial need; and the element of danger involved had about as much appeal for me as using faulty electrical household appliances.

3. Even meeting Joanne would cost time and money. It would be pointless, embarrassing and disappointing. I would either annoy her by wasting her time or go along with something I would come to regret out of politeness and misguided lust.

4. In all honesty, her letter had really stirred nothing more in me than disappointment and slight irritation.

5. She was involved in a relationship with someone who was obviously far more important to her than I was, whatever difficulties they were going through at the moment. Her feelings towards me were faltering and ambiguous at best.

6. We had had sexual intercourse three times.

I rang her that evening.

She offered to come over and meet me. This meant I would have to clean the flat, but it was a positive suggestion and I had not thought of an alternative. So it was agreed. She would come on the train 'So Tom can have the car' and we would meet in the station buffet at one the following Wednesday. I booked a nearby Chinese for lunch, to remind her of the meal we had shared when we had been young and in love.

****

She had clearly prepared what she had to say well in advance, making good use of the time which I had spent worrying about the state of the bedroom, and half-heartedly preparing an application form for a job with The World Wide Fund for Nature in Tunbridge Wells on £18,000.

"Right," I said with exaggerated brightness as she finished, pausing very slightly between the 'h' and 't' of 'right'.

"What do you think?" she asked. I hadn't really been listening. It was some kind of ridiculous fraud back at Hanlon Hall.

"I'm interested, obviously."

"But you need convincing? I've done it once already," she said, triumphantly. "It was with a friend, and we split the £1000 her company was paying. She pretended the name on the card was hers. Obviously we couldn't do that very often. But it was just a test. And it worked."

"Right." I paused. "OK. Impressive." I spoke slowly and deliberately to suggest that a huge amount of thought was going on in the background, but as I didn't know what she was talking about I couldn't add much more. Another mental note: try listening to what people are saying rather than concentrating on appearing to do so.

"Perfect," she said. "I knew you were right for this. You're cautious."

"Sometimes."

"You take a cynical view of things - and I need slowing down a bit. I think you probably have lots of ideas, but are very careful about doing anything about them. "

"Thanks."

"As a rule. Without encouragement. You're very sensible."

"Do you think so?" I felt insulted.

"It's not an insult."

"I didn't think it was."

"I can get carried away. I need a wet blanket sometimes. Again not an insult. You're a very nice wet blanket - and a lot more than that, as you know."

"May I take these now?" asked the waiter, lifting the starter plates with the crumbs of prawn toast, seaweed and spring rolls. I poured some more wine.

"I like working lunches - never actually been to one before," I confessed.

"I'm enjoying it as well."

"Yes. And power breakfasts."

"Pardon?"

"Sorry. I think they're the next step up in glamorous business meals." She still looked puzzled. “Power breakfasts? No?" I petered out, unsure what I meant myself now; probably just trying to get her thinking about breakfast and what went before. "Anyway - your plan. Perhaps a bit more detail?"

"Yes. You're right. In its present form it's limited. I can see that. Which is where Rachel comes in."

"Rachel who works there?" She nodded. "John-and-Rachel Rachel?"

"Please don't tell her I let that slip."

"One thing I don't understand is when did they have the time?"

"Not when we were there. Before. Last year. Now, can we get back to business? Rachel's got access to who's going on the courses, the money being paid in, the issuing of cards."

"You've spoken to her about this?"

"Yes. She's up for it. Graham - her manager - is useless. She'll have no trouble getting things past him."

"Sounds like the ideal manager."

"Starting to see the possibilities?"

"Yes." No. And still nothing about going to bed for the afternoon.

"I thought you would. After all it was your idea in the first place." I looked blank. I was blank. "At lunch about halfway through the course? About selling courses on a Privilege Card." It was flattering she had remembered.

"But you could do it by yourselves, couldn't you? I could hardly sue you stealing the idea, so why do you want me involved?"

"It feels right."

"Because. . . ?" Tony, you are irresistible.

"Partly because it was your idea, and partly because you say things like that. You're sceptical. You need persuading."

"Is that what you're doing now?"

"Do you remember there was a big house just at the gates to Hanlon Hall?" I nodded. "Empty. Perfect for a Bed and Breakfast. It's up for rent. How much do AJA charge for a week's accommodation at Hanlon Hall? Two or three hundred? We could have people up there at half the cost. Give us a reason to be there and make some money totally legally, to blur the money we are making illegally."

"By running a Bed and Breakfast?" I'd rather work in IT for The World Wide Fund for Nature. Much rather.

"It's one of many possibilities. All I'm saying is," she slowed down, and looked at me. "That place is a honeypot." She smiled. "And no-one is guarding the honey." Her eyes widened.

Watching the widening of someone's eyes, it is hard not to copy them. I widened mine back. I was still listening but I was hearing words rather than their sense and I was more interested in the body they were coming out of than anything else.

"Businesses like that are wide open to attack. They deserve it. You could almost say they need it. Law of the

Business Jungle."

I had to make it look as if I was considering all this so I went for the cautious thing that she seemed keen on.

"It's all a bit vague, though, isn't it?" I said as the waiter put down sizzling beef in a heavy black iron dish, and a tray of rice beside it.

"Yes, yes I know," she said, and smiled thanks to the waiter as he went away, "Having said that, I've already made £500." She spooned me some fried rice.

"And it's easy enough to set up a company. Just a couple of hundred quid and a friendly accountant. And I've got a name."

"Have you?"

"Yes." She was obviously proud of this because she paused as if she was expecting a drum roll. "Love," she said. I was lost again.

"Pardon?"

"Love Training Limited. Love Training. Do you get it?"

"Yes – but is it not a bit . . .?" Shite.

"It's memorable, isn't it?"

"Well – yes. But it doesn't sound very business-like."

"Would you prefer some Eighties-style acronym? Like AJA. That's out of date. Like them. The important thing is to be memorable. It's all that matters in Marketing. Everyone's doing it. Even the Trade Unions, for God's sake. Unison. And think about it. Love - no-one's going to forget that, are they? Would you?"

"What about Rachel?" I asked hurriedly. I was beginning to blush. "How does she feel about me being involved?"

"She is," she stressed the next word, "Happy for you to be involved. And she's had a few ideas. She thinks, in time, we could actually have people staying in the Hall itself. It's so big, and according to her it's so badly run that nobody would know. Nice rooms too. Honeypot," she reiterated, smiling.

It was like a big, juicy rotting plum and we could be the wasps, sucking what we wanted from it.

"In the meantime it'll run courses for us, provide accommodation, the lot. It's so simple. We intercept their customers and sell them places on courses which they are running for the rest of the class. We'll always undercut them; we haven't got any overheads."

"What about the training rooms?" I chipped in, feeling it was time to contribute. "We could probably run courses ourselves in their empty training rooms. We could steal things as well. Why not? It's all the same really."

"Yes. But only for a while. They can't go on like this forever. From what Rachel says, it's chaos; it's just a matter of getting what we can before it all blows up."

"And we'd need to be able to get away when the auditors arrive."

"Yes," she nodded. "And there are take-over rumours, but they are still just rumours at the minute. But it is definitely on the skids - it won't be like this for ever."

"Perhaps in time we could buy them out."

She liked that and laughed. Impossible things become possible if you gave them a chance.

"Good way to launder money - the odd take-over bid."

"Especially for a company whose business we know and understand so well." She was smiling all the time now.

"If the tax people queried us, we could always say we won it on the horses," I suggested. The conversation was steered where I wanted it, and we exchanged memories. "I enjoyed that week - some parts more than others."

She didn't reply. Instead she toyed with a mushroom in chilli and ginger. It glistened in her chopsticks. She squeezed it tight, then released it and pushed it slowly through the sauce on her almost empty plate. Then she smiled.

"So did I - especially the session on Gantt charts," and she popped the mushroom into her mouth. I felt I should laugh, and then I ate a little more before speaking again.

"Was your thingy OK about last Friday? Me ringing up like that."

"Tom? I told you. He sulked. But then he sulks about everything at the minute. If he has a problem and hasn't got the guts to talk about it well then, that's his problem."

"Did he not ask about it?"

"He wouldn't, would he?" she said shaking her head.

"Things not great?" I suggested helpfully.

"Not as great as they might be, shall we say. That's all, though," she added, warning me off.

"This is a really good Chinese, isn't it?" I said, warned off.

"Plenty of it too."

"So, while you're weakened by food, will you tell me what happened with John and Rachel?" There was something very satisfying in talking about other people's sex lives.

"What about them?" she said playfully.

It was time for my Bryan Ferry impersonation. I let my eyes drift slightly out of focus and fluttered my eyelids while executing a parrotesque swivel of my head and pushing my lower lip out slightly with my upper front teeth. The whole was meant to show that I was interested and willing to play her game, by her rules if she liked, but only up to a point. And to ooze sophistication.

"Are you OK?"

"What? Yes. Fine." I readjusted my face.

"John. I know he's a friend of yours . . ."

"He's not a friend of mine. I've told you. I work with him."

"But Rachel is a friend of mine."

"Right. Good."

"Who probably wouldn't thank me for telling you about her."

"Then she's right to be your friend." Nice one, Tony. We finished with liqueur coffees.

"Nice and healthy, isn't it?" she said, "Cream, coffee and rum", before pushing her lips into the thick cream. I realised I was staring at her. She noticed, and didn't seem to mind.

"So," she raised her glass to toast, "Love Training. Me, you and Rachel?"

"Probably," I said and she laughed.

"Her and John. It's hard to imagine them actually..." It was not a good idea to encourage her to think I spent a lot of time imagining other people in bed. "Did she..." I faltered, "Was Rachel... bothered a lot?" was the best I could manage.

"She liked him. I don't really see why."

"Me, neither."

Once I stopped asking for information about what had happened she gave it.

"They met when he was doing a course there last year. They had a night or two together. Didn't tell her he was married or anything of course. Not at first. And then he goes down there again without even warning her."

Was there no end to the impressive depths of John

Mulholland?

"And then when they bumped into each other – like they were bound to - he arranged to see her and then cried off."

"Family first?" I said.

"Perhaps."

"Seeing the reflection of his wedding band in the temptress' eye."

“What?”

“It’s from a song. Almost Persuaded. Tammy Wynette.”

“I’m serious.”

“It’s a good song.” I was about to explain, but then I remembered she was more a Billy Joel woman. “Sorry. Didn’t mean to appear flippant.” Time to shut up, Tony. Another ploy that always works if you want to appear sensitive.

"Rachel's a good friend of mine. And he treated her badly. Which is why I started having my doubts about you. That morning in the park when you said you wanted a lift and didn't turn up."

"Sorry. I explained. The phone thing. Not having one."

"In case you were playing games, like him."

"I know. I wasn't."

"And that whole thing about his ankle."

"What do you mean?"

"It was a very convenient excuse. He'd arranged to meet her; then couldn't because of that." It had never in a million years occurred to me that John had faked his sprained ankle. Perhaps we had more in common than I thought, but he was better at it.

"I'm not sure he didn't get some kind of perverted power kick out of it. It was all just a bit shabby. And there is something about a married man away on business."

"Like you?" I asked, despite myself.

"I am not a husband and father away on business who doesn't know whether or not to deceive his wife," she replied, unamused.

There were a number of possible clever replies to this, but I backed down, because I wanted to sleep with her. Then I surprised myself with a really clever one.

"Do you always know what you want to do?"

"Why do you say that?" she asked, with the coffee glass covering part of her smiling face.

"Just... you seem to most of the time, whereas I'm pathologically indecisive - most of the time. Unless I'm definitely sure about something," I paused for exactly as long as it would have taken to say 'like wanting to see you naked again', then continued.

"So this scheme of yours - I'm genuinely unsure. I need to think a little."

"Of course. Nothing ventured, nothing lost?"

"Well yes, I know that's not always true." This was

better. “I need some time. I'm just being straight with you."

"That's what I like about you. One of the things. But what does your instinct tell you?" She leaned forward eagerly.

"My instinct? I think that, well, perhaps, I really don't know." She laughed. "Once you start trying to work out what you feel spontaneously, it gets very difficult." She wanted more. "To answer your question honestly," I liked her eyes scrutinising me, "My instinctive reaction is what I've said - to think about it seriously. Very seriously."

She accepted that. It sounded adult and honest. It wasn't. I wanted to sleep with her, but I didn't want to get into this mad scheme of hers. It meant taking too many risks for no good reason. I didn't really know or trust her, and she was unwise enough to trust me. And I knew how quickly your feelings about someone, especially someone you wanted to sleep with, could change. I would be too vulnerable. And she was too close with Rachel.

"Is that OK as an answer for the time being?" I asked. She smiled and nodded. "Good. It means I'll get to talk to you again anyway."

"That'd be nice," Then she added, "But don't do it for that reason."

"No. Of course not. It's a good idea and I'm seriously thinking about it."

I would be mad to get involved. For at best a few thousand quid and some much unwanted excitement. No, thanks. And if we were caught? A criminal record; a big, dirty, black mark on the CV, even prison. No. That was my instinct on this one, and I was definitely lying when I said I was seriously thinking about it.

CHAPTER 11

And yet by the summer, I was happily falsifying accounts for Love Training, and organising guests in the Lodge near Hanlon Hall. I had always thought of myself as an honest person, or at least someone who was afraid of the consequences of dishonesty, but I knew I could adapt; running a Bed and Breakfast, though, was something I could never have imagined.

My change of heart was not motivated by sex. This might not sound convincing, even though Joanne had made it quite clear during our Chinese banquet, and afterwards back at my flat, that sex and business were utterly unrelated in her mind.

"Neither is in any way whatsoever dependent on the other," as she put it.

I stopped kissing her shoulder for a moment to make my contribution. I was glad I had tempted Fate by tidying the bedroom.

"If anything, they could get in each others' way," I said, like an intelligent scholar wanting to encourage his teacher.

"And if they did, they could kill each other," she added. I agreed wholeheartedly.

"And we don't want that." And she agreed wholeheartedly.

Sometimes people say things they don't mean; and sometimes they say things they mean at the time but know they won't mean later. Neither was the case here, though. I meant it. I had no intention of getting involved with her scheme.

****

For several weeks following the revelation in the garden, I had not seen Richard. In fact I had not spoken to him at all, mainly for fear that I'd give myself away. Having no idea what to do, I did nothing.

Then one day he turned up at my flat. This was something he never did. If he was making a visit, it would only be after a minimum of two phone calls, one to arrange, one to confirm. I was never sure why. It wasn't self-importance. It might have been our genetic lack of spontaneity; it might even have been humility. Whatever the reason, he never turned up like this, unexpected, unannounced, anxious-looking and bedraggled.

"Can I come in?" he said eventually.

I hadn't invited him in only because of my surprise. First, copulating with parishioners in his living room and now visiting his brother without arranging it in advance. Truly we were experiencing the marvels of the Millennium.

He was very hesitant. My accidental lack of hospitality

had made him even more sheepish, so I ushered him in quickly, hoping this would alleviate his discomfort. It was becoming infectious, and I could hardly explain what was behind mine.

"You haven't got a brandy or anything?" he asked in response to my offer of tea.

"I don't think so," I replied. This wasn't strictly true. I knew for a fact that I didn't. I always knew the location and quantity of any alcohol in my flat. There was none at the moment, as was usually the case. Any alcohol was generally consumed on the day of purchase, long before it had the chance to make it to a cupboard, let alone become part of the fixtures and fittings.

I was also glad of the opportunity tea-making gave me to hide in the kitchen. But then Richard loomed up to me like a fidgeting ghost as I was pouring boiling water into the teapot, apologised as I almost scalded myself, and then turned and trotted out again.

I took his agitation as a warning of impending confession. When it began I would not admit to any knowledge. Confessors aren't supposed to come out with 'I know what you're going to say' as the punter settles down on the kneeler and clears his throat, and I would adopt a similar tactic of discreet attentive pastoral silence.

"Have you heard from Susan or Robert lately?" he asked as I brought the cups through to the living room which he was exploring as if it was all new to him. They were always referred to in that order - the order in which they were born. I was about to reply when he spoke again. "I spoke to Robert, briefly."

"Too busy with the troubles of a hard-working family man?"

"And Susan's been away - Malaysia I think."

"The Maldives. I got a card."

"It's been a long time since we saw each other," he continued. That was half-true. "But then we've both been busy, I suppose. How's work?"

The question was bolted on suddenly, perhaps as he remembered what 'being busy' meant in his case.

"It isn't."

"Oh, right. Like that is it?"

"No. Redundancy."

"Oh. That's bound to have a bad effect on morale. So short-sighted as well as a rule."

"Yes."

"You're OK though?"

"I've been made redundant."

"Oh. Sorry."

He didn't know what to say. I had also knocked him off course for what he had really come round to talk about. He sat there, becalmed, and sipped his tea; or at least lowered his top lip into it. He didn't seem to drink, he just left his mouth there.

"It shouldn't be a problem. There's loads of work

round at the minute. The Millennium Bug."

"Never really understood that."

It was a safe topic.

"Any programs with two digit years need to be converted to four digits, otherwise they'll crash on 1st January 2000."

"Will they?"

"Yes."

"Right." For the second time I felt some sympathy for Mr Campbell.

"Because any calculations using years will fail because '00' isn't bigger than '99'".

"I see." He obviously didn't. "Tony, have I... do I seem... strange at all lately?" My diversion hadn't worked for long, unsurprisingly

"I haven't really seen you much to talk to," I replied, not strictly speaking dishonestly. "But you do seem a bit," how to put it, "Preoccupied, I suppose, now you mention it." He looked sombre and said nothing.

"Did you drive over?" I found myself asking, to fill the silence. I don't think he heard me anyway.

"There is something."

He was right there. But I didn't help him tell me. I must be a bad and cowardly person, I thought, watching him in his gloom. I wasn't enjoying it much myself either though.

"There's something I've got to tell you."

It sounded as if he was going to tell me he was pregnant. For the last few seconds he had been staring at his cup, which he was gripping tightly in both hands. Now he gave me a sudden nervous glance. Come on, Richard, get on with it.

"And ask you. Ask you to forgive. And please don't say anything to anyone."

"OK, Richard." I prepared to act shocked.

"Vows of chastity are... no." He tailed off, then tried again. "I've been having a relationship - a sexual relationship - with someone... a woman, you know."

I did a shocked face for about a second then went into what I hoped was compassion mode by closing my molars together and nodding gently and encouragingly, as I waited for more.

"What do you think of that?" It was an unexpected and, I couldn't help but feel, rather inadequate ending to a priest's confession. It sounded like an explorer boasting or a schoolboy showing off a scar.

"Depends, I suppose. Are you OK?"

"It's too much pressure."

"Right. It must be difficult. Do people know?"

He shook his head in a flurry, like a dog shaking itself dry.

"God, no."

"So it's hard to meet up with her?" And the rest.

He looked surprised at how calm I seemed. Then he

must have realised how little he had told me.

"There's more than that - and I'm so sorry it's got to be you I tell. She's pregnant. I don't know what to do. I'm desperate. She's not. She can act so fu - bloody cool can't she? She says we'll work something out, but I don't know what, and all the time it's growing, getting nearer. I don't want to stay calm like she says. I want to know what I can do. She talks calm as hell but I'm sure she's not, I know she's not - I wish she'd admit it."

"You want to stay a priest?" I asked.

"That's why I thought to ask you this," he was speaking very quickly now. Until this point it had just been a painful spectacle, unpleasant but nothing more dangerous. Someone else's car crash. Now I suspected I was about to get more than a request for advice and comfort.

"It's a lot to ask," he said. Yes, there was room in this crisis for one more, and he was called Tony Palmer. "If you would, well consider, saying that it's yours, if that was something you'd consider?" he tailed off.

"Pardon?"

"It's just a sort of idea for the time being - just a thought because of the situation being such a."

It was the old story - he had known more than me after all.

"What does she think of this idea?" I asked coldly.

"I don't know. I haven't asked her."

"Do you not think you should?" I was being hard and sensible, which was easier than saying 'No'. I began to doubt his sanity. Perhaps the pregnancy was imaginary.

"Yes, yes you're right of course. I will. I just thought I'd see how you were about it first, instead of going through it with her. I will though. I'm glad you're taking it so well, Tony. Nobody could... And this is all just an idea and because well, you know."

"Hang on," I panicked, "I'm sorry you're in such a mess but this doesn't seem much of an idea to me at the minute, to be quite honest."

"Perhaps not - no," he agreed hurriedly, "Not even on an temporary basis? No."

That began as a tentative question and finished as a disappointed statement. I shook my head to make it clear I was not simply asking for time to think it over.

"She thinks a lot of you, you know."

That seemed an odd thing to say, even among all the other odd things he was saying. Did he talk about me in bed?

"But you seem...not so surprised." He seemed to think that this was good in some way that was utterly beyond me.

"Do I not?" This was my last chance to mention my visit to his garden. It was the honest thing to do. "I am surprised. Of course I am. I'm concerned for you." He seemed touched by that, which was nice. "How long have you been ... seeing each other?"

"Well more or less ever since, you know..." He looked at me for help. "A month or so after. It wasn't deliberate or planned, you know, by either of us. We spent a bit of time. . . a lot of time really, and... I was concerned, worried about what you'd feel, but I suppose other things just took over."

It was happening again. He seemed to be trying to drag me in to his madness.

"Is it months, years?" I said, trying to keep things at the hard and factual level. He looked very surprised, and then gave a puzzled smile.

"Can you not remember?" He said. "It was well after you'd split up. It was - I promise you."

"What are you talking about?"

"You and Louise - when you split up."

"What's she got to do with it?"

"Louise?"

"Yes. Louise." I stared at him. He realised that I hadn't realised yet.

"There wasn't any overlap," he said. I realised now. "At least a month – nearer two."

There's a George Jones song, The Grand Tour, in which the singer promises to tell you the most chilling account of a world being torn apart that you will ever hear. I felt I'd like a word with him.

On the positive side, it meant that my brother was not

actually mad. There was a reason for what he was saying. I knew from experience that a sexual relationship with Louise was unlikely to add to anyone's mental stability, even if they weren't a priest and she was carrying his child, but I was still not pleased.

"You hadn't realised," he told me.

"No, of course I fucking hadn't. And you've got the fucking nerve to try and foist your fucking baby off on me. Fuck."

And I launched into an angry tirade which took in priesthood, abortion, and fucked up families. I followed up with an attack on Louise, including my knowledge of her sexual preferences, and a small mole on her left buttock. He left as I started throwing things - his full cup of tea to begin with.

"I'm very, very sorry," he said as he reached the door. The cup missed him. "You're right to be angry. I'm sorry. This was mad. Sorry."

I punched the settee a few times, then lay there. When I got bored with this, I went out and bought a jumbo bottle of gin. I drank most of it and it was dark when I woke up on the settee. I stumbled to the phone and rang him. I ignored his polite 'Hello', and demanded to know details of their relationship, which he refused to give, possibly because she was in the room with him - half-naked and pregnant.

I slammed the receiver down and flopped on to the

settee again.

I remembered how Richard had been so friendly and generous and understanding and supportive to both of us at the time. Supportive - I hate that word. He had been one of the very few people we were both able to relax with, even when things had apparently been going well. Then, quite suddenly, things weren't going well at all. I had been bewildered and then scared.

"Are you getting sick of me?" I would ask her.

"No."

"I don't believe you, Louise."

"God's sake, Tony."

"What?"

"Perhaps I'd better go."

"You see."

Conversations like that had become more and more frequent. As had these.

"You're scaring me, Tony."

"What? I'm scaring you?"

"Yes."

"That's ridiculous."

I stopped trusting her and she became afraid of me. She couldn't understand why I didn't trust her, and I didn't believe she was really afraid of me.

Looking back I had wanted it to be like the first few weeks forever, and she wanted a grown-up relationship. I see that now, but then it had just been a mess. So who could have been a better and safer confidante than my trusted brother with his sworn vows of chastity? At first his friendship with us as a couple had seemed to be proof of my acceptance into the adult world. Then he had listened so patiently for so long, and tried to help us see each other's point of view. When this failed, he helped me realise how sometimes you just have to let things go, and when we finally split up, his wise counsel had helped me to survive.

And she had been so mature and thoughtful when we separated. I hadn't been so nice, and I had always felt a bit guilty about that. I didn't now.

I hadn't recognised Louise's body from the garden. I had recognised bits of him, though, sticking out between her legs and above elbows and over shoulders. Where would it stop? What was he going to do to me next? Would he add incestuous buggery to his interpretation of his priestly duties?

He rang up and suggested that the three of us meet up and "Try to talk this through. No. Sorry. Bad idea," as he received my aggressive and blasphemous response.

At least he was in no doubt about my attitude to fostering their less than immaculately conceived child.

Louise rang up, initially to apologise, and then to see how I was coping. I gave her a reprise of my attack on Richard. She said it wasn't like that at all. They both felt terrible – Richard especially.

"I'm not surprised. It didn't do a lot for me either - as far as I remember - sleeping with poison."

Richard rang up again to try to 'save the situation'.

I told him that I was sick of getting lectures every time they broke from their conferences. He told me it wasn't like that at all. I hung up.

Louise rang up to ask me if I knew what this was doing to Richard. I told her I hated her and couldn't work out whether he needed sympathy or a good kicking. She told me that, actually, I was being childish. This was a difficult time for all of us and we needed to support each other.

"Do you think I'm even more stupid than I am? Than you've made me feel?," I said, "And don't ring back. Either of you. Ever," and I hung up.

Richard rang again. I managed to bring their calls to an end by asking if he thought Louise was planning on screwing Robert to collect the full set of Palmers. That worked. No more phone calls, but I was left sitting in wretched silence on the settee until I managed to drink myself to sleep. Just before I did I realised I wasn't making much progress on the redundancy, alcohol and loneliness fronts.

Next morning I rang Joanne and my life as a rural fraudster began.

CHAPTER 12

Obviously, I changed my mind a thousand times. Even as I sent emails to the list of leads Rachel had provided I knew I could (and probably would) pull out before any of them tried to book. When I put my flat on the market and caught the train down to sign the lease on The Lodge, I told myself nothing was fixed. My course might appear set, but it could be changed. It had to be. There was so much to go wrong. Perhaps nothing would happen. Despite the triumph of Capitalism in the Cold War, most new businesses failed, why not this one? Besides, as I was the person fielding calls, it was in my hands. I should relax, treat it as a holiday. I was committed to nothing until we had our first customer.

"Our delegate is called Bill Stapleton," said the voice at the other end of the phone. She sounded serious. "For a place on The Data Security Implications of the Millenium Bug Course 24-26th of June."

"Are you sure?"

"Pardon?" Exasperated.

"Sorry?" Worried.

"Is there a problem?" the voice said. She was getting more exasperated. It was still just in my power to stop this happening, and prevent a hundred other similar conversations.

"No, no problem at all. I'm booking it now, our pleasure," I heard myself saying, like a lunatic. "Course Code MBDS1."

"And you have budget accommodation in The Lodge?"

"I'm afraid there's none available at present."

"Hanlon Hall, then."

"Yes. We'll mail you out the details. No worries." That wasn't true; there were lots of worries. This was a disaster waiting to happen.

"That's brilliant," said Joanne, when I rang to tell her.

"Yes. Fantastic." She knew me well enough to know that wasn't sincere.

"This is the start of great things. I know it. But you're not sure, are you? You're cautious. You don't want to celebrate until we get the money. You think it might not happen." That was true; it was the hope I was clinging to.

"Is our delegate staying at The Lodge?" she asked next.

"No, he. . . I couldn't persuade him."

"Never mind. And look, Tony, it'll be fine. They're a bona fide company booking a course with another bona fide company. The cheque'll be on its way."

"And what about you?"

"Saturday."

"You sure?"

"Of course I am. I said, didn't I? Look why don't you tell Rachel the news. Cheer her up as well."

I would have felt more secure if she had been a little wary about throwing her single friend and her lover together like this, but she was right. If we were operating as a team we had to communicate. But I always found it awkward communicating with Rachel. She had a directness and simplicity which I found difficult. When she first came over to the Lodge, instead of suggesting a drink to celebrate, she pointed out all the things which she thought needed doing before we could take paying guests. Curtains for example.

We worked together on preparing the Lodge, but we worked in different rooms most of the time. I am pretty sure this was not accidental on her part: it certainly wasn't on mine. I don't think that she thought I was a fool, exactly, so much as someone it was dangerous to trust with too much. She might have been protective towards Joanne, or she might have associated me with John. It needed talking through.

"I'm sorry about John."

"Why?"

"Way he behaved."

"Why should you be sorry?" She was right. There was no reason. "Joanne says you aren't that close with him," she said.

"God, no. I'm not."

"That's all right then. I think he's a shit."

"Yes."

"You agree?"

"Yes. From what I know about him."

"Which seems to me like a good reason not to talk about him."

I still suspected she didn't believe me about John, but now he was a banned topic it would be tricky trying to persuade her otherwise.

Rachel's reasons for being involved were a lot simpler than mine. It all came down to her health. She thought that a medical condition she had (it was explained to me but I wasn't really paying attention) would benefit from a warm climate and she was planning to move abroad - Italy or Greece or North Africa or somewhere - and she wanted a little extra money to make the move.

Despite our differences, we had a common role of trying to harness Joanne's enthusiasm and energy. Joanne would pour out ideas, and usually if she met our reasoned disagreement, she would just accept it and move on to the next. She was getting a kick out of this. I suppose she was just bored - with her job, her partner, with turn of the century England. She wasn't used to being naughty and she was enjoying it.

I wasn't. I felt slightly sick when I received the envelope containing the cheque from Bill Stapleton's company.

"What? Has it? That's brilliant," said Joanne, pulling herself out of our post-coital embrace. "But why didn't you tell me earlier?"

"It just arrived today - a few hours before you."

"So?"

"I thought it might have distracted you."

"From doing what we've just done?"

"Yes."

"How wrong you are, Mr Palmer. You see, we've got something to celebrate now. And I know just how." She lifted up the quilt, and slid herself down my body.

We had just finished, and in all honesty, I would rather have waited a little, before starting again, but experience had taught me to make the most of these opportunities. Similarly, I could also have been offended by the fact she seemed more excited by the cheque than by the proximity of my naked body, but I had not learnt nothing in twenty eight years, so I stayed quiet, and concentrated on overcoming all my instincts and upbringing by enjoying the moment.

"I've had a lot of time to think," I said, when we were back in the talking position.

"Should I be worried?"

"I was thinking about legitimising things - the business," I added quickly.

"We haven't even broken the law yet. Not til you pay the cheque in," she added. I never thought anyone's eyes could glitter as they spoke, but I would have sworn hers did then.

"We could sell software."

"You want to be Bill Gates now?"

"Not writing it. As an agency for software houses: small software houses with no business sense. It's a bit like Love Training, really. Other people do all the work, we just sort of act as a go-between. We find customers and take a healthy percentage." She didn't look impressed. "I've found one already. Doing library software."

"Libraries?"

"Yes."

"And you think running a B&B is dull?"

"Got to have something to occupy my time."

"You could do something about this place."

"Are you suggesting I'm not pulling my weight here?" This could have been our first argument.

"No," she said. We both knew she was, and I was surprised how easily she had backed down. I felt the need to justify her decision to do so.

"I've spent a lot of time chasing customers, you know."

"I know, Tony, you're right."

"And I'm the one whose sold up to come down here." She acknowledged this; and the unspoken 'While you stay at home, in your well-paid job, with Partner-Face'.

The next time I spoke to Rachel, I was surprised at how much she knew about my business plan.

"Has Joanne been talking to you about it?"

"Yes. Of course," she said. I braced myself. It was time to stand my ground. "And it sounds a really good idea," she added.

"You think so?"

"You've more business acumen than I realised."

"Right. Thanks."

"We have to make Joanne realise that this scam has a limited shelf-life." I agreed with her on that. "I got you this," she added, handing me a Platinum Card. "For getting access to the Hall. Totally authentic. I'm sure you won't need it, but like Dumbo's magic tail feather. . . "

She laughed so I laughed. I knew Dumbo was a flying elephant in a Disney cartoon, who presumably had a magic tail feather but I failed to see the relevance. I made a mental note to look it up.

"And I was going to charge it to your former employer. Do you think they'll manage to trace the fact you've left?"

I shook my head.

"Me neither. I even got commission. I'll pass it on to Love Training."

I spent some time getting to know my way around Hanlon Hall with the Platinum Card in my pocket, but she was right, I didn't really need it. I inspected the teaching rooms and sampled the leisure and catering facilities; I took the opportunity to stock up on complimentary mugs, mouse-mats and pens, along with floppy discs, cutlery and training manuals; and I repaid them by putting helpful ideas in their suggestion boxes.

I enjoyed this petty industrial espionage. It gave me something to do to keep my anxieties at bay and it kept me away from town where I might bump into Gary. I had seen him once, across the road with some heavy-looking colleagues; I had ducked into a shop before he saw me (I hoped), but avoiding his gang remained one of my chief concerns.

As part of my research I spent a couple of nights in Hanlon Hall in the role of a guest. Apart from anything else, the Lodge felt very empty when Joanne wasn't around, so it seemed a good time to test standards of accommodation and security on behalf of our future customers. I was relieved to discover that the former were reasonably high and the latter very low.

Sex with Joanne, the presence of Rachel and these scouting missions to Hanlon Hall helped build my confidence, but I was still very worried about the impending arrival of Bill Stapleton, our first, and possibly last, paying customer. There was so much that could go wrong. All he had to do was mention Love Training (sole known operative, Tony Palmer) and we were done for.

The others advised keeping out of his way but I couldn't resist hunting him out on his first morning. I knew it was pointless and even counter-productive but I still did it. I loitered by the Registrations Desk until I heard him say his name. As I caught his eye I was blushing nearly as much as I had on my training course a few months earlier.

He was all I had feared. He had a silly moustache, a personal organiser, a state of the art mobile and a shirt with a contrasting collar. I knew to look at him that he was a complainer.

I was right. I heard him complaining that (a) there was no cranberry juice in the Hospitality Room and (b) there was no security camera in the car park. He was the sort of person who labelled his lists with (a) and (b). This was going to be a disaster. I knew it. Joanne had asked me about my instinct. My first instinct had been to run a mile from this madness, and it looked as if I was about to be proved right. I was only glad that he wasn't staying in The Lodge.

"What are you doing?" asked Rachel, when she saw me hanging around the Hospitality Area.

"Keeping an eye on him."

"What for?"

"I know what I'm doing. He's trouble."

From the way she shook her head as she turned to walk away, I knew that I still had a lot of work to do to persuade her of my value. But I wasn't going to sit in The Lodge waiting for disaster to strike, I had to be there to see it happen.

Stapleton re-appeared complaining that there was no "ordinary coffee", and that the course was not capturing his imagination. Tricky – as that would have required him having one.

I sat on his table at lunch. The Thai Green Curry, some of which had smudged his moustache, contained too many different spices, and he wasn't happy about the range of satellite channels in his room. It was only a matter of time before he complained at the desk. When he went back for the afternoon session I stalked the Hall nervously. I had no idea what I could do to prevent the inevitable, but when he came out for the afternoon break I introduced myself to him.

"Enjoying your course?" He looked suspicious - like a suspicious weasel.

"Not especially."

"What are you doing?"

"The Data Security Implications of the Millennium Bug."

"Y2K - eh?"

"I'm not impressed with the course materials either."

"That's a surprise."

Sarcasm was completely wasted on him. Much as oxygen was. But I couldn't help myself; he was like a scab I couldn't leave alone. I had to find out more about him and stop him screwing my life up. He started picking his nose - I wanted him to stop that as well.

"I mean they're normally very good. Did you stay here last night?" I asked.

"Here?"

"Yes."

"In Hanlon Hall?" No, in Bad Wurtenburg. Of course here, you gormless fuckwit. "Yes."

"I am. More's the pity. I've already made a written complaint. Much good it'll do."

"Have you?" I managed to utter audibly

"For what it's worth. The Dolly Bird on reception didn't seem very interested." Dolly Bird? Who, since 1975 has ever said 'Dolly Bird'? He was a bit special this one. I gave him a hard pat on the shoulder which he didn't like. Good. I did it again.

"Good for you, mate. Not enough of it about complaining. Did you book direct?"

"Eh? Done through work. Company called Love Training or something."

"Stupid name."

"Yes. Girl at reception said she'd never heard of them. Beyond belief."

I alerted Rachel and told her I wasn't hanging around any more. She told me not to worry, but to go back to The Lodge and lie low. I phoned Joanne. She said the same.

For once I took advice. Actually, I had no real choice; I had nowhere to go and it would take considerable detective work to find a link between Stapleton's letter and the Lodge B&B.

I drank a couple of bottles of wine, watching videos and tormenting myself by trying to imagine the moment of detection. Perhaps when Rachel was called in by her boss; or when the bank queried the cheque I had paid in; or when the police appeared at The Lodge. I could have fled. I could have followed my instincts, but I stayed.

I was lying on the settee in my underpants when Rachel's phone call woke me next morning. She had intercepted the letter and was working on getting Love Training on to their database as some kind of recognised agent.

"Right. Good stuff. Well done." I wasn't convinced this was the end of it.

"And stop stressing, Tony."

"I'm not."

"You are."

"I'm not. This is the way I am."

Nothing had happened - yet - but I knew it would. To Rachel's annoyance I followed Stapleton occasionally and at a distance over the next two days. He didn't seem to recognise me. At the end of the last day I stood in the car park and watched him drive away. His cheque cleared and the following week his company booked another two delegates on a course through us. It had worked. Deep down, I always knew it would.

CHAPTER 13

The pleasure of being in Hanlon Hall on expenses was nothing compared with the pleasure of walking its carpeted corridors knowing that I was making real money out of the place. I liked being there and I felt I belonged. After a couple of weeks genuine employees began to smile and nod at me. When the opportunity arose Rachel would introduce me to members of staff, formally but vaguely.

"Tony's on the marketing side - you've probably seen him around."

"Right. Marketing?"

"For my sins, ha, ha."

And I would give a firm handshake and friendly eye contact with smile, then disappear before the questions became any more specific.

I did a lot of smiling. Like lying, it was good for business. It cost nothing and it was becoming a habit. Life was good. I was eating better, taking exercise, drinking less, taking pleasure in the beauty of the countryside for God's sake. I was getting real satisfaction from making money, and from watching it mount up in the company account, even though we were taking out more in cash than I felt was financially prudent. I was working when I wanted and when it was necessary, which were the same thing. I enjoyed wearing a good suit and tie and talking business with clients.

Everybody was right.

Joanne was right. She had come up with a piece of business magic. The only difference between booking with Love Training and booking direct with AJA was that we were a little cheaper and we kept the money for ourselves. It could be done and we were doing it.

Rachel had been right as well. She knew that AJA was a very disorganised organisation, and she was in the perfect position to intercept bookings and dangerous queries and manipulate the accounts. She destroyed correspondence and stole addresses, and she would be the first to know if we were in danger of being discovered. She had already dealt with a woman from a Law firm who had tried to get through to senior management about a discrepancy on her bill; and if she could deal with a female lawyer querying a bill, she could deal with anybody,

I was right for going against my better judgement, disregarding my instincts and allowing myself to be swept along by Joanne's enthusiasm.

Even Gary had been right. It was a nice place to live. I was surrounded by trees, cottages and rich farmland. All the things I had expected to miss about urban life - activity, chaos, change, choice, crowds - I was happier without them. For the first time in a long time I felt happy about everything. It flowed through me.

With some help, I had finally prepared the Lodge for guests, with a room set aside as my bedroom and office. There I would happily work into the night on business plans, fictitious company accounts and spreadsheets showing projected growth figures, with a cup of strong tea at my side and Mozart or Bruckner playing lightly in the background. I had never listened to classical music much before but it seemed the perfect accompaniment. Hank Williams and Jimmie Dale Gilmore didn't seem to belong in an office dedicated to creative accountancy.

Joanne came down every two or three weeks. We would spend some time together and meet Rachel to discuss new schemes and talk through any problems, and I would give them a financial report. They were very trusting, but they were right to be. I also tried to push the legitimate side of the business. Joanne and Rachel didn't try to stop me but they were less interested in it than I was. That was fine. I knew that it was, initially at least, only a sideline, and that the core of our business and the real money-earner was the other side of our operation. I understood; we were a team; we made joint decisions. They would come round when they saw how much money there was to be made from my ideas. Joanne and Rachel sometimes went for lunch together without me: I was happy enough about that. I was becoming good at spending time by myself, now that my life had purpose.

I enjoyed Country Life. I read through dozens of back issues one rainy afternoon and I learnt a lot. There were still people in England living lives more appropriate to the 1790's than the 1990's; and they really lived in the type of places I had thought only existed in pictures reproduced for biscuit tins and jigsaws. There was one feature in particular which I loved. Every issue had one page set aside for a photograph of this month's star bride - which sat very comfortably with the pictures of horses and houses for sale around it. It was the wealthy rural equivalent of Page Three, right down to the description of Pamela, a sparkling, vivacious follower of the Staffordshire Hunt, or Georgina, the star of Hampshire's fast set.

And the things I did. I found myself on a horse, for God's sake, walking - trotting sometimes - across the rich pastureland of Southern England, with a healthy meal inside me, considering how best to present our books to the Inland Revenue, and what new methods I could devise to increase our undeclared income. My sense of well-being was further reinforced by the memories of textbook sex two nights earlier with a woman who was starting to feel more for me than I did for her. She still wouldn't tell me the truth about the bomb scare and after a while I had stopped giving her the satisfaction of hearing me ask. The Tony Palmer who had pretended to sprain his ankle to hide embarrassment seemed like another man entirely. I had grown up and I understood the value of concealment.

I knew without checking what was happening in the next few weeks. Our most recent booking was a Peter Mason who would be attending a database course run by AJA Training for which his employer was paying us nine hundred and fifty pounds plus VAT. Two of his colleagues had provisionally booked the same course: they needed to confirm or lose their deposits. We were accommodating three other delegates from an accountancy course in unoccupied rooms at the Hall at a cost of a hundred and forty pounds each. We would also have five genuine guests for Bed and Breakfast at The Lodge (with forged meal cards for lunch at Hanlon Hall provided) paying sixty-four pounds each for two nights. Or forty-five as we would tell the Inland Revenue.

Later in the month, we had two delegates booked into Mr Campbell's Project Management course and I had four provisional bookings to chase up. At a date I had yet to decide upon, we would be holding a phantom open day at Chimera Ltd, for which we would be claiming over two thousand pounds in expenses. I would also be trying to sell a copy of a library package to a Peterborough law firm for three times what the authors of the package would receive.

One thing I was putting off, was preparing my

training course. Joanne had brought it up.

"Me - teaching?"

"It was your idea. Do you not remember?"

"It was a joke."

"You'd be surprised how many good ideas started off as jokes."

"And how many bad ones."

"Never been in a relationship with a teacher before. Might lead to some interesting role play."

Rachel identified a little-used room on the third floor as the ideal venue. My first class was to be three days on 'The Prevention of Computer Fraud and e-Crime'. It seemed appropriate.

We already had nine delegates paying a total of five thousand seven hundred and sixty pounds including accommodation. I still had my doubts. I knew I would be nervous, and most novice teachers don't need to worry about the police bursting in to remove them. Even without the police, I had a class to convince, and I had visions of one of them standing up and denouncing me as a fraud. After working through the applications I suspected this would Clive Hunter, whom I visualised as a thin, pointed-nosed man in glasses.

I was going to do it, though. We had a full set of course notes from AJA, and Joanne had more or less convinced me I was good enough. For her part, Rachel had done everything bar receiving a signed authorisation from the MD to reassure me that I wouldn't be interrupted. My experience with Bill Stapleton had made me bolder. I was learning how to bluff, and enjoy it.

AJA was in a state of financial and organisational chaos despite the steady flow of business into which our customers merged. Rachel kept us up to date with the latest rumours of mergers, friendly take-overs, hostile take-overs and everything in between. There was constant talk of boardroom putsches, redundancies and bankruptcy. All this made it easier for us to operate our business and, for example, to wander out of the building with new PC's, which Rachel had ordered specially, in waterproof covers under our arms.

Love Training was doing well. We even joked about launching our own Platinum Card scheme. All the time, though, we know that we had to be ready to fold convincingly at any moment, especially if one of the rumoured take-overs actually materialised, or the panicking senior management finally broke and let the auditors through. In either event, Rachel would stay on long enough to fend off any unwanted enquiries and collect her redundancy money. This gave our adventure a reassuring safety net.

The horse below me trotted forwards comfortably and at times even seemed to be following my instructions. The stable lass had enough confidence in me to ride ahead without looking round. I had never really considered the attractiveness of women on horseback before, now I began to understand.

I filled my lungs with country air, and refreshed my eyes with the lines of autumnal golds, browns and reds. At the edge of a field, I made a passable 'click-click giddyup' noise with my tongue, and moved the reins to turn the horse back to the yard. He turned as requested which was very satisfying. He probably wanted to go back to the yard anyway, which made it a lot easier, but that was fine. Ballet in London tomorrow night with Joanne, and a business meeting back in the Lodge the next day.

****

The ballet was good; the business meeting less so.

"Liquidation? First I've heard - and I'm there remember."

"So am I, Tony," said Rachel. "They're accepting the first offer that will get them out of it."

"But that's been on the cards for ages. We've known that."

I looked at Joanne. She said nothing.

"This is different," Rachel insisted. "And we've already had one serious scare. That solicitor."

"That was weeks ago."

"It could happen again. Or they could come back to

us."

"I thought you sorted it."

"I did, eventually - but even Graham thought it was a bit strange. I'm not sure he'd let it go again."

“You didn’t sound so worried at the time.”

“Perhaps I should have been. Anyway, it’s all changing now. They’re bringing in a team from outside. Auditing, spot checks, the lot.”

“When?”

“Soon. I don’t know exactly.”

“We could scale down - see what happens.”

“No, Tony, it’s time we got out. And Joanne agrees.”

“There’s a surprise.”

Joanne still said nothing.

“It is different now,” Rachel repeated. Time’s running out.”

I had a moment of hope. If Joanne agreed with her why wasn’t she saying anything? Did she just want to ditch Rachel? Perhaps she wanted me to bring her into this so it looked less of a betrayal to Rachel.

“You don’t agree with her do you, Joanne?”

“No, Tony. I do. She’s right.”

“Which you know how? Woman’s fucking intuition?"

"Listen, Tony."

"No." I stood up. "You listen."

****

The following morning I sat in the main dining room with a cafe latte and a couple of croissants, looking out over the great expanse of grounds that I had come to consider my own. They issued my meals now without even a cursory glance at my card. I could quite easily have lived there for years, and if they tried to get rid of me, I could probably have got on the payroll and claimed redundancy. That would have required a little help from Rachel, though.

"End of the picnic, bye-bye honeypot," I mumbled.

It had always been temporary of course. I knew that. It had been agreed from the start, and frequently reasserted. It had been the only sensible approach and its temporary nature was one of its attractions for me, but I wasn't ready for it to end yet. What else would I do? That had been one of the reasons I had been pushing the legitimate side of the business. I had already sold three copies of that library package, and I was sure we could sell more. Joanne and Rachel had listened, but not with any enthusiasm.

"You could do that anywhere, without the rest of this set up, if you wanted to," Rachel had concluded.

But that wasn't the point. The weather had turned, and her mood had turned with it. She was impatient to get away, and she had won over Joanne. Her acquiescence was infuriating. Rachel's arguments were solid enough in some ways. We could leave under cover of the take-over chaos, in safety, with the money we had made - but I wasn't satisfied. There were other options. This was just a convenient excuse, I was sure. I told them as much. Rachel was proposing to kill a thriving business. It was wrong. She had never been happy about me and Joanne either, and she probably liked the idea of killing that too.

"Yes," said Joanne, "It doesn't stop you doing whatever you want with your share."

"No problem at all," said Rachel, "And I'll wish you all the luck in the world - and mean it."

"That means so much to me."

Rachel stood up.

"I'm going home. You OK, Joanne?"

Joanne nodded. I watched Rachel go to the door.

"Talk to you later," said Joanne.

"About me?" Neither of them said anything, so I gave Rachel a last parting shot as she left the room. "I'll say 'Hi' to John for you, should I? God, he had a narrow escape."

"Did you have to?" said Joanne.

"We never liked each other. Paddington Bear stuff and Disney references. Probably has a pink bedroom as well."

"She's right though, and you know it. We've said it all along, and we've taken this as far as we can. Enough's enough."

"I never knew you to be against taking risks."

"There's a point when a risk becomes too big to be worth taking."

"But there's no risk involved with the software business is there? And it's a good idea, you said."

“It is.”

"But not such a good idea that you want to be involved?"

"To be honest, at the moment, no."

"You just want out, don't you?" She didn't disagree. That was bad. Now for the next bit. "So - what about us?"

"Honestly?" she asked.

"Yes." I said it firmly, but suddenly I felt scared.

"Look, Tony, I really don't know. It's never happened before."

"I thought you did this all the time - in your 'open relationship.'"

"No. I haven't. And the thing is - I care about you."

"Funny way of showing it." She was going to say she loved me next. I braced myself.

"But it's not fair on Tom."

"What?"

"Well it isn't."

"So what? You want to go back and play Happy Families do you?" It was a bad phrase - Mrs Bun the Baker's wife. But the best I could do.

"I'm not saying that."

"Sounds like it to me." Again she said nothing. "You want to split up but you haven't got the guts to say it."

"It's not that."

It came to me suddenly. The Golden Rule. Never ignore the blindingly obvious.

"Are you pregnant?"

"No."

"Thank God for that."

"But what if I wanted to be?" I would run a mile. But I wasn't going to let her ludicrously change the subject like this and somehow make it my fault.

"Don't tell me you want children all of a sudden."

"I always have."

"You haven't."

"How do you know?"

"You said."

"I didn't"

"You implied it." She was about to argue, then decided I wasn't worth it. Never a nice thing to see.

"Tony," she explained, "It doesn't matter anyway what I said or you'd thought I'd said."

"It does to me." That made her look uncomfortable at least, which was a start.

"Sorry."

"It's them I feel sorry for. These kids you've apparently always wanted. They'll be just another craze for you. Then what'll happen - when you get bored with them?"

She looked upset at being told she wasn't a good mother.

"You're angry."

"And you're a stupid bitch."

"Tony." She was pleading for me to stop, but also telling me this was the last time she would plead.

"A stupid, selfish, fucking bitch - Tom has my sympathy. He must be some doormat."

We were not about to have sex, nor was it likely that we soon would, so I thought I might as well storm out.

"And listen, Joanne, just to give you some practice for domesticated living, you can look after the guests tomorrow. Breakfast starts at seven."

This wasn't very satisfying but it was the best I could come up with before I did my storming out, after which I was faced, like all stormers, with the practical problem of where to go when the show was over.

Hanlon Hall was a possibility but it was late and I hadn't got my Master key. I wasn't going back for it, and I didn't know which rooms were free, and couldn't find out without Rachel's help. I walked up the drive and rang for Security. Simon, one of the regulars, was on.

"Could you do me a favour, Simon? I can't face the drive back home - I've had a drink anyway - I just need a room for the night. Any chance?"

He grimaced, but not in an unfriendly way.

"Don't tell anyone. I'm not supposed to... Mind the

way things are at the minute," and he disappeared into the back. He emerged after half a minute with a room key. He was about to hand it over when he stopped.

"I need to ask you something." There was something about his expression that worried me. Surely Rachel hadn't left me a trap. I felt exposed and vulnerable, and he was stalling now for no good reason.

"Listen. . . "

"What is it?" I checked my route to the door in case I needed to make a run for it. He came right over to me, and touched my arm. He wasn't a big man or a very fit one. Unless he had already pressed an alarm, I'd be able to push him away and break free.

"Do you know what's really going on with this take-over?" he said, "Off the record so to speak."

"No, I'm sorry, I really don't."

I wished I did. He was a decent family man who had no intention of getting me arrested. The least I could do was give him some worthless reassurance. I had become a very adept liar over the last few weeks, and he deserved the benefit of my talents.

"I've heard lots of rumours, but nothing's set in stone. I think there must be something happening soon - you don't get this much talk for nothing - but as to what. . ." I shrugged.

"No more than that?" He pursed his lips. "I just thought - but if you've heard nothing definite."

"All I can say is - I think you'll be OK."

He smiled. "Yeah?"

I smiled. "Can't guarantee anything though. Not enough information."

"That's just for them at the top, isn't it? We find out after." We both sighed. "Thanks for the key, as well, mate. I'll just pop it behind reception in the morning?"

"Without mentioning my name."

"I've forgotten it already, Simon." He smiled. "I owe you one."

"No you don't. You're all right."

He was a nice man. He had no control over what might happen to him, and anyone dependent on him was like a castaway clinging to a flimsy crate, but he might as well be happy for a while.

****

I had passed a restless angry night. They didn't realise how much I'd put in, how much I'd given up. All I wanted in return was some support in carrying on. I'd sold my flat; risked my neck on a number of occasions and put in some very long hours. Suddenly, all that counted for nothing. I could hear their replies. 'We've got to deal with the situation as it is', 'It's what we agreed' well rehearsed by the two of them in earnest supportive meetings where I had been the agenda. I had thought I was so happy in our triumvirate. Now I realised they had been colluding against me, I didn't know for how long, in what, on a cold autumn morning looked like the premeditated murder of the operation and the exiling of Tony Palmer.

I had always thought that because she was less crazy than Louise, and not as attractive, that Joanne would be easier to negotiate with. I was wrong. She had outflanked me. I should have asked her who she had in mind as the father of her children. Would I have been so bad? If I was, I could always die in a car crash when my second eldest son was twelve.

I carried on brooding over my solitary breakfast. John Mulholland had been right to keep his distance from them. I felt a pang of disloyalty at agreeing with Joanne and Rachel's assessment of him. He had got what he wanted and left. I had under-estimated him. He read people well, made wise decisions, and everybody loved him.

I popped a small piece of cold croissant into my mouth. I knew, deep down, that I was afraid of trying to do anything by myself. I would never have dared to try teaching that course without Joanne's encouragement, and knowing that Rachel was in the background keeping guard.

Even if I could have kept the business going by myself, I knew that here, on my own, I would fast become a lonely oddity. What was I doing riding horses badly and listening to Mozart at three in the morning while tinkering with a spreadsheet? The pair of them had made me dependent while using me for what they wanted. When they withdrew their support, they were surprised at me for falling, and displeased at my resentment.

On the positive side we – I – had succeeded. The money left in the company account was proof of that. Viewed in a detached way, what was happening was simply what was always going to happen. It had all worked very well and it was just unfortunate that its ending coincided with the end of Joanne's interest in sleeping with me. But all the same, I knew that I was being betrayed before I got the chance to betray them. And I probably wouldn't have. I plucked out a piece of croissant. I wanted them to know that I was not going to give in so easily. I wanted to hurt them back.

Then it came to me. I would go on strike, like men used to in the good old days. I would stop them doing what they wanted with the money we had left – which was not as much as I would have liked because they had kept taking those cash dividends. I suspected I knew why now.

Well - not any more. They could hardly prosecute me, and they would be stuck without me. I had more knowledge about our finances than anyone else in the world. I wouldn't actually rob them of their share. Apart from anything else that would have invalidated all my careful book-keeping, and the pride I took in the dignity of my labour. The two of them would have stolen from me quite happily if they had decided they needed the money - and they would have found some way to justify it.

My revenge would be less practical, but that would give it more moral force. I would simply refuse to co-operate for a while. That would make them aware of how much I had contributed and how much I was now hurting. What had Joanne done anyway, apart from exaggerate my ideas and sleep with me when it suited her? And what had Rachel done, apart from defraud her employer and moan about the English weather? The croissants were now a dozen torn and squeezed and pummelled pieces of golden and white dough.

The paths and verges were thick with leaves. I kicked my way through them, muttering to myself like a beneficiary of Care in the Community. They had got me to sell my home. I had no reason to be here any more either, no reason to be anywhere. I had no desire to spend my share of thirty-one thousand pounds on moving to the Mediterranean to develop carcinomas, and no primordial urge to invest it in crates of Pampers.

I would have to find a job again, find somewhere to live again, find someone to sleep with again. I would have to account for this time on my CV. But I was an adult now and I would have to handle that by myself without Mummy or Daddy or my big brother to help me. I hadn't thought about Richard and Louise for a while. Now I did and a few more leaves were angrily scattered as a result.

I was alone. We were all alone really, but the lucky, the cowardly and the stupid don't realise it. I did. And these others – Joanne, Rachel, Richard, Louise, everybody – there was no point in protesting to them, no point in telling them the truth. Anything I said or did would just be twisted and used as justification for the actions which provoked it. I had been trapped and tricked, but it meant I knew more than them, more than anyone. I also knew that I could do with a drink.

CHAPTER 14

I hit the brown firmly into the corner pocket, leaving myself very tight on the blue. My next shot was a good one, but unlucky. The blue ball hit both jaws of the pocket and then stuck on the lip. Meanwhile the cue ball had come around perfectly for the pink. It looked as if I was still trying for position even with such a difficult shot.

Benny gave me a sympathetic shrug and stepped forward to the table. He potted the easy blue and pink with some deliberation.

"Tough. Good game, mate" he said, picking up the notes.

"Yes," I nodded. A good game. Close. I was playing better than I had ever played before. No inhibitions, I smiled to myself; playing for money with hard men.

I had been worried about coming to the snooker hall alone, a friendless failure. When I tired of tearing up croissants and kicking up leaves around Hanlon Hall, I had gone back to The Lodge. Joanne had seen to the guests, got them checked out, and left me a letter, now crumpled up and in the bin. She had asked me to make sure that I cancelled any outstanding bookings. I would not have been so callous; not after dumping me the way she had. To her it was the practical thing to do; and not asking me would have been some kind of admission of guilt. I knew it had to be done, and we both knew I would do it, so I had found myself following her instructions, resentfully.

I had trouble contacting Peter Mason, our last delegate. At three o'clock I finally got through to someone in his office who knew he was on holiday. I left a message and Joanne's number. She could deal with that. There was nobody staying tonight, and tomorrow was the weekend. I finished off a bottle of whisky that had been provided for guests and went to sleep.

When I woke up I had nothing to do and nowhere to go, and there was no drink left in the place. I would go out of my mind shuffling round like Miss Haversham. I wanted company and the only place I could think of was the snooker hall. Why not? There was no need to avoid Gary any more. Things had been wrecked without his involvement, and I couldn't bear to sit here for long by myself. Before I left I snapped my classical CDs (all four of them) and binned them, put on my jacket and emptied the petty cash into my pocket.

As I approached the snooker hall, I warmed to the idea. It was something Joanne - hypocritical, suburban, Yummy-Mum-to-be Joanne - wouldn't understand. I had friends in armed gangs, and they understood loyalty. Gary wouldn't have betrayed and humiliated me. Deep down he was all right. He didn't pretend to care about your every feeling as long as it suited him. He was under-educated and occasionally violent, but he was fundamentally all right. He was solid. He was a friend of mine. From way back.

I went to the bar and looked around. There was no sign of Gary, but someone from that Saturday at the races recognised me and came over. I remembered his name, which was a relief. Brendan Price. It was ironic that I had believed it would have been my companion at the races on the Thursday who would be so important in my life, but she had gone and here I was shaking hands with Brendan. He greeted me with real warmth, then insisted I let him buy me a drink.

"While since we've seen you in here. Been back in Newcastle?"

"I've actually just moved here now - in a way." It was too difficult to explain. Especially if I followed it by trying to explain that I was now moving away again: once I found somewhere to move to. Fortunately, this was a world where it was understood that a man might have good reason for not explaining.

"Gary's away himself at the minute - would you like to join us?"

"Yes, thanks"

He led me to a small group of his mates, introduced me and then disappeared. Over the next twenty minutes three more people volunteered the information that Gary was away. This was obviously news, and I began to suspect that it was probably not good news for Gary. I was starting to feel uneasy when Brendan came back.

He was still friendly and he seemed to be well-respected by the others, despite his social skills. If Gary had fallen out of favour, it had clearly not coloured his view of me. There was no reason why it should. Brendan's approval helped, but even without it, I could justify myself. I was a solid man among solid men. I had until recently been running my own illegal operation here successfully and without fuss. Then came my turn at the snooker table with Benny.

“Benny always plays better when there's money on the table,” Brendan said, when we came back.

"Don't we all?"

“How's your luck been – since you came down here?”

“Off the snooker table – fine.”

Perhaps it would have done no harm to tell him more, but I didn't want to take any risks, especially with the others nearby. Brevity and silence were respected here, and they could fill in the blanks from their own imagination.

"Yourself?"

"Not bad, not bad. This place is doing OK for me now as well," he added casually.

"Oh I thought... it's yours is it?" I asked awkwardly, not sure how much I was supposed to know.

He seemed not to have noticed my surprise. Perhaps it was just tact.

"I'm a partner, you could say, but I wouldn't make a very good minor partner. It's a long time since I was up Newcastle," he continued. I wasn't sure if this was a change of subject or not. "Must be seven or eight years. South Shields. You know it?"

"Yeah right."

"Not a bad place. Lively. Friendly. Good people." I felt pleased, even flattered. I needn't bother explaining that I hadn't lived there for years. "Most of them, most of the time."

"You known Gary long?" I said, enjoying the hint of treachery. He laughed, which was a relief.

"Five or six years. Sound, great crack most of the time. And everybody makes some unwise decisions, don't they? I don't blame him myself. Do you know Fiona?"

"His wife?" I shook my head. "No."

"I'm sure she's a great wife and mother. If that's what he wants... But for me it's like the fire's gone from him, and what's somebody like Gary without the fire, know what I mean?"

"Yes," I said with feeling, "They do that to you."

"If you let them. I'm not one of those that say they should be in the kitchen or looking after the kids all the time, if they don't want to." I watched him with interest.

"Margaret Thatcher, Indira Ghandi, that woman from

the Body Shop," he was about to add another name but stopped himself. "No, any idiot can read the news. But they are different."

"Hormones."

"Yes."

"Worst is being in business with them," I confided.

"Not sure I've ever done that."

"Wise man. You think you're speaking the same language, then suddenly the hormones kick in, and everything changes. All very civilised and caring, but actually they're dropping you in the shit. It's like you've been thinking and seeing and hearing completely different things all along, and it's only now you realise. They are different." Brendan nodded and smiled. Misogyny was easy and satisfying. I should have tried it before.

Someone came over with drinks, then went away, knowing better than to interrupt for too long. We seemed to understand each other very well. It was certainly easier then talking to Gary.

"Was this in Newcastle?"

"Was what?"

"This business that went sour?"

"No. That was here. That's what brought me."

"You moved here for this business?" He sounded impressed. "I like that. Lot of people here don't have the same energy, you know? Like Gary used to."

"It helped that I was screwing her as well." That got a big laugh. It wasn't really fair on Joanne; she had been more than that. She still could be if she'd had the wit to realise. But I wasn't going to wait forever.

"In fairness it was partly her idea. But it was me who ran it and made things actually happen. I took the chances."

"Someone always has to." Too right. "It's all about ownership. So what was it? The business? I'll understand if you don't want to tell me. But I am a discreet man." I liked the fact he could use words like 'discreet'.

"You know that training place just outside of town?"

"Hanlon Hall? Computers isn't it? Business courses?"

"We put people in there. On their courses and took the money. Eight hundred quid a pop on average and no overheads."

"Simple as that?"

"I'd still be there now, if that woman I was telling you about – well there two of them. . . "

"Outnumbered as well? Shit."

"Too right."

"How long was it going?"

"Not that long. A few months. Had other things on the go as well. Some of it legitimate - not quite as lucrative but they helped us spread the money. That place is just asking for it. It's on the rocks, going to get taken over soon, but until it is...honeypot. One of them wants to go to Greece for her health for fuck's sake and the other one wants to have babies." I shook my head.

"Sounds a bit messy, mate," said Brendan.

"Messy is right."

"But I don't understand why you had to walk away as well."

He was right.

"You're right." It wasn't Joanne's idea, it was mine. And they had held me back, managed me, let me do all the work, while making me think they were helping me. Sex. It had blinded me again.

"I hadn't seen that," I admitted. "Sleeping with someone can cloud your judgement." Brendan smiled.

"I didn't want to say, but. . . "

"Women are different. The only reason, fundamentally, that a man who isn't gay doesn't have sex with almost any woman who's willing to, is other women. And it's not the same with them."

"Either that or they're better liars," he added.

"Which they are," I said, pleased with my wit, and Brendan laughed again.

"Drink?"

"My shout."

"No – I get them in here, Tony. Please."

"OK, then. Bitter, thanks. Hope I'm not boring you."

Brendan reassured me I was not. As I smiled back, a man I did not recognise approached our table a little hesitantly. I welcomed him and he joined us, although he had been expecting to get approval from Brendan. Well he was getting it from me now instead.

"Paul, Tony. Tony Palmer." Nod and shake as Brendan went to his bar.

Tony Palmer made small talk with Paul. Tony Palmer, who had been about to get on a train and run away; who thought he had no friends and no status. I had never thought about status before.

"You're from Newcastle?" said Paul, impressed.

"Aye, been down here a few months now, though."

"Like it?"

"Yes, I do. There just seems so many possibilities here."

There were. Getting away from Joanne and Rachel made me realise that. I could do it all again. My way. And no mistakes this time. There really were so many possibilities. Brendan came back from the bar with a tray. And so many drinks. That wasn't a problem either. I'd show them how much I could drink; they were my kind of people and I understood their code.

CHAPTER 15

I peered out from behind the curtain. It was light now but still quiet. My memories of the night before were vague but worrying. The faces and voices at my table had become blurred as time went on, but I knew that Brendan had gone and come back again a number of times, and I had carried on drinking and talking. So much talking. I had woken suddenly out of a dream in shock. The dream had been a disturbing one, but the details melted away before I was able to catch them, and anyway I was too busy trying to piece together the real nightmare of the day before.

I went down to the lounge. The television was still on and my shoes, socks and two open cans of beer were on the floor by the settee. There was the note from Joanne lying there as well. I had fished it out of the bin when I got in last night, though I couldn't remember getting around to reading it. Wearing only my jeans and standing barefoot on the prickly carpet in the middle of the room I looked it over again.

Dear Tony,

I've sorted out the guests and everything is where you would expect it to be. I've gone back home but I'll try and get in touch over the weekend or early in the week. I'm sorry - genuinely sorry - but things were going too far and too fast. I very much hope we will be able to sort things out properly next week. I'll try very hard. I've got so much out of this adventure. Thank you for sharing it with me. I'm so glad I went on that Project Management course.

Look after yourself and have a good weekend,
talk to you soon, take care

love,

Joanne.

PS Could you sort out cancelling any outstanding bookings?

I put it back on the table, and slowly, thoughtfully pulled on my socks. I seemed to have spilt beer on them. They were still damp but I couldn't be bothered to go and get clean ones. I picked up the note and read it again, taking more in this time. It didn't seem like the same note I had read the day before; it seemed friendlier, more conciliatory. My brain was very gradually picking up speed, and had now linked up with my memory and vocabulary store.

Had I rung her last night? No, I didn't think so. Good. She was obviously feeling guilty. I didn't think I'd ever been wished so much happiness and good fortune in such a limited space of time before in my life. How did she propose I go about having a 'Good weekend'? I had been planning on spending it with her - what would I do now? Poor Tony. I felt sorry for myself. Then I moved back to more pressing and worrying matters.

I had talked about the business a lot, I felt sure of that, but I hadn't actually taken my new-found friends to the main doors of Hanlon Hall to launch a hostile take-over. The fact that the possibility had occurred to me was disturbing enough. Just talk. I had a dim memory of arranging for Brendan to come around here - but I wasn't sure for what. To discuss business? To sell him the business? To try to impress him a bit more? I could hardly ask him what I had said.

I wished Joanne was here, then again I was glad she wasn't - especially if I managed to get away with this. Brendan might just dismiss it all as drunken rubbish. He could laugh it off; his opinion of me could fall as low as he liked. I didn't care as long as I could just sneak away. Just a little bit of luck now please, I prayed. I was still standing and I twisted one skinny leg around the other in supplication. If he didn't come by mid-day I could assume the whole thing was forgotten about.

The bell rang. It had a heavy, hollow, echoing ring, which filled the building, then left it very silent. My mouth tasted awful. I hadn't had a cup of tea or even a drink of water yet. At the very least I needed a chance to think and even that was being denied me. I could pretend to be still in bed, but I didn't want to upset the people at the door.

Time was passing, and I had not even moved from the spot. I wanted to go to the window to see who was there, but I didn't want to be seen sneaking around behind sideboards and coat-stands like a comedy fugitive. Besides it might be someone else entirely, someone unconnected with the criminal underworld - a window cleaner, the Betterware man, a tourist looking for rooms, a knife-sharpener. If it was, I would not have any knives sharpened; I didn't like the idea of there being potential weapons around.

The bell sounded again. I was going to have to go and find out who it was. I could make out a silhouette through the frosted glass of the door. For a moment I let myself hope that perhaps it was Joanne, rushing back to acknowledge her mistake and help me through this predicament between episodes of agonisingly pleasurable sex. But that was not the way she operated.

After tugging at the door for a moment, I realised I must have managed to put the deadlock on last night, so by the time I actually managed to open it, I was already in quite an advanced state of panic. It was sufficient to bring on my hangover headache.

It was not Joanne, nor a harmless innocent selling

household goods at low prices. It was a small man with pallid skin tight on his face, and cold, murderous eyes. He was wearing a good suit and spoke slowly with a trace of a London accent.

"Mr Palmer? I'm sorry to disturb you. I know I am early." I indicated that this was not a problem. "I hope I find you well this morning," and he smiled with a pretence of warmth.

His eyes were almost black, and bulged like two grapes. He was the most frightening person I had ever opened a door to. "I am Gordon Proctor - Mr Price's accountant."

"Oh," I managed, trying to dry my palm before it met his small leathery hand.

"Mr Price will be along shortly, as arranged, but I hope you have no objection to me coming along in advance. Perhaps you have some accounts I could see while we are waiting." I stumbled through an "Oh do come in" routine and begged him to sit down while I ran around opening curtains and windows.

I didn't know whether to feel frightened or foolish (I suspected both were appropriate), and my head was now clanging too much to permit coherent thought. I knew I hadn't got away with this one though; and I knew I was sweating. I wondered how I looked, and smelt - a mixture of sweat, and stale alcohol, and fear, in the crumpled clothes I had slept in.

I kept our bodies as far apart as possible while I escorted him up to my study. I hope he wouldn't misunderstand anything from the fact that the first thing he would see was my unmade bed. He made no comment, and I sat him at my desk with a spreadsheet on the PC, a pile of floppies by his left hand, and a few folders containing letters, receipts, addresses and advertisements by his right.

I made my excuses and raced to the bathroom to freshen up. I locked the door and turned on the shower; then checked again that the door was locked before undressing. I had one foot and most of one leg under the spray when the bell rang again.

I stepped straight out again; rolled on some anti-perspirant in a frenzy, pulled on my shirt and trousers, grabbed my shoes and socks and rushed out of the bathroom. I didn't want to inconvenience Gordon by making him answer the door, but at the same time, the idea of disappearing through the bathroom window and letting them move in and help themselves to whatever they wanted appealed to me immensely.

Halfway down the stairs, I stopped. There was no sound of movement from Gordon. I grabbed hold of the banister with one hand, pulled my feet into the damp flapping socks, and forced them into my shoes. Then I bolted downstairs, my feet squelching slightly in my unfastened shoes, my shirt flapping open and, I suddenly realised, smelling strongly of Boots Freshwood, like a nervous teenager on a first date. I steadied myself in the hallway, wiped my hands on my jeans, fastened a button or two on my shirt and opened the door to two men.

"Well, hello there," emerged from me with a jauntiness more appropriate to Leslie Philips at the tennis club than my present situation.

Brendan looked surprised but he managed a gruff and not altogether unfriendly 'hello'. The other man, whom I could not remember seeing before, had the look of a tough, successful small businessman, who did not mind using unorthodox methods when necessary. I felt a fresh wave of fear as they crossed the threshold. I wanted to cry, but that would have embarrassed Brendan, so I stopped myself. Already I was afraid that he was ashamed of me in my present state: damp, hungover, half-naked and friendless. I fastened another button or two but decided against tucking my shirt in at this moment. My face was still prickly and wet. Brendan made the best of things.

"This is Tony Palmer I was telling you about. An old friend of Gary's," he paused, "From the old days. Before he lost interest in snooker clubs and the more adventurous side of business."

The two conceded each other tough smiles. I grinned despite my growing nausea. Among the fears jockeying for position in my mind emerged one that I would vomit on the carpet in front of them. I breathed in heavily and slowly and deliberately. Brendan introduced his companion.

"And this is Alex Gianolli."

I made an involuntary unvoiced 'R' sound, like someone blowing on a window to steam it up, and I leant forward, a little further than I intended, as I shook hands with him, so that I was slightly off-balance. His hand was big and solid and warm and strong. He even smiled slightly and I felt absurdly pleased - I wanted him to like me. The situation could have been worse. I could have told him how impressed I was with his handshake and asked him if I reminded him of Leslie Philips. I nearly fell over when he released my hand.

I wouldn't do well under torture. At times, particularly during the seams of piety and austerity which shot through my childhood and early adolescence, I had believed that I would have been stoical and strong. Perhaps then I would have been, but not now, when adulthood saw me reduced to record-breaking levels of suggestibility.

"I hope you didn't have a problem with Gordon coming along first. We thought it would be useful to have some idea of the financial realities of the operation before talking, and Alex has got a lot on today." Including clean underpants and dry socks, I thought, bitterly.

"No, you were quite right," I managed, "Always a pleasure." That received a strange look.

"Right, then. I mentioned one or two things to Alex about your . . . operations next door," he threw his hand in the direction of Hanlon Hall, "And he detects possibilities. As we all do."

"Not just possibilities," Mr Gianolli corrected gently, and to me, "I hear talk of fifteen thousand a week, possibly twenty."

I shrugged politely and modestly, to suggest that this could be a slightly optimistic view. I thought it best not to tell him we had actually been making about a tenth of that.

He acknowledged my qualification.

"You think that may be an optimistic assessment, but we have a large organisation - and our own methods. I understand you wanting to grow your business; good ideas deserve to be developed."

He did seem genuinely interested, even impressed. Perhaps this was unsurprising; it was hard to imagine any of the snooker hall thugs coming up with anything as original or daring as we had. I wished he had been a little less impressed.

"Where's Gordon?" asked Brendan Price.

The idea of being in my bedroom with the three of them was too much.

"I'll get him." I offered.

"We'll come with you," said Brendan.

"No. It's fine."

"We'll come with you."

So that was settled. They were coming with me. I had the feeling that this was a taste of things to come.

"It's just a temporary office space," I explained on the stairs. "We are converting from a B&B."

"Why?" asked Mr Gianolli. It seemed a very good question.

"That's what it was," I said.

It did not sound like a good answer. Not only did it sound childish, it could have been interpreted as implying that I thought the question was a stupid one. That wasn't my intention. It was a good question, and I certainly did not want to give offence to the man asking it.

Gordon turned from the screen as we came in. I felt very vulnerable. The only time I had had company in this room before it had been Joanne.

"Well?" That was from Brendan to Gordon.

"Would you like to sit down?" I interrupted clumsily, but they paid me no attention.

"Possibilities, definite possibilities," said Gordon.

"Not too many outgoings there, eh?" I joked. "Of course it's all up in the air at the moment."

"I'll need two or three days," Gordon said to Brendan who was now at his shoulder, "There's a lot to wade through; and they could have done with a proper accountant."

There was no need for that, I thought. I found myself looking at Brendan for support. He gave me none.

"What are you planning exactly?" I said, quite loudly.

Brendan didn't reply immediately, but he did turn around, for which I was grateful.

"What you have here interests us. Isn't that right, Alex?" Alex nodded slightly.

"We may wish to become involved, once we've had a chance to assess the financial situation, and the logistics and risks a little more thoroughly. Then we'll come back to you."

Gordon had turned away from the spreadsheet in the middle of this and was watching me. I felt I was being assessed as well and I didn't like it much.

"But of course nothing's definite yet, I suppose, is it? Would you like a cup of tea, coffee?"

"No," said Gordon.

"No thanks."

That was Brendan being polite, rather than me correcting Gordon. I turned to Alex who shook his head once, and then spoke.

"In the meantime we will need full access to your information, and yourself."

"Right."

"Who else is involved in your operation? Brendan tells me you mentioned a woman."

"Oh there are - were - partners," I was terrified they

would ask me for their addresses, "But there's no need to worry about them. Perhaps if you went away and considered it, and came back with your proposals - if you were still interested."

They didn't like that. There was a change in Brendan's tone when he next spoke.

"You're an outsider, Tony, so perhaps you don't fully understand. We run things in this town. Ordinarily we wouldn't allow something like this to take place here without our involvement or at least our approval. We are making an exception here, but that will only be continued if we are sure we have your full co-operation. If that changes... " He waited for a few seconds before continuing.

When he did, he resumed his lighter tone. It was such a relief I could have kissed him.

"But as you say everything can be discussed once we have all had time to consider. You have compete freedom of movement around the Hall?" I nodded. "Perhaps you will take us around later."

Of course I had no keys, and anyway I could think of nothing more foolhardy than wandering round there on a Saturday morning with two conspicuous and possibly well-known criminals, and their sinister accountant. I might have disagreed with Joanne and Rachel at times, but this was altogether different, altogether worse. I didn't want this at all. I felt something like anger rise up in me, buoyed up by fear, and wanting rid of fear.

I needed time, a little chink of time that I could lever, first into a definite gap, and then into a larger space through which I could escape. I decided to risk voicing a slight disagreement.

"Yes, but we would be very conspicuous on a Saturday morning."

From their faces I could see that my gamble had paid off. They had to accept I had a point. Brendan half-nodded in acknowledgement. I grew bolder. After all, they needed me more than I needed them. I ought to remind them of that. Perhaps they would respect me more if I stood up to them.

"We all need some time to think this through," I said. "Clarify our positions. Can I get back to you and talk it through later in the week, after we've had some time?"

For the first time, Alex reacted. He glanced towards Brendan, with the hint of a frown. I realised the weight of disapproval this implied, and tried to pacify him.

"As I say everything's up in the air, and I'm obviously flattered and very interested in your interest," I was faltering, "And of course I'm sure that we'll be able to co-operate to our mutual advantage."

"I think I will have a coffee," said Brendan quite calmly. "I'll come with you," and almost before I realised it he had steered me out of the room and towards the staircase. It occurred to me how much damage the human body could suffer in falling down a flight of stairs. Brendan made me walk in front of him so I held tightly to the banister while we descended in silence. I reached the bottom without sustaining any broken bones.

"Kitchen's there," I said, half raising my arm to point and explain where I was going and why.

He remained silent, but I knew he wanted me to lead the way so I did. I knew I had crossed some line and I was afraid of what was coming at the end of this silence. My scrotum tightened, and I realised I was beginning to shake at the thought of boiling water. As I plugged in the kettle I heard him close the door. I went to the cupboard to take out cups and sugar. Had he said tea or coffee? He watched me placing the cups on the side.

"Sorry, but was it tea or coffee?" I asked, and finally looked at him. He was playing with a delicate bone china milk jug, dropping it slowly from hand to hand now.

"I don't think," he said, slowly and thoughtfully, "You are fully aware of your situation. And I don't think it is wise for you to demonstrate that in front of someone as impressionable as Mr Gianolli."

Impressionable, I suspected, was a euphemism for psychotic. The beat of my heart was affecting my ability to hear and I didn't want to miss anything but it was hard to concentrate while anticipating the shock of the jug falling from his hand and breaking. I wanted to ask about tea and coffee again, to pretend that was the reason we were here, but I stopped myself. I didn't want to upset him more than I already had. He was probably very impressionable as well.

"There may be a place for you in our operations. We will tell you if this is the case. We may choose to incorporate your business directly, or allow you to operate with our protection.." He was watching me closely, in as measured a way as he was speaking.

"We have the means to enforce our decisions which it would be unwise for you to bring upon yourself. We even have valuable influence within the police. We'll go now. Will you make sure Gordon has all the information he might need?"

"Yes. Of course."

I felt very grateful towards him again - just as I had in the club the night before. He was good at that.

"If there is anything you need in that time, you may arrange with him to borrow it, although from what you told me, your affairs are in suspension at the moment?" I nodded. "Are you free on Monday morning?" I nodded again.

"Then I will see you here at ten. This could be profitable and rewarding for both of us. If you meant what you said last night, then this could be your opportunity. Don't mess up, Tony."

"No. It's all just a bit sudden," I hoped he might understand. I felt better when he said my name. His tone had softened, and part of his threat had been, I almost smiled, the police. Perhaps he was as soft and reasonable as he had seemed last night. Best of all they were leaving.

"If you withhold anything, it will be taken as a sign of non-cooperation, and I would advise you to cooperate."

I remembered the bookie who had been killed a few months earlier. He looked hard at me. He had something else to say; probably a reminder of what happened to those who did not cooperate. Like the bookie. Or possibly Gary.

"Do you remember Victoria?" he asked. "She works for me."

He smiled contemptuously, then he threw the jug, underarm, and not hard, towards me. I caught it with both hands, just below waist height, then followed him back out of the kitchen still clutching it.

"I'm going now," Brendan said at the bedroom door. Alex got to his feet and came towards us.

"Yes. I've seen enough."

"I'd like to take some material away with me," said Gordon. Alex puckered his lips and raised his eyebrows in assent. He couldn't be expected to work in the bedroom of a man like me.

"Of course," I said. "I'll get you a bag to carry them in."

All I could find, apart from suitcases was a plastic Harrods shopping bag. I gave it to Gordon who gently dropped files and floppy discs into it without a word.

"If we need anything else we'll let you know. I've got your number here. Otherwise, I'll see you on Monday."

"Thank you. Goodbye," I responded. "Goodbye. Thank you."

I followed them to the door, which Brendan pulled shut behind him, and then they were, finally, gone. Leaning against the door, I listened to two BMW's drive away; then I slouched despondently back into the lounge.

My first instinct was to blame Joanne. I had known all along that I shouldn't have got involved in this. I had known I was not suited to crime - and now I was dealing with proper criminals. I realised I was still holding the jug. It was something Joanne had bought in an antique shop a few weeks ago. It had seemed like a waste of money, a very middle-aged thing to do, but it was the same as one she remembered her Grandmother having when she was a little girl.

Then I blamed myself. I had given them all our information, and nearly let them break her precious milk jug. It was all down to me getting drunk and shouting my mouth off in front of all those men. There was no chance of going back now; I had ruined everything. If they had asked me, I knew I would have given them her address.

I bent down to put the jug on the low coffee table and then sat on the floor next to it and cried a little. Brendan Price was not a nice man. He had fooled me last night, and now he scared me.

"There's absolutely no talking to him," I sobbed out ridiculously.

After a while I raised my head and looked about me like someone just waking up. The house was quiet and empty. I felt bereft, as if someone I loved had just walked out. Perhaps they had; I didn't even know what I felt any more.

There was an unpleasant sensation inside my skull. I could feel the chemicals of depression being released and seeping through my brain like liquid through a sponge. I knew from experience that the answer to this was activity, but what activity? I wished Joanne was there to hold me and reassure me, and perhaps take me to bed for a while. But she wasn't, and if she had been, then I knew that I would have been disappointed in, at the very least, the last of these things. If I had been stronger I would have been glad she was not there to see me humiliated, and at risk herself, but I wasn’t that strong. A plan was forming in my mind. Flight. It was not a clever plan, but I could see no alternative, and it was activity of a sort.

I emptied the safe of cash, and put the cheques in my wallet. I went upstairs to dress properly, definitely feeling less nauseous now. It was a temporary respite. It would come back, but I was grateful for it. I just had to get to the station and away. The telephone rang. It was probably Joanne. I rushed to the top of the stairs and then stopped.

No. I let it ring, and went back to the bedroom to pack.

CHAPTER 16

Before I left the Lodge, I set the place up to look as if I was intending to come back. I set the video to record the Brookside Omnibus, and I left a copy of 'Computer Weekly' on the television open at an advert for a computer warehouse in Reading. I even circled Monday in the calendar in the kitchen and wrote "Brendan 10-00" inside.

I had packed the biggest bag I could find with clothes, leaving enough behind to make it look as though I would be coming back. I put Joanne's new letter in the folder with my other mementoes of her, along with any other papers which might lead them to me, and crammed them in as well. I walked to the station because I was afraid Brendan might have friends in mini-cab firms. I kept off the main streets for fear of being seen, and finally I reached the station, sweating with the exertion and the stress. I bought tickets for both Reading and London, and waited anxiously behind a photo booth, until the train came in. When it eventually arrived, I walked briskly to an empty carriage, sat in a corner with another 'Computer Weekly' open in my lap, then closed my eyes. I wanted to avoid recognition, even casual conversation with strangers who might have dangerous connections. When the train finally shuddered into life, I opened my eyes a little to check that the carriage was still empty. It was. As we pulled out of the station and picked up speed, the thrill of successful escape shot through me. There was no need to get off at Reading, but I stayed wary. I wasn't safe yet.

Just past Reading, a youth with a Birmingham accent got on and tried to strike up a conversation.

"On holiday, mate?" I made a noise. He had been looking at my bag. "I'm living down here now myself. From Birmingham originally, like. Names's Jason."

He would have put out his hand for a shake given any encouragement but he got absolutely none. Normally, I would have chatted back, mate, but I didn't want to be remembered on this journey, so I said nothing. It was rude. But it worked; he went quiet. These were amazing times: first I had discovered the pleasures of lying, and now the advantages of being rude

The Home Counties countryside flashed by. Then houses sprang up and place names familiar from the Boat Race, and the Thames with its bridges and Parliament looking like a life-size model of itself, and finally Waterloo, and the end of my journey. I was reassured by the size of the city we had passed through; it seemed like a good place to hide.

In Waterloo, I glanced around for any familiar unfriendly faces. There were none. I was glad I had dropped my idea of changing trains on the way, to check that I wasn't being followed. It would have been so typical to have messed things up by over-complicating my plans, and walking straight into Brendan on the next train.

I took a tube to Victoria and booked into The Regents off Buckingham Palace Road for a week as Mr Lawson. I was upstairs and safe in my hotel room within three hours of leaving the Lodge.

I sat on the bed to ponder my next move. I had not really given it much thought on the train. I had been enjoying the drama of my escape too much; I remember surprising myself humming at one point. Now that I had got myself away, I had to think clearly. I had less than two days before Brendan and the rest would find out that I had gone. It was the only advantage I had, but I didn't know how to use it. I had no idea how they would react, and no way of finding out what they were doing. They were not reasonable men. This hotel room now, before they found out I had betrayed them, was the safest I would ever be. I had nowhere to go. And I was lonely.

I had to tell Joanne and Rachel before they found out for themselves, or something unpleasant happened to them because they did not know. I felt a pang of guilt at exposing them to this risk, even though Joanne hadn't felt much guilt at what she had done to me. Best done now. I picked up the phone, and then put it down again. Hotel telephones could be listened in on. Besides they were twice as expensive as phone boxes, and I would have to be careful with my money.

I thought about money again as I went down in the lift. I could withdraw it from the company account, but doing that would show where I was, and Brendan would be looking at the company bank statements, possibly with his friends in the police. It was too much to think about right now. One thing at a time.

Once outside I headed towards a call box. I walked across a small park with railings around it. It was more like a large shared garden than a park. I wondered if I was trespassing. Another crime. I had to be careful now.

This conversation was going to be unpleasant. I looked enviously at the birds tweetering away happily in the branches, and at the gormless, carefree tourists and students intent on their pointless anxiety-free activity. I felt jealousy I had not felt since Louise. God, she was back in my head again.

The phone box was empty and smelt only slightly of alcohol-rich urine. I lifted the handset cautiously. The display indicated that it was working. I took two deep breaths, away from the possibly polluted mouthpiece, tapped in Joanne's number, and then waited, reading advertisements for 0898 numbers offering humiliation at the hands of strict, blond sixteen year olds. That would definitely be preferable to this.

"Joanne?"

"Hello, Tony," she replied neutrally.

"How are you doing?"

"OK. I've been trying to get hold of you." She didn't sound friendly, although if she knew what had happened, surely she wouldn't be sounding as calm as this.

"Something's happened."

"Yes, I know."

"You do?"

"Yes, and I'd like to know how they got my home number."

"God. Sorry. It wasn't me - not deliberately anyway. It must have just been in the stuff they took away." I had been wrong thinking I was safe even for today in my hotel bedroom.

"It was difficult - I wasn't on my own when they rang."

"Sorry, Joanne." But the fact that she sounded so calm gave me hope that she had somehow managed to get us out of this. Please, miracle. Unless she had sacrificed me to them. I mustn't say where I was. I couldn't trust her now even though she had nearly loved me once, and would probably would have loved me properly, if circumstances had been different.

"What are we going to do then?" I asked.

"Eh?"

"About . . . them."

"I just told him we couldn't do it," she said simply.

The miracle was happening. I would have given

anything at this point just to be free, and she had somehow just done it.

"I said there'd been a mix up. I think they were satisfied with that." She was amazing; I missed her more than ever now. "Anyway they aren't coming. But they shouldn't have been in the first place. I knew nothing about it."

"They aren't coming," I repeated slowly.

"No. And I think it's a warning. We'll have to check we've not missed anybody else. I did ask you to cancel any outstanding you know."

"We are talking about the same thing aren't we? Brendan?"

"Brendan? Who's Brendan?" she said. We weren't. "I'm talking about Peter Mason. If the money's gone they'll need a refund."

"No. There's something really bad happened." I put in a pound coin, "Very bad. Seriously."

"Yes, you've given out my home number to a customer," she said.

"We've been found out."

"Found out? Who by?" she said quickly, but calmly. She didn't sound frightened or angry. I could have loved her again for that. It gave me some hope again.

"Brendan. He's a local gangster," I added helpfully.

"A gangster? What are you talking about? Gangsters?"

"I know. You wouldn't think you'd get gangsters there

would you - in the countryside?"

"Are you drunk?"

"No, no, no. Look, I'm in hiding."

"You're what?"

"I had to get away. It's not safe there - for any of us."

She wasn't sounding frightened yet, but anger was surfacing.

"I still don't know what you're talking about. This isn't some kind of joke is it?" I was impatient and at last she had given me the chance to correct her.

"No. Of course it isn't." Better not overplay it though.

"I should have asked you before, Tony, but have you ever had mental health problems?"

"No." She didn't sound convinced. I tried to sound as sane and organised as possible.

"Listen Joanne, we'd all better keep away until things calm down. I'll check everything's cancelled. It's finished, I know that. But look, these are dangerous people, and they want to take over. They've got friends in the police as well. There's an Italian. You know what that might mean. Mafia. Not definitely, but... I know it sounds," I struggled for a word, "Fanciful. But if you'd been there. . . Sorry."

"Look, Tony, this is making absolutely no sense to me. What do you mean - the Mafia? And slow down, for God's sake."

I decided to begin my confession with a statement

that she would agree with.

"It's all my fault." I paused. "I let one or two things slip - in the snooker hall."

"What snooker hall?"

"Brendan's. He's a gangster with an accountant and a friend called Signor Gianolli, and they want in. And I don't know what to do. I'm sorry. Very, very sorry. And I had to give them all our books, finances and stuff. Had to. They would have just taken them anyway. He's a frightening man, Joanne. If I don't co-operate, I don't like to think what might happen, and I'm not co-operating. I've run off. They're involved with lots of bad stuff. Prostitution, gambling - do you remember that bookie who got killed when we went to the races?" That seemed a very long time ago.

"You have got me worried now. You'd better not be making this up."

"No," I wailed and that seemed to convince her. "I'll explain properly when I get the chance. I've been wrong about things before but not this time." She was quiet. "Just tell me you'll keep away, for your own safety. And will you tell Rachel?" I put in another fifty pence.

"No. Apart from anything else I don't know what it is I'm telling her."

"Please, just tell her to keep away, and be on her guard. I picked up the last cheques," I added in a vain attempt to strike a positive note. "Look I'm out of change and the money's about to go."

"Don't you dare," her anger was rising, "What's the number there?"

"There's people outside waiting. Look, I'll ring you back. When? Er - Monday? It's going, sorry, goodbye. Tell Rachel," I reminded her.

"No - you tell her."

Her last syllable was swallowed up as I pressed the end call button. It had been a while since I had fallen so far, so fast in someone's estimation. I walked back across the little park to the hotel. The queen lived only half a mile or so down the road.

"You've had yours," I muttered. "I think my Annus Horribilis is just about to kick in now."

I had a drink in the bar - a half of lager, which cost two pounds forty. There was a piano player in the corner, entertaining Americans with extracts from musicals, and there were complimentary newspapers. For the same price, I could had eight times as much alcohol if I'd gone for cider in a plastic bottle in the park. That was ahead of me, but for now I treated myself. I loved it, and more so because I knew I'd have to leave it to ring Rachel; Joanne had been adamant about that.

I eked it out for as long as I could, then trudged back to my phone box and dialled Rachel's landline. I tried to control my breathing and my heartbeat as it rang. After six rings, it clicked - an answering machine. She was out, that was good.

"Hello, Rachel. This is Tony, Tony Palmer. I'm ringing to tell you that there are a few problems at work. Some people we don't want to, have started interfering." That sounded strange, but it was too late now to change it.

“I'd keep away from things to do with it, until you've spoken to Joanne. If you give her a ring she'll be able to give you more details. Don't do anything until you've spoken to her."

I didn't like speaking on answering machines, but it was far preferable to speaking to Rachel herself. I wondered if she was sitting in the room listening, and about to cut in.

"I'll try and get hold of you later," I lied, speaking more quickly, "But ring Joanne." This message was recorded. It could be kept and listened to by others, "I'm in Birmingham by the way. T'care, bye." I hit the follow on call button.

It was a relief, but an unsatisfactory one. I was escaping due punishment, and I was afraid it meant that my real punishment was to come later. And I oughtn't to leave Joanne in any doubt about the risk of going back to Hanlon Hall, especially with Rachel to explain to. I dialled Joanne's number again, anticipating the attack which she had now had time to prepare. It rang without response. I would let it ring five more times before hanging up. It reached four and a male voice spoke.

"Lo?"

"Oh hello." This was him. Tom. The partner-cum-buffoon-cum-cuckold-cum-father-of-her-children-cum-reason-to-live. He had access to her mobile. Things must be looking up between them.

I wondered if she had got around to mentioning me yet, or if she would ever feel the need.

"Best left," I could imagine her saying to herself or a murmuring, supportive female friend. "It's over. He's history. What's the point?"

This was my chance to blow the whole thing wide open.

"Is Joanne Carr there, please?" I said, "It's work I'm afraid."

"No. She's not, I'm afraid. Not at the moment." She was probably in bed, where I had dragged him from a pleasurable attempt at conception. "I can take a message."

He didn't sound as if he wished to be particularly helpful, but he wasn't actually hostile either. People from work were probably always bothering her. It was annoying but inevitable, and Joanne wouldn't want him to be rude. He was doing just the right thing. No wonder she had dumped me for him.

"Er, could you just let her know I rang, please - Tony Palmer, from work."

"Tony Urquhart?"

"Palmer. Tony Palmer."

"Palmer," he confirmed. "Yes, OK."

"Thanks, G'bye."

"Goodbye," he said with finality and ended the call.

Urquhart. I stomped away muttering. And I was still no further forward. I would still have to ring her again and I hadn't asked him when she'd be available. I hadn't wanted to be a nuisance. I was too considerate of her feelings. Had she really thought I had mental health problems? It was an insensitive question whatever the answer. Perhaps I hadn't realised quite how peripheral I had been in her life.

I just wanted to do right by everybody and escape from this mess back into my own life, but I had no idea how. If I went back to my hotel I knew I would end up getting drunk, and I needed to stay sober to ring back Joanne. I walked to Victoria and bought a Time Out. There was nowhere to sit and read, so I bought a one day travelcard and got on a tube heading north. I needed to do something. I began with the cinema pages. Violence and crime were a little too close to home, which ruled out a large proportion of films. I also knew that watching floppy-haired successful young people leading interesting lives would have just depressed me. As none of the lavish costume and scenery, return to a non-existent Golden Age stuff appealed either, there was actually not one film in all eighteen pages that tempted me. I tried theatre, music, mime, dance, comedy and I ended up going to the zoo.

I tried talking to some of the less popular birds and apes when no-one was looking. They did little to help. I suppose it was unreasonable to expect sympathy from bored creatures, probably feeling the cold, who had been put in cages by other members of my species.

Until now fear of Brendan had dominated my thoughts and I had not really considered the possibility of being incarcerated myself. Now I did. On the whole I thought I would rather be a gibbon in a zoo cage than a human locked away in some cold, overcrowded Victorian institution with the smell of other peoples' stale shit in the air, the prospect of beatings and buggery in the cells, and nets hung below balconies to turn suicides into trampolinists. On the other hand, as long as I did not become implicated with Brendan's other activities, my crime was more or less a middle-class one, so I should have a good chance of ending up in an open prison. I might be able to survive in one of those places that are always compared to holiday camps by right-wing Tories who can't have been near either; the sort of place where everyone writes poetry and takes Open University courses.

"Presumably," I said to a gibbon, "The judge doesn't actually say, 'I sentence you to three years imprisonment in one of those nice Halls of Residence type prisons, rather than a toilet-dungeon.' So who does? Be useful people to know."

The gibbon scratched his left breast, then swung his head away to indicate that he had no wish to hear any more of my mawkish meanderings, especially with something far more interesting to stare at in the neighbouring cage.

I might be in trouble, but he had absolutely no chance of escape. If his cage was left open and he was not too demoralised to notice; or if he overpowered his keeper at feeding time, and worked out how to use the key; even then, if he managed to get out into the open, even out of the zoo, he would not last long on the run in London. He would have no chance against the traffic and the dogs and all the other dangers he would have no hope of understanding. He had no chance of changing his name and blending in; or raising the money for a boat overseas and slipping away unnoticed.

I on the other hand, was theoretically capable of all of this, but first I had to ring Joanne again - an ordeal the gibbon was free from. I thanked him for cheering me up a little and said goodbye, but he still paid me no attention.

I walked past lions and antelopes (separated) and cages of monkeys. Looking at them, it was obvious. We really were the same - monkeys that had got out of hand, whether through sex with alien astronauts, or because of the way our thumb had evolved collecting walnuts. Anyone who thought otherwise was an idiot. I must become a vegetarian. Like Helen. I dialled Joanne's number, pulling a face and feeling foolish, like a naughty monkey looking for help and trying to avoid punishment.

At least her mate did not answer this time. "Yes, Mr Palmer," said Joanne.

"Is it difficult to talk at the moment?"

"Yes that's right."

"Should I ring back later?"

"Yes."

"What time?"

"That's difficult to say at the minute."

"Oh, I see," I paused.

"When do you think, then? So I can let you know if it will be feasible." What did that mean?

It meant that she was trying to sound businesslike for the benefit of anyone who might be listening.

"Oh right," I said, "Certainly." There was no need for me to use the same language, but it seemed the thing to do. What time? I needed to keep a clear head so I could explain things to her properly. I didn't want her walking into danger, but on the other hand I didn't want to put off drinking for too much longer. "Half six?"

"No - that's no good. Perhaps I should call you?"

"No," I said. "I'm... I'm not at home still."

"Where are you ringing from?"

I looked through the glass at a sign for the Penguin Pool and the Bear Park.

"You wouldn't believe me if I told you. Anyway hotel calls can be listened in on."

"This is not helping." She was just managing to control her irritation with me - her ex-partner and co-conspirator.

"Do you want me to suggest a few times that you can say yes or no to?"

"I'd go along with that," she said.

"Eight?"

"No."

"Nine?" Please no later.

"Thirty."

"Nine thirty?"

"Yes."

"Tonight?"

"Yes. That should be OK. Thanks for calling." She sounded weary.

"And I've not been able to speak to Rachel; just her answering machine."

"Then I would suggest you try again."

"Right. Thanks. I'll talk to you again at half nine."

"Yes. Goodbye."

I could see her looking heavenwards. Tom would be sympathetic and admire her maturity and restraint in the face of the office incompetents bothering her at the weekend, when all she wanted was to be with him, and perhaps little Junior inside.

It was on the Tube back that I first felt at home in London. The carriage wasn't full. There were a couple of anxious-looking women in expensive fawn coats clutching shiny plastic bags, a wild-faced youth in a leather jacket and two or three days' stubble, staring intently in front of himself in a way which was possibly the cause of the two women's anxiety. Standing by the door was a quiet group of Italians and a noisier group of English student-types. I had no bags to guard, and no problem with a thorough shake up of the existing world order, so I felt fine being thrown through dark tunnels at speed in the society of strangers.

I enjoyed walking around my hotel room rather less, trying to use up time before ringing Joanne without resorting to the bar. I was too nervous to eat and there was nothing on the television to hold my attention.

I gave up after about ten minutes and headed for the bar. My room was on the second floor, but to use up more of my life, I pressed for the lift. When I heard it arriving I went to the stairs and descended them slowly. At the bar I ordered an orange juice, and decided that what I needed to occupy myself was electronic chess.

I drained my glass and went back to Victoria Station. The shops there sold a mixture of the mundane (TCP, bread and toilet rolls), the ludicrous (dancing coke cans, fake knives) and the exotic (African stone carvings and oriental electronic goods) alongside London souvenirs, pornography and cigarettes. Finally amongst Game Boys and Savlon, I came across a batteries not included set endorsed by a Ukranian grandmaster and retailing at £21.99.

It was one of the most exciting purchases I had ever made. I could hardly wait to get back to my room with it. There were sixteen levels, the book informed me, and its special features included Reverse Play and Save Game. Wow. It was the same size as an ordinary travelling chess set, but a little deeper. I peered into the box, and pulled the board half out. There were two rows of red lights to indicate which square your opponent wished to move from and to.

"So that's how they do it."

I decided that I would begin at Level One with white, and then when I was winning a good majority of games at that level, I would switch to black, and then go to Level Two with white and so on. If I got really good I could go on to try to become a Grandmaster, although I might have to change my name. I might even achieve popularity and respect through my talent. It was important I got started as soon as possible. But first I had to ring Joanne.

A slow walk to the phone took me to ten past nine. There wasn't a queue so I waited nearby, trying to work out how I would explain myself. After five minutes of this, two women arrived more or less together and the first embarked on a call which she expected to cost her a small pile of pound coins. I went and stood behind the other. She looked suspiciously at me, but after a minute, I spoke to her.

"Are you going to be on long?"

"Yes," she answered grimly, without giving me eye contact.

I went to look for another box. From having too much time, I was now entering a state of mild panic about being late. Round two corners, I found one without a queue, but with a young woman inside. There was no money showing on the display. This was a bad sign; she had been rung back by a concerned wealthy parent or some brainless big-jawed boyfriend. It was another old-fashioned heavy phone box and some of the glass panels were smashed. I could hear her talking.

"... and it was set off by the cat ah hee, hee, hee. Gareth. Ah ha, ha ha." It got worse.

"Arabella I told you about, yes, who melted the mixing bowl on the cooker, well yesterday she melted the colander as well. Hamish says we've got a matching set now." And more sweet innocent laughter. I stalked away. Hamish probably wasn't even Scottish. Finally, at five to ten I arrived back at the original box which was now free.

"Sorry I'm a bit late. I've been looking for a phone

box."

"Where are you?"

"London."

"So why did you tell Rachel you were in Birmingham?"

"Oh, did she ring you?"

"Yes."

"What did she say?"

"It doesn't matter. Leave that to me - not that you haven't already. Why did you have to lie to her?"

"It was her answering machine and I didn't want to leave anything incriminating, anything that could be traced. Should I ring and explain?"

She told me that I shouldn't; and then gave me her opinion of my intelligence, common sense, trustworthiness and wit. She had apparently met a not inconsiderable number of (I think exclusively male) people whose reason she had occasion to question, but that if there was a competition for stupidity, I would win, without question and in every year I chose to enter. I could also compete with distinction at international, even interplanetary level. And through it all, did I know what the worst thing was? It was that, despite the mountains of incontrovertible evidence to the contrary, I seemed to think that I knew best. Arrogant and pathetic.

I carried on shovelling in more pound coins to hear more criticism and abuse - one of those 0898 numbers probably offered much the same service, but without the same degree of personal customisation. Meanwhile the shuffling of feet and sighing from outside built up. Finally, she let me explain what had happened. I kept it simple and she seemed to take it in.

"And you expect me to sort it all out?"

"No. Not sure you could."

"So what do you propose to do?"

"Nothing," I said, bracing myself for an onslaught.

"Well it would be an improvement I suppose." Pointed, but better than an onslaught. Then I got the onslaught.

"How could you be so stupid? You've ruined everything. You're an idiot. Rachel was right about you. What about the money?"

"It's in the bank - they can't get it; we all need to sign for it."

"Yes, I know."

I didn't remind her that I could still take money out with the cash card.

"And I don't know if it would be safe at the minute.... Should I...?"

"No. Don't do anything, anything at all. If you even think you've had an idea, check with me, so I can tell you how stupid it is."

She sounded more exasperated when I refused to tell her my whereabouts. I explained I was moving around a lot and using different names. She groaned at this. In truth though, I no longer trusted her. If anyone had to take the blame and suffer the consequences, I was sure that she would think that it should be the feckless, drunken loudmouth with no responsibilities, rather than a potentially pregnant woman who had done nothing wrong, or her ailing and equally innocent and reliable friend.

"God, I could have done without this," she added. "Just when everything had gone so well, and we were out of it."

That was unnecessary and insensitive, considering how recently she had dumped me, but I decided to say nothing. Any disagreement would prolong the call and keep me from my chess game, which I was at that moment reading about from the side of its box.

We re-confirmed that I must tell her if I was going to do anything which might possibly affect her in any way whatsoever, and she agreed to talk to Rachel. She felt that Rachel would not be very responsive to me at the moment. This was a relief, but also clear proof of my inadequacy.

"Well, look after yourself, Tony," she said finally, and I thought I detected a hint of warmth. I could start loving her again if she would let me. With her, perhaps, things might just be OK.

"You too. Take care, Joanne," I replied, to which she

snorted down the phone.

I left the phone box and smiled at the young woman bubbling with anger at the front of the queue. It could have been worse. I could have tried to save myself by blaming her for getting me involved in the first place, or for betraying me so abruptly that I had turned to the first friend who appeared. Either of these would have led to a longer and more painful conversation and apology, so I was glad I kept my mouth shut. Also I needn't worry about Rachel any more, and I was surely out of the clutches of Brendan and his mates. If you had to be on the run, a hotel in London with mini-bar and room-service was the place for it, especially with a brand new electronic chess set.

My opponent was not a brilliant player at the lower levels. It concentrated too much on its next move; taking an unprotected pawn at the expense of a possible checkmate two moves away. I assumed it was making long-term mistakes as well, but I wouldn't have noticed them. I suppose all games of chess are just a series of mistakes of a greater or lesser degree - like everything else in life.

From about Level Six, however, I stopped progressing, by which I mean winning. As my opponent now planned several moves ahead, it took a lot longer before deciding on its next move, and I was enjoying the games less and less. Any mistakes I made now were punished - terribly slowly, with almost cruel circumspection. I was growing frustrated with my electronic chum.

It also took a long time over its response to my opening move. There are only twenty possible opening moves, some of them fairly silly, so it should have had an instant reply to each of them. I suppose to my opponent, with infinite patience and no memory for anything but the rules, each game was its first. Given this, it did play rather well.

We had spent the first few days together in our hotel bedroom, like a honeymoon couple. As the novelty waned, however, I began to yearn for pubs and betting shops, despite the harm they would do to my health and pocket. I combined the chess with these other pursuits for a while, but soon I was playing no more than a game or two a day.

I left my chess behind one day and headed for Ladbrokes and put on a pound a stake Heinz. For fifty seven pounds I got a very pleasant hour working out what I would get if they all won; and a miserable afternoon as not one of them did

Next day I moved to Plan B. This involved backing favourites and increasing the stake after each unsuccessful bet to cover outstanding losses and a small profit until I had a winner.

This system is infallible as long as you have an infinite pool of money and are prepared to make small profit from large outlay. I stuck to it for four days making ten pounds a day, but on the fifth day, joint favourites, boredom, and the tiny profit margin weakened my resolve. I succumbed to the temptation of sudden inspiration and lost a hundred pounds. It could have been worse; I could have got to the stage when the requirement for infinite funds kicked in and I lost everything I had, so I took it as a warning.

But now what? I had a few drinks and felt the desperate need to talk to someone other than a barmaid or bookie. I rang Richard. He was so shocked to hear from me that he wasn't able to interrogate me about the very edited version I gave him of my story. I asked him to ring Joanne and exchange numbers, so that each could contact the other in an emergency, but also so I could make a crack about asking him not to sleep with her. Otherwise I remained cold and factual, but being quite keen on forgiveness myself at the time, I weakened.

"And how are things with you?" I asked finally.

"Oh, OK you know. Just trying to decide what to do." He didn't sound happy, but he wouldn't say anything more. At least he didn't resurrect the idea of me playing Joseph to his God.

I didn't ring Joanne and Rachel for a while, in order to avoid domestic upset, or induce panic that I was about to 'do something'. I wasn't. Having exhausted my social circle, bored myself with chess, and no longer able to afford to gamble I spent most of my enforced leisure on my bed, half drunk, watching television. Not that different to most people really.

PART THREE
NEW LABOUR

CHAPTER 17

I have always disliked Crimewatch. The programme had started when the remote was lying on the floor at the other side of the room, and I couldn't be bothered to move. I slouched there drinking gin and tap water and daydreamed, while concerned reporters scared middle-England with their crime reconstructions presented like footage of exotic holiday resorts on a game show.

I was dimly aware of a change in subject to the murder of a bookie, perhaps linked with 'callous gangland crimes in the heart of rural England', and then I saw a picture of Brendan's snooker club, followed by Hanlon Hall. That got my attention. In my three quarter drunken state, it was hard to concentrate on the details of the people the police were trying to trace. The description of myself was quite flattering; and they got my age about right and said I had a 'slight Geordie accent'.

They were describing me on Crimewatch. This was happening. I desperately tried to tear myself out of my stupor and understand more, as if this in itself would somehow change things. Ten million people with nothing better to do were watching this with cups of tea and biscuits and disapproving expressions on their nasty little faces. I was scared. I couldn't believe that Tony Palmer, could really be wanted in connection with murder. I clung on tightly to my glass. If the police wanted to find me, then no doubt others did as well. Brendan and Alex, for example. I sipped my drink. My life would never be free of this.

For the first time, outside of nightmares, I felt aware of my mortality. Never mind the police and the legal system, I had crossed people who punished those who crossed them, and broken codes you were violently punished for breaking. There were more of them; they were far more powerful than me and they were capable of anything. And I had no idea where they were, or what they were doing.

All I could do was hide. I would be like a gazelle running from lions, escaping and then stopping a little distance away before moving on again. The report had mentioned prostitution, gambling, protection and drugs. Brendan had said he had friends in the police. Could he be setting me up for his crimes? It would be very convenient for everyone now if I was found dead, unable to testify, and presumed guilty. The police were preferable to the alternative, but then once you were in prison you were as vulnerable as a penned sheep.

I had no idea what had happened since I had fled and no way of finding out so I watched the television avidly all night and slowed down my drinking, in case I missed some important detail, like my photofit, or an interview with Brendan presented as a concerned citizen, offering a reward for my capture.

I had no idea if I would be recognised as soon as I left my room, or if I could trust myself not to blurt out the whole thing to a stranger in the bar. I desperately wanted to get out of here, and talk to someone. I even had an urge to ring up and confess. I strained hard to forget the Crimewatch phone number. I knew the penance for a secular confession in a police station would be a lot more painful than a handful of Hail Marys and a blush in the dark of the confessional.

I wondered if Rachel or Joanne would ring in if they were watching. They had no reason to protect me. I was fairly sure there had been no reference to them, and if they had been arrested or attacked, it would have been included in the report. If they could have linked it all with our adulterous affair they would probably have extended coverage to fill out the whole programme, including bedroom reconstructions and interviews with leading sexologists.

I felt a little ashamed for mistrusting them. After all, if there was anyone who had shown they couldn't be trusted, that was me. Even now I had lied to Rachel about my whereabouts. A little dash of shame wasn't going to make me change my feelings though. So much had happened since we last saw each other that even Joanne was fast becoming a stranger I could hardly believe existed; never mind someone that I had once shared a bed with. No, this hotel room, the gin, the television, the chess, my meetings with Brendan and Alex, the phone calls, Crimewatch - this was my life now.

Things were becoming more dangerous. I had to do something but I had no idea what. When Newsnight finished without a mention of me, and there were no solid leads boasted about in Crimewatch Update, I wrote down a promise to myself not to touch the phone or leave the room, as conditions for getting to finish the gin. I kept my word and managed a long, heavy sleep on top of the bed.

Next day I ordered some sandwiches from room service, and when it was dark I put on a coat and sneaked out of the hotel with my head down and my collar turned up. It was a relief to be out in the fresh air.

I rang Joanne one last time. Tom answered the phone again, so I put on a shrill Scottish accent and asked for Hamish. Then I rang Rachel, resolving to do the same if she answered in person, but I heard with relief the click of the answering machine. Perhaps I shouldn't do this. Perhaps her phone was being tapped, and I would now be incriminating her in addition to all the other acts of folly

I had visited upon her. But I was never very good at prudent inactivity, especially when the adrenaline was already racing.

"Hello, Anthony here. I'm going on holiday. Can you tell anyone that I might have forgotten about that I won't be in touch for a while. Hope you're OK - really."

Just as I finished, I heard the sound of the receiver being picked up, as someone went to override the answering machine. I think it was Rachel, and I think she said "Wait". I didn't.

Finally I rang my brother Richard again. It must say something about the strength of our relationship that he was the one member of my family I wanted to talk to despite all he had done; or perhaps it says more about how weak my relationships were with Robert and Susan.

Now I was pleased that there were students waiting outside my phone box, stamping their feet impatiently in the cold as they wasted their night waiting to tell Mummy and Dad on reversed charge calls all about their exploits in grown-up land. I would take as long as I wanted. Louise answered, but I asked for Richard straight away.

"He's out, Tony. It is you, isn't it?"

"Yes."

"How are you?" she asked, with genuine concern.

"I'm OK I suppose."

I felt touched by her warmth. This was the first proper

conversation we had had for a very long time, and when it came down to it, I was much more antagonistic towards Joanne and Rachel, whom I had let down, than I was towards Louise who had dumped me for my brother.

"And you? Richard told me about the baby."

"Yes. And his plan." She tutted. "That was stupid and insensitive. I'm sorry, genuinely. You're a lovely man, you know."

My reaction to this was a burst of lust - I remembered her body vividly, and how it felt being inside it. I could hear my voice softening.

"I was just ringing to say that I'm going away for a bit - but not to worry."

"Sounds like a good idea," she said brightly.

"Hope so. You wouldn't know if he's been in touch with somebody - Joanne from work would you?"

She shook her head.

"Sorry?" I said after a few seconds.

"Oh sorry, I mean no. I don't know. Richard is worried about you, you know. I'm sure if you wanted him to he would have done."

"It's just," I continued. "No. Look are you OK - all of you?"

"Yes, Tony. Is there anything we can do to help?"

"No. You're OK, but thanks. I mean it. Tell Richard I hope he's OK as well. And the baby. I'll get in touch soon. Take care."

"You as well. I mean that as well, Tony."

I couldn't help but be pleased, and I knew she did mean it in her own way.

"I know. Thanks. Goodbye." Well, that was nice.

I walked slowly back to the hotel thinking about her. When I got back to my lonely room, my confidence began to ebb away. I knew I needed to do something. I needed a new name, cheaper accommodation, and a job, although I had no idea how I would ever manage that.

I decided to grow my hair long; and grow a beard as well. I toyed with the idea of glasses, but vanity stopped me, along with fear of damaging my sight.

I looked along the padded carpet from my double bed to the veneered dark wood of my door. Now I had decided to leave this place, I was already beginning to miss it. I would give myself another two days here before moving somewhere cheaper. I knew I was spoiling myself for a future of mouldy bedsits, the pavement and prison, but I might as well enjoy now what I would later regret. Next week I would hate the selfishness of the person I was today, lying on a clean bed and getting pissed in front of the hotel movie channel. 'Thelma and Louise' seemed appropriate.

I thought it would be a good idea to shake off anyone who might be hunting me. Next day I took a train to Portsmouth, humming songs from the film to myself. I had decided to send a letter to my brother from there, and a postcard to the snooker club. The card would be anonymous but it would contain enough hints to tell Brendan or an intelligent detective that I had sent it. And the only reason for me to be in Portsmouth was the ferry to France. I used the business cash card as well and then bought a couple of postcards showing views of the Tricorn Shopping Centre.

I changed my mind about sending one to the Snooker Hall. I didn't want to risk antagonising anyone more than I already had done, and the card might be taken as an insult. I didn't know for sure they were looking for me, so it would be obtuse even by my standards to stir them into activity.

It was too obvious a fake lead as well. I wanted my disappearance into mainland Europe to be as convincing as possible. The police were more likely to give credence to intercepted post to someone I was believed to trust, like Richard. I was continuing a great and long line of Twentieth Century disappearances - Agatha Christie, Lindenberg, Lord Lucan, Idi Amin, Reginald Perrin. I used a second class stamp, so that I could have been well out of Caen or Cherbourg or St Malo by the time it reached the sorting office.

Dear Richard,

For reasons which you may be aware of I am going to have to go away for a while. I don't know exactly what you have seen on television but I know that a lot of things which are not true are believed about me, so I have to get away. I'm OK though and I will get in touch again when I can. I sincerely hope everything works out for you and Louise and the baby. If my feelings seem to have changed, it is because I've had the world turn upside down on me these past few weeks and I've come to realise more what really matters. Could you let Joanne know that you've heard from me and that she has absolutely no reason to worry. The only reason I'm not in touch is because I'm out of the way.

I wrote another to Joanne.

Dear Joanne,

I have decided to go away for a while. Things seem to be getting out of hand and I just need to escape. My brother Richard may be getting in touch. If he hasn't and you want to talk to him, I'm enclosing his number and address. Please could you pass on any news to each other and I'll be in touch with one or both of you when I can.

You can trust him with anything you want to say or

pass on, although I haven't told him any details of why I have to go away - just the television he might have seen. I hope everything's going well,

Take care,
Tony

I posted both letters in what looked like a little regarded box, but one which was public enough to make it an unlikely target for the lighted newspapers of bored teenagers who never got any post themselves. As I released them, I thought that I should have posted them separately. Then again, if that could be detected from postmarks or something, it might make my actions look more suspicious. But it was too late, and it was a relief to be able to stop worrying about it.

In the end I sent the Tricorn Shopping Centre postcards to Susan and Robert with a scrawled ambiguous message about a holiday. In the unlikely event that anyone connected them to me, it might add to confusion about my whereabouts.

I didn't know if I was worrying too much or too little. It was very difficult with no-one to talk to. As the train back to London pulled out of the station we passed a large cemetery, I found myself wondering if any of the gravestones were fitted with satellite dishes. It was understandable. Given the pressure, I wasn't doing that badly; it was just sad that Joanne or Louise or somebody else wasn't there to tell me that and make me feel better. Butch Cassidy and the Sundance Kid, Thelma and Louise, Bonnie and Clyde, Terry and June, Tony and his electronic chess set.

The simplest cure I knew for loneliness was alcohol and TV in bed. This worked in the short term, but always left me feeling more depressed afterwards. There were other methods. I had been tempted by some of the cards in the telephone boxes. My experience with Victoria didn't seem relevant here - it would be easier with a prostitute I didn't feel the need to impress - but I was afraid to go beyond the voyeuristic thrill of the cards themselves, and scuttled back to the warmth of my room.

I felt more like an outsider than ever. The streets were full of shoppers and trippers and other groups who all seemed happier and more purposeful than a drifter with dwindling resources. Drifters tend to be solitary, male, and stubbled. I fitted right in. They tend to wear long coats; they are misunderstood; and they are likely to suffer random beatings and wrongful arrest before consumptive or violent death. We are not a happy group, and we aren't big on Chrismas. Even before this stage in my life, I had not liked Christmas. Now it was less than two months away, and making its presence felt more and more on the streets of central London with each passing shopping day. At least I had an occupation which matched my natural predilections. There were no drifters' office parties to dread.

I paid a months' rent in advance and a month as deposit on a bedsit in Willesden. It was sparsely furnished but there were no obvious signs of damp or vermin. I had left The Regents Hotel with tears beginning to form in my eyes and all the nostalgia of a student saying farewell to his beloved Oxford for ever; or a country lad taking one last look at the land he loved so well, as he stepped on the gangplank of the boat for Americay.

I signed the lease as Tony Lawson - on the principle that if I ever found anyone to love me I wanted them to call me by my real first name at least. And this was before I even began to brood in earnest. I wondered how long I would last. Still, I had to try.

CHAPTER 18

I spent the next two days aimlessly traipsing the streets of North West London; the following two in my room writing and tearing up confessions. On the fifth day I decided to try to do something. Recalling accounts of how people in hopeless conditions find it important to try to preserve the appearance of normality, I washed, shaved and changed into new clean clothes and resolved to do so every day.

While shaving, I decided to look for work. Then I remembered that the reason I hadn't shaved was that I was supposed to be growing a beard. I looked hard at the half-shaven face in the mirror.

"In case you've forgotten, Tony, you've changed your name and you're on the run from the police, who have given your description to the nation. You are also possibly being hunted by a set of murderous gangsters who feel you have betrayed them, and made a fool of them. They may even be in league with the police. You have no home. You are in hiding. That is why you were supposed to be growing a beard. OK?"

I stopped at this point and finished shaving. There was no point being too hard on myself and I did feel a lot better with a clean smooth face again.

My search for work was unsuccessful and

disheartening. My room was dull and claustrophobic, and I suspected I had been wrong about the damp. Having moved from the extravagance of a hotel to the dinginess of bedsit land, I became more grudging with money. I was unwilling to buy a second hand portable TV or a cassette player or a decent electric fire. The convector heater in the room had difficulty overcoming the chill in the air and only succeeded after an hour-long struggle at full heat. Soon black mould began to appear on the wall above the bed. Scrubbing with a damp Jey cloth (eighty-five pence for three) forced it to retreat, but only temporarily. When I moved the bed to check the wall lower down I found a death certificate, presumably belonging to an earlier tenant. I tried to work out if it was more likely to be the tenant's own, or a possession of theirs. This was not a healthy way to spend my time so I decided to start a diary. As part of my economy drive I resisted the temptation to buy a shiny new exercise book and used the only paper I had to hand which was in my old Delegate Reflections folder. That seemed a long time ago now. I had been happy then, if only I had known it.

Monday: Decided to keep a diary. Haven't done anything like this since I used to get those little red Letts schoolboy ones, and recorded which lessons were worst and what was on TV and whether or not there were any new signs of puberty. It feels easier now. More to say I suppose, although I'm doing less. Money left =

(This next bit was crossed out in case someone broke in and reading the diary, demanded that sum of money, which by then I would not have).

Played chess three times. Sober, but seem to have got a pawn and bishop mixed up which cost me the third game. I had definitely got up to being white at level seven. I'm sure I'd got as far as trying black at seven as well, so I must be getting worse. Tried three pubs and a MacDonalds today for jobs. Nothing. Really don't want to end up queuing in the morning for hotel portering jobs and sleeping in piss beds. Answered some ads so at least there'll be some junk mail arriving for Mr Tony Lawson.

That death certificate. Trying to forget the woman's name. I've hidden it away in the back of a drawer. Trying not to think about it too much. Half inclined to go back to the Regents, get a nice room and give myself up when the money runs out. Prison'd be worse though. Remember that and work to avoid it. I hadn't been going to mention the death certificate for superstitious reasons, but I'm superstitious about giving in to superstition.

Tuesday: Realised reason for erratic chess playing is that the batteries are on their way out. That's another £3-50 I can't afford. Tried bleach on mould. Wall went a funny colour so I moved the wardrobe with the door that doesn't shut in front of it. Believers, why in the infinite wisdom of the Almighty was mould created? And on which day? If everything has a purpose why is there dry rot, bluebottles, John Selwyn Gummer? Could add myself to that miserable list. Wondering about Joanne's mental illness question again. No-one who is mad thinks they are mad, do they? Not at first at least. On dangerous ground if that is only argument for my sanity.

Got batteries for chess. Not the long life ones. Newly refreshed, it beat me on white at level six. Bastard.

Wednesday: Got up very late. Couldn't be bothered to shave. Bad. Too mean to heat up water for a bath. Must try to remember what hostages or whoever said about keeping up appearances. Impossible to imagine ever having sex with a real live woman again. Hard to believe I ever did. Pissed now I suppose, but not enough. Pissed off. Waste of paper. Very. At least it's got late now. Hate the half past seven sort of time (people going out laughing, Tony Lawson staying in trying to work out if he's mad or not).

Friday: Yesterday was very like Wednesday. Probably worse as I didn't do anything at all - even this. Had a shave and a bath this morning. Good thing about long washes is they use up a lot of morning. Friday is a bad day to look for work - not sure where I've got that from. Had a large sensible breakfast - lots of fruit, don't want to be getting spotty. Going to spend this afternoon with my friend William Hill.

Saturday: Woke up wearing all my clothes, with the

radio and the light on at six o'clock this morning. Farming Outlook. Not much in common with those bastards; although I was on a horse once.

Hadn't even locked my door - worrying. William Hill actually gave me £55. It had been nearly £200 at one stage. Went for a Chinese meal - but ALL BY MYSELF. On my lonesome. No Joanne. No Louise. Not even a Victoria. Felt stared at by other diners, then found an eyelash under my soup bowl on the saucer thing which put me off completely. Got very pissed around Soho. Saw somebody I was sure was Dave Allen coming out of a theatre. Shouted something aggressively friendly with "Dave, mate" in it as far as I remember. He looked scared. Got talking to some Scottish blokes who live near here. Said I might see them in the Belvoir Arms tonight. Don't think I'll bother though. Have to make up reasons for being here and remember not to mention gangsters and how my girlfriend took up with my priest-brother. Keep my stories straight. Unlikely they'll all get together to compare notes - though with my luck I'll be at the altar rails with Louise when they do. Louise. Not Joanne. Interesting. Worrying.

Sunday: Got stood up in the Belvoir. Tried a once and for all bet with William. £25 each way on an outsider in a big handicap. Could have won £3200. Came seventh. Stupid. Went to church this morning. Say it again, Tony-who-thinks-he-might-be-losing-the-plot. Went to church this morning - empty and quite nice. Don't have to buy anything or say why you're there and on your own. Might try religion next. Prefer physical comfort though. Love a shag or even a hug. Wonder if I should have responded to that pissed woman last night, but scared about disease - not so much AIDS as something more instant and squalid that'd just make things a bit worse. Also scared of getting beaten up by husband and brothers. Got enough enemies already. And who's going to sleep with me? You need a selling point - what's mine? Not my soul or biceps. Anybody who'd sleep with me either wants something or they've got mental health problems.

Strange smell from the flat upstairs. Nasty, smoky, sour. Noise on the stairs just then. It's night time. Had a look out, pretending to be checking my post (unlikely - even if it wasn't a Sunday). First time I've seen my neighbour - thin coughing man called Michael. He looked scared. Good.

Monday: What a day it's been for neighbours - I never did. Lawks it's quite the little village here at 170 Grosvenor Court; and everyone is in such terrific form. In the afternoon, a girl of about 17 by the payphone smiled at me. A big smile with eye contact. She asked if I had change. She gave me 50p for my twenty and three tens. Her coin smells beautiful, of teenage perfume, cheap but not harsh. I would gladly marry her if I thought there was any chance she would have me.

8 o'clock there was knocking at the door. Hoped it might be her - so fascinated by the coins I gave her that she couldn't bear to squander them in the telephone - come back to offer herself to me. It was a large angry man asking if I had seen his giro. He eventually calmed down when I managed to convince him of my innocence. Played the simple Geordie card, and massive relief when he ambled away down the corridor.
But it's not a good idea for people to know where they can find a stray solitary Geordie called Tony – especially one who can't even be bothered to grow a beard. Especially one who never has any visitors, never gets any phone calls, and who neither works nor gets giros. Decide to write myself a letter. Also to send off for more catalogues and junk mail.

Tuesday: Bored and lonely. I know I'd feel better with some activity - anything. But not today. Bloody Tuesday. Fed up. Fed up.

Thursday: Went for a few jobs in pubs yesterday. Nothing. Gave up in the Marquis of Granby and got a pint of Guinness. There was a band on. Only just realised how much I've missed music. They looked like a rock band at first with a tight-trousered singer who was attractive in a romantic, raunchy way (this bit is half crossed out), but they were Country. They played good stuff - even the stuff you weren't supposed to like; and she had a strong throaty voice with a faint catch in it. Great.

****

I had actually left the pub, and I was on the pavement outside when I heard her voice from the upstairs room.

"Last night all alone in a bar room, Met a man with a drink in his hand, He had coal black hair, baby blue eyes and a smile that a girl understands."

The song is about resisting temptation for the sake of a marriage, but I had never before heard it sound so much as if she hadn't resisted at all. Or at the very least, that if she had resisted, then she regretted it. On "For temptation was flowing like wine," I decided to call a halt to the job-seeking, and "I was almost persuaded, To strip myself of my pride" floated down the stairs to me as I went up.

By the time I had got a drink and moved away from the bar they were doing Honky Tonk Masquerade. It carried on - Tonight I Think I'm Gonna Go Downtown, Feel So Lonesome I Could Cry, Ring of Fire, All My Exes Live in Texas. Then they were off. They encored with a rowdy Heaven's Just a Sin Away. I wasn't drunk enough to approach them after the show, but I asked the barman their name. The Fugitives.

I bought a Time Out the next day, but there was no

mention of them. Nor the week after. They seemed to have disappeared. I felt cheated. Then, two weeks later, I was in the Marquis of Granby, and there they were on a small corner stage downstairs, halfway through their set, doing 'Just Between the Two of Us'. I had tried to stay in that night, but I cracked at about ten to nine and I was very glad I had. It was like bumping into an old friend - as far as I could remember.

They took a break shortly afterwards and, still flushed with the pleasure of stumbling across them again, I went over to speak to them.

"Loved the set," I said to the singer.

"Great. Stay for the second half then."

"Don't worry. I will."

"I'm Kate." She put out her hand.

"Tony," I said. “Have you got any cassettes?" There was a pile on sale but they were by The Outsiders.

“Barman said you were called the Fugitives.”

"We used to be. We're The Outsiders now.”

“Right. Better name. But that was why I couldn't track you down."

"Not one of our better ideas,” the drummer interrupted. “To confuse the few fans we have."

"Well, you've got one more now," I assured them.

“We had no choice,” she said. “Terry - our last manager - left and set up his own band with the same name.”

“Dickhead.” That was the drummer again, presumably talking about their old manager.

"Do you play yourself?" she asked.

Right; time for a witty reply. I thought one would come to me, but it didn't and time was passing and the smile was starting to freeze on her face. I had to say something

"Er - no.” Not brilliant. “But you sound like you’ve been singing all your life.” Not sure where that came from, and it sounded a bit corny but it saved the conversation.

"Long as I can remember," she replied, with a big positive smile. I usually had trouble with people with lots of positivity, but it made a change from arguing about stolen giros.

"Always country music?"

"Since I was about thirteen. My cousins from Tennessee came for a visit, and that was it."

"Well I'm glad they did." I bought my cassette and turned to go. As I did, someone bumped me in the back.

“Sorry,” I said, turning round. It was their roadie. He glared at me and stomped past.

"Great," she said to him. "Great way to treat the public."

I smiled slightly to show that it wasn’t a problem, though I understood how she must feel. I applauded loudly through their second set. They closed with

'Tennessee is not the State I'm In.'

****

Little changed in the house. The only development was a banging noise from the top storey. I hoped it was not connected with the smoky stew smell, and made sure my door was locked. I had never worried about cannibals before, but once a thought like that is in your head, it is very difficult to shake it off.

For the sake of my sanity, I bought a cassette player. I accept that listening to country and western music in a solitary bedsit on an alcohol-rich diet, might not be a widely recommended cure for depression, but at least it would make the drift into insanity less unpleasant. After a few days, as an economy measure, I resolved to cut back on drink. It was probably best to keep the maudlin influences within some bounds anyway.

I was listening to Hank Williams when I got a knock on the door. I couldn't think of a single person who could want to be calling who knew where I lived. I opened the door as Hank began 'I'll Never Get Out of This World Alive'.

It was Giroman. He filled the doorframe. I considered praying to the God I had told on several occasions that I didn't believe in, but he put out his hand.

"Sorry about before," he said, looking a little less massive. "Didn't mean to accuse you of anything." I didn't tell him that was exactly what he had done. "It's just there's been some robbers in this place before. Bloke in Room 4 - one before last. Coppers came to take him away in the end."

I reassured him I had not taken offence, and asked him his name.

"Sammy", he responded happily; and was calling me Geordie by the end of the conversation

I was finding my way in the world again. At The Outsiders' gig that night I became embroiled in a conversation with a drunk from Darlington. I would normally have ignored him, especially as I was sober myself, but it was a good idea not to seem friendless, especially if the band were getting suspicious of my solitariness. Perhaps me, him and Giroman could go out together.

I edged away from him, and towards the stage during 'How Much I Lied'. At the end of the set, when I had finished shouting for more, I went over to speak to the band, whom I was beginning to look on as friends. I grinned as I approached them. I was the sort of fan they wanted - loyal, well-informed, and witty. And not a total scary loner.

Halfway there I stopped dead. I saw myself for what I was. I knew what I was going to say to them - 'Enjoyed the set. Great tape as well. Do you know where you're on next?' And I was thinking of these people as my friends. The reality was that I was more like a stalker.

It was clear. This was hopeless. Easing off alcohol was helping me see the truth about my situation. Once my money was gone I'd have to come out of hiding anyway - if my mind lasted that long. And until then I was skulking in a bedsit, trying to keep on the right side of thugs, and lusting at the perfume smell a seventeen year old left on a fifty pence piece. The other high points were pestering semi-professional country and western bands in upstairs rooms in North London pubs. And developing a hopeless crush on their beautiful singer. I should stop now and hand myself in. At least I had made that decision myself. It would be worse in every way if it was made for me.

All the fear and tension drained out of my body. I smiled at Kate. It was a different kind of smile now; it was calm and valedictory, although she probably didn't notice as she was in the middle of a conversation with another fan. It didn't matter. I started moving again, but altered my route subtly to take me past the band and straight to the toilet. I was controlling where I was going.

Suddenly there was a crash, followed by a shout. I turned around to see the roadie punch the top of the guitarist's head as he was trying to get to his feet.

"Hey," called out Kate.

I rushed over at the same time as she did, and together we pulled the roadie away. He shook his arms free and swung around angrily, but not too near anyone. His hand was probably too sore to punch again.

"That's it," said Kate.

"Too bloody right it is," he replied. He brushed aggressively past her on to the stage, stumbling as he got up, and then with a bellowed, "Fuck off. Losers," disappeared behind the back of the stage and away.

"Are you OK?" Kate asked me. I nodded bravely and smiled.

"Thanks anyway," said the guitarist.

"Drunken prick," said the drummer, “Should have got rid of him years ago. What you get for feeling sorry for people."

"Do you want a hand shifting any stuff?" I asked.

"You're fine."

"No. I don't mind," I pleaded.

"What about your friends?"

"My what? Oh, they'll be all right. Just people at the bar, y'know."

"Well, thanks."

They let me help them with their gear and I was given a lift home in the van. The atmosphere was good. They were relieved the storm had finally broken and they were rid of Saul, which the roadie claimed was his name. They seemed to like me. I didn't invite them in, which I was sorry about, but there was just a chance they might have accepted and I was ashamed of what my room said about me.

"We'll need a new roadie," Kate said to Guy - the guitarist.

"I'll do it," I interrupted. Then I regretted sounding so eager and pushy.

"Are you sure? There's not a lot of money in it."

I hadn't even thought about money. I'd get money as well as friends and a reason to live? And the chance to talk to Kate? In order not to appear too desperate, I thought I'd ask about the money.

"How much?"

"Quarter profit after expenses," said Guy, "Same as the rest of us. Not a fortune. You'd probably get fifty quid if we played three times in a week, thirty/thirty-five if it's twice. It is cash in the hand though."

"You drive the van as well," added John, "You can drive?"

I nodded. I would have accepted anything short of legally binding slavery but I thought it best to look as if I was weighing up their offer. I used the time to do some quick calculations about how much longer the money I still had would last with this extra cash. I could probably spin it out for about a year if I settled for a bean-centric diet. Perhaps more.

"Give it a try, yes. I really do like the way you play - I

think you really could get somewhere. I'd like to help you try." They seemed surprised at their good fortune.

"Be good to have someone enthusiastic like you on board," said Kate.

"Couldn't be any worse than Saul," said John.

"He was a bit too fond of his drink," admitted Guy with a smile.

"And everyone else's," added John.

They had obviously been impressed by my temperance - now almost a fortnight old. I had worried about appearing a bit staid, but sober and reliable was what they wanted; and that apparently was me. Stranger things had happened, but not many. They seemed genuinely concerned for me.

"I do hope you know what you're letting yourself in for."

"I think I'll enjoy it."

"You might regret saying that."

"I'm sure I've had worse jobs," I laughed, soberly and reliably.

"Well, if you're certain."

All this was on the corner of my street.

"I'll be fine, here. And, the job - I'm certain."

"Sure?"

This was starting to remind me of those computer endgames from my earlier life.

"Are you sure you wish to close this file? (Y/N). Do

you wish to overwrite the existing file? (Y/N). With this? (Y/N). Do you wish to quit the package? (Y/N) Are you absolutely certain? Y/N). Look, how can you want to quit the package - we put a lot of effort into this you know. You don't really want to quit do you? (Y/N)." And as usual it was "Yes. Definitely. Jah. Oui. Si. I do."

They asked me my name - which was still Tony Lawson, for the same reasons as before.

"When do you want me to turn up next then?" I asked. Always a good idea to ask a meaty question at the end of an interview.

Apart from driving them around in the Transit, with an out of date A to Z on the dashboard, my job involved carting equipment round and helping them set up.

Like most technical things, this was a lot more straightforward than it might appear to an outsider, and I was puzzled at first as to why they needed me at all. They were a three piece country band playing pubs, not some rock leviathan. Their idea of showmanship was saying 'Thank you' and doffing the odd Stetson. They could all drive; I was sure they all knew London better than I did. Perhaps it was just as pointless as all the other jobs I had done.

It was only when I tried to imagined them without a fourth party that I realised that I did serve a useful purpose. None of them would have wanted the responsibility for driving, getting lost and being late for gigs; nor would they have wanted to hand the job to one of the others. My job was to be sensible and dependable; something between a civil servant and a tranquil mystic behind the wheel. I drove very carefully, not least for fear of what would happen if the police stopped me and asked to see my license. They laughed about my cautious driving, but I think they liked it. I enjoyed the sensation of submerging my ego into an orgy of selflessness, restraint and dependability. Three was a vulnerable number. Four was a group, and that was, after all, what we were. The fact I had no musical aspirations of my own probably helped as well, after their experience with their last manager.

Most weeks they played a couple of times, plus occasional practices. Guy was a very good guitarist. His playing was generally understated, but there were occasions when he'd really let go and take over the stage. Kate was the real star though. Her voice was powerful and rich, and she moved as she sang, holding the attention of the crowd both with her voice and her swaying body. She played competent bass as well. Guy shared the singing; his style was relaxed, less macho than hers, almost throwaway, English perhaps, like his guitar playing.

John, the drummer, was harder to like. He was short-tempered and I was convinced that he had once had, or nearly had, or would like to have, a sexual relationship with Kate. I was worried about the effect this might have on band dynamics. Guy was a much more stable influence. He always appeared very calm and content, as if he had his life sorted out. He lived for his guitar and his wife, who worked in the City. I was watching him play before a practice when Kate rushed in.

"Got my ticket for Nashville," she announced.

"You're not moving are you?" I had a sudden panic for the future of the band. She laughed.

"God, no. Too much competition out there. Holiday. See my cousins."

"Been before?"

"This'll be my first time. I'm so excited. I could do with some spending money though."

I resolved to do what I could to improve the band's income. They were usually paid between eighty and a hundred pounds for a night, and they generally had audiences of thirty or forty. There were, however, some places where they attracted more people, and were paid no more.

"How would you go about asking for more money?" I asked Guy.

"What? Do you want a rise already?"

"No," I laughed. "For the band."

I was careful not to say 'all of us', as John was already looking at me suspiciously.

"Never thought about it. Terry used to do all that."

“Before he ran off with the name and dreams of stardom for himself.”

"Mind you he was shite," contributed John. "A parasite." It was important to distinguish myself from Terry.

"What about the places where you get good crowds? Like The Eagle or The Fountainhead? Could ask for more there.” No response from John, but he could hardly disagree.

"Would you want me to see what I could do?" They were all listening now and they shrugged non-negatively.

"Well, 'slong as you don't lose us any gigs," said John.

I wouldn’t. I had acquired negotiating skills with Love Training, and as soon as I started talking to the Bar Manager at the Eagle, I remembered how much I had enjoyed the game.

"You know, they don't really make enough money for it to be worth their while coming all the way out here."

"No? Be a shame if they stopped. Not bad for Country and Western.”

“Get a good crowd in here – especially for a weekday night.”

“Think that’s down to the girl.”

“She's got a great voice."

"Yes. Fit as well."

“Thing is they asked me to see if I can get them a bit more cash. They’re barely meeting expenses at the minute."

"I'm pushing my profit margins as it is. And if I give you more, then the other bands'll be asking for more."

"Can they bring in as many punters on a wet Tuesday night?" He couldn't argue about that. "And they're getting bigger. This place could be the start of something."

"Only got your word for that – and let's face it, mate, you're biased. Not saying they ain't good, but this is business."

"Exactly."

I listened but I could tell he was weakening. He didn't want to lose control, and he wanted to talk, so I let him.

It seemed as if all I had to do to succeed in life was to stop behaving as I normally would. Finally he stopped.

"You know your business," I said, "I respect that. But, look, if you think it's too risky, leavc that to us. No fee and we keep ticket money. Simpler for you. Getting the audience is our problem then."

"Tell you what - another twenty a night," he said.

"What about nothing more unless they clear fifty in the crowd? And if they do - an extra fifty quid."

"Fifty extra?" He was more shocked than I thought necessary. I hadn't just asked him to throw in a night with his wife.

"That's only a quid a punter. You get admission and a night's spend for that. Can't complain about that. Can you?"

He couldn't, and with that agreed, it was easier to persuade The Fountainhead to do the same. I began advertising properly, and as often as possible we made concerts ticket-based. I wanted people to come to listen, not treat them like a sideshow. They were good, and there was no reason to undersell them. As the band became convinced that I knew it, they started to believe it themselves, and they knew the change was down to me. Like most artists, the criticism they most trusted was financial - and I was improving their notices.

And best of all, leaving it at that.

CHAPTER 19

London grew colder and darker day by day. As Christmas loomed, Oxford Street was in overdrive, and I enjoyed picking my way along the road, carrying nothing and with nothing to buy, watching the stressed shoppers playing their proper part in the ceremonies. A bedsit Christmas with an alias would be lonely and gloomy - not a lot of cards would be landing on my non-existent mat at 170 Grosvenor Court. I would pay for my freedom then; but at the moment my state was a very agreeable one. Being on the outside of this nasty folly was just fine. I was drinking very little, and toying with the idea of becoming a vegetarian.

This time, only a few weeks, was very short, but it constituted a definite episode in my life, as much as being a schoolboy or a software engineer or a fraudster, and it was the most carefree. I liked London and I relished this aimless sight-seeing of non-sights, especially if the band had played the night before to a good audience. Being on holiday from a job you enjoy is just lovely. Some mornings, I set my alarm early so I would be up in time to watch the commuters heading for Willesden tube, before going back to bed.

Money was a worry but not yet an urgent problem. Thanks to my new found abstinence and thrift, along with the money from the band, my capital was still diminishing, but slowly. Then, tricked by the insidious Christmas spirit and buoyed up by my success with a couple of pub landlords I jeopardised the whole thing.

"You can be more ambitious," I said.

"How?" asked John.

"Go upmarket. What about an Outsiders Christmas Show?"

"You're our manager now are you?"

"No. But you can do it. Get a venue for a few hundred quid, plus publicity, put on a bit of catering, and ticket through the venue. Be good for press, make a few quid and help build up the following."

"That sounds brilliant," said Kate, her eyes shining. I'm sorry but they were.

"Catering?"

"Yes. Go for it. Jambalaya and ribs. Sweetcorn. Chilli dogs." (Whatever they were).

"When?"

"I was thinking the 20th of December. It's a Friday."

"You've looked into this have you?"

"You are something else, Tony. I am so glad we found you."

"No bother."

It was a nightmare even finding a venue for the 20th. I finally got a cancellation at The Wagon for which they wanted a five hundred pound fee plus the same as a deposit. Ticketing would be another hundred. As I handed over the cash I realised I hadn't the first idea about getting publicity material produced. The posters on the pub wall looked pretty good.

"Are there any printers you use, for posters and stuff?"

"Yes."

"Great – have you got the number handy?" This was not a good way to get value for money but I was panicking.

"Can't see them getting it done this short notice, mate. But you can try."

Now the time I had been happily been spending smirking at shoppers was spent in libraries writing up what I hoped looked like proper press releases and ringing up uninterested and very cynical local newspapers. Catering was almost impossible to get at short notice before Christmas ("Jamba- what mate?") without paying over the odds, and with printing costs I was over a thousand pounds out of pocket in a week and it kept going up.

If we sold two hundred tickets, though, we would cover costs, and perhaps I could take a bit of a loss myself to convince the band it was worth it. Even without a big profit I hoped a decent crowd and a bit of press would be enough to raise their opinion of me again. I wasn't being entirely honest when I said I didn't want to be their manager.

I called in at The Wagon on the 15th to check on ticket sales.

"Twenty-three."

"Sorry?"

"Twenty-three, mate."

"That's disappointing."

"Probably get some on the door."

"Yeah, right," and I slunk away. I had thought that if my Christmas Day was to be the painful event it is meant to be for those who are failing to live their lives properly, I could have made the 20th special instead. It didn't look likely now; and having blown all that money on the gig I might as well spend some more on beer. I could write a few Christmas cards while getting morosely pissed to 'The Fairytale of New York' in some dingy North London pub, although actually this year I had so much news it would have justified a Round Robin style Festive newsletter.

Tony had a great start to 1996. Things were going well at work; finally being appreciated for his contribution to the war against the Millennium Bug by being sent on a residential training course where he met and slept with (once successfully, once, less so) a woman called Joanne who has a dull long-term partner. The week of the course was spoilt somewhat by a disastrous encounter with a prostitute, but that's the kind of thing from which he might, possibly, learn.

Following redundancy, however, Tony became involved in a criminal operation, a fraud, in partnership with the above-mentioned Joanne and her Paddington Bear-loving friend Rachel. Things went well initially. They made money faster than they could have hoped, but then the two women decided they wanted out just as it was taking off. Joanne also decided to turn Tony into a footnote in her life, and concentrated on having children, and trying her hand at faithfulness to her partner.

In an emotional state at these developments, Tony became involved with some violent criminals who had designs on his operations. To cut a long story short, he became a murder suspect (perhaps you saw him on Crimewatch in October), and fled to London to avoid both the police and some rural gangsters, neither of whom wished him well. There, following a change of name and a brief sojourn in a hotel on Buckingham Palace Road, he is now living in a bedsit, roadying for a Country band and anticipating a lonely Christmas. Following a ludicrous attempt to promote a Christmas gig for this band (including spending over a hundred quid on Jambalaya), his money is running out and prison beckons as the only real alternative to sleeping rough.

But enough of Tony. Big brother Father Richard has taken up with Louise - Tony's ex. In fact, if truth be told, he was not uninvolved in the process of her becoming

Tony's ex in the first place. She is now pregnant by him; in fact she should have had the baby by now. In an emotional scene, Tony refused to pretend to be the father of this child. God alone knows what is going to happen to them all.

Baby brother Robert is carrying on as a boring, sanctimonious family man, ageing and avenging himself on his siblings by producing children in the approved fashion and wearing very dull suits and jumpers. Sister Susan, still theoretically artistic, selfish and self-satisfied is God knows where doing God knows what with God knows who, but is probably planning a nice holiday somewhere. They don't deserve their own paragraph.

The nuclear family really is falling apart isn't it?

Tremendously looking forward to 1997. Talk to you in the New Year - if we're spared of course.

In the end I bought a pack of Oxfam cards with penguins on the front and 'Merry Christmas and a Happy New Year' inside. I didn't have to buy a big box. My shortlist was very short. I worked through the possibilities. Joanne? Not sure - should I address it to Tom as well? Would she understand the irony? Richard and Louise? Possibly, yes probably. Robert? Susan? It seemed unimportant whether I did or not. Who else? A lot of the casual acquaintances you take to be friends disappear as soon as you stop living in the approved fashion.

As well as Richard and Louise, I sent one to Aunt Eileen. It was only her second Christmas as a widow. I should make an effort. For the first time, I tried to imagine what it must have been like for her, all those years ago, being suddenly entrusted with four children who only wanted their mother and father.

I sent Kate a card as well. I wanted her to have something to remember me by. Perhaps when the band were successful, I'd be mentioned in interviews. I could look for oblique references to myself in their songs.

Again I had the dilemma of deciding where to post from. If I wanted to, I could drive to some remote location in the band's van. I would never again be able to buy my own car, or hire one, or use a credit card, or collect a pension. I was denied the right to pay tax. It was another proof of the effectiveness of my disappearance, even more than my aimlessness in the Christmas rush and the size of my Christmas card list. No-one who knew my real name knew my real address.

In the end, I posted them in the centre of London. I had told Richard that I was fine, hoped 'everything was OK with Louise and the baby' and that all was well with him too. I hoped they would be pleased with my benediction. I meant it, more or less.

****

I sat nervously by the door in the Wagon on the 20th. Ticket sales were up to thirty. That wouldn't exactly fill the room, and there wouldn't be much dancing if they worked their way through food meant for two hundred. A few extras came up and paid on the door. It was heading towards the mildly catastrophic fifty when a twenty-five year old in a jeans and leather jacket appeared and asked for his comps.

"NME. Did they not ring through?"

"Not a problem."

The presence of a journalist cheered the band up a lot and even though there were only about fifty people in when they came on, they were fired up for it. For all I had tried to organise an occasion, and pull off an astute piece of business, it was the music that mattered. Kate reached new heights, Guy did his stuff and John was unrecognisable from the sulky thirty-something I had left behind in the dressing room. They were very good and the crowd seemed to recognise it. Something had changed I was sure.

"That was fantastic," said Kate as the journalist walked away.

"Not quite two hundred people and huge profits, though."

"Have we lost money, Tony?"

"No. Nothing to speak of. Called in a few favours."

"But not enough to make a profit?" said John.

Kate gave him a 'there's no need for that' face. There was no need for her support, but she meant well so I let it go.

"You were good," I said.

"It was a brilliant crowd. Felt like an occasion."

"You made it one."

Guy was mainly interested in the food.

"It's good stuff," he said. "And these ribs. . . "

"All down to the journalist now," I said.

"Seemed very interested in you." said John. "Is he reviewing?"

"Said he would."

"God. I just hope he gives you a good notice. That's what matters most."

"No," said Kate, "It's the music. And the occasion. Thanks, Tony."

"Can you freeze Jambalaya?"

Kate stayed behind by herself afterwards which surprised me. John went off with some friends for a drink, and Guy had gone back to the Barbican. She talked happily as I drove her home. Her endless optimism began to annoy me after a while. She was so clean, so enthusiastic, so uncynical. I was happier with less fragile, less pure people - like Joanne, or seriously unhinged like Louise. Apart from our early encounters, I had not felt any real strong attraction for her. She still looked beautiful, especially on stage, but there was an earnestness about her which didn't attract me at all. Despite her singing voice, her face was the wholesome, innocent face beloved of. . . well, beloved of country music clichés. She was beautiful, and, I realised, there were few things I found less attractive than beauty.

"You're smart, aren't you?" she said. "And you don't push it but I know you've got passion." I liked her more for that.

"No point in having one without the other." I wasn't sure what that meant but it fitted in.

"I could tell how excited you were about tonight. You've taken us somewhere we always wanted to be. Like the next level." It was true.

"It's worth it, just to hear you singing - the expression on your face when the crowd are reacting."

"All of us."

"Yes." No, just you actually.

"We owe you. We've made real progress - and a lot of it's down to you." A lot of it? Bit more than that.

"Thanks - well I'd like to think so."

"So modest."

"I hope he really is with the NME", I said, at the risk of spoiling the moment and she just laughed. And kept on laughing.

A little ice in the gutter cracked under the tyres as I stopped the Transit outside her house. She was spending

Christmas with a gang of old friends who had hired 'a big old cottage in a forest somewhere'. I expected it would feature a roaring fire, and lots of food and drink and casual sex.

My bedsit would be cold. She would get out when she had finished her happy talking and I would go back to begin my miserable Christmas vigil. It annoyed me that she didn't know about my life, even though I worked hard to hide it. None of the band knew anything about me. And no-one from my past could know about them. I felt a kind of vanity in my loneliness. But it was still loneliness, and I had to get through six days until the day after Boxing Day.

"Tony, would you like to come in?"

I said that I would. Of course I would, even though this was only delaying the inevitable, perhaps making it worse when I finally had to confront it. I wanted a glass of sherry, but knew I would feel silly asking.

She seemed to brush against me at the door. I was afraid of misinterpreting this, and I was doubtful if Country Angels flirted so deviously, so I made no move to reciprocate, but I didn't pull away either. When she brought me a small glass of wine, her hand definitely waited longer than was necessary just touching mine. When she went to the window to look out into the night, I counted to twelve, then I went over and stood next to her.

If I was wrong here, I'd never be able to face her and the band again – NME review or no NME review. The last shred of hope I had would be gone; no more Svengali, no more van-driving. It was a huge risk. Then she turned and launched into me with a kiss. She was so beautiful. I launched right back, loving everything about her. We hardly spoke.

Next day, I was rushing down Oxford Street buying jokey Christmas decorations and trying to find a present that showed affection and even hints of love, but without presumption or surrender. Regents Street and Bond Street were better but more expensive. Earrings? Not too small, because she had so much hair. Not too big either, in the name of taste.

I loved being in bed with her. In everything she did she was single-minded, enthusiastic and loveable. I found myself playing the role of a shy dreamy Englishman who could break out of his reserve in moments of high passion, and retain fragments of that passion when he resumed his reserve.

She cancelled her Christmas in the forest.

"Look - if you. . . "

"Don't be ridiculous, Tony."

We spent all Christmas Day together. She liked the earrings and wore them all day. We didn't have turkey. She agreed with me that it always tasted like fishy cotton wool anyway. We had vegetable pate on crackers, grapes, tomato and basil salad, mushroom risotto and Bordeaux, a selection of cheeses. We said a variety of things.

1. Mm, that's gorgeous.
2. Mm, you're gorgeous.
3. You really, really are gorgeous.
4. Take me over, please just take me over.
5. Just there.
6. You are so beautiful, I could.
7. Do you want me to?
8. I love the taste of your fingernails.
9. I want this to go on forever - do you think it will?
10. I love your thighs.
11. Is that nice?
12. I feel so strong with you.
13. I feel like I'm a baby born. I just can't touch enough of you.
14. Do you mind if I kiss you there, like that?
15. You've got beautiful eyes.
16. It's gorgeous when you stop and start again.
17. Just put the pillow there.
18. I'm knackered, absolutely (with a smile, a happy reciprocated smile).
19. Do you mind me asking if there's - if there's anybody else?
20. This is the best Christmas I've had since ever. Best before was when I was ten - I got a cowboy outfit. If

you kiss me now there'll be no competition.

21. You are a real one-off.
22. I can just feel you all over.
23. Do you like that?
24. Please, oh please.
25. I'm very glad we met.
26. And what about you, mysterious?
27. Is there anywhere open we can get them today?
28. Would you rub some of this on my back?
29. Would you rub some of this on my front?
30. Does that? Does that not?
31. No, sorry, but I will not sing.
32. I love absolutely everything about you, every inch of you, you are so gorgeous, you deserve everything (whispered in the ear).
33. You look beautiful in that dressing gown, your hair crumpled - and out of it you're just...
34. Wonder what time it is.
35. You're very ticklish.
36. Wonder what the Pope's doing now.
37. There something about the underside of your nose that makes me want to come - completely.
38. I'd like to put you in a cake and eat my way through.
39. Just there now, bit more round.
40. I love you doing that.
41. If I were to grip the cracker there, would you do the same at the other end - yes, just there - and try to

pull.

42. Is there. . . ?
43. What?
44. Anything else you want me to?
45. Lovely strong hands, haven't you?
46. Is there?
47. Just lovely.
48. Do you mind me asking - anyone else?
49. I always thought.
50. What?
51. You and John.
52. (After laughing) I always wondered.
53. What?
54. Never saw you with anyone. Not that there's anything wrong with that.
55. Perhaps I'm just shy.
56. Don't seem very shy now.
57. Happy Christmas.

"Do you feel we know each other?" I asked

"Mm."

"Really? You're very trusting aren't you, with this mysterious young roadie here?"

"Well, I've known him long enough and well enough."

"But you don't know anything about me."

"I do."

"But my background," the word sounded hollow. "There are things."

There had been a chance of a gig in Reading, which I had never followed up or told them about. Good money and a good venue, but it was away from London where I felt safe, and too close to the places where I didn't feel safe at all. It had been an opportunity and I had concealed it. It was a bad thing for a lover to do - never mind a Svengali. I would confess, but not now, not until I trusted her in a mundane way, and at present I was too mesmerised by the shape and warmth and movement of her body to know what I was doing.

"Do you think you're bad?"

"No - stupid sometimes, which can be worse in a way - but no, not really bad."

"So many words," she laughed, "And do you mean me any harm?"

"No."

"And you're telling the truth there, that's what matters. Details whenever you like; I know enough. We've all done something. We've all stolen from shops or stolen a lover. We've all done something we aren't proud of later, but that's no reason not to trust. And there's worse things than trusting. Like not trusting."

There were times when she sounded like a Country and Western singer or something.

"Now come on, lover boy, and give me a kiss. It'll be

nice, I promise you. Trust me."

On Boxing Day there still wasn't snow on the ground. That would have been too much, but there was a coating of frost early on, and when we opened the bedroom window, the moisture in our breath turned the air silver grey as it passed through. The special magic was that some of that warm moisture had been born in the mouth of one person and passed over to the other in a beautiful slobbery kiss, the way infection is passed.

CHAPTER 20

We, sorry I mean the band, played half a dozen times in January, and, especially considering it was the quietest time of the year, things were still improving. The NME didn't give us a review in the end, so much as an honourable mention which concentrated on Kate, but our audiences were steadily, if very slowly increasing. I thought that we could benefit from having someone else in, to play a bit of pedal steel guitar or extra rhythm. I talked about it with Kate, and she mentioned it to Guy, who shrugged in non-disagreement, and John who made some comment about the money having to be split into smaller shares. I suggested advertising for someone, but in the end, we decided that it would be best to wait until Kate came back from Tennessee.

For me, things were better in every way, and not just because of the glow which new sex puts on everything. We had another special concert on the fourteenth of February. I meant it to be ironic, but I don't think anyone else realised. Ironic or not, it brought in two hundred and ten people paying six pounds each. Kate would have something to add to her spending money.

John injured his wrist before the next pub gig, but we managed to find a replacement, Archie. He picked up our songs very quickly, and he had a slightly lighter touch than John. He had a friend who played pedal steel guitar, he said, in case we were ever interested. John missed the odd practice later in the month. It was not important in itself, but it was annoying that he didn't always give us a lot of notice. If we could, we went ahead without him. It was nothing to endanger his status in the band, of course. He was an integral part of it and always would be - as long as he wanted to be.

His sulky temper added to the richness of the mix; with Kate's beautiful strong voice and Guy's subtle but reliable guitar and singing. It was because he was so much part of it that it didn't matter if someone else took his place when he couldn't make it. On one occasion we didn't manage to let him know before arranging a practice. I did ring, but there had been no reply. Archie was available and he asked if the pedal steel guitarist he knew could come along. It was a shame John wasn't there because it went so well. But it had always been understood that the band took priority, and he had started forgetting that himself, with missing practices and picking fights.

Guy's wife, Imogen, was at this practice. I liked her; she wasn't at all the stereotypical City woman.

"I tend not to tell people that I'm married to a Good Old Boy," she said.

"Oh, I thought you were married to Guy," I said and she smiled. "He is very talented, isn't he?"

"And committed," she said. "He says you've brought them on a lot. Apparently you're the great organiser and ideas man."

I blushed happily. She was all right.

"Well I couldn't play an instrument to save my life, and I want to do something musical."

"They deserve a chance - I like that new, what is it, pedal steel guitar?"

"Yes. Sean. Friend of Archie's." We stopped talking to applaud.

"I love this one," she said as they played the opening to Tennessee Waltz. "Her voice is beautiful in this." Guy did the harmonies.

John got very drunk at the next rehearsal, and stormed out complaining about plots. He apologised the next day and we apologised for not managing to tell him about the previous practice. He had been out of London anyway, and I think he assumed we had made more effort to contact him than we had. This helped calm him down and it was all forgotten.

All the same, it was probably as well that the band would be having a break for a few weeks while Kate was away. It would give us all a chance to cool down and consider things.

"Is your cousin the same one who came over when you were thirteen?"

"You have some memory."

She'd had a hard time back at school for preferring Country to Duran Duran, but it hadn't threatened her love for the music. Knowing her, it would have just made it stronger and more passionate.

I was a bit worried about this cousin of hers. He'd been about seventeen when he came over, and the glamour of being a singer in America must have made a big impression on her at the time - the kind that often doesn't go away. Women don't forget their first good impressions of men, apart from me. Louis, he was called. Another to add to the ever-increasing list of names I hated. It wasn't impossible that her love for country music was a sublimation of her love for Louis. Besides, he lived near Nashville, which is a fairly obvious place for a beautiful English country singer with a handsome cousin involved in the business to want to stay.

We were spending a lot of time together at her flat now, although I still had the bedsit, and the promise of a cheaper room in a much nicer flat after Easter, sharing with a friend of Guy's. I was working occasional nights in a pub now, as well, but otherwise I had nothing else to do outside the band, and I knew I would miss Kate when she went away.

"I'll miss you as well," she said, "Very much."

It was no time to ask about her cousin's marital state, or that of all the broad-shouldered, tanned Tennessee boys she would meet out there. I knew she meant what she said now, most of the time. She had been the first to say 'I love you'; I had responded in kind and it had quickly become an established fact, but we had never hammered out exactly what it meant. I assumed it meant monogamy but it was a tricky question to ask, especially when she was about to leave the country. I was worried this trip might change our status even before I knew what it was. The anxiety intensified my love again.

She left in early March. We had frantic sex in the days before she left. I hoped it would make her miss me more. Also, I have to admit, I suspect that I was trying to sate her and tire her before her holiday. This was rather ambitious, considering that she would have three weeks in which to recover her energy and appetite, but I thought it was worth a try, so I felt ashamed when it became obvious that it was not her who would tire first. And more ashamed because she would never have done it with the same pathetic possessive motive as me.

"I do worry." I had meant not to say it, but I did.

"What about?"

"Well - you."

"That's sweet, but don't. No need. I'll be fine."

"Good. I hope so." She looked at me, guessing that there was more. "I don't just mean you, though," I confessed, "I mean you and me." I knew this kind of wheedling never got anybody anywhere. You're never going to manage to beg someone to become as besotted with you as you are with them - but it was out now.

"Trust me," she said and kissed me.

"I do." Although it was obvious from my previous question that I didn't. "Course I do."

"But what I really want reassurance on is that you'll be coming back with a Southern Belle accent." I said, to lighten the tone and try to claw back some self-respect.

"Ah surely wiall, boy."

I fell on her and we played the tiring game again. Even when we were doing it, I couldn't ignore the fact that she had never asked if I wanted to go with her. No wonder I didn't trust her.

"Tony," she said later. "I'll understand if you don't, but would you like to come with me?"

It was the question I dreaded.

"Thanks - I'd love to but . . ." But if I try getting through passport control, you'll find out that I am suspected of involvement with a gangland murder - ridiculous though that may sound.

"Then do."

"I wouldn't want to cramp your style." That was exactly what I wanted to do; I would have loved to have cramped her style - big style.

"Is it money?"

"No. Well, I could get it together, but even if you say I'm not, I feel I'd be crashing in. Actually do you know I haven't even got a passport - an up to date passport?" She took that to mean I couldn't get the money together, and was too proud to ask, so she tactfully let it rest.

We agreed that I would stay in her flat when she was away. It was a lot more comfortable than my bedsit and it had a telephone. I felt closer to her just being near her furniture and it made a warm and welcoming refuge. Actually, I felt I needed a hiding place less and less as time passed and I tried to move back into financial and legal respectability. As well as my cash in hand work in the pub, my name was on a Council Tax payments book and I had sent in an application to join the Co-operative Bank. A credit card would be next, and a drivers' licence, then perhaps direct payments into the account from a job, followed by who knows what. Anything that didn't need a Birth Certificate. I saw her off at Heathrow, then headed back to her flat with a Tandoori King Prawn and a bottle of Fitou to console myself.

The following night, as I sat gazing into her gas fire, with a cup of black coffee and a plate of refried beans inside me and the old computerised chess waiting patiently on the arm of the chair, I found myself thinking about families, more specifically babies. Without them there are no families, long-term at least. This I knew already, even I had worked that out, but it had never seemed like a personal issue before. Dwight Yoakam had just been singing about leaving his coal mining family in Kentucky to work in the city, so that might have had something to do with it. On the other hand, Dwight had been preceded by Steve Earle tearing through town with wild gangs, breaking hearts, throwing child-seats into dumpsters and heading out into the night, and I had not developed an urge to hit the highway, and live each day like it was my last. The telephone rang.

"Hello?"

"Hello, Tony."

"Kate?"

"Expecting someone else? Course it is. How are you?"

"Fine, fine. Not bad at all. Just sitting in front of your fire day-dreaming. How about you?"

"Great, well, fine. Bit tired but it's great. My cousins and their friends are all very nice. Really friendly."

"What's it like there?"

"I like it. It's more modern than I thought, and bigger than I expected and I miss you so much."

"I'm glad," I said. "Not that you miss me in itself. It's not nice. I know." I added hastily. It was one of those points where telephone conversations can lurch uncontrollably into spirals of misunderstanding, anger and hurt. I concentrated on preventing a crisis. "I'm glad because it means you're thinking about me."

"Of course I am."

"I miss you a lot as well." I had been going to tell her what I had been thinking, then decided against it. It was too open to misinterpretation over the phone and across the ocean. "Already really looking forward to seeing you again."

"So am I."

"I hope you have a really good time, though." And I did mean it.

"Be really good if you were here as well - I'm sure you'd love it. It's amazing; I look out of the phone booth and it's Nashville outside, looking just like you expect it to. I've shown them all your picture and told them what you're doing for the band - and me. All dying to meet you."

Yeah, right. I was always really excited about meeting female friends' boyfriends too.

"Real shame you're not here."

"Next time. Definitely." Change the subject. "Bet it's warmer there as well."

"Reckon you're right."

"Seen anybody famous yet?"

"Three people who look like Johnny Cash, and the odd beard that might have concealed Waylon Jennings."

"Better than nothing I suppose."

"It's not really late there is it?" It suddenly occurred to her.

"No - you're fine. About ten."

"At night, yeah? I'm hopeless with the time thing. Anyway, the money's going anyway."

This was the call box (had she just said 'phone booth'?

She'd only been there two days) equivalent of the 'I'll let you get on' of domestic phone calls, but I understood.

"OK, take care. Feel better for talking to you. Looking forward to seeing you. Really am. Send a card, yes?"

"Oh, yes. Bye, bye. I love you."

I understood that as well and said the same in reply.

But you could love someone and still settle in Nashville with cousin Buck, or you could start off loving someone and just change your mind while on holiday. It is an unreliable word. All the same, I loved her, or if I didn't, then I knew I was on my way to it, and she sounded much the same. But I did feel better. By the time I did the washing up I found myself singing.

“Heaven's just a sin away, ah wah ah whoah...”.

A few days later a card arrived from Kate at Kate's flat. It had a picture of the Grand Ole Oprey on the front. She was still having a good time. In fact from the date on the card, it was the same good time she had been having when we spoke on the phone. I'd probably laugh, she said, but she had been to the place on the front of the card. She was a tourist after all.

She had heard, and was going to hear lots of music at lots of different places. There was so much choice, and though some of it was very commercial, the place did have a spiritual feel about it as well. More than London anyway. She missed me a lot and sent me all her love. No mention of Louis. She phoned the same evening.

"Got a postcard this morning," I said.

"Oh. Who from?"

"Oh, I don't know. Haven't bothered reading it yet. America somewhere."

"Wonder how they got the address."

"So you're enjoying yourself still?"

"Yes. It is really special here. The country - it's not countryside like we think of it - tidy roads and little fields and oak trees and bushes." I hadn't known she was a tree expert. "So vast here. And the people are really inspiring. Everything seems to be artistic or spiritual or both. It takes a while to realise that. It's because it's all so whole-hearted and sincere here. TV, churches, bars, music. You don't have to hold back. I know it sounds corny, but it's real."

"Right - feels young sort of?" I suggested.

"Yes, but very aware of the ancient past. In the names even. You know, like Memphis?"

"How's your cousin?" seemed like a good link with the ancients.

"Which one? There's so many."

"The guitarist one you met the other time. The one who came over."

"Oh Louis. He's fine, but I don't actually see much of him. It's my other cousin - Liz - I see most of. Her and Gabe, her husband. They're really nice, hospitable, open."

"Good."

"Tony?"

"Yes."

"Are you - are you annoyed or worried or anything?"

"No, not annoyed or worried or anything," just irritated by so much positive energy. "Why?"

"Just. . . last time. . . it was as if there was something you wanted to say but didn't."

"No. Nothing I can remember. No." This was making me feel uneasy. "No. Made me feel really good that call."

"Do you know how I feel?"

"I think so." She sighed. Obviously honesty was too ambiguous. "Course I do. You said it on your card. It was really good to get that as well."

"But it's different on a card to saying it. When you're away. Isn't it? Do you not find it hard?" It was back to all that spontaneity and sincerity. Very difficult to deal with. Always made me feel devious.

"It's much easier when I'm with you - that's probably why I sound a bit - if I sound a bit." I was floundering.

"Well say that if you feel it. You should never be afraid of saying what you believe." That wouldn't take long.

"Yes, you're right. You help, you know. I do miss you."

"I'm missing you a lot as well. Wish you were here. There's things here I can get into very deeply, though. That makes it easier for me than you, I know. But I don't want to waste my time here - just because there's somewhere else I'd rather be. Do you know what I mean?"

"Yes," I said. I was getting fed up with this now.

"I feel everything very strongly now, which makes it all the harder not to be with you. Sometimes I miss you so much it really hurts. I've done some singing - just with a few of Liz and Gabriel's friends and that was great, really uplifting. They think I sing in a real English accent, and I'm putting on an American one. Or at least I thought I was." At last we both laughed.

"We can do some great things with the band when you're back - expect you're learning a lot. Lots of new ideas you'll probably have. Be good to be in bed with you as well."

"Why?" And we were laughing again. It was a good phone call in the end, I thought, but then it wasn't the end yet. There was the 'I'd better get on now bit', and the agonising over how to say goodbye bit, and the 'if I really loved her I wouldn't be relieved we were finished' bit.

"It's great to be able at least to talk to you, but I'm on Gabriel's phone and it'll be costing them a fortune and I know they won't take any money for it. I said could I reverse the charges, but they wouldn't have it. Better to accept just as we accept from the Lord as they say here." I laughed. "I've learnt a lot here. I love you more than ever."

"OK. Thanks for ringing, brilliant to hear your voice.

And thanks for the card."

"I'm sorry it was the same day."

"No, no," I protested, “It’s made it a doubly good day. Trebly.” There are things you say in the early stages on a relationship which are not really fit for public consumption.

"Anyway - goodbye. Take care. Be great to see you again and touch you again."

"Yes it will. Can't wait. You enjoy yourself. Love you."

"Goodbye - me too."

****

"Did you hear about Sammy from downstairs?"

"No," I said.

"Got caught. Fighting dogs again."

"Fighting dogs?"

“Pitbulls. For the betting." At least that was better than fighting them himself.

"Dodgy is it?"

"Yes. They broke it up. It's not legal."

"No."

"It's illegal."

"That as well."

"Saw on the telly about it - just the other week there. Loads of blood. They really lay into each other. Both of them get killed's often as not."

"Aye - thought they'd banned them."

I began edging away past him towards my door. As far as I remembered he was called Michael, and he lived in the bedsit next door. We had exchanged no more than 'You all rights' in the past, when I wouldn't have minded a conversation with another human being, but now I had moved on. I just wanted to grab a few clothes and get back to Kate's. I backed away while he spoke, and twisted myself round to unlock the door and get into my room while wishing him all the best. I hoped I'd never have to stay here again. If I could take enough with me now, I might never have to come back.

I collected clothes and cassettes, and checked for anything that could identify me. There was my diary and various papers which needed shredding before I binned them. I had just started when the police car pulled up. I caught a glimpse of it before I ducked down and waited for the bell to ring. It went off in one of the other rooms. I waited. Then they tried a different bell. And then mine. It wasn't the kind of place where you personalised your door bell so they must be guessing. Then I heard my neighbour's door open and footsteps.

It was hard to believe that they had tracked me down now, when my life was perfect – and I couldn't see how they could have found me. They mustn't know I was living at Kate's or they wouldn't have been watching for me here. Perhaps there was some dingy reward that someone like Michael would shop me for. It was Michael who had gone to the door as well. Or perhaps I had used my cash card once too often and been followed. It didn't really matter why; they were here.

My room was on the second floor and the only window gave out on to the street where the police car was. I was too frightened to move anyway, and even if I hadn't been I would probably have only succeeded in breaking my back trying to climb down a drain-pipe and that wouldn't have helped anything, so I waited. I was like a character in a Country song – a fugitive glad he had at least given his real first name to the woman he loved so that she had called him by it, until she found out the truth.

After a few minutes, I heard Michael's door open and close as he returned to his room alone. Then I heard the police car leaving. I peered out through my dusty curtain. No sign of danger. I quietly collected everything, even the half-shredded papers while counting up to one thousand. When I reached it, I opened my door softly and padded down the corridor. Michael leapt out as I passed his door, and I got a sense of what it must be like to die of shock.

"Away out again?"

"Yeah. Cheers. Bye."

There was no sign of anyone on the stairs.

"Did they not try your bell as well?" he said.

"Who?" He laughed at that.

"You hiding from the Law as well?"

"No. No. Of course not. No."

"If you say so, mate."

"No. I mean it," I mustn't raise suspicion now.

"Looks like Sammy's been doing more than fighting with dogs. You see him, give him the nod. I said I'd not seen him."

"Right. Me neither."

Michael grinned and put out his hand. I seemed to be accidentally gravitating towards criminality again. I didn't belong there. I was a maverick urban cowboy. I wished Kate was here. It was hard to believe how much I had moved on since that night in the Marquis of Granby.

I realised I was going to have to shake his hand.

"Michael," he told me, and did that thing where he put his upper arm against mine as we shook.

"Tony. Short for Antonio," I said, in an attempt to confuse any pursuing posse, and I disengaged as quickly as I could without appearing unfriendly. He smelt slightly stale.

"Take care, mate," I called out as I walked carefully down the stairs. I realised I was shaking, so I held tightly to the banister. The police might well be waiting around the corner and this was not a time to go over on an ankle and draw attention to myself. At least Brendan was not following close behind me this time; I looked back and saw Michael disappear into his room.

There was no sign of the police outside, and I saw a bus pulling up, so I jumped on. It took me in the wrong direction, but with every stop we passed I breathed more and more naturally. When we reached the end of the line I thought Archway had never looked more beautiful and I didn't even resent the twelve pounds it cost me to get a taxi back to the paradise of Kate's flat.

It was hard not having anyone to tell, but then I couldn't have told Kate, even if she had been there. But being alone in her flat was very different to being really alone in my miserable bedsit. Guy gave me a ring that night to see if I had heard from her. They had had a card. He thought she was sounding very American. We laughed. I was becoming established again. I really liked that; and I really liked Kate. I was going to have to tell her the truth sometime, but perhaps not until I was sure quite how established I was.

There were three other callers (two male), but I reasoned that if they were anyone important, they would know that she was away. Another postcard arrived with a big whitewashed church on the front. She'd got me a present she said. A souvenir of Tennessee. That was nice.

****

She gave me a big hug at the airport. I had forgotten what it was like to touch her and I found it hard to believe how good she looked. She had a slight sunny glow about her; her skin was warm and soft; and she was female.

"I'm really glad you managed to get here, Tony."

I smiled back. We put her bags in the back of the van. She was wearing a jumper that showed her neck and the tops of her shoulders. I kissed her. She smiled as she turned her head.

"It's cold here. And so grey. Nice to see you though; you're neither."

"I got your card - the church one - a couple of days ago."

"Good. I'm glad you got it before I was back."

"So how was everything?"

"That can wait. Are you OK?" I smiled back. "I've got loads of photos, and things to tell you - it's just a different world out there. Helps you see things clearly. What's important." She looked at me meaningfully.

I felt, on the whole, glad to be part of what was important, although I hoped her portentous style of speaking would be rubbed off again by England before too long. I leant across to kiss her over the gearstick. Once I managed it, I pulled back. I still had to drive carefully; I remembered it was one of my most attractive features. She talked about people and towns and music and churches. It was a very one-sided conversation so I felt it was reasonable to stop listening and concentrate on her body, with occasional glances at the road ahead. Back at the flat, she was still fired up, excited but tired from her journey.

"Do you want to go to bed?" I asked.

She smiled at me. She was doing a lot of smiling, but it was a purer type of smile than I would have liked; the sort of smile when you have good news to announce, or a surprise; or perhaps the kind you get after very draining sex. Beatific. I smiled back, but mine was more a sly pre-sex smile. I was right to anticipate disappointment.

"Can I do something first? They've been very good to me. Shown me a lot." Them. Her cousins. I listened to her making the call.

"Yes I will, Liz, don't worry and thanks again for all you've done. It was great - life-changing. You've got no idea, or perhaps you have. Say to Gabriel as well. Sorry if I've got you out of bed or anything. Good. OK, yes then, thanks so much. Bye and God bless." Didn't sound like anything to worry about there. Unless it was in code.

When the call was over, I brought her a cup of tea.

“Mm, great. That's one thing I've missed about being here. One thing,” she smiled. Then she handed me a carrier bag, smiling even more. My present was a Stetson. “Do you like it? Really like it?” It really seemed to matter to her.

I did, and I said I did. She was delighted and gave me another hug. I tried to turn it into something more sexual, but all she was giving me was love and affection.

"Can I show you some photographs? Make me feel I'm back with you properly by sharing them with you. Wish you could've been there."

I felt disappointed that she wasn't feeling the same way as me, but then she hadn't just spent the last few weeks hanging around the flat with an erection, waiting for this moment. If it was the other way around, and I had just got off a plane, perhaps I wouldn't feel like jumping straight into bed with her. Perhaps. There were a lot of photographs - Nashville, Memphis, big American cars and smiling children and cousins and farms; men with guitars, and churches in the wilderness.

After her tea she said she was going into the bedroom and gave me a look that nearly made me faint.

Will you come along in five minutes?" She bit her lip. "I'll be in bed then."

When my time was up, I pushed open the bedroom door, aching with lust. She pulled the covers back from her naked body and told me in a whisper to come over to her, slowly. She had never played games like this before, and I loved it.

"Don't bother, Tony," she said when I started fumbling in the drawer for Durex, "No need."

"You sure?"

She started doing that smile again. I wasn't sure. On the positive side, this did suggest she hadn't been sleeping with anyone over there, but the idea still worried me. She had always wanted to use them before. I felt the pure fire of my lust fading. That smile, though.

"Shit. You're not pregnant are you?" The smile became a laugh.

"No. Not yet anyway."

"In that case," I turned back to the drawer, but she turned me round with her hand on my shoulder.

"What will happen will happen," she informed me.

"Not if you stop it. Just common sense."

"There you are again, Tony. You'll never be happy that way."

I muttered disagreement, but I tailed off as she started kissing my neck and shoulders.

“Let go,” she urged me. “I want to make you feel so, so good.” Perhaps she was right; perhaps I had to learn to trust and give and accept. I hadn’t found any Durex yet anyway.

I was turned on by her recklessness - different to the measured rebellion of Joanne, or the madness of Louise. Her face was lit up by it, and I was in such a state that if this was to be a conception it would be a very rapid one. Then we did it again, slowly, and it was easy to ignore my better judgement under the weight of so much pure pleasure.

It came back with force afterwards, though. I was angry with myself for being so stupid as to be guided by her stupidity. This was as nothing compared with the stupidity to follow.

"Tony, it'll be OK - with God's help."

"Who?"

"God."

"What's God got to do with it?"

"Everything. God's part of everything."

"God is?" I looked at her, smiling kindly at me. She nodded beatifically.

"You haven't signed up with some crazy church out there have you?"

"It's not like joining the army or something, Tony. More like finding out you've always been a part of it." She smiled at my puzzlement. "Joining is just an outward sign. Like we join each other when we make love. You know? A sign. A beautiful sign."

"What?" I leant on my elbow and tried to stare through her eyes into her stupid brain. "You have, haven't you?"

"Yes," she said, still smiling. "It's different, though, to becoming a Catholic or something and taking on their rules." She explained it slowly as if it was me that was the idiot. "It's as if I've recognised the church in me. It's what's right for me and the Lord. It's what's within that matters. You can be in a church like you can be in a band or in a relationship."

I spoke even more deliberately than her.

"That doesn't mean anything."

"It does, Tony. I only wish you knew."

"Bollocks."

"I love you so much - do you know that?" She was forgiving me, which really pissed me off.

"At the moment - with you talking like this, I'm concerned about what that means."

"That's it again, Tony. Always worrying, taking the pessimistic view. Why waste time on the little details that don't matter? God will provide."

"No he won't. And do you now why? Because he doesn't fucking exist."

"Then explain the Bible."

"Seriously, Kate. I was brought up with this shite. Fourteen years of Catholic education. Not a couple of weeks of born-again nonsense in a cottonfield."

It was a shame I couldn't think of something better than 'cottonfield'; the only alternative was 'honky-tonk'; but she just smiled at me again. I could tell from the smile that I was being forgiven again. I prayed to God that I had not just made this woman pregnant.

"Two thousand years," she said slowly, as if she had never used such a large number before, "And still he is not being followed by so many people - and why? No faith. No trust. No giving." She looked at me, accusingly, "No accepting. But it will change."

"Because it's prophesied in some bit of the Bible you

haven't read?"

"Do you know what I thought on the plane coming here?"

"Surprise me."

"Well, you know when we first slept together, made love?" She had that face on again. "Christmas," she added, with one of those encouraging nods intended to bring out a nod in response. Doctors, social workers, psychiatrists and psychopaths use them.

"December 20th, Year of Our Lord 1996. Hallelujah."

"And do you remember what you said then?"

"I said lots of things."

"You said you felt like a baby." That was embarrassing.

"No."

"And don't tell me you haven't been thinking about babies when I've been away."

That was alarming. A bit like imagining your parents are dead and then finding out they are.

"Kate - tell me you aren't pregnant."

"I've already told you. Although now. . . if it's God's will."

"Shite."

"It all makes sense."

"Course it fucking doesn't. Anybody who thinks that wants locking up."

"Don't be angry. Listen. Don't you see? We give birth to each other like Jesus does to us. And you are like him."

"Pardon?"

"We are made in his image and likeness." This was off the scale, beyond the scale. And I had just had unprotected sex with this woman – twice.

"You felt it as well, I know. It all makes sense now. And over there I learnt to express everything that I might once have turned away from. Now I know. It all fits in. Think about it. My cousin Elizabeth, like Mary's cousin Elizabeth; and Gabriel, like the Archangel Gabriel. They showed me how to welcome the warmth of truth and Revelation." Then she hit a climax, "Tony, we could be the Holy Family."

"We could what?"

"Don't you see? Christmas, Elizabeth, Gabriel, and love."

"One possibility."

"What others can there be?"

"That you are just the latest and stupidest in a long line of stupid women I've been stupid enough to fuck."

****

"That wasn't nice."

"No."

"But she was so sure of herself. I just wanted to shock her, so I told her anything I could think of. I told her who I really was, and about our parents, and you and Louise and Joanne and Victoria and Crimewatch and Brendan and the killing and the money - all to upset her."

"Right."

"It didn't though. You could see her, just forgiving everything. They're like that - religious types."

Richard smiled wryly.

"They love it when you exhaust yourself pouring out venom and leaving yourself wide open so they can just ooze in and collect the pieces and explain it all back to you. Bastards."

Richard didn't challenge me or question me. He didn't even seem very surprised. I suppose priests are used to opening their doors to all kinds of stragglers, which is what I was, having gone straight from Kate's bed to the station without even packing a bag.

"I don't feel good about bringing Mam and Dad into it. Using them to score points."

"I'm sure they wouldn't have minded," said Richard. "And then what happened?"

"I stormed out. Well, I grabbed a few things - very few things - and then stormed out. Went to the station and came straight here."

I hadn't thought about it at the time. I just went to the station and bought a ticket. A less nice brother would have made some comment along the lines of "Nice if you'd checked first"; but he just offered me a bed and a change of clothes if I needed them.

Louise appeared and joined him on the settee. I had forgotten about her but I was glad she had missed the misogynist rant. She was like someone from another life. She had changed. Her hair was longer, and she was older, less slender – definitely less elfin. She looked like a mother now, domesticated. But there was still a flash of something dangerous in her eyes, even though it was subdued at the moment.

"I know circumstances are a bit weird, but it's good to see you."

Richard nodded in agreement and before I could work out how to respond, their baby's crying crackled into the room through the monitor, and Louise went to see to her. I wasn't as nice a brother as Richard, and once we had watched her leave the room, I turned to him.

"Did you tell her your plan to pass that baby off as mine?" He looked hurt.

"Yes. She wasn't impressed. Sorry, Tony, I wasn't thinking straight. Sorry."

I tried to stop feeling sorry for him by reminding myself he must have discussed me with Louise in the sanctimonious way couples do about people they have shat on. I still did though.

"No. And look - thanks for putting me up. I know it's not a good time. I hope it's not putting you in any danger."

"Danger?"

"I know it's a while ago, but in case the police were still watching or anything."

His bewilderment cleared.

"Oh you mean with things at that training place." It was obvious he thought I was imagining it all, but he was worried about me, which was nice. "I never really understood that. Are you sure the police are after you? I rang Joanne like you asked and she didn't think so."

"You mean she thought I was mad."

"No. Unnecessarily stressed, perhaps," he tried.

"But it was on Crimewatch," I moaned.

"Never watch it myself."

"But there was someone stabbed. They might have been killed - I never found out. Earlier, when I was doing that course."

"But that was nothing to do with you," he said. He was reminding me, but I thought I detected the tiniest hint of a question there. Perhaps not, perhaps that was more what I would have thought about someone in my position.

"No. Course not. But they don't know that. They think I'm part of it all. It said so." I hadn't looked at a paper or seen the news for ages, I realised. Ever since I had got involved with Kate I had lost interest in the outside world. "It was probably on the news. You didn't see anything?"

"No," he said, apologetically, "But then I have been

busy." We fell into silence. Louise came back into the room.

"She's OK," she said, to Richard. She had put slippers on. I'd never seen her in slippers before.

"Teething or something?" I attempted.

"Bit early for that."

"Is it?"

"But it's like that."

"I was just saying to Richard, I appreciate you putting me up like this."

"We're glad you feel able to come here," she said.

"What have people been like?" I asked.

"Some great, some awful."

"And the church?"

"Well I'm sure it will survive and so will we. Our most pressing problems are practical ones." Like any new parents. "I need to get a job, but there are very few vacancies for errant priests at the moment," he said with a smile.

"Or runaways." We all smiled.

"And look, thanks again for letting me stop. I'll not be too long I promise. Just need a couple of days rest. Two or three days."

Most couples would have conferred before agreeing; they both just nodded straight away.

"I can't really decide what to do. And now there's Kate as well. I've made a real mess of things."

They didn't disagree, but reminded me that I was hardly unique. Suddenly, a great wave of tiredness swept over me, and I shivered, although half an hour in this living room had warmed my body through again, and I was in a dry shirt and jeans.

"You must think we're some family," I said to Louise as we passed out of the room. She laughed. It was, I'm sorry but I have to say it, a sexy laugh, always had been.

"Well I've been very keen to get into it one way and another, so what does that say about me?" she said and laughed again. That was more like the Louise I had known – startling, reckless, possibly flirtatious.

I fell asleep the moment my head touched the pillow. Yes, cliché, but it was exactly, literally true. I remember undressing quickly and pulling back the quilt, my body thrilling at the prospect of lying down, my head about to touch the pillow and then I was asleep. I slept heavily and long, dreaming about a stray dog I had met in my walk around town and about booking into some big comfortable hotel and ordering sandwiches, crisps and blankets from room service. Louise was room service.

CHAPTER 21

It was late morning when I woke up. I was hungry but I felt a little anxious so I lay still in the foetal position, hoping the feeling would pass. It was subsiding when I heard footsteps and a gentle knock at the door.

"Hello?" I called.

It was Louise asking if I wanted anything to eat. She didn't come in, which I took to be an acknowledgement of the continuing sexual tension between us. I said I'd like a cup of tea, and promised that I'd be up soon. Ten minutes later she came in with a cup of tea and a plate of biscuits - Hobnobs and Fruit Shortbreads.

"Thanks. I promise I won't be like this for long - just today."

After she left, I reran the scene a few times looking for signs of sexual tension. Disappointingly few. None really, so after a while I persuaded myself in stages to sit up, get out of bed, wash and dress. A spare towel had been left at the bottom of the bed when I was asleep. Considerate - but hardly sexually charged.

I went down to the kitchen where Louise was chopping turnips and parsnips. For all they were disgraced priest and semi-incestuous cuckolder, they seemed to be falling into nice suburban couple roles very quickly. She read my mind as usual.

"Richard does cook as well," she assured me, "And I'll be back at work again quite soon. I think he's a bit apprehensive about looking after Claire. But he'll be great. Can't be easy for him either. Must be bored."

"Well, he's got you two - hard to imagine how he could be bored." That pleased her. Now I was getting used to being around her again, I could see more of the Louise I had known, despite all the changes.

I absorbed TV and warmth and solid food and a good few glasses of brandy. When they went to bed I had the house to myself, so I took my shoes off, lay on the settee and watched videos. They had a small but classy collection. I was half-way through The Godfather before I realised that I was watching a film about my most recent profession, and I was pissed enough to smile about the fact. I woke up on the settee at about three and went to bed. I was woken by Claire's crying two or three hours later, but went back to sleep until midday. Then I had tea and toast and mooched around the house getting in Louise's way. My brother was out again doing something which he hoped might lead to a job.

"The cost of a child-minder's going to cancel out most of the money for any job he's going to get. Still, he needs a start."

"He's not the only one."

"Who's Victoria?"

I had mentioned her name the previous night, in

passing, as part of a list of people I had come across in my stumble on the wild side, and Louise had registered it. She missed nothing.

"Just someone I ran into on the way. You know me."

She knew I was hiding something but let me off. That was nice. I stayed in all day, which was also nice. I had intended to go for a walk, but I didn't; officially in case the house was being watched by the police, but more because I just liked being in the house, warm and comfortable, and with Louise. Despite her new persona (She was now obsessed with the baby's cough. Did she have croup? What was croup?), she still looked very good. I could see how this might become a problem, but in the short term I would indulge myself. I felt safe in the house, but not free, as I had done in London.

London. None of the people who knew me there could possibly have guessed where I was. I felt that I owed Guy at least an explanation. And Kate. I was beginning to feel bad about being so hard, but I knew I was right to get away. Why was nobody sane?

Richard had had a frustrating day, and didn't seem pleased to see me when he came into the kitchen to seek solace from Louise. She was on edge herself over the baby. I provided an outlet for their frustration and an opportunity for blame and recrimination as well. I was the unwanted guest, the elderly child who refuses to leave the nest.

One day they would sit me down at the kitchen table and talk to me.

"Look, Tony, we've been thinking - about what's best for you and for all of us. And you know, some day soon, you're going to have to get out there and do something with your life. You can't just fritter away your time sleeping, watching videos and drinking your father's good brandy. There's a job going down at the steelworks - make a man of you. The money's good as well. So how about it? Your own payslip, your own place, chance to do some courting. . . "

Tony B. Goode. Death of a Couch Potato. And I'd only been there two days.

I asked her if they'd mind if I used the phone.

"No problem."

"It's someone in London. Won't be on long," I said quickly. "I won't say where I am or give any definite information."

"Fine."

"Just want to smooth things over a bit."

"Sounds like a good idea."

My life was becoming a series of self-contained episodes each linked to the preceding only by a thread of unreturnable phone calls. This reminded me that Joanne and Rachel still existed somewhere, and should be telephoned. They seemed impossibly far away now though, part of somebody else's life. I couldn't go back further than my time with a Country singer in London. Even that seemed a long way from here, the carpeted provincial comfort of a conventional turn of the Millennium family home. For an unspontaneous person I was spending a lot of time in the present.

Next morning Louise asked me to keep an eye on Claire while she had a shower.

"Cuckoo, cuckoo," I said to her softly. I meant me. She was asleep, but at six months old she wouldn't require an explanation anyway. She looked happy enough; peaceful. I must have been like that once.

There had been a lot of set-piece conversations based on the Apology Gambit.

"I know I'm in the way here, but..."

"No, no, not at all. It's nice having you here, isn't it?"

"Yes - makes a change - no trouble at all."

"It's very good of you to say that, but I'd just like to assure you that I will be going in a few days. Not that I don't enjoy being with you, and appreciate and enjoy your hospitality."

"Don't feel pressured - it's fine really."

"Oh, I don't. Thanks. I just want to let you know that I'm not taking you for granted."

"Oh no. No, no, no." That was them.

"And to tell you what I'm doing."

"Well as long as you don't feel you have to go."

"Oh no. No, no, no." That was me.

This is a very popular family game, despite the fact that it almost always results in stalemate. The only alternative is for one side to crack and either lose their temper or break down and beg the other to stop. This takes a while, and I was hoping I would have left before that stage was reached. I wasn't doing much about it though.

They went to bed earlier that night, which was good, and I finished off two bottles of sherry. They were both open - nearly empty, in fact.

"I'll get some to replace it - but I don't feel quite ready to go out yet."

"Oh, no. No, no, no. Don't worry about that."

"I'd like to, though. I will."

"Don't worry about it."

That was the first game of next morning. The second followed soon after. My own fault for initiating it.

"I did telephone London last night, sorry, but I wasn't on for long. Just left a message on Guy's answering machine saying I wouldn't be round for a bit." I didn't like the idea of the band going on without me, without my help.

"I rang Kate as well, sorry, but no-one has any idea where I am. It wasn't for long either. Just to make sure things are reasonably OK - you know."

"Oh, no - that's fine. Didn't we say? And are things OK?"

"Yes - think so. And don't worry, I'll not do anything daft when I'm here. There's no-one coming here or anything. They don't know where I am."

"Who?" Richard asked, suddenly anxious.

"My friends."

"Oh."

"Not criminal friends. The band. Guy's in the band. He plays the guitar," I added, to make the truth more plausible.

"What did Kate have to say?" asked Louise.

"She's OK."

"Really?"

"Yes."

I hadn't been looking forward to speaking to her. I had expected hostility, but she was friendly. Then I remembered. She was a Christian now, and I knew how enthusiastic I had been to forgive those who wronged me when I was a little boy in a religious phase.

"Hello," she sounded fragile. Shit. "Hello."

"Hello, Kate," I was speaking quietly, "It's me - Tony."

"Where are you?"

"How are you?"

"Fine, fine. Missing you, but OK."

"Have you seen the rest of the band or anything?"

"No. Not yet. When will I see you again?" The Three Degrees. Prince Charles.

"I'm not sure what I'm doing. Not for a while. I need

to do some things. I just wanted to tell you that I'm OK and see if you are."

"Right. That's nice. When then?" I strengthened myself by remembering why I had left.

"I don't know, Kate. I'll telephone."

"Is there a number I can get you on?"

"No - I'm ringing from a call box."

"Do you want me to ring you back?"

"No. Thanks. There's no need. It's OK." There was a pause - a dreadful telephone pause.

"You left in a real state, you know. I was frightened. Never seen you like that."

"Sorry."

"There's no need for that. You didn't mean all those things you said, did you?"

"No. Course not," I lied.

"Good. I knew."

"Not all of them. Not the way it came out. But it was a reaction."

"Shock," she explained.

"No. I just find all that religious stuff... I can't agree with it. It makes me. . . " Sick. Say it. "Sick."

"Faith is difficult to understand sometimes."

"You can say that again."

"But I'm not trying to force you or anything. I love you, Tony, I really do, and I want to tell you how I feel and what I think. We're bound to argue sometimes if we do that; but we mustn't hide things from each other."

"Right."

"So you're saying you need a bit more time? That it's all a bit much at the moment?"

I remembered the time with Joanne when I should have plunged in and used the 'Open Relationship' phrase. This time I cliched obligingly.

"I need some space." It worked a treat.

"Right. I respect that. But I'm not going to stop saying what I feel, what I know. It's the same as wanting to show my love in other ways - ways I know you do like."

"Oh." I remembered what these were.

"I need to know things are OK."

"They are. I just need some time."

"I'm praying for us, and that helps - me at least." She laughed which was a relief, "But I know I want to see your face."

"And yours. Look the money's going. We both need some time to think things through - least I do. Sorry about dropping the band in it as well, if I have. I'll telephone next week - OK?"

"OK."

"OK then. Goodbye and take good care of yourself."

"Mm, bye." I dropped the handset back on the rest, and let out a large quantity of air from puffed out cheeks. Then I picked it up again to check the line was dead. It was. I sighed again and had a sip of sherry. It appeared that she still loved me. That was something I hadn't thought about at all.

****

It was strange, being there, with them. It was a little like being off work sick. There was the same feeling of confused guilt at being somewhere other than where you were supposed to be. It was cosy but stuffy, indoors in warm carpeted rooms, and sitting on armchairs. With your parents, I could have added. That was how it felt. The weirdness of the situation was starting to get to me.

Another two days passed. It was high time now for Tony to leave home. I was spending too long indoors, and it was unhealthy. Lethargy was taking over. I still showed no signs of doing anything, even going out, let alone going away.

"Have you thought any more about what you're going to do?"

"Not really, no. Look I'll be going soon, though, very soon. I promise."

“No, it’s fine, Tony. When you feel ready, not before.”

But I had no idea what I was going to do. I could apply for jobs, and try to lie about my past; or I could try explaining to the interviewer openly and honestly that I had recently spent time on the run. Alternatively, I could return to a small but very determined branch of a

Tennessee church in London with a woman who seemed to think that either I, or our probably as yet unconceived child, was the Messiah. Details were vague.

"Do you think I should confess?" I asked my brother. He looked startled. "I mean go to the police. Find out what, if anything, I have to be afraid of."

"Well, that's got to be your choice."

"Yes, I know that," I snapped back like an adolescent, and I got the usual forgiveness shit.

"Do you regret the truth coming out – about you and Louise?" I asked him.

"No," he said, "Not at all."

That was the end of his answer. He was that kind of person. The priesthood was a strange choice of profession for someone who seemed so little interested in the sound of his own voice. Perhaps he could have made a very good monk had he been born in a different age. As it was, there was a framed Monet print on the wall behind him, his girlfriend was in the kitchen, and his baby was asleep in a cot.

CHAPTER 22

"What is it you want to report?" The sergeant had a fat face, with lots of burst blood vessels spread across it. I had never been in a police station before, but I knew from television that he was a desk sergeant.

"It's not exactly 'report' as such," I said quietly, so that the others sitting on grey plastic seats along the window could not hear me.

"Pardon," he said loudly, irritated.

"I need to ask something. Find out if I'm guilty, or at least accused of something." He looked unimpressed. I smiled, which didn't help.

"Would you like to take a seat Mr?"

I hesitated, "Palmer." The name was not familiar to him.

"All right Mr Palmer, sir, I'll have someone here with you soon. Anywhere there," he added with his last ounce of patience, indicating a row of seats with his head.

The place reminded me of a dole office, except that the clerical officers were burlier and in uniform. Richard had offered to come with me, but I preferred to do it alone. I had to go and see Mr Tomkins and tell him that it was me who had been stealing his apples, and I didn't want to do it with my big brother next to me. He had looked unambiguously relieved, which made me appreciate his offer all the more.

It was a long time since I had confessed anything formally to a figure in authority. In my early life it had been done most frequently in an empty wardrobe, and through gauze, to an elderly cleric, who would listen to a catalogue of sins ranging from 'being dishonest and telling lies,' through to 'I think I've committed masturbation and smoking and being dishonest'. It had finally reached the stage where I had become too embarrassed to confess to being disobedient, and then I had stopped going completely.

As an adult, confessions at work had been no more than non-committal acceptance of an unspecified part of corporate responsibility for what was perceived to be a failure to fully communicate how goals had been achieved. Otherwise, there was confession to a landlord that the damage had been done while I was having a party; and to a girlfriend that I had spent the night after the party with one of her enemies.

"I can imagine how you must feel, I'm very sorry - me and her together like that."

"You can imagine how I feel can you? I very much doubt it, Tony. It's not the physical side that matters most - can't you even see that? It's the intimacy. You must have said things."

"Very little," I had replied with no deliberate irony. That had made it worse.

I had been well trained, though, and I knew how to confess. I would hold nothing back. The full and abject plunge into total confession is quickest and cleanest. Then there is penance and relief. I remembered that and looked forward to it now. It was like an addict's rush - sweet and joyous and pure.

As for the penance, as I looked around the drab station, I realised that it was to be boredom and a little humiliation. I was going to try to confess the barely comprehensible to bored and suspicious people doing tedious jobs. The sardonic 'sir' was the beginning of it. I had thought I was going to be confessing a crime; I was actually confessing to stupidity.

It was all clear now. There was nothing to tie me to serious criminal offence. Anybody looking at me could tell that; and as for what Joanne and Rachel and myself had done, it was more like a children's prank than a crime. Still I had to go through with it. Richard had been right. There had been no need to spend all that time in hiding. I had been very stupid, but I knew that when I walked out of this station it would all be over. I would be able to do just what I wanted again. That would be good. After this, I could deal with Richard or Joanne, or anybody, as an equal.

Quarter of an hour went past. Then another one. A drunk veered towards me, alarmingly large and wide-eyed. I was worried that he might be an unexpected addition to my penance, but he swerved before reaching me, and headed towards the desk like a remote control toy. A bored-looking constable grabbed him and bundled him away, protesting.

Finally, I was called to come through. A tape recorder was switched on and then I asked for forgiveness from a plump middle-aged man in a buff coloured jacket and what I would have to describe as slacks. I didn't mention any names; I told him about Hanlon Hall and he looked puzzled.

"What do you want us to do about it?" I had no idea. Like all badly planned projects, my confession was floundering.

"Sorry for wasting your time. Perhaps I should go." He thought about it.

"Hold on, please."

He went out of the room and left me on my own with the tape recorder for a while. I thought it was a shame I hadn't brought a Merle Haggard tape with me to pass the time. Then he came back with a colleague.

"Good cop, bad cop?" I joked. They weren't laughing.

"Do you know Brendan Price well?"

"Pardon?"

"Brendan Price."

"I met him. I played snooker. In his snooker hall. I didn't know him well."

"We know you met him."

"Do you?"

"Did you know that he is currently on a murder charge?"

"No."

"How often did you met him?"

"Two or three times, I suppose." They wanted more. "I tried to sell him the business - the business I was talking about before. Love Training," I hated that name more than ever now. "Sort of tried to. By mistake."

"You tried to sell him your business by mistake?"

"I was drunk. That's why I had to get away."

"So you came here?"

I panicked in the face of their scorn.

"I just wanted to make sure everything was OK." That sounded ridiculous. I was confronted with disbelieving stares.

"Mr Palmer, what are you really doing here?" I couldn't mention Crimewatch. That was too ridiculous.

"I saw something on Crimewatch."

"Crimewatch." He uttered the word slowly, disbelievingly, pronouncing every letter.

"Mm - yes," I giggled. No-one else giggled. "You know - the television thing."

"Tell me more about it."

"About Crimewatch?" No. "I was described on it."

"Which is why you came forward?"

"Yes."

"When was this?"

"Before Christmas."

"Taken your time."

"I've been mulling it over."

"And now you've decided to confess?"

"Without being specific about what you are confessing to?"

They asked me a lot of questions about Brendan and his cronies. I answered them honestly. Halfway through, I felt a thrill of panic at the thought of testifying against them in court, but it was hard to see how I'd be much use as a witness; I knew nothing. The police became irritated with me as this became more obvious. I took this as a good sign. Then the new policeman left, which I took as another good sign.

"We are going to let you go now."

"Great. Thanks. Sorry for wasting your time."

"This isn't the end of the matter."

"Right."

"You must not leave the area without notifying us first - we may need to speak to you again."

If they wanted a laugh presumably. Or to charge me with wasting police time. He was just doing this to humiliate me. It was part of the penance, and I felt suitably humble.

"We need your address."

"I'm staying with my brother, Richard."

I was handed paper to write down his name and address. The policeman looked it over.

"Is he involved with this?"

"God – no."

"What does he do?"

"He's a priest." That surprised him. "Or at least he was." That surprised him even more.

The early evening air was cold but fresh. It was a delightful shock. A friendly light reached out a few feet through the windows of the Market Tavern. I went in and drank a pint of Guinness in four or five gulps. I was Tony Palmer again. I had brought on myself the anguish and humiliation and embarrassment of unnecessary confession, but I had nothing more serious to face than that. A stupid punishment for a stupid crime. But now it was over. My life was my own again, and I could choose what to do with it. And I would be less stupid in future.

I exercised my right to choose by going to the bar again, for another pint and some cheese and onion crisps and some dry roasted peanuts. I could spend money freely again; I could look for a proper job again. I ate the crisps and nuts together. I liked the contrast of the crisp crunch of the one with the mushy crunch of the other, so I did it again. This was true salvation. I could tell Kate a thing or two about how it really felt.

Everything that had happened after that night in the snooker hall could have been a dream. Or even earlier. I could be back to the point where I had fallen asleep in bed with Joanne knowing her scheme would never work and our relationship was going nowhere. I was even spared the chore of disentangling myself from her because she had done it for me. She had opted for dull domesticity, and she would always be saddened, deep down, by the knowledge that she could never have the one relationship that would have given her life true meaning. Poor kid.

It was not too bad being me after all. OK, I irritated myself sometimes, and I was capable of acts of sublime stupidity but my sins were relatively minor and my punishments were bizarre rather than painful. And now, should I choose to, I could fit in again, with these people in this pub, in late Twentieth Century England; and I chose to, more or less, and it felt good. We knew where we stood. We didn't believe in anything but we took a lot on trust, and it was working out all right at the moment. And that was fine.

There were two women talking animatedly to each other a couple of tables away. They were discussing plans for what sounded like a business they were setting up, and flirting with a young-looking barman who had been over with their food, and was now collecting their empty glasses. While he was enjoying their attention, he was also treating them a little warily. If I had wanted to, I could have joined in. My choice. The worst that could happen was that I would get on someone's nerves, and the best could be anything.

Then the juke box kicked in and, after the shortest of intros, Tammy Wynette's voice came through, telling us how last night all alone in a bar room she had met a man with a drink in his hand. This man had had coal black hair, baby blue eyes and a smile that a girl understands. I sighed. It was good being here. She moved into the chorus. There was more passion in that word 'Almost', before 'Persuaded', than most people could get into a declaration of undying love or an electoral address. And again, that ambiguity about whether or not she really was going to resist. Somebody somewhere in this bar had chosen to put this song on. Quite possibly a woman.

If I wanted to, I could push my own conscience aside, go to the phone, ring up a woman from my past and see where it lead. Or I could get involved with the conversation at the nearby table. Temptation was flowing like wine. One of the two business women caught my eye, and we smiled. But resisting temptation had its own exquisite charm as well. I owed it to Richard and Louise to go back. They would be worried.

I decided to have one more pint before I left. Standing at the bar, I saw that the music was a tape being played by management, so there was no soul mate there. Not this time anyway. I had one more pint before I left. I chuckled to myself as I walked down the happy lane.

Spring was here. If it had been daylight, the birds would have been twittering in the trees. There is nothing quite like relief for making you feel relieved. Nothing succeeds like success. Laugh and the world laughs with you. Fact is stranger than fiction. You are what you eat. Everything we do is driven by you.

At that moment, a large bird - an owl I realised, it was so quiet - swooped low in front of me. It turned to look at me and then away again as if beckoning me to follow. I did, and it left me at a hedge, through which I could see the remnants of a tiny fire smouldering. The fire was neat, almost exactly circular - the size and shape of a chimpanzee's head.

I stood staring into it. Tiny flames were still flickering up every now and then across the surface. The embers around the edge began to grow brighter and formed a glowing red ring. Then the whole fire seemed to move, uncertainly at first and then clearly and determinedly, and lift itself, like a cow getting to its feet. The flames and the brightest of the embers crumpled into the shape of the head and neck of a ruby red and golden bird. The rest of the fire fell away, and the bird rose from the heat, and flew straight up into the air. I watched after it, staring up into the clear night sky. The bright shape gathered speed and flew away across the darkness until it faded to almost nothing, and then was swallowed up in the gloom.

I was left staring upwards humming (or at least

making a half-whistle in the front of my mouth) Phoenix the Cat. It was the best response I could make to this. I was not in Ancient Athens or Crete - this was the England on a cold March evening. I was not drunk. I believed then that I had not imagined it. As soon as it disappeared, I began to wonder if I had. Now I really don't know. I have been wrong so often that it is usually a safe bet, but not always.

And then I was standing on my own in a suburban side street, not too far from my brother's house. I had forgotten about him and Louise. I should share my good news with them.

I hoped I did not smell too strongly of drink, but now that I was fully free and once again myself, I should have no fear of others' disapproval. And after all, while still a practising priest, Richard had stolen and shortly afterwards impregnated my girlfriend. He was in no position to cast the first stone. And it was me - Mr Stupid, Mr Insensitive, Mr Too Selfish to be a Priest - who would never dream of upsetting anyone by trying to get her back.

Sometimes, I ought to stand up for myself before these Sadducees and hypocrites. I should stop doubting myself so much. I was not that bad, and I was prepared to take chances. I was in my prime. Career opportunities, health, youth (relative), global economics and politics were all on my side. I lived in a hideously corrupt and unfair world, contorting itself for my convenience.

I walked back home like a conquering hero, somewhere between Richard Coeur de Lyon and William Brown.

They were relieved to see me, and to discover that I wasn't headed for Rampton or Devil's Island. Once this was established, though, they made it clear that I should have told them sooner; and the more I talked, the more irritated they became. I had only to suggest going for a drink, to bring upon myself a torrent of tuts and sighs and shakes of the head.

"Anyway," I said angrily. "What right have yous got to criticise me? "

"What do you mean by that?" Richard replied, daring me.

I dared.

"One minute you're everybody's favourite priest with nothing more sinister on your mind than saving the world from eternal damnation, the next. . . " The fact that Louise was there increased my determination not to shrink from this.

"The next you're sleeping with your brother's girlfriend, and then you're trying to fob your baby off on to him. You're missing your pulpit now, I suppose, that's why you've decided to preach morality to me because I went for a few pints of Guinness after going through a hell of a time - my own fault admittedly - but a hell of a time at the police station."

"That isn't what we meant."

"No?"

"We were worried." The old honesty ploy. I had forgotten how good a priest he was. I saw no alternative but to look back insolently and continue being unpleasant.

"I could have rung and I didn't. Right. But it's not like that's what matters. It's just such a great excuse for telling me off that you can't resist it. I'm a valid target again now that I'm probably, probably mind, not definitely, not going to be done for murder.

"I'm going out again. I'm going to The Grey Goose, and if either of you or both of you would like to join me at some stage I'd be very pleased to see you. Is it OK if I take this?"

I picked up a copy of The Independent, and as I headed for the door Louise finally spoke.

"Tony, will you never learn?"

"Oh, I've learnt," I said, in what I hoped was an enigmatic tone of hurt.

Richard appeared in the bar half an hour or so later.

"Sorry'f we were killjoys before a bit."

"No, no. You were right really."

"And I know how you feel about me and Louise now, anyway."

"No, that was a bit... To be really honest with you, I

don't particularly... Not that she's not...But well that's not really a problem. Not that it wasn't the worst thing anyone has ever done to me."

He nodded. He was turning the other cheek like a punch-ball. All this agreement was difficult to combat. And coming out to the pub was a major peace offering.

"You are my elder brother, as I'm sure you know, and in some ways I'm just wary of being too much in awe of you."

"In awe of me?" That did surprise him. "After the mess I've made of everything?"

"Have you, though, really?" He frowned. I explained. "At least you haven't just spent six months on the run from a law that wasn't after you anyway, in the company of a Nancy Griffiths clone who thinks you're about to father a Messiah."

He laughed at that, so I gave him a few new details from the last few months, including entertaining gangsters first thing in the morning with a hangover; pit bull terrier fights; and how to post a card from a place you haven't been to.

"Makes my exploits sound very tame."

"Fairly tame," I corrected him. "What about the rest of our family? I suppose I ought to tell Robert and Susan."

"Who do you think they'll disapprove of more?"

"Have you not told them?"

"Sort of never got around to it." He smiled with pride at his cowardice. "God knows what they'll make of it all."

"Has He not told you? The Man Upstairs."

"No. And I'm surprised you don't know - I'm just a priest - you're being lined up to be His father."

"Again."

****

I woke at about ten with a mild hangover and a strong feeling of well-being. I lay in bed for a while chuckling over memories of last night, and the months before. Louise was moving around downstairs. When I had showered and dressed, I went down and asked if there was anything I could do. She looked at me and shook her head.

"Sorry if we were a bit noisy and pissed last night. Me and Richard."

"Well, there's a baby in the house, in case you hadn't noticed, so I'm quite used to being woken up at funny hours."

"D'you want a cup of tea?" I asked, and she nodded.

"I would have liked to have gone for a drink with you last night as well, you know," she said turning towards me. I was standing next to her, waiting for the kettle to boil. "But only one of us can get out, obviously, with the baby. I'd like to sometime, though. Lot to talk about. It's good to see you two getting on again anyway. Richard thinks the world of you, you know."

"I hope everything..." I was going to say 'works out'. She knew what I meant anyway.

I poured water on to the two teabags into the pot as a burst of sunlight came through the kitchen window. A faint sweetish aroma of tea rose up. The baby was asleep in the living room. The doorbell rang.

"I'll go if you like," I offered. She smiled.

It was the police. My hangover grew worse as I was taken back to the station for four hours' hard, repetitive questioning from two new officers. They were more business-like and persistent than before. I was asked a lot of questions about Brendan and now Gary; apparently he was the Geordie who had been described on Crimewatch. Not me. He had disappeared. I suspected something bad had happened to him. I could give them no useful information; they already seemed to already know everything I could tell them. It was Gary and Brendan they were interested in, and they found it hard to believe I hadn't been working for them, but as I gave them proof after proof of my naivety and stupidity, they began to accept the possibility.

A solicitor appeared. I hadn't even thought about getting one; further proof of my stupidity. Richard had organised it. The solicitor was called Johnstone, and he seemed to know the police well. It quickly became obvious that he regarded his main job as persuading me to plead guilty to conspiracy to defraud. Richard agreed with him.

"I mean you've more or less confessed to it anyway".

"I suppose that's a point."

"And it sounds like they've given up trying to link you with anything else."

"I hope so. I'm knackered."

"Johnstone says he doesn't see how they can."

"I hope he's right. I've had enough surprises."

CHAPTER 23

A few months later I was a long way away from that mature and sensitive adult conversation in the kitchen with Louise, watching teabags floating around in an Ikea floral teapot. I was sweating into my suit, staring with desperation at Justice Collins and trying not to upset or offend him in the slightest way. I had never been so worried about anybody else's feelings in my life.

As I watched him, he seemed to be moving closer to me and then further away. He grew blurred around the edges and then excessively clear. He was about sixty, plump and pompous, and he had real power over me. I didn't like it, and I didn't like him, but I tried hard not to let it show. He could authorise the uniformed strong men in the court to take me and lock me away for as long as he saw fit. I was frightened of wetting myself; and I knew he wouldn't like that.

Now I had to stand and wait respectfully until he felt ready to tell me whether he was going to have me put in a concrete room with a heavy door and a big lock that I wouldn't get the key to. I had a feeling I had been lucky so far and I was afraid it might not last. I tried not to sway as I stood there, though the muscles in my legs were aching.

I had only spent five days locked up and that had been

enough to terrify me into agreeing to anything. I remembered being led through a concrete Seventies building which reminded me of a multi-storey car park, with flickering fluorescent lights and white-painted breize blocks and into a cell. When the door shut behind me I had not cried, though I felt like it. I had just sat down on my shallow mattress with my head in my hands, trying to understand how nice clever little Tony Palmer had ended up here. More helpless and scared than when he really was little Tony Palmer.

I knew I was unlikely to have the cell to myself for long and I was petrified every time footsteps approached. I couldn't rest, let alone sleep. I tried writing a diary again on some writing paper I had been allowed.

'Here I am. I can't even sleep - watching my life just going away and wishing it away. Locked in concrete waiting for someone else to be locked in with me, thinking, worrying about more of the same, and worse to come, knowing that even after this there's nothing else good.'

That was about as far as I got.

There was something else which I wouldn't have ever put in my diary in case it was found, and I was beaten for it, but there was a smell in there, a prison smell, and I realised that I was part of it. If I had had a wife on the outside, Vinny would be shagging her.

It was shocking how very easy it was to get here, and

how fast, and how impossible to get out. In a few hours I had gone from that nice house to an interrogation room and then this cell, via a van that stank of alcohol and stale sweat. I had no idea what would happen next, and no say in the matter. It was frightening, because I knew it could get a lot worse.

I had the first night on my own, listening to footsteps and voices echoing in the dark, and pipes banging and dripping. I was too afraid to sleep and I was glad that my door was locked. First thing next morning, Howard was moved in. He was massive, with darting, slightly manic eyes. As the door closed I stared at him, not knowing whether to smile or not, only hoping he couldn't smell my fear. I finally grunted out a greeting. He walked over to me, and put out his hand.

"Hello, mate. Name's Howard."

"Oh, right. Tony. Tony Palmer."

Now he wasn't presenting a threat, I could see that he wasn't actually much bigger than I was, and the movement of his eyes had more to do with confusion than aggression. He talked a lot, especially about his 'business plans'. He had spent a lot of time in and out of prison, but despite all the evidence to the contrary he was convinced that he was lucky and he was determined to become rich.

When he found out that I had worked with computers, he couldn't believe his good fortune, and he started coming up with numerous, ill-formed schemes for beating the bookies, harnessing my computing expertise and his instinct. I knew this was not the best of synergies, but he was preventing the bed being taken by someone worse, so I was inclined to forgive him a lot. All I had to do was consider possible alternatives (a large hairless man with tattooed biceps and a shrill Scouse accent was in the cell next door), so I was as happy to talk business plans with him as I had been in bed with Joanne.

It was all that was going to happen next and for how long, and who would replace him that worried me now. I didn't like being locked up here, but I was afraid I would be moved somewhere more frightening and there would be nothing I could do about it. I couldn't stop myself being pushed into another van and driven off to some huge red-brick computerised dungeon littered with bowls of stale excrement, and populated by corrupt officials and brutally violent cell-mates.

Visits were not much of a relief, as I was too concerned with what might be happening in my absence to really enjoy being out of the cell. Richard came first. He was very apologetic about encouraging me to confess.

"Although I don't know what else there was to do."

I watched him as he sat, slumped and twitching with guilt, at the other side of the table, offering sorrow and sympathy and having no idea what to say. As time went on, he grew straighter and physically stilled himself. It couldn't have been too hard to believe in yourself with the memory of Louise's encouragement and support in your mind, and even the smell of her still on your skin. And knowing she would be waiting to offer more when he went back home. I knew, I had been part of a couple myself; once with her, although on reflection it had never felt secure like that.

I didn't say much to him. After all, it was him that had come to see me. I did ask him for money, though.

"How much, Tony?" That was not a question I could answer precisely.

"Well, as much as you can give me. And what's happening with bail?"

"I'm seeing Paul Johnstone at two. I'll know then." Richard and the solicitor seemed to be making all the decisions. I didn't mind. In some ways it felt like the old days again.

Richard carried on talking. I think he felt he should chat. He must have done prison visiting professionally in the past, so I was probably getting some of the benefit of his priestly training and experience. This was different though because he was entangled with me. Once or twice I thought I caught him looking at me with real antagonism. He had to be here, but he really didn't want to be. It was as if I was carrying out some kind of mutually destructive revenge. What would I going to do next? Denounce him to the press? Commit suicide?

Become a proper criminal? Take Louise away from him? I watched him, interested that he thought I had so much power when I felt absolutely powerless. At least Howard was still in the cell when I got back.

Next day, Richard was different. He began with a flood of self-recrimination for which I provided an audience. He told me that when he was here, in this awful place, to see me, he should be able to stop going on about his own feelings and concentrate on mine.

"I agree." He looked surprised. He just wasn't ready for sarcasm. "You were seeing the solicitor," I reminded him, "Johnstone."

The day before, I had used up two phonecards trying to find out what was happening to me. Richard's two o'clock meeting had been cancelled; I had spoken to Johnstone's secretaries six times and they were as sick of me as I was of them. Richard finally managed to see him on the way back.

"Oh, God, yes, sorry. It's thirty thousand for the bail."

"What?"

"Johnstone's working on getting it reduced and I'm seeing what I can do to raise money, and so's Louise. I'm trying Robert and Susan. Any other ideas?"

"I've got some money in my account. Not much though. I suppose I can just write a cheque. Can I pay towards my own bail?"

"I don't see why not."

"But - thirty thousand. I could be here for months."

"I know, Tony. I just feel so useless. I'll try Robert and Susan - you don't mind?"

"No, no." I shook my head as well to make sure there was no chance of any ambiguity. I was alarmed that he felt the need to ask the question. "No. This is urgent. Anything to get me out of here. Anybody. Anything." I told him my PIN number and the pocket where my address book should be. "And there's the money in the company account..."

"I'm not sure we can do that." He screwed his face up. "I don't know. I'll ask Johnstone."

"If he doesn't disappear again. People doing jobs like that. They just don't realise, do they?"

After some optimistic mental arithmetic, and assuming moderate generosity from Robert and Susan, we arrived at nearly ten thousand pounds.

"So we need to borrow twenty thousand?" Richard did not look optimistic. Unlike me he had not come from a world of instantly available limitless credit. His was a world of collection boxes, fund-raising walks and fetes to pay for church roof repairs.

"Thirty thousand is ridiculous. Johnstone thinks so as well."

"It's because they think I'm involved with Brendan Price."

"But that's so unfair." I almost felt sorry for him in his

belief in fairness.

"Perhaps I should apply for an overdraft."

“Yes," he said. "Perhaps. Do you think so?"

"I was joking."

"Oh."

"So what else is going on?" I said, to help him out of feeling useless.

I wanted him to stay longer now, a few minutes at least, even if it was keeping him from his money-raising activities. He told me his stories of hopeless job hunting and harrowing interviews.

“Both our CV’s are going to be fairly interesting after this,” I said and we laughed.

"If you want a reference..."

He was gone soon enough, though, and I was led back to my cell. I lay down and tried to sleep, even though I knew it would make it even harder to sleep at night.

Robert came the next day. It was clear that he didn't like the place. "Very smoky, isn't it - and grey. I find it depressing."

"So do I."

"You must do, still..." It's your own fault.

"And I know you must have found it hard to get the time away from work and," I tailed off, not being sure of his children's names. "The family." So don't bother coming back.

"Is there anything you need?"

“Money? I need to get out of here.”

“Yes. Richard spoke to me about that."

"There's rumours a man down my corridor has just had his faced slashed open with a sharpened spoon."

"I should be able to get a couple of thousand - from Amanda’s parents,” he added, hoping that I understood quite how distasteful he found that. “A loan, though, I must insist that they understand it’s a loan. I’ll try to get it as soon as possible." I actually need the money now please; to get me out of prison.

"When?"

"They are away at the moment - at their place in Tuscany," he added, as if that was of any interest to anybody. Perhaps they could die on the way back, leaving him a fortune. He’d probably have scruples about lending it to me even then.

"Can you not ring them?" I knew my tone was not appropriate to my status but he was, as usual, driving me mad.

"I'll have a word with Amanda."

"Good." Ideally before I get beaten up, raped or lose my mind. "If you could find out - as soon as possible."

"Of course." I was driving him equally mad, I could tell. It wasn’t easy for him, he had brought his damaged family into contact with Amanda’s happy and fragrant family. Her parents have a house in Italy, he was thinking. I have a brother in prison.

"You haven't got any cash on you now, have you? Just to get things here. I'll pay you back when I get out."

I could see him deciding that this would be his last visit. After all he had a wife and children with more urgent and more rightful claims than me. "Oh, yes, Right."

"Thanks, that means a lot," I said reaching over. He gave me thirty, which was all he had in his wallet.

I couldn't think of anything else to say. I wanted him to go. If he wanted to do something useful he could get another job in the evenings to raise some cash. Or put his children to work on the streets.

"So what are you going to do when you get out of here?" he asked. I wondered if he was preparing my case for Amanda.

"Don't know." He did not look pleased. But then he rarely did. He seemed older than me, older than Richard. But I was his big brother - a human being to whom he was linked and therefore a burden to add to his stack of burdens.

He had a lot of problems, and he told me about them. Problems with his wife; with George, Oliver and Sarah (whom I took to be his children); with Andy Bowers and Roger Ketley (at work); Clemson (a neighbour with garden fence issues); Mark (his wife's cousin); John Major; Tony Blair; Saddam Hussein; Bill Clinton; the Abbey National Easy Access Saver Account; the M6 and, of course, me.

I gathered that Richard mustn't have told him about his own recent activities yet. They would have sat nicely on his list; he would be convinced there was a family conspiracy against him.

Susan came later the same day, in what appeared to be Gypsy Rose Lee the Fortune-Teller fancy-dress. She didn't like the place either.

"Everybody's smoking and it's so institutionalised, and all this strip lighting - you must find it awfully depressing."

"Yes, I do."

"I just don't see the need for the denial of colour."

"Perhaps grey's cheap."

I could tell she wouldn't come back and I was glad. I had been afraid that she would enjoy the drama too much, and decide to visit conscientiously. She could have quite easily have become a dedicated prison visitor, addicted to our tortuous conversations over the table, before embarking on a doomed romance with a fellow prisoner - ideally one with convictions for mindless violence whom she alone could reach.

As she was on her way out of the visiting room, I saw a woman with long, wild blond hair coming in. She looked like Kate. She was Kate. She looked good in jeans and a tight checked shirt. Susan glanced disapprovingly which made her seem even more attractive. She had two buttons open on her shirt, just to the point where her breasts began. I looked her in the eye with a new respect. I had forgotten about her body in my shock at her mental deterioration. There was nobody in the world I could have been happier to see. I was glad Richard had been so thorough with my address book.

I almost forgot about getting out. We chatted easily. The band had broken up. Guy was getting into session work and the two newcomers had set up their own band playing rockabilly. John had disappeared angrily.

"That's not like him," I said. She had been serious until now; she looked even better when she laughed.

"And then re-appeared playing the same places with a younger band. They're supposed to be good. And they've got a pedal steel guitar."

"Wish we'd thought of that. Do you miss it?"

"No," she smiled. "Well, I get nostalgic sometimes when I pass one of the old places - but if I want to badly enough I'll get another band together. Might even need a roadie."

That was nice, but after I had finished smiling, there was silence. She asked me about the food. Every time the flow of conversation began to splutter, I worried that we would run out of things to say. Perhaps this was because we weren't as we should be - on our own, in bed. She did look good, and sexual desire was about the only pure feeling I ever had.

Unfortunately conversation is always awkward when you're hiding something - like debilitating lust for a friend. I hoped she wasn't hiding something as well. It is the convict's stereotypical nightmare to discover that his woman was pregnant by somebody else. Mine was a variation on that

"And how are you keeping, health and all?" I asked. She looked a bit surprised, which I took as a good sign.

"Fine. No problem."

"How's things with God?"

"They're fine too," she replied unprovoked, "More than fine." Still none of the outpourings of before. Her face looked beautiful, I would have loved to touch it. Perhaps I had left too hastily. The idea of being in her bed seemed unbelievable now, as I thought of the shallow scratchy bed in my cell.

"What do you do about it?"

"Do?"

"I mean in church or whatever."

"It is a church, Tony," she laughed. "Not a whatever. It's a big part of my life now; I'll not pretend that it's not."

"What's it called again?" This was a genuine request for information.

"I've told you before. The Church of Jesus," she said, her mild annoyance turning to pride as she said the name.

"Nice name. What does it believe in?"

"We," she said pointedly, "Believe in the Bible - living it as much as possible."

It had happened in bed and now it happened again – a surge of lust at her proud stupidity. I tried not to let it show.

"I can't say I've ever heard of it," I said and she looked puzzled. "The Church not the Bible."

"It's American," she said warily.

"Tennessee?"

"Yes."

"Right."

"But our numbers here are growing. I do a lot of work with them now, that's one of the reasons I don't miss the band so much. I miss you though."

I was happy enough to watch while she talked about her church. It sounded relatively innocuous. Although officially based on the Bible, they seemed to draw more on The Family, groundless optimism, George Jones and the Flag. No popes or bishops, but spicy chicken wings and apple pie to compensate. She spoke about it without preaching, which was nice. Then quite suddenly she changed the subject.

"After you left, and after you'd been gone a while and never phoned again or anything, I went through some of your things. Perhaps I shouldn't. But I was just trying to find out more - see if I could find out where you'd gone."

She waited to see how I'd react. Compared with being locked up in here, it didn't seem so very important. Still, you have to stand up for yourself even if you don't care.

"There was no need to spy on me," I said.

"It wasn't spying. I was just desperate." I shrugged. She looked at me, sizing me up, then went on. "I don't know how or why. It's so different to the way you talk, yet it is so clearly you as well."

"What is?"

"I found something. Something you'd written."

An embarrassing Country and Western lyric? Something to do with Hanlon Hall? More worryingly, something personal? Joanne? Louise? Shit. I really needed to keep these women apart. No, I had no idea what she meant.

"What was it?" I tried to sound calm, but I wanted to know. What had I done with my diary? I didn't want her to know how desperate I had been when we met.

"Perhaps you don't even remember, perhaps it was inspired."

"What?" I almost shouted; then looked placatingly at the men in uniform, promising to keep the noise down. "Sorry, look - I have no idea what you're talking about, Kate. Can you put me out of my misery, please."

"I came across your diary."

"Oh." Oh. I tried the moral high ground. "That was private."

“I know. I shouldn’t have, but I was desperate to find out - anything I could. And I’m glad I did.”

“You read it?”

“I had to.”

“You didn’t.”

“Well I did, anyway. It’s done.”

“I suppose it shows how low I was – before you. But you still shouldn’t have read it.”

“And I’m glad you saved yourself from that life. You sounded so sad.”

“I’m not very happy now.”

"But it wasn’t that I’m talking about. It was something else. It was like a prayer.”

What was she talking about now? Madonna songs?

“If you can’t recall,” she continued, “Perhaps that proves you were full of the spirit.” She was more unhinged than I had realised. Best not to alienate her though; I was in no position to turn away support, even from the insane. I smiled blankly.

“That prayer you wrote,” she explained. “All about destroying your devils and loving your angels. It was there with the diary. In that folder.

“It was so powerful. So spiritual. I was thinking, if you finished it, I could try to get it in the Church Newsletter. I thought you could call it The Battle of Good and Evil. They call them pamphlets like in the olden days to inspire other believers."

"But, Kate, I'm not a believer."

"You were once, in a different way."

"Because I was brought up with it, but once I had the chance to think for myself . . . ."

"If you can change once, you could change again."

"No."

"God moves in mysterious ways his wonders to perform," she informed me.

"It was a joke. I was bored," I said, "Stuck in a Bed and Breakfast. I'd been subjected to some religious cable channel..." Then I stopped. I could see that she had picked up on the religious TV as a proof of divine intervention. What was the point?

"Can we change the subject?"

"Yes, Tony. Course." She smiled. "For now. What are you going to do, anyway? Your brother Richard said something about bail."

"Oh, yes I'd forgotten," I didn't really want to ask her.

"Talk about impractical," she laughed. "Do you know how much you need?" I wasn't sure any more. I had been more bothered about getting cash for today from my visitors. My concerns were becoming more and more short term.

"Best ask Richard. Anything you can."

"How much – altogether?" OK,

"Altogether? Last I heard thirty thousand." She didn't flinch. She wasn't good on practical things like money, I remembered. I had surrounded myself with other-worldly financial innocents – although it was me that was in prison.

"I'll see what I can do."

"Anything at all, Kate."

"Thirty thousand, yes?" She was mad again.

"I know there's no way you can, but thanks."

"There is. I'm sure the church can help."

"Are you?"

"Yes. And if you finish your Battle of God and Evil piece it might help. But I'm sure they would anyway." It was blackmail. Blackmail was fine.

"OK. Just bring it here next time you come." It would be good to know she was coming in again at least.

"No need." She took the Delegate Reflections folder from her bag.

"You'll need to clear it with them," I nodded to a watching officer. (I didn't feel able to call them 'screws' yet – I hadn't been here long enough and I wasn't sure if it was still the right term. Perhaps I could ask Howard). "But, yes, no problem."

"Will you need a pen?"

"No. I'm OK there."

After this she moved on to the same prison questions as anyone else, and I could tell she was ready to go.

"And I can come back, Tony. If you'd like me to. But only if you'd like me to." There were a lot of complicated answers I could give, but I thought I had to keep this simple.

"Yes, Kate. I would. A lot."

“Good. Thank you.”

CHAPTER 24

With God involved, things suddenly started moving. Richard finally coaxed the solicitor into actually doing something about my case, and with the help of The Church of Jesus and some serious borrowing, I was out in two days. I went back to London to stay in Kate's spare room, and soon I had an answer to everybody's favourite question.

"What are you going to do when all this is finished - one way or another?"

"I'm going to work for the Church of Jesus."

I had a friend years ago who worked at a Catholic school in Southport called Christ the King. This meant that when he answered the phone in the staff-room, he was able to say "Hello, Christ the King here," without being dismissed or sectioned. This didn't quite elevate me that high, but it would stand out among all the dull IT posts on my CV.

"Doing what?"

"They need someone to look after their databases."

"Will you get paid?"

"Yes."

Richard remained dubious. It is amazing how often people are dissatisfied when you do what they want.

"How?"

"The usual way. You know - money."

"They've got some have they?" He could have made a convert of me.

"Yes."

"Where from?"

"Bank robberies mainly. Kidnapping, extortion. I don't know, Richard. I would have thought church funding was more your area of expertise. Your lot were bankrolled by the Borgias and the Nazis as far as I remember."

"It's not got anything to do with drugs has it?"

My sister got in touch again as well. That was a surprise. I thought I might have misjudged her; but it soon transpired that she was ringing to disapprove.

"It's got something to do with a woman hasn't it? The one I saw coming in when I visited you? She got you into all this in the first place."

"No she didn't. That was a different one."

"Will you never learn?"

She never got around to sending any money and we haven't spoken much since.

But the Church genuinely did need a database manager and I went for an interview. I convinced them of my professional expertise, and suggested a few innovations, including some they couldn't possibly understand. I guessed that church management, like everybody else, was inclined to give a ludicrous amount of respect to anyone with a command of intimidating jargon and experience of working in the private sector.

They didn't seem concerned about by my impending prosecution. Perhaps the idea even appealed to them. I suppose my case must have been helped by Kate's advocacy and my own casually disclosed biblical knowledge. One of the things I noticed about these fundamentalist Christians who insist that every word of the Bible is God's word and therefore literally true and precious, was how few of them had actually bothered to read it, even in translation.

A Catholic Grammar School, unimaginatively perhaps, made its victims read whole chunks of the Bible and regurgitate it, with the recommended interpretation, in essay form. This made it very easy for me now to make reference to the Sermon on the Mount; tongues of fire; the bread and wine offered by his priest Melchisedeck; Martha and Mary; the pros and cons of picking corn on the Sabbath; those who are not with us are against us, and those who are not against us are with us, with the result that I was soon being treated with all the respect prophets aren't accorded in their own land and by their own people.

They made me an offer. It wasn't a difficult decision. A judge might be impressed that I had a job when deciding on my sentence; and I needed the money and something to occupy my mind. I was still sleeping in the spare room in Kate's flat. Attempts on my part to open discussions about what other rooms I might sleep in were gently discouraged. She was still beautiful and she was clearly taking it upon herself to help me, and I was grateful, whatever her motives. The occasional sight of her half-dressed in the kitchen gave me a thrill like a mild panic; but I am ashamed to say that I was more excited about the prospect of a job than the possibility of sex.

I started work two weeks before my trial date. I would be pleading guilty to fraud and obtaining money by deception. Johnstone was convinced this was my best chance of staying out of prison, which was my only real concern. It also meant an end to the questions. The police seemed to be as relieved as I was about this. They were sick of the sight of me, and I was proud of the fact that I had managed not to mention Joanne and Rachel.

Work helped keep my mind off the thought of court and what might follow. When I got back to the flat, though, I found myself brooding, and sleep was hard to come by. There was nothing I could do to make my prospects any better, plenty that would make them worse. All I could do was wait, but I found inactivity very difficult.

It got worse as the hearing grew closer, and my own memories of remand and other people's horror stories became more vivid. To pass the last few nights, when all I could think of doing was to go crying into Kate's room,

I tried writing myself to sleep. I couldn't face my prison memoirs, they reminded me that I might be about to go back there for a lot longer than five days, so instead I launched myself wholeheartedly into pamphleteering for the Church. Flight seemed an appropriate subject. For those not familiar with the Church of Jesus Inspirational Journal, I quote the following example.

'The release from life is death. Death is not an end. Death is the flight for which life is no more than a preparation, but a preparation as important as motoring down the runway is to a take-off. And it is terribly short compared to the everlasting journey to follow, which is eternal life.

'And when death releases us from our earth-bound captivity in these decaying bodies, we can, with God's help, fly anywhere. If we choose God, they will be to His places - to bliss and joy everlasting. But if we do not choose God, if in our preparation for flight we have not lived for Him, if His Bible has not been our training manual, then we will fly not upwards towards glory but down - to wretchedness and perdition. And that crash will be as great and terrible as any earthly disaster we can imagine, but far, far worse, for it will be total and eternal.

'And in exchange for what? What are the things for which we would trade eternal bliss for eternal agony? They are sinful things. They are sordid, squalid pleasures that fade as soon as they are touched and turn foul as soon as they are tasted. They weaken the mind and oppress the spirit, and even on earth bring only misery. We know this. We all know it in our hearts; but we often forget the lessons we have learnt.

'But with our Church as our craft, our Christian brothers and sisters as our fellow passengers, and our ministers to guide us in our short stay here before departure, then God our pilot will fly us sure and safely to righteousness and joy in the skies above.

'Before then we must strive to avoid any other shadowy craft which might tempt us with their promises of cheap tickets and easy pleasure-filled journeys. For if, on those other craft, we were to make our way down the aisle to the front, and past the luridly clad and falsely smiling stewardesses into the cockpit itself, to see the pilot to whom we had entrusted ourselves, there we would see, beneath the fine-looking cap, not a face at all, but a rotting skull with a mad, evil and desperate grin frozen across its features.'

I had not known it at the time, but the Church was in the process of buying its own aircraft, which helped make this one particularly successful. Kate told me that they were so pleased with my efforts that they were considering using me in their publicity material. 'Convict Rescued by the Church of Jesus Discovers Divine Inspiration'. I wasn't sure about this. In the end, either because of my reticence and atheism, or because they decided it was unwise to publicise the pamphleteer at the expense of the pamphlet, they dropped that idea. This was a relief. They paid me for it as well, perhaps because I was not a believer. Two hundred pounds. Kate thought it might be a good idea to donate the money back to the Church. I didn't.

Pamphlets, work and a return to drink were not enough on the last two nights before the trial though, and it was Kate who listened as I whimpered and ranted and sulked. And it was Kate, not family or friends, who took me to court.

But now I was on my own staring at Judge Collins. I could tell from his tone that he was coming to an end. He hoped that I was aware of my past folly. I was. I had dodged and avoided the consequences of my actions for too long. I could see that.

It was time to grow up and accept responsibility for my actions. I nodded at him firmly to convey my full agreement. He appreciated the efforts I was now making with my life (for which he, on behalf of the legal system, seemed to be taking credit), and my willingness to confess.

Surely he couldn't send me back, all alone, to prison after that. But it was in his power. I tried not to cry. Or vomit. Then, through increasing dizziness, I made out 'two years' or was it 'three' and I thought 'suspended', and Kate was smiling and my solicitor nodding in satisfaction, and I swooned like a Victorian heroine.

I held on to the bar in front of me, so I didn't actually fall, and I came round to dazed handshakes and hugs and congratulations. Everybody was so happy that I was saved. Then the crowd dispersed and it seemed entirely natural for Kate to be driving me away.

We headed into rural Sussex, to an old country house hotel sometimes used by the Church for conferences and meetings and managerial contemplation. My nausea and dizziness passed as we left London; I wound my window down, and stuck my elbow on the ledge.

"Bit of Steve Earle?" asked Kate.

"Yes. Steve Earle would be perfect."

She pressed play and we both smiled big smiles as 'Fearless Heart' began.

"Tempting fate, wasn't it – booking a room before you knew the verdict?" I said.

"I had faith in the power of my prayers," she answered. "And it's rooms." Not room.

Although neither of us said anything about sleeping together, and I knew I was pushing my luck, I still felt disappointed and annoyed, so I criticised her driving. When that didn't get a reaction I asked what there was to do in this hotel place she was taking us to.

"It's a really good one. I thought you liked hotels."

"Will I have to pay?" I heard myself saying. I was amazed at my ingratitude and arrogance. She remained calm and patient and matter of fact. I didn't have to pay.

"What are you up to?" I asked her that night, after a few drinks.

I watched her for signs of disappointment or anger. I got mild surprise, and a 'go on' noise.

"I mean why are you doing all this?" I said.

"It just seems the obvious thing," she said simply. "You need a job." I had meant our chaste stay in the hotel, but I let her continue. "And I think you are perfect for an organisation I care deeply about. And I care about you."

"And you're not trying to convert me?" It was simple; now I had the threat of prison lifted, I was less afraid of hurting her feelings.

"That's not why I'm doing all this. Yes, I'd like you to join us, but this is not some kind of trap. I'm being straight with you. We've got a lot to give, but it's up to you if you take it or not. I respect you for not pretending to believe in the Church when you might have thought it would have served your interests."

She had spoken clearly and calmly, with authority. I had not. I didn't get any better.

"And what about us?"

"There are problems there aren't there?" Right. It was time for me to mock the woman who had saved me and the church which had bailed me out and given me a job.

"I jumped naked out of your bed and ran away

because you had turned into religious nut who wanted me to help her make a Messiah."

"Seems a long time ago now," she smiled. "I got carried away."

"And now." No reply. "You know I would have loved to last night and the night before..."

"Yes, Tony. You know I believe in marriage now?"

"Like a good old country girl." She said nothing, so I tried a different tack. Remind her of what we had. "Do you not want to get out and sing again?"

"A bit. Sometimes. I told you, didn't I?"

"Yes, you did."

"But it doesn't seem so important right now."

Everything I said sounded glib and flippant and false and calculated – with good reason. Whereas she was just saying what she meant. That must save a lot of time, I thought.

"So you don't believe in sex outside marriage?" I said, asking for unnecessary clarification. She indicated with a leftwards movement of her head and slight shrug of her left shoulder that, with a certain reluctance, this was more or less the case. "And I do, as much as I believe in anything."

She made no reply. She was right; there was no point. The job, though, was different.

"OK. Well you know I'm far from convinced about this church, but I'm glad of the job. And see what happens with us after."

I wasn't really in the position to pretend I was being magnanimous, but she let me. It was very nice of her, but intimacy with the All-Powerful puts things into perspective, I remembered. With Him watching, it wasn't all about me.

"And you still shouldn't have read my diary." If she wouldn't react, then at least I could remind her of her wrongdoing.

"Yes, I know. You're right about that, sorry." I wondered if she was thinking how much I'd changed since the judge had set me free. "But I wasn't thinking too clearly then. As you know. Because of how I feel about you."

I had no reply to that. She was right and I was a failed manipulator.

****

When I got back, the Church of Jesus had given me an office with a desk, a PC, a telephone and no religious pictures. There I sat, happily working on a specification for the design of a Believers' database, and at the same time fine-tuning a piece for a pamphlet, and working on the outline for a computer game called Salvation.

The game was based on the Christian's route to heaven. I was enjoying it, but I anticipated a problem. In any game with the object of reaching a target, players tend to lose interest once that target has been reached. It would be unfortunate if believers became bored with achieving salvation. They might take this as a sign that I was dangerous. After all, I was a non-believer, and perhaps, ultimately my faithlessness would out and undo any good I might have done them. Those who are not with us are against us. And I really didn't want to lose the job. I had never had my own office before.

But then I never knew how significant my paganism was thought to be. Even if I was not a believer, I was promoting the cause of the Church so was I not, in effect, on their side? Those who are not against us are with us. After all what did they believe in but the good of the church itself?

I was never sure about their doctrines. At first I tried to check with Kate. I wanted to know if what I wrote smacked too much of Free Will or Predestination; of Medieval Catholicism or Industrial Revolution Methodism; Songs of Praise Anglicanism, Atheism or anything else which might sit uneasily with the Church's beliefs. But she reassured me. No. No problem at all. When I asked about their beliefs I never received an answer I understood. Not only were they fundamentalists who hadn't read the Bible; they were believers who didn't know what they believed in - and they didn't seem to think that was important either.

The practical side of my job presented different problems. Up to now my working life had been an exercise in cloaking inactivity with an impression of professionalism. Now I actually had to do things. They had a network of PCs and a number of databases for which I found myself solely responsible. To strengthen my own position in the organisation and my future employability outside, I wrote a lengthy, cogently argued and well-researched report recommending they bought in an Oracle database. They agreed because they liked the name. I realised that the Church wasn't different to any other large organisation; if you knew what you wanted, who to approach and how to spin it, you would get it.

As soon as I discovered I had the power to take on staff, I began recruiting. New staff would be the perfect excuse for mistakes, while increasing the chances of successes which I could share in. My superiors were a little surprised at first by the speed and scale of recruitment, but once it had begun, it acquired its own momentum, and I soon had a small team established. Nobody knew what we did and nobody knew how to ask. Salaries were good. As I explained, we had to be competitive.

With my new staff responsibilities I was given a pay rise and a larger office on the fourth floor. There I could sit, tapping my mouse every fifteen minutes to restore my timed out screen, looking through the smoked glass as people with faces resembling, to a greater or lesser extent, carp, swam past and occasionally in. I wore a suit most days, and I bought a nice flat on the outskirts of Lewes.

At the end of a month I usually find that I have money left over. I am drinking far less, and I am gambling with about the same frequency as I did when I was eighteen. I've been given a mobile, and I see the point of them now.

I see the point of lots of things I never did before. Like the new government, I see the point of finding accommodation with a lot of things I would have felt uncomfortable about in my naïve past. I am happy. There, I've said it. I think to be happy we must feel we belong, and the late nineteen-nineties were when I began to belong.

I'm still not really sleeping with Kate. There is kissing and physical contact, but I am not sure of our status. It reminds me of being fifteen again except that she talks about marriage from time to time. It's a point of view. Most points of view aren't without some merit, if viewed from a certain angle in a certain light, and she has a way of making her point of view attractive. The temptations of stability have never been so clear.

If it sounds as if I am being sucked into some sink of religion, then I insist that I am not. My defence is to be open about what I think. If I am asked about my beliefs I tell the truth. I have none. The head of the Church is a man called Wesley Fordham. He is due to visit before the end of the year, and if I am introduced to him, I will show the same insincere deference I would to any head of an organisation this size, but if asked, I would tell him a polite version of what I would tell you about my beliefs if we fell into a casual conversation. But he won't ask. Why would he?

They may listen in on my telephone calls. They must overhear fragments of my conversations anyway, as my office door is usually open, and I speak as I would anywhere, perhaps louder, again as part of my defence. My last call to Richard could demonstrate.

"Oh, hello Richard, it's Tony here."

"Yes, I know. How are you?" There is something in the way he says it which suggests it is a genuine question.

"Fine, fine. Just ringing up to say hello. What about you?"

"Not bad."

"Claire?"

"OK. She's got into that nursery I was telling you about - Cherubs." He laughed, "But it seems OK."

"Good."

"Give her the chance to socialise early. Good for her. And takes some of the pressure off Louise - I mean us."

"And work?"

"Well it's OK. Not as glamorous as yours."

"Still Claims and Benefits?"

"Yes. Mind you there's not a lot of difference between

working in them and getting them, apart from where you spend your day."

"Not even the pride in being an honest working man?"

"I've just realised how interesting being a priest was."

"Lots of things are interesting compared with being an honest working man."

"Are you still coming up next week?"

"Yes, if it's still OK with you. I know I just invited myself. Didn't ask if you had anything planned."

"What would we have planned?"

"Another child?"

"Getting into this uncle thing are you?"

"Louise still on the mend?"

"Yes. Might have been a touch of Flu, they reckon, and she's still very tired. Back at work, though. She'll be glad to hear you're coming up. Be good to see you. And Tony, if you want to bring anyone with you..."

"You mean Kate?"

"If you like."

"OK. Thanks. I might. But I'll warn you in advance who to expect."

"OK. I need to get on – I don't have employers who are as flexible as yours." He stopped abruptly. "Are you really able to talk there, properly?"

"Mm - course."

"And things really are OK? They've not..."

"Tried to get me this week? No, and they haven't even tried to make me take a vow of chastity."

"All right. But, Tony, watch yourself. Don't let them make you do anything you don't want to."

"It's OK. I don't spend my entire life making stupid mistakes you know."

"I know. But be careful. You're not as clever as you think you are, you know."

"I know."

He gave up.

"I could try to get you in here, if you like. I'm sure your experience would be relevant."

"Goodbye, little brother," he interrupted.

"OK. Look forward to seeing you."

"Yes, and you. Take care and hello to Louise, bye."

Richard has read some of my pamphlets and said he thinks they are clever, which I think means he disapproves. I think he disapproves of Kate as well. He would try to get on with her for my sake, but he might find the religion a bit of a problem. Still, Claire will probably go to a Catholic school, and I'm not altogether sure Louise isn't pregnant again. They've told me they don't want an only child. We all agree about that, which is nice. I have recently written a piece for the Church based on baby and child development.

I don't ring Joanne from the office, or anywhere else, and if I did, it would not be in the same carefree fashion.

I have the feeling it will soon be a Christmas card relationship, if it isn't already. She was grateful that I managed to keep her name out of the court case, although I'm sure she suspects that is more due to police incompetence, than my tenacity and discretion. As usual, she is right. It is also not in her nature to forget that I put her at risk in the first place.

We said a while ago that we would meet up in London when we next had the chance. It hasn't happened yet, and probably never will. The time between our last proper conversation and now is already as long as the time which elapses between conception and the average child starting to walk. She had her baby three or four months ago. I wrote a card but didn't send it.

I've been back to Hanlon Hall once, quite recently. The Church of Jesus put me on a Database Management course run by the company who took the place over, not long after Love Training went off the radar.

I had an hour train journey watching dawn break over the pale late winter scenery while eating my breakfast of expenses paid sandwiches and tea. Second class this time, and I wasn't keeping any of the money, but I was looking forward to my stay.

I was a little nervous as the train slowed down approaching the station, but it was more because I had expected to be, than because I really was. Nobody there would have the slightest interest in me now, and my anxiety had changed into bravado by the time I walked out of the station into the fresh air. The fact it was early morning helped. It was a virtuous, positively energetic time of day.

The changes I saw were small but definite. The station had had a makeover, and there were a choice of cappuccino bars nearby, one of them also selling fairly tasteful contemporary art. The payphones had gone; and there were flats going up where the house with orange curtains had been. There were even a couple of taxis waiting at the taxi rank. Everything was two and a half years older, and it was no longer in any way my town. I was here from Sussex for a course as I told the taxi driver.

"Residential, three days. Been here before, nice town."

Hanlon Hall was much the same, except for new corporate colours and lots of new glossy brochures bearing the new logo. I recognised no-one on reception, and if anyone recognised me they didn't show it. There was no sign of Simon, the friendly security man. If he had gone, I hoped he had got a decent severance. The nobility were still there looking down at us from their picture frames.

The first day of the course was reasonably well-taught and about the right length. Short. I wondered how that course I was all set to teach would have gone. I also wondered if anyone had turned up for it; I suspected I hadn't been as efficient as I should have been with cancellations.

The Church had booked me in Residential in the Hall. The bedroom was very comfortable, much more pleasant than prison and a lot bigger. And private. There was no in-house Christian cable channel, with toothy American megalomaniacs saving souls, either.

The first evening, I took a taxi into town for what I thought might be a nostalgia-inducing walk, but I felt very little, not even regret. I didn't know the place as well as I thought; I was shocked when I turned a corner and found myself looking at the snooker hall. It was closed up and there were To Let signs outside. I walked past it on the other side of the round. I enjoyed the nervous feeling, and the relief as I got past and out of sight. I felt sure I was out of its grip.

I was more conscious of the cold wind than anything else, so I went into the next pub I passed. The Bluebell. I had a Guinness and a Shepherd's Pie, then went back. I rang Kate, watched TV (Seinfeld and Larry Sanders) and went to bed. My sleep was not disturbed by prostitutes or drug dealers or even wide-boys offering me a discount on an extra training course as long as I paid them cash.

If required, I'd come back here again. If not, it was unlikely I'd ever feel the need. I didn't particularly want to be known as the criminal on the fourth floor, but, if pushed, I would tell anyone who wanted to know everything that had happened, without feeling guilt or shame. I don't know if middle-age is this kind of self-sufficiency slumbering into smugness, but if it is, then that's what I am. I have grown into my time. I slept soundly and woke to the radio alarm – Tony Blair was being reassuring about the future of Northern Ireland on the Today programme.

As the Millennium turns, it's not a bad time to be an IT manager with a position of influence in the Church of Jesus. It captures both of the obsessions of the time, and it pays well. Religion, which once looked like a well beaten outsider seems to have come storming back into the running, and it's good to have your bets covered. There is an IT department in the Vatican; I could probably get a job there helping administer a database of angels and saints, and their associated miracles.

Besides, every month that I manage to keep Kate and the Church happy, is another hundred or two in the savings account, another month further from prison, and an increased chance of submerging the whole thing that little bit further into the swamp of my CV. There's only one problem really.

On the second day of the course the weather was dismal. It was cold and still raining when we finished class. I had no great desire for another disappointing night walking around town, so I stayed in the Hall. I had a meal in the Training Centre Restaurant, using my genuine and valid green ticket, and afterwards I went through to the bar, still situated in that long, high-ceilinged room. I bought a drink and sat down to read the paper. I had phone calls to make, and work to prepare, so I enjoyed lounging around reading about floods in Holland and the economic crisis in Brazil. The Church does not disapprove of alcohol in moderation, so I had a second charged to my account. After a while, I put the paper down and looked out of the window through the drizzle to the floodlit summerhouse.

I daydreamed about a man a little younger than me, and what he and a couple of women had tried to do in this place not so very long ago. I was so deep in reminiscing that I did not notice someone coming towards me until they had stopped, only two or three feet from my chair. I looked around. I recognised her from the course - we had spoken briefly in the coffee break on the first day. I wasn't sure of her name. She had a glass of red wine in her hand. She looked back at me and smiled in a very friendly way. Then, still not saying anything, she moved a fraction closer towards me. I found that I was gazing up at her warmly. I liked the way she was looking at me, and I liked her, very much. She had coal black hair, baby blue eyes, and a smile that a boy understands.

A Questionnaire

How Good a Reader Are You?

1. Do you feel that the fate of the central character in the novel (Tony Palmer) is

a. What he wants
b. What he deserves
c. The opposite of what he really wants
d. The opposite of what he really deserves
e. Arbitrarily inflicted, and neither nothing nor something
f. Fluid

2. Did you feel that the Oliver Twist references were

a. Well-judged
b. Overplayed
c Underplayed

3. Were there any aspects of the story which you feel required more explanation?

a. Yes
b. No
c. Not sure

4. Which of the following do you think the novel had?
a. A sense of history
b. A sense of place
c. A sense of pain
d. Sense.

5. Did you find the presentation of the difficulties of human sexual relationships close to your own experience?
a. Yes
b. No
c. Quite close
d. Rather not say.

6. How do you feel about the late 1990s (the era portrayed in the novel)?
a. I can't remember them
b. Glitzy, glamorous, and hedonistic
c. A time of social and cultural conflict
d. Hard to say really.

7. Do you think a medal should be struck to commemorate the great work done by the men and women of the IT industry to prevent the chaos threatened by the Millennium bug?

(a) Yes

(b) No

(c) Only if it is made of dried dogshit

8. How important do you feel is the omission in works of literature of the 'I beg your pardon, I didn't hear what you said' followed by the exact repetition of the preceding statement, type of exchange?

a. Extremely

b. Quite

c. Not very

d. Don't know

e. Don't care

9. Did you find the portrayal of the relationship between Tony and Joanne

a. Convincing

b. Unconvincing

c. Neither nothing nor something

d. What relationship?

e. Who?

f. Sorry I didn't quite catch that

10. Do you consider yourself a friend of any of the characters?
a. Yes
b. No
c. Rather not say

11. As above, substituting the word 'lover' for 'friend'

12. How do you feel about living at this time?
a. Blessed
b. Worried
c. Cursed
d. No choice and nothing
e. Other (give details if you wish)

13. Do you feel that you know more than you did before reading this novel?
a. Yes
b. No
c. Less
d. Yes, but not because of having read the novel
e. Haven't read the novel

14. You are at a party, and an attractive man/woman comes over to you and strikes up a conversation. You are possessed with lust. In an attempt to impress and seduce them would you

a. Talk about literature - especially this book
b. Talk about literature - excluding this book, except perhaps to deride it, and its author
c. Flatter them outrageously, and only express an opinion about literature if they have already done so; and then only to reflect and amplify theirs
d. Roll your tongue about your lips a lot, touch them as if in fun or mock anger whenever possible and make it clear that you are healthy and solvent and sane and free

15. Are you healthy and solvent and sane and free?

a. Yes
b. No
c. Are you?

Scoring

1. A(1) B(1) C(1) D(1) E(1) F(1 - if you can explain what you mean)

2. A(3) B(0) C(1)

3. A(0) B(5) C(-1) (If you are not sure then should you not have chosen B?)

4. 1 point for each chosen

5. A(8) B(1) C(3) D(1 - why not?)

6. A(0 - That was the 60's) B(1 - That was the 70's) C(2 - That was the 80s) D(7)

7. A(2) B(2) C(2)

8. A(2) B(3) C(1) D(1) E(0)

9. A(5) B(1) C(2) D(8) E(-1) F(5 - How convincing did you find the portrayal of the relationship between Tony and Joanne?)

10. A(2) B(3) C(4)

11. A(1) B(2) C(3)

12. A(2) B(3) C(2) D(1) E(2 - if you didn't feel the need to go into detail, 0 - if you did)

13. A(5) B(5) C(5) D(5) E(-5)

14. A(3) B(0) C(1) D(3)

15. A(2) B(1) C(5)

Over 70: This is well over the maximum possible. You have problems.

65-70: Still more than the maximum possible but only a little. Perhaps you should check your mathematics, but if this is a minor miscalculation it can be forgiven in one of such sensitivity, insight and intelligence.
40-64: Excellent. Well-read. Can I say that it was as great a pleasure for me to have you read this as it seems that it was for you to read? May I suggest you buy more books by the same author or further copies of this? Perhaps the favour could be returned if you can provide proof of purchase. Bless you.

20-39: You have persevered with a book in which you have felt some interest, and your effort has not been totally unrewarded. This shows good sense and judgement. Thank you for your qualified endorsement. Perhaps you didn't concentrate quite as much as you could have done (Television on? Music in the background? Children in the room? Noisy neighbours? Things on your mind?), but this is not an ideal world, and you should be judged no more harshly than you yourself judge.

10-19: Well, thank you so much for being so good as to press on to this point. Perhaps this indicates that you found the book not utterly without merit. It is unfortunate that its qualities are a little too sophisticated or subtle for you to appreciate. Would footnotes have helped? Or are you beyond help? As for the novel's sharply observed and trenchant detail, perhaps you don't like sharply observed and trenchant detail, or perhaps your own life is so blurred and generalised that you can't recognise it.

0-9: Sorry. Is that what you want - an apology? You can make do with the analysis above but bear in mind that even they are better people than you are.

Less than 0: Again, not possible. Even if you had all the minus scores; selected none of the possibles in question 4; screwed up question 12; and chosen 'Fluid' for question 1 without being able to explain what you meant, you'd end up with zero points. In case that's not clear I'll try again. Zero is the minimum possible score. You haven't been doing this properly. You've made a complete mess of this and you've only got yourself to blame. There is no point in making notes to self if you don't take them to heart.

It's enough to make a body despair. You can't score less than nothing. It's all very well having freedom, but you can't, can't, can't do the impossible. You have to learn from experience. Has life taught you nothing?